JUGGERNAUT

A STRAIN NOVEL

AMELIA C. GORMLEY

ACG Publications
www.ameliacgormley.com

Juggernaut (A Strain Novel)

Cover art: Danielle Fine
Editor: Danielle Poiesz

ISBN: 978-1-62-622618-0

First Edition
August 2015

Second Edition
April 2018

They helped destroy the world. Now they have to survive the new one.

NICO FERNÁNDEZ has a charmed life. Working as a high-end rentboy for the agency his mother started beats the hell out of being trafficked for slave wages in some corporate brothel. And no one needs to know about his occasional side jobs, seducing political and military dignitaries and "nudging" them with mind-altering agents to swing their votes and opinions to favor his favorite client.

Zach Houtman's life *should* be charmed, but isn't. His father, the Reverend Maurice Houtman, has insisted Zach advise him as he pursues his political aspirations, ignoring Zach's calling to minister to society's most vulnerable outcasts. Politics, however, are gradually turning Zach's father away from Christ and into malicious zealotry, and his campaign is courting violent fundamentalists.

When one of Nico's "special jobs" results in military approval for a weaponized virus that mutates, unleashing a deadly plague, Nico and Zach are thrown together. Each burdened by terrible guilt for their unwitting roles in the calamity, they find safety and solace in each other. But the new world is a dangerous, violent place, where the handful of survivors are willing to do anything and kill anyone to get by.

READER DISCRETION ADVISED

Each reader is unique in their tolerance for graphic material. As such, please be aware that this novel may contain material or references which may be triggering for some readers. If you worry that this might be an issue, the author fondly encourages you take the time to read some of the reviews others have left at Goodreads and various ebook retailers to see if it contains subject matter you may find disturbing. Thank you.

For my husband and son, whose faith and love make it all possible.

And for Chris, Angie, Elin, and all the other people who helped me brainstorm this story and the books that have gone into this world.

The events of *Juggernaut* take place roughly ten years before the events of *Strain*.

1

PAWNS

LATE MARCH

The rains had abated to a persistent but bearable patter that rapped against the car's windows as it wound up into the Blue Ridge Mountains. The winds had died down enough that it was once again safe to venture out of doors, but the damage Hurricane Lilith had wrought on Virginia was readily apparent in the downed power lines and fallen tree branches lining the road. The Commonwealth was still tabulating the toll in both lives and dollars, but whatever it ended up being, it would be too damned much.

Of course, federal relief for the disaster would be considerably easier to get out here. The debris and damaged utilities would *inconvenience* politicians fleeing DC's sweltering heat in the summer to come. Other areas smashed by the catastrophic storm would be shit out of luck.

"We've got about a half hour until we reach the cabin, Mr. Costas," the driver informed Nico over his shoulder. "If you wanted some time to watch the news, you might do it now."

Nico smiled with genuine warmth. General McClosky's people were always friendly beyond mere professional courtesy, which wasn't something he could say for the staff employed by some of his clients. He never got that cold, *I'm looking down my nose at you but it's not my place to say anything* vibe from anyone when he had a contract with the general. And there was no question that the driver knew exactly what services "Octavio Costas" performed for McClosky; he was, after all, the one who had to clean the upholstery and air out the car whenever their contracts involved travel.

"Thank you, Darrin."

"How's your thesis going?" Darrin asked as Nico tucked his memory cards and projection glasses into his bag and tidied up the back of the car, where he'd been working for several hours.

"Slowly. How's yours?"

He caught Darrin's grimace in the rearview mirror. "Public course servers and connections were damaged in the storm," he answered. "Everything has been offline for weeks. The only students getting any work done are the ones who can pay first-tier tuition. Apparently their servers are up and running just fine."

Nico sighed and shook his head. Due to setbacks like this, Darrin had been working on his degree for as long as Nico had been seeing the general as a client—some six years now. Each delay meant his degree took longer, and he was paying for more terms than should have been necessary to finish it.

"I'm sorry," Nico murmured.

Darrin shrugged. "Not your doing. It's not like I plan to stop working for the general, anyway. Finishing it is mostly a point of pride at this point."

Reading between the lines, it sounded to Nico like Darrin was giving up, or at least contemplating it. There was nothing he could say to that. The fact was, Nico could afford first-tier, private university tuition and all the preferential treatment it entailed, and both he and Darrin knew it.

"Anyway," Darrin continued, "if you want to watch the news, go ahead."

"Thanks," he said again, and Nico raised the privacy partition. "Display," he called. A heads-up display appeared on the partition. "Video. News. Politics," he instructed. An image quickly came into focus on the HUD, revealing the familiar face of one of the ubiquitous Sunday-morning pundits, Daniel McNary.

"Here with us now is the Reverend Maurice Houtman, communications director for the Righteous Word Party. Reverend, with this latest wave of attacks, accusations are once again being leveled at the RWP, claiming the Righteous Action League is the terrorist arm of your party, operating with the RWP's knowledge and cooperation. How does the RWP respond to this?"

"The same as we always have, Mr. McNary." Even through the video screen, Houtman's eyes burned with a zealot's fire and the smile on his gaunt face stopped just short of smug. "The Righteous Word Party is dedicated to—"

Houtman's diatribe—which had all the earmarks of becoming the same sort of sermon that was broadcast to millions of people every Sunday morning from Houtman Ministries mega-cathedral in Indianapolis—was overridden by the chime of a call coming in on Nico's tablet. He pulled it from his bag and redirected the signal to the left half of the HUD, compressing Houtman's creepy mug on the right.

"What's up, Mom?"

"You rearranged the schedule." On the display, Silvia Fernández's artfully painted lips were pressed together in a tight line, her eyes narrowed with annoyance. Nico allowed himself a moment of amusement, wondering if the rest of the nation—who knew his mother as Marina Costas, owner of the wildly successful escort agency Costas Companions, outspoken advocate for sex worker rights, detractor of the corporate brothel system, and easily the most recognized madam in the western hemisphere—had ever seen her wearing any expression other than a charming smile. Certainly they'd never seen her play the role of mother hen. "Marcus was supposed to have the McClosky job tonight."

"McClosky is *my* client."

Silvia dipped her head, acknowledging the point. "For personal engagements, certainly, but this is one of his other jobs."

"All the more reason for me to handle it."

"Marcus has taken special jobs for Logan before."

Nico blew out an impatient breath. "I prefer to do it myself."

"Nicolás—"

"Is there a reason you *don't* want me to take this job, Mother?" he demanded sharply.

Silvia sighed. "The information Logan gave me made it seem like it wouldn't be very pleasant. To the point where it seemed like *he* would rather I assign it to someone else."

"Well, wasn't that considerate of him?" Nico smiled softly. "I appreciate that the general was thinking of me, but it doesn't change the fact that he's my client and we shouldn't be distributing these *special jobs* to our other employees if we can avoid it. I don't mind if it's not the most enjoyable evening I've ever passed."

Silvia's eyes narrowed again, this time with an assessing look. "You don't have to prove anything to Logan, you know."

"Don't worry, Mother. I'm not in love with General McClosky." He rolled his eyes, flicking a glance at the right side of the HUD where another talking head was heatedly countering something the Reverend Houtman had said.

"Of course not." Silvia smiled with open amusement. "I know you're not that foolish, and if you were, you'd never have another engagement with him again. But I do think you very much want to impress him, for whatever reason."

Nico shrugged uncomfortably. "He's been a good friend to me. To us. And my point remains: the fewer people we involve in these special jobs of his, the better. I'm fine doing it myself." Nico reached for the controls on the armrest and turned up the volume on the talk show. "Are you watching McNary?" he asked, changing the subject.

On the left side of the display, he saw his mother reach for her own controls. "I am now."

"He's talking about the attack on the Buffalo *Yes on 46* campaign office."

Houtman was back to pontificating. "—bringing the Lord back into our system of government and overcoming the corrupting and immoral influences in our society by peaceful and legal means."

Nico suppressed a snort. Houtman's moral stance would be a lot more convincing if most of the funding for the RWP's campaign against legalizing independent sex work didn't come from the corporate brothels. For obvious reasons, enabling sex workers to operate as independent, contracted service personnel—which Costas escorts already did in states where it was legal—wasn't a notion the brothels approved of. Because God forbid whores might work for something more than a starvation wage, operate outside of facilities that claimed most of their income in "fees" for leasing and managing their work space, schedule their appointments as though they *weren't* on an assembly line, or have the right to refuse service to abusive clients.

Beside Houtman's image on the HUD, it was Silvia's turn to roll her eyes. "It's all well and good for McNary to ask the question, but the RWP had too many highly placed supporters for any serious investigation of their connection to the Righteous Action League to get off the ground."

Nico shrugged. "*Someone* is shunting money to the RAL, and it's damned convenient that their targets just happen to be whoever is the subject of Houtman and the RWP's rants du jour."

Until last year, the league had only carried out their attacks on reproductive clinics and shelters for queer youth. Then they had branched out to hit the administrative offices for grassroots organizations trying to get sex work out of the hands of corporate brothels. Since Costas Companions was making significant contributions to those campaigns, and Silvia was acting as a spokesperson for them, this impacted Nico's livelihood directly.

"So the RWP condemns these attacks?" McNary prompted on the display as Nico and his mother fell silent.

He smiled at the screen, letting his eyes roam over McNary's chiseled jaw and piercing eyes. No political pundit had any business being so gorgeous. Unfortunately, according to all the rumors, he was completely devoted to his wife. Of course, many of Nico's clientele were attached to similar rumors, but he had been to five functions at which McNary had been in attendance and he'd never gotten so much as a lingering glance from the guy.

McNary was also damned good at not letting people on his show off the hook when their responses reeked of bullshit, which made him a veritable treasure among pundits, as well as Nico's favorite fix for his political-talk-show addiction.

Idly checking his immaculate trousers for lint or wrinkles, Nico flicked his gaze to the display as the reverend tilted his head in a half shrug, his expression obnoxiously complacent. "The RWP is in no way complicit in these attacks, nor do we know who the perpetrators are."

"Sure you don't," Nico muttered, and the corner of Silvia's mouth lifted.

"It doesn't matter what they say, *mijo*," she murmured. "Momentum is on our side. People can overlook the human rights abuses in the retail and industrial sectors, but once you add in the element of sex work, that brand of wage slavery becomes human trafficking, and that's a lot harder to ignore."

Nico chuckled. "That's nice. Was that from the speech you gave at the last *Yes on 46* fundraiser?"

"Paraphrased," Silvia said with a blithe wave of her hand. "The point stands."

Yes, the point stood. Getting corporate brothels legalized some fifty years ago had been an easy sell; they'd campaigned on a public health and safety platform, claiming it would reduce crime and the spread of sexually transmitted infections. But the more the brothels began operating like the industrial tenements, the more obvious the human rights abuses in the whole system became. The sex element got people's attention like nothing else did, which made it harder for the brothels to resist grassroots efforts to legalize independent sex work. That was why most of the arguing against legalization efforts was coming from religious fundamentalists like Houtman, quietly backed by the brothels. And now, apparently, the extremist terrorist groups were getting in on the act.

"How is security at the fundraisers you've been doing?" Nico asked with a frown. "Do you think they could—"

"Not likely." Silvia shook her head. "We've got the entertainment industry taking our part. Too many notable names at those events. They wouldn't dare."

That was true. Attending awards ceremonies and opening nights with a Costas Companions escort on one's arm had become a status symbol, a way for cinema, televid, and music bigwigs to revel in being shocking and controversial. Some flaunted the fact that they were hiring a rentboy or call girl for the evening, while others truly appreciated the services Costas Companions offered beside the obvious. His mother's contractors were trained to provide far more than just a sexual experience.

Nico was about to caution his mother to be careful of her security anyway when something Houtman was bloviating about on the HUD caught his attention.

"—Nevertheless, it must be said that one need only look at the targets to discern the hand of God behind the tragedies. The United States has become a modern-day Sodom and Gomorrah. The more corrupt and dissolute we become as a society, the more often we will see the Lord allowing His servants to smite the wicked in His name . . ."

Nico's jaw slowly dropped. "Oh my God. Did he just . . .?"

⋀⋀⋀

ZACH CHOKED, coughing as he stared in disbelief at the video monitor. He frantically looked down at the computerized notepad of talking points they had gone over before the broadcast. The reverend was off script. As usual.

A headache began to throb in Zach's temples, and his stomach started to burn. Fumbling, he tucked the notepad under his arm and dug into his inner breast pocket, withdrawing a prescription bottle. He stuck one of the quick-dissolve tablets under his tongue and resumed perusing his notepad, waiting for the pain to ease before he put the bottle away. By then, his father had doubled down on his hardline rhetoric, prompting Dan McNary to call for a commercial break, ending the reverend's segment.

Zach produced a handkerchief, holding it out before his father arrived at his side. The reverend dabbed his sweating brow, and Zach saw the disgruntled look in his peripheral vision.

"Look up and greet me properly, Zacharias. Don't just fling a rag at me like you can't be bothered."

"Sorry, sir." Zach lifted his gaze from the notepad and fixed it on his father. "I was just checking our notes. You veered off the talking points."

The reverend spared an indolent shrug. "The audience wants to hear something exciting, something that will get them charged about the message we're putting out."

"By 'the audience' you mean 'the voters,' don't you, sir?" Zach shook his head, accepting the now-damp handkerchief back and tucking it into his pocket. "Yes, I'm sure people will get plenty excited over the implication that God is working through *terrorists*. If you're serious about running for Senator Davis's seat, those are not the sort of quotes you should be making headlines with."

His father gave him a repressive look. "The people want God back in our government, Zacharias. That means they need to see His hand, active among us, and know that He will not abide the current, immoral status quo."

Zach's headache renewed and stabbed at him again, like an ice pick drilling into his eye. His vision blurred, making his father swim before his eyes. He wanted to get out of this studio and get home to his dark, quiet bedroom.

"I can guarantee you, no one is going to vote for a man who claims innocent people died because God decided to use terrorists to smite them."

The reverend scowled. "The targets of those attacks were not innocents."

Zach hung his head. Why did he bother? There had once been a time when his father would listen and heed the voice of moderate reason, a time when the message he preached from his pulpit had been about God's love and mercy, but since he'd helped found the Righteous Word Party, those occasions were becoming increasingly rare. Now his sermons were about God's wrath bringing down the wicked.

"They were a cancer in our society, corrupting us, and it needed to be destroyed," the reverend continued. "I won't compromise my beliefs to get votes. If the people can't handle God's truth, if they are happy with a government that sanctions the fornicators and sodomites and idolaters, then they're not going to vote for me anyway."

"God's truth includes 'thou shalt not kill' and 'love thy neighbor,' and 'vengeance is mine, sayeth the Lord.' When does the voting public get to hear that truth?"

"It also says 'honor thy father,'" came a sneering voice behind him before the reverend could spit out the blistering retort twisting its way to his lips. "Or are we ignoring that commandment today?"

Zach turned to see his little brother standing there with a smug smile. Jacob was seventeen, the youngest of Maurice Houtman's five children, and as such, Zach knew his brother had a tendency to feel shorted and overlooked. Unfortunately, he also had a habit of trying to offset that feeling by currying favor with their father. Or so Zach carefully reminded himself when he grasped for the love he was supposed to feel for all God's children, especially his little brother. In his less charitable moments, though, he was inclined to accuse Jacob of being a suck-ass. It had become worse since their father's dogma began to take on more shades of fire and brimstone, too.

Zach forced himself to smile. "Of course not," Zach conceded. Locking horns with Jacob was just as futile as trying to sway his father, and it certainly wouldn't help get rid of his headache, so he kept that bland smile pasted on and turned to retrieve the reverend's coat.

⚠ ⚠ ⚠

STILL AGHAST AT the Reverend Houtman's faux pas on the McNary show, Nico ended the call with his mother and idly skimmed from one broadcast to the next for the remainder of the drive.

". . . I think we need to look at the economic conditions that led to these efforts to begin with, Michael. The tenements operate like the mining camps of the late-nineteenth century before unionization forced reform. Employees amount to little more than feudal serfs serving at the mercy of their corporate overlords . . ."

He was about to change the channel again when Darrin called back to him over the intercom, interrupting the congresswoman's rant. "We're almost to the cabin, Mr. Costas."

"Thank you, Darrin." He smiled and sat up straighter, smoothing his hair and then the fine wool of his suit coat. He switched off the HUD, popped a mint into his mouth, and shifted into the rear-facing seat of the limousine.

The car decelerated with a soft whine and turned off the two-lane mountain highway onto a long, wooded driveway. Five minutes after that, they came to a stop before a cozy, rustic-looking cabin. Nico remained seated as Darrin parked and got out of the car to ring the doorbell. He waited patiently for nearly another ten minutes before a broad-shouldered man with graying black hair opened the door. Darrin escorted him to the limousine and opened the door, then returned to the cabin and emerged with a suitcase, which he stashed in the trunk while McClosky slid into the seat opposite Nico and closed the door.

"Nicolás. It's good to see you." A warm smile split the general's ageless face, and Nico ducked his head at the reminder that this man —the first and favorite of his clients—had known him long before he'd adopted the professional pseudonym Octavio Costas. To the general, he was still Nicolás Fernández.

"It's always a pleasure, General," Nico replied with complete sincerity.

"You know you can call me Logan." As General McClosky looked Nico up and down, Darrin returned to the wheel and pulled the car away from the cabin.

"It wouldn't feel right, sir." Nico's formality in no way diminished his fondness for the general; any more casual form of address just rubbed at his nerves, chafing.

The general gave him a fond look. "Thank you for coming out all this way to meet with me. I wasn't going to have time, otherwise."

"I didn't mind the ride at all. It was relaxing."

"Still working hard on your thesis?"

"Yes, though, I think I'll be done with it before the holidays. But of course, my schedule is usually booked fairly tight with clients, so finding time for something other than school or work can be a challenge. A nice afternoon drive in the mountains is a refreshing change of pace."

McClosky favored him with another warm smile. "And how is Silvia?"

"Devoted to you, as always, sir." Nico grinned, settling back against the soft leather. "She sends her regards and hopes you'll be able to come by and see her sometime soon. She also asked me to assure you that the usual precautions to make the transaction untraceable are all in place."

"Excellent. I might be able to arrange a visit sometime next month. Worst-case scenario, I definitely wouldn't miss her midsummer celebration." McClosky reached for his briefcase and pulled it into his lap, popping it open. He withdrew a memory card and handed it to Nico. "This is the man. You'll find all the information you need and a picture so you'll be able to spot him. He'll be staying at the hotel after the convention tonight, and he'll be in the bar looking for companionship. All you need to do is make sure he has a smile on his face in the morning for our meeting with the joint chiefs. I very much need this recommendation to go my way."

"And should subtle hints and pleasing smiles not work?" Nico's hand drifted almost unconsciously to the vial of oil in his pocket.

"You have my permission to use whatever means are at your disposal." McClosky knew exactly what was in that vial. Hell, he'd provided it specifically for occasions such as this.

Nico took his HUD glasses from his bag and put them on, then slotted the card into them and fell silent, perusing the file. His intended mark looked like an appealing enough man. He'd certainly entertained far less attractive clients. He ejected the card and handed it back to McClosky, folding and putting away the glasses. "As usual, I can't guarantee his vote, or recommendation, or whatever you're after from him, but I can certainly guarantee he'll have a smile on his face and he'll be feeling reasonably amenable."

"I have every confidence in your abilities." The general nodded and relaxed in his seat, his knees parting. Nico slid out of his coat and laid it on the seat beside him before slipping to his knees on the floor of the limousine. McClosky reached out to stroke the side of Nico's face as Nico reached for the fly of his uniform. "It's been too long, my boy."

"It's always a pleasure, sir," Nico repeated, smiling, and dipped his head to suck the general deep into his mouth.

He'd lost track of the number of people—male, female, and all points in between—he'd pleasured, but McClosky would always stand out from the masses. When Nico had declared his intention to work for his mother's escort agency once he turned eighteen, Silvia's first order of business had been to hire one of her best rentboys to tutor him. Then, for his first job, she'd booked Nico for a week with McClosky. That engagement had been something of a graduation, and it had taught Nico more than six months with his "tutor" had.

He supposed he *would* be in love with the general if he were idiotic enough to fall in love with anyone at this point in his life and career. There was an edge of danger to McClosky, despite the fact that he was always very proper and courteous outside the bedroom. Nico suspected that people who dealt with McClosky on a daily basis would say he was not a *good* man, that he was firmly convinced that the ends justified the means, but moral ambiguity had a certain appeal.

Pushing all that aside, Nico refocused his attention on the cock in his mouth, on the general's groans, taking him deeper, working him with tongue and lips and throat, using every bit of skill he'd acquired since that first week-long engagement. McClosky shuddered and came down Nico's throat. Nico rocked back on his heels, smiling as he wiped the corner of his mouth. McClosky's fingers gently petted his hair, and Nico closed his eyes in pleasure at the touch. He wondered if the general noticed he was doing it.

"Will you be going straight to your town house in Arlington, sir?"

McClosky nodded, tucking himself away and fastening his trousers before he dug through his briefcase for a tablet and his own HUD glasses to plug into it. "Yes. Though, of course, you're welcome to have Darrin drive you into DC if you need."

Nico discreetly pressed his own unattended cock into a more comfortable position in his trousers and moved back into his seat. Clearly McClosky had too much going on to make this more of a mutual encounter, and Nico wasn't here for McClosky's pleasure this time, anyway. The blowjob had simply been a freebie. "Thank you, sir, but I'll take my own car. I know it's not likely anyone will notice me stepping out of the limousine and trace it back to you, but why take the chance?"

"Very well. If the secretary doesn't attend to your accommodations tonight, take a room and add it to my bill."

Nico contained a frown. He'd really hoped the general might

invite him back to his house after he'd done his job. "As you wish, sir."

One corner of McClosky's mouth tipped up, and his eyes passed over Nico slowly from behind the projection goggles. "Will you be heading back to Princeton in the morning?"

"I have no reason to remain in DC, but I certainly have the availability. You told my mother that the secretary can be a little *rude* when he plays with his toys, so I don't have any clients scheduled for a few days."

"I told her that in the hopes that she would send someone else for the job. I wouldn't want to see you hurt."

Nico licked his lips, smiling slowly. "I don't mind some wear and tear. *You* taught me to enjoy that, if you recall. Though, it has been a while. I find I rather miss it."

"Well, then, I hope the job doesn't disappoint." The general's eyes darkened, his nostrils flaring slightly. "But just in case, come back to the Arlington house after you check out tomorrow. There's no reason you can't stay there a few days to recuperate. I'll leave instructions with Peter to let you in if I'm not home yet."

A tingly surge of anticipation seized Nico's nuts and squeezed gently. His ass clenched almost greedily as his hands gripped his knees. "Like I said, it's always a pleasure, sir."

⚠ ⚠ ⚠

HAVING dinner guests had become a nearly nightly event since the reverend had thrown his hat into the political ring. Strategists, consultants, fund-raisers, and donors all seemed to converge upon the Houtman's Indiana home, an overdone—to Zach's eye, at least—mansion in the country, surrounded by corn and soy fields. They all seemed to have an agenda, and very little of that agenda appeared to have anything to do with the Lord. His father assured him that their motivations were irrelevant, but Zach couldn't accept that God's work was being done by people whose only interest was earthly power and wealth.

Not for the first time, Zach wished he'd stuck to his guns and gone to seminary. But by the time he was getting ready to choose his major in college, his father had been laying the groundwork for establishing the Righteous Word Party and moving Houtman Ministries into the political arena. The reverend had insisted that Zach could do far more good studying political science and marketing, working as an aide and adviser to the RWP than he could as a pastor. It hadn't been the work Zach felt called to by God; he'd wanted his own ministry, perhaps do some missionary work in the tenements or inner cities. But the reverend had been relentless. He'd painted a rosy picture of Zach shaping a movement to redirect the government toward principles according to Christ's teachings, principles of charity and compassion. The actual party line had been quite a disappointment.

Zach would be expected at dinner. He wasn't sure why his father insisted on it, since his input as one of the RWP's political advisors —which was his official title, though more often than not he just held the reverend's notes—was uniformly disregarded.

With a reluctant sigh, Zach concluded a brief, silent prayer for patience, a necessity before these dinners. Then he adjusted his tie, straightened his glasses, and made his way toward the den where his father's colleagues were enjoying a drink.

". . . instant polling shows a strong response to your appearance on McNary's show this morning," said George Welshman, a media consultant so greasy Zach needed a shower after shaking the man's hand. Welshman had no principles, much less anything as powerful as ethics or morals. All that mattered was winning and getting his consulting fee. If Zach truly had the influence his father had promised him, firing Welshman was the first thing he'd do.

"It's as I've been saying all along," he continued. "The harder you come out swinging, the more impact you're going to make. Building momentum right now is crucial."

"That all depends on the kind of impact you want to make," Zach replied, coming to a stop in the doorway. He felt his father fix him with a narrow-eyed look for interrupting, much less contradicting, the consultant, but he refused to meet it. "What sort of momentum is a negative impression truly going to build?"

Welshman waved the question off with a negligent flap of his hand. "Doesn't matter. At this point we're after brand recognition.

Maurice could go on the talk shows promising drugs and orgies for everyone who votes for him and it wouldn't matter what he said so long as the voters remembered his name once he declares his candidacy."

A low chuckle rumbled from across the room, and Zach's stomach twisted. Jacob was sitting next to their father, practically beaming at being admitted to the inner circle. The avarice in his smile made Zach uneasy, as always. He'd tried for years to reach out to Jacob, tried to counter that sense of entitlement and superiority and model humility and compassion for his younger brother. But Jacob's spite was just too strong, and Zach didn't have the energy to be the voice of reason in his father's campaign *and* be continually rebuffed by his brother.

"We need to keep hammering this prostitution business," another voice added. Zach glanced over to see Bishop Karl Craven nursing a tumbler of whiskey. "The liberal media is determined to make a tragedy out of those bombings. We need to focus people on the positive side of these acts."

"Positive side?" Zach blinked incredulously. "I wasn't aware there was a positive side to wanton slaughter."

The bishop's mouth pulled into a tight, disapproving line. "The targets of those bombings were panderers and whores."

"Yes, they were, but when Christ came upon the adulteress about to be killed, He invited anyone without sin to cast the first stone. He told her to go forth and sin no more. He didn't tell His apostles to firebomb her home."

His father's gaze bore down on him, making his chest tighten. Sweat beaded on his forehead, but he refused the silent command to back off.

Jacob jumped in before the reverend had a chance to dress Zach down. "No one wants to see God as some toothless old geezer who lets sinners traipse off with only a stern lecture."

Zach smiled tightly. "I'm fairly certain that only applies to *children* who have inflated ideas of their own self-importance."

A ruddy flush darkened Jacob's acne-marked cheeks. A rash retort twisted his lips, but their father laid a hand on his arm before he found his voice.

"Enough, boys." He stood and gave them each a quelling look, the fury in his pale blue-gray eyes carefully masked until his back was to the room. His voice was perfectly modulated, just the right tone for patronizing affection. "Despite his blasphemous phrasing, Jacob is making much the same point I made to you earlier, Zacharias. Clearly you've been working too hard lately and the stress is beginning to tell. We can do without you at dinner tonight. Why don't you go check in on your youth group, see how they're managing since you retired?"

Being summarily dismissed was as infuriating as being required to attend in the first place. Having the reverend use his youth group as an excuse to get rid of him—the same youth group he'd made Zach sacrifice to free up more time to work on the campaign—was the final insult. Zach glowered at his father for a moment before he spun on his heel and strode from the den and toward the front hall.

"I'm going downtown," he threw over his shoulder. "If anyone needs me, I'll be helping out at the Center Street Shelter."

2

PREDATORS AND PREY

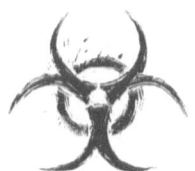

Secretary Littlewood was unfortunately named. It also didn't describe his physical stature very accurately. It remained to be seen whether the name was apt in other regards or not.

What Littlewood was not—at first glance, at least—was the brute the general had led Nico to believe he was. He seemed a quiet yet charismatic man, cautious when Nico started chatting him up. But there was something lurking in his eyes, a predatory gleam, avid and hungry. Held in check but definitely there.

He was also sending out so many mixed signals that even Nico, who was adept at reading physical cues and the subtext beneath the banter, was bewildered. The general's dossier had said Littlewood would be seeking companionship, and he certainly looked keen whenever Nico caught the secretary studying him, but the more amenable to passing time Nico let himself appear, the less interested Littlewood became.

"I guess I'm just in the mood for an adventure," Nico remarked, trawling out careful bait when the opportunity arose over their second drink.

Littlewood cleared his throat, his eyes darting to the side as if concerned someone might be listening in. "What kind of adventure?"

Nico looked down at his glass, flicking a few rapid glances at Littlewood without meeting his eyes. It would come off as covert admiration while Nico surreptitiously assessed the secretary. This was where he'd normally come right out and tell a client he was perfectly amenable to being held down and pounded into the mattress, maybe even bruised and welted a little, but the vibe he was getting warned him against it. If he came on that strong, Littlewood would walk away, he was sure of it.

"Oh well." Nico shrugged awkwardly, as if making a shy admission. "You know, something . . . maybe a little unusual. Possibly even dangerous."

"Oh." The secretary's mouth tightened, and he tipped back his whiskey, giving Nico an irritated look. "I'm not interested in that."

Nico blinked. Was Littlewood ashamed of his predilections? But no, that didn't track, either. Nico was used to smoothing the way for clients who were embarrassed to admit what they truly wanted. Hell, he was *good* at it. The key was putting them at ease with it, making them feel like it was all normal and that Nico wouldn't be repulsed by anything they requested of him. But any attempt Nico made in that direction with Littlewood had the opposite effect. He didn't like Nico being comfortable and open-minded and unapologetic.

He accepted his third glass of wine, his other hand lightly brushing Littlewood's knee. Perhaps the secretary didn't know how such games could be played with the consent and satisfaction of all involved. But Littlewood didn't come across as that naive. He hadn't seemed confused by Nico's hints, but rather, *annoyed*. That hungry look in his eye was being replaced with disinterest. In fact, the more worldly Nico acted, the less engaged Littlewood became.

What was his kink? Did he want an ingenue? Someone he could instruct? A virgin? Someone maybe a little reluctant that he could "convince" to play his game?

"That? You mean— Oh no, not *that*." Nico laughed lightly, pushing on Littlewood's knee as though the secretary was joking with him. He couldn't quite manage a blush, but he ducked his head to convey embarrassment. Maybe even inexperience. "Not anything, you know, *perverted*. Just . . . exciting. Out of the ordinary. I'm making a fool of myself, sorry. I, um, don't usually do this."

There. That did it. The interest was back and stronger than ever. He looked at Nico like he wanted to devour him. Instead of satisfying Nico that he was finally on the right track, though, his nerves started jangling with unease. Suddenly he didn't feel safe, and that hungry look in Littlewood's eye was far less sexy than it should have been with Nico's admitted penchant for alpha males. His smile wobbled, and Littlewood's eyes grew darker in response to that hint of fear. Something wasn't right; all his instincts were screaming at him, telling him to be careful. And Nico's mother and tutor had hammered into him the importance of listening to those instincts.

Littlewood liked it rough, but he didn't want *Nico* to like it rough?

Everything fell into place, and a shiver ran through him.

Littlewood wanted someone innocent and unworldly, someone shy and easily embarrassed, someone with no taste for rough play, so that he could—what?—force it on them?

Oh. Oh shit.

The general's dossier hadn't prepared Nico for this.

One of the first things he had learned when he'd started training to work for Costas Companions was spotting the warning signs of a potentially violent or abusive client. It was standard training for all his mother's employees: how to avoid dangerous situations before they became dangerous. That was what had him alert. If Nico was right, he was looking at a wolf in sheep's clothing, a true predator beneath that understated demeanor. Possibly even a *criminal* predator who hadn't yet been caught, or against whom charges never managed to stick. A white man with enough money could get away with everything up to and including murder, especially if the victim was brown. A charge brought by a Latino rentboy would be laughed out of court if Littlewood had the money to hire a half-decent attorney.

No self-respecting practitioner of the arts of pain and dominance would have anything to do with this man. Littlewood's desires had nothing to do with games of mutual pleasure agreed to by both parties. He wanted to hurt Nico, and he didn't want Nico to enjoy it. He didn't even want Nico's *consent.*

Nico swallowed hard, draining his glass faster than he'd

intended. Had McClosky known about this? That Littlewood was so dangerous? No, surely not. He would never have sent Nico here if he had. Would he?

With an uncertain smile that Littlewood lapped up, Nico turned away under the pretense of ordering another drink, his mind racing. He should get out of here. His mother would kill whatever Littlewood left of him for carrying through with the job knowing what the secretary was. She'd refund General McClosky and that would be the end of it.

But then McClosky would be left without the recommendation he needed, and Nico desperately didn't want to disappoint him.

Nico made a show of craning his neck, stretching out the sudden tension while looking for the waiter. Anything to avoid that predator's gaze Littlewood had fixed on him, while he quickly weighed his options.

Okay. Littlewood wouldn't kill him. He likely wouldn't even injure him seriously. He just wanted to force something unpleasant upon Nico against his will. But . . . the secretary was hesitant about that desire. Did he feel guilty, perhaps? No. That didn't ring true. More likely, he was afraid of being caught and charged. Or even just exposed. He knew he should lay low, but hurting others was a compulsion for him. He *had* to have it.

Someday he could be truly dangerous if he had nothing to lose by cutting loose. But right now he had other forces keeping him in check.

That's what Nico needed to use to his advantage.

He turned a self-conscious smile on Littlewood. "Oh God. I was so hungry and tired and stressed out when I got to the hotel that I forgot to check in. Would you mind waiting here for a moment while I take care of that?" If he was going to do this rather than call the whole thing off, he needed to get the secretary alone in a space he controlled.

"How long are you here? Do you live with parents? Roommates?" Littlewood asked. His smile was attractive, even a little charming now that he thought Nico was what he wanted. But there was something sinister under the question. What Littlewood might very well really be asking was when he was expected elsewhere, who might notice if he was hurt or scared or showed up late and worse for wear. Did Nico have anyone to look after him, and how much trouble could they make for Littlewood?

"My plane doesn't leave until late tomorrow morning. I'm heading home to see my parents."

Nico watched the secretary do the math. Jesus, he was scary now that Nico could see how much of what was going on behind his eyes was a cold calculation of the amount of hurt he could inflict, and for how long, without risking anything.

"You didn't say what brought you to DC, did you?" Littlewood ventured, and Nico had to stop himself from squinting as he tried to figure out the point to the question. Leverage, maybe? Looking for something he could use to coerce Nico into not making any waves for him?

"Oh, right! I'm here for a job interview. I graduate in the winter, and I might have something lined up. But gosh, you know, DC . . . Being raised in upstate New York never prepared me for living here!" He chuckled and ducked his head shyly, playing it just right. Harmless enough to keep Littlewood on the hook, but with enough of a hypothetical support network to keep him from getting reckless with whatever he had planned. "Stupid, huh? I was trying to impress you, acting like I was all sophisticated. I should have known better."

"That's fine. You don't need to impress me. You're charming just the way you are. Very sweet." Littlewood's indulgent smile made a cold knot of fear settle in Nico's stomach. The hungry look in his eyes flared into something downright voracious.

Nico stomped the urge to get the hell out of there under his heel and continued playing the innocent. "So, would you mind excusing me for a moment? I'll get checked in and then . . . I don't know, would you like to . . . maybe . . ."

"Come up to your room?" Littlewood lifted a smug eyebrow, amused and magnanimous. Of course, the idea of having a naive target was even more appealing than the idea of having a street-smart one. "I'd like that very much."

"All right." Nico bit his lip, feigning the nervous habit that he'd long ago broken. "Just give me a few minutes? I'll be right back."

Fuck, his mother was going to kill him when she found out he was playing this close to the edge. He'd be lucky if she didn't fire his ass. But he wasn't about to let McClosky down. He couldn't.

He quickly checked into a room, charging it to his personal account rather than the Costas corporate one—he'd still bill McClosky for it, but he didn't want it directly traceable back to the general or Costas Companions—and sent his small bag up with a bellhop before rushing back to the bar.

"Done!" he declared, looking breathless and hoping the flush from scurrying would make him seem excited rather than afraid.

Littlewood unfolded himself from his chair and rose, reaching to hook one hand around Nico's hip and tug him closer. Playing it like a seduction. "Good. Let's go, then."

The whiskey on his breath as his lips brushed Nico's face smelled rich and heady, which was horrifying because it seemed like he should be foul in all ways. The only thing that made him appalling was the knowledge of what he was.

Whatever Littlewood was being cautious about, being seen with another man wasn't it. The elevator doors had no sooner closed behind them than the secretary pushed Nico face-first against the wall, gripping his ass hard, gnawing on his neck. Not quite enough to be painful, but if this was the starting line, Nico knew he was in for some hurt.

It wasn't hard to come across as nervous, though he tried to play it off as shy. "Wait. What if someone else gets on the elevator?"

"So what?" Littlewood grunted. "I thought you wanted something *exciting*. Different."

"I know, but . . ."

"Just shut up and go with it. I know what to do with you."

Nico swallowed hard and closed his eyes, his forehead pressed against the cool metal wall of the elevator. The nipping at his neck was replaced by suction. Not pleasant, teasing suction, but hard and merciless, leaving what Nico knew would be a vivid mark on his skin. Branding him.

He had no expectations that he would enjoy what was going to happen once they reached Nico's room. Yes, he could take pleasure in some rough play, but this wasn't that. On Littlewood's part, at least, it was entirely real, an act of violence and corruption, and even if Nico did like his sex that edgy—which he didn't—knowing it wasn't a game for Littlewood was enough to strip any potential for pleasure from it and just creep him right the fuck out.

He'd had clients who hadn't bothered with his enjoyment before. He'd had clients who had been rough and hurt him before. But it had all been negotiated in advance, part of the fee, with boundaries firmly established. His mother insisted on it for all their clients, citing the abuses of the brothels as her rationale for conducting business differently. A couple of clients had wanted to renegotiate on the fly, but Nico had shut that down quickly—per her rules—and anyone who had tried to press the matter beyond that had ended up watching Nico walk out the door and hadn't had their money refunded, as stipulated by their contract.

But that wasn't what Littlewood wanted. He didn't want a playmate, or a toy, or a masochist, or a submissive.

He wanted a *victim*.

Nico's hand shook as he fumbled with his card, trying to swipe it past the scanner. He got it on the third try and opened the door, turning on the light as he stepped inside.

"I have a diffuser," he stammered, playing his near-virgin role to the hilt for the secretary's benefit. "You mind a little cannabis oil?"

"If you wish." Littlewood smiled. Nico knew that idea would appeal to him. It had been nearly seventy years since marijuana was legalized across the nation. Sonic diffusers had become a popular means of getting the effects of THC. And anything that could lower Nico's guard and weaken his ability to fight back would appeal to Littlewood.

What the secretary didn't have to know was that the oil was laced with a drug that wasn't even remotely legal. Officially, it didn't even exist. McClosky had entrusted it to Nico and his mother for times when he needed an intended mark to be particularly suggestible. After plugging in the diffuser, Nico slid a data card into the entertainment unit and turned on some low music, playing off the puttering as nervous dithering. Nico had programmed the playlist that afternoon, layering a subliminal message under the songs that extolled the virtues and benefits of McClosky's new project, Juggernaut. Nico had no idea what it was, but it didn't matter; that was McClosky's business. His job was getting Littlewood on board with it.

And the opportunity didn't get much better than this. The secretary was so focused on the assault he had planned for his victim, he'd never even suspect he was being influenced.

"That's enough." A harsh note of cruelty crept into Littlewood's voice now that they had privacy. His eye was on the prize, and the predator was beginning to emerge from behind that unassuming facade. "Take off your clothes."

Nico affected a pout, then shrugged and began stripping. "Jeez, that's not very romantic." From beneath his lashes, he watched Littlewood's eyes narrow dangerously. The secretary jerked his tie from his collar and tossed it, along with his coat, on the bed. He pulled his belt out of the loops and ran it almost lovingly through his hand before dropping it on the bed too. He began unbuttoning his shirt, revealing a chest that looked like it had a substantial slab of muscle underlying an inconsequential layer of middle-aged paunch. It was enough to make Nico's lithe twink's physique seem fragile in comparison.

When Nico was down to his minuscule briefs, he stepped closer to Littlewood with a flirty smile, hoping the fear he knew showed in his eyes would come across as inexperience and nerves. "I, um, I haven't done this much," he murmured, ducking his head. "What do you . . . What would you like?"

Littlewood grabbed Nico by the arm and shoulder, and tried forcing him to his knees. "I want you to suck my dick."

"Ow! Not so rough!" Nico tried to jerk away, making a display of his wince when Littlewood's grip tightened. He half wished Littlewood would react angrily. It would be comforting to see some sign of human emotion, but the secretary's eyes were reptile cold.

One hand released Nico, the other still digging in hard enough to leave bruises on Nico's russet skin, and Littlewood backhanded him almost casually. Nico didn't have to feign the cry of surprise or pain. He would have fallen against the bed if not for the grip on his arm.

"Shut up and do it." Littlewood took advantage of Nico's momentary disorientation to drive him to his knees, jerking his fly open and shoving his trousers and underwear down with one hand.

Shit. The name wasn't apt. Not at all. It would be worse than Nico had anticipated. For a moment, he considered calling the whole thing off, incapacitating Littlewood, and getting the hell out of that room. Only the fact that the job was for McClosky kept Nico from sweeping the secretary's legs out from under him, breaking his kneecaps, and running away.

Littlewood wouldn't kill or maim him, he told himself, fighting back the panic and drive for self-preservation. McClosky wouldn't send him into a situation *that* dangerous. Anything else was endurable—as long as he *chose* to endure it—and no matter what Littlewood thought, Nico was *choosing* this, however little pleasure he might take in it.

Littlewood's cock jabbed at Nico's mouth. "Suck it."

"No—" Nico began to shake his head, but the secretary grabbed a handful of his hair, yanking hard. Nico cried out in pain, and Littlewood took the opportunity to ram his dick down Nico's throat. He didn't even have time to suppress his gag reflex.

"That's right, you bitch, choke on it." Holding Nico by the hair, Littlewood began to pump his hips, fucking into Nico's mouth as reflexive tears streamed down Nico's face with each barely suppressed effort his gorge made to rise. Time ceased to mean anything, each instant drawing out into an eternity as Nico wondered if he'd critically, maybe even fatally, underestimated Littlewood. His battered throat convulsed around the secretary's cock as he gave one last brutal thrust and came with a groan. He jerked out almost immediately and let Nico collapse to the floor, coughing and gagging and trying desperately not to retch.

Littlewood panted feral breaths, his fists clenching at his sides. Nico cringed, forgetting everything he knew about self-defense for that vulnerable instant. He wondered if Littlewood was going to beat him.

He lay there longer than he actually needed to, trying to collect his thoughts and strategize. He heard the soft music in the background under the rushing of his own pulse in his ears. He could smell the pungent cannabis oil as the diffuser vibrated molecules of it into the air. The longer he kept Littlewood in this room, the greater his suggestibility would be.

He had to keep Littlewood distracted while the oil and recording did their work. If McClosky wanted Littlewood smiling and content when he went to their meeting in the morning, Nico was in for a long night.

Coughing against the slime of cum that still coated his throat, Nico rolled to his knees and pushed to his feet.

"What the hell?" he protested. "You didn't need to do that. I would have gone down on you. You didn't need to—"

Another careless backhand sent Nico sprawling back on the bed. Littlewood straddled him, pinning him down before Nico had a chance to do anything more than roll onto his back.

"How many times do I have to tell you to shut up?" the secretary snarled, his hand clamping around the front of Nico's throat, cutting off his air. Terror screeched through Nico, and he began to thrash desperately. "You say another word, you even think of screaming, and I'll wring your neck, got it?"

Frantically, Nico nodded, and Littlewood released the grip on his throat just as black spots began to speckle his vision. He snuck in a breath before Littlewood stuffed his discarded tie in Nico's mouth. The secretary seized Nico's wrists in one large hand, stretching them out above his head, then grabbed the belt and wrapped it around his wrists, cinching it until his fingers went numb.

"Don't fucking move," Littlewood growled, and set his teeth in Nico's shoulder.

With the end of the belt pulled taut and the secretary's weight pinning him down, Nico was helpless to fight as those gripping teeth sought a handle on his flesh over and over. He didn't break the skin, thank God, but that didn't mean it wasn't agony. Nico screamed around the wad of silk in his mouth, thrashing to the full extent of his limited mobility as more and more hot, throbbing rings of pain ignited on his neck, shoulders, arms, and chest. Even now, Littlewood hadn't done anything that Nico wouldn't have allowed for fun in other circumstances, or under negotiated terms with another client, but knowing what Littlewood was, what his intentions were, made it something else, something entirely horrific.

He found himself trying to mentally escape it by focusing on other matters. Shit. He was going to have to cancel his clients for at least a full week with as bruised as he was going to be. How long could he hide out of his mother's sight so she wouldn't know the extent of the situation he'd deliberately placed himself in?

Damn you, McClosky. This had better fucking be worth it.

It would help if he could dissociate totally. Detach his mind from the ordeal, let his body's own pain-dampening responses kick in, and let go, but he didn't dare. Littlewood was too dangerous to relinquish control to him like that. When there wasn't a single inch of flesh showing above Nico's waist that didn't burn and ache from the biting, Littlewood flipped Nico onto his stomach and began work on his back.

Nico didn't have to feign the tears. They dripped into his nasal passages, clogging his already compromised breathing. He choked on them each time Littlewood seized him by the back of the head and ground his face into the pillows, muttering all the painful things he'd do to Nico if he so much as hinted at fighting or crying for help. Nico fought against the surges of panic that kept trying to rise, telling him—not inaccurately—that he was in danger. He tried to convince himself that he was in control of this, that he had chosen it of his own free will for a reason. He would be fine when it was over, but the animal drive for survival and safety was having none of it.

The drug-laced oil was affecting him as well, heightening his own suggestibility. He hadn't considered that before, hadn't realized just how merciless and violent Littlewood would turn out to be and what the ramifications of that combo were. No doubt that was why he was having a hard time remembering that Littlewood wouldn't actually kill him. All the secretary's threats and insults were going to take root and fuck over Nico's psyche for ages if he didn't do something to overwrite them. The last thing he needed was to go all post-traumatic every time he entertained a client. He tried to block out the secretary's vicious words and shouted a mantra in his own mind.

I'm safe. I'm in control. I'm no one's victim. Nothing happens to me that I don't choose. I'm safe. I'm in control . . .

The mantra screeched to a halt when Littlewood jabbed two thick fingers inside his dry ass, a jagged edge on one of the nails scratching his sensitive tissue.

Fuck!

Nico's panicked thrashing resumed, more violent than ever, as Littlewood sawed those fingers in and out. He wasn't trying to prepare Nico. No. This was just to add another layer of pain. No matter how knowingly he'd gone into the situation, he was not going to be able to endure it if Littlewood fucked him without lube, especially if he was already abraded from the rough fingering. He kept struggling until the secretary ground his face into the pillow again and he nearly lost consciousness. He was still clearing the oxygen-deprived fog from his brain when Littlewood dragged him up to his knees and attempted to drive his dick into Nico's dry, aching hole.

I'm no one's victim. Nothing happens to me that I don't choose. I'm safe . . .

Eventually, Littlewood grunted with discomfort and gave up the agonizing struggle to force his oversized cock into Nico. He spat into his palm, rubbing it along his length before trying to shove it inside Nico again.

Nico wasn't sure if he was tearing or if it just felt that way, but whatever it was, his awareness was limited to white-hot sheets of pain washing over his body, radiating from his ass outward. The brush of Littlewood's dick across his prostate did nothing to make it better; Nico was flaccid and had been since before they started, not even the smallest bit of arousal present to ameliorate the pain. All he could do was weep and scream into the pillows, trying to drag his mind back to his mantra and program the affirmations into his subconscious.

Thankfully, it wasn't long before Littlewood went still and groaned, pulsing hot semen into Nico's guts. Good thing he was up-to-date on all his immunizations, as all licensed and registered sex workers had to be. There was nothing Littlewood could give him that couldn't be cured with antibiotics or postexposure prophylaxis.

Perhaps the worst part of it was the way Littlewood changed once it was over. Suddenly he was jolly and indulgent, as if he and

Nico had just had a mutually delightful roll in the hay. He flopped over onto his side, released the belt that still bound Nico's bruised wrists, and patted Nico's ass.

"That was great, baby. Thanks."

3

ORDEALS

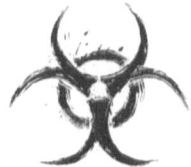

Nico wriggled his hands free of the now-loose belt around his wrists and pulled the spit-soaked tie from his mouth as Little-wood rolled off the bed and strutted to the control panel on the wall, his clothes still open and in disarray. He called down to room service and ordered a bottle of whiskey, apparently unconcerned that it would be charged to Nico's room.

Nico moved carefully, every muscle in his body aching as he sat up and pulled his knees to his chest. It took all his self-restraint not to lash out now that he was free. Even hurting as he was, he knew at least a dozen ways he could have Littlewood on the floor in seconds, writhing, bleeding, nursing broken bones and dislocated joints. Fury at the sick fuck was clawing inside Nico's chest, screaming to pay back the man who had hurt him, but he had to quash the instinctive reaction and consider his options. While Littlewood undressed, humming contentedly, Nico rested his forehead on his knees and centered himself so he could think rationally.

He still had a job to do, and if he didn't do it, everything he'd just gone through would be for nothing. The longer Littlewood lingered in the presence of the additive-enhanced THC oil and the subliminal recording, the more effective the tactics would be. The ideal situation would be for Littlewood to fall asleep here.

Fuck. That meant Nico had to keep him happy and complacent.

Nothing happens to me that I don't choose. I'm safe. I'm no one's victim . . .

But that was what Littlewood wanted—a victim. A hapless innocent to abuse and defile and degrade. The more vulnerable Nico made himself seem, the more satisfied Littlewood would be.

Nico's injured sniffle was affected, but the tear he wiped away was genuine as he braced himself for more. "Why did you do that?" he whispered plaintively, his voice raspy with the abuse his throat had received. He gave Littlewood a saddened, bewildered mien, trying to appear every inch the sacrificial lamb. "Did I do something wrong?"

Jesus. Littlewood looked amused by the question. Even fond. He finished stripping off his clothes, and he was already half-erect again. "That's just the way I like it, sugar. You wanted to make me happy, didn't you?"

Nico widened his eyes, trying to appear sweet and desperate to please even as loathing twisted his stomach and threatened to make him spew up the load Littlewood had shot down his throat. "Yes, but—" He shook his head as though confused. "You won't do it again, right? You'll be nice, now?"

The secretary looked away, his smile barely disguising a sneer. "Only thing you need to do is what I tell you. You just stay right there while I shower, baby. I'll be out in a minute. I'm not done with you yet."

Nico nodded and lay down on the bed, curled into a fetal ball, and watched Littlewood with wary, wounded eyes. Littlewood practically lapped it up. Nude, he strode to the bed, grabbed Nico by the throat and hair again, and seized his bottom lip between his teeth, biting until Nico tasted blood.

"You behave yourself when they bring my whiskey, or I'll make you very sorry, little boy. This is Washington, and I'm an important man. I even have the president's ear. If you're not here when I get back, or if you do anything to upset me, that company you interviewed with today will find out you're a hustler picking up tricks at the Watergate Bar."

"But that's not true!" Nico suppressed the urge to laugh at the irony and aimed for hurt and confused outrage. Even if it were true, he would have broken no laws here in DC and being a sex worker should have no more impact on his employability than having spent his college years manning a fast-food counter, but he pretended not to know that. Littlewood smirked, clearly thinking he'd found a way to ensure Nico's compliance.

"Think that will matter?" He licked Nico's bleeding lip and sauntered away, closing the bathroom door behind him in a gesture so idiotically arrogant and self-assured that Nico wanted to pummel the guy's face in.

The whiskey arrived while the shower ran. Nico wrapped himself in a hotel robe and answered the door, keeping his face turned away to avoid drawing attention to his split lip or what he suspected was the beginning of a swollen bruise on his cheekbone from that first backhand slap.

It alleviated some of his despair to know that underneath it all, Littlewood was dancing to Nico's tune. Honestly, his manipulations couldn't have gone more perfectly. Littlewood was so egotistical, so secure in his power over others, it never occurred to him that he was being corralled into the position Nico wanted him in. That would help offset some of the trauma and feeling of helplessness, and keep him on an even psychological keel, Nico thought, checking his bruises in the mirror. Of course, it would be even better if he didn't need to dance to McClosky's tune in this, but at least he'd chosen that dance willingly.

He could have dug in his bag for a drug to knock Littlewood out, which was a common self-defense measure Silvia Fernández made sure her employees had access to if they needed to get out of a dangerous situation. But if Littlewood awoke in the morning suspecting he'd been drugged, it would unravel all that Nico was attempting to do here. His only choice, other than to declare the job a failure and let his favorite client down, was to endure the rest of the night as best he could.

I can do this. Just because I've chosen not to fight back doesn't mean I'm helpless. I'm no one's victim.

He repeated the mantra as he poured Littlewood a drink and folded back the covers on the bed, grimacing at the pink-tinged smear of semen on the bedspread. Damn it.

He was still staring at the stain, wondering if he could actually go through with the evening, when Littlewood emerged from the bathroom, already stroking himself erect.

Nico didn't have to fake the fear in his eyes when the secretary ordered him to get on his knees on the bed and not to even think about taking his face out of the pillow.

A A A

LITTLEWOOD MUST HAVE BEEN on some performance-enhancing drug—probably Khumitrol or Climaxxis, depending on if it was legal or if he'd gotten it off the street—because he managed to fuck Nico's ass and mouth seven more times before he collapsed into a short, exhausted slumber. Now welted from the belt, and bruised from bites and slaps, Nico passed out as well, and awoke with a scream when the secretary drove three fingers into his wet, torn ass, then rolled him onto his stomach again for one more go.

Littlewood departed before dawn, his mood jovial, even gregarious. As he dressed, he seemed doting and half-smitten.

"You were amazing, baby," he hummed, kissing the top of Nico's head as Nico continued to play his half-fearful, half-eager-to-please role of the injured innocent. "I don't remember the last time I had someone as good as you."

If he asks, Was it good for you? *I'm going to puke.*

Nico smiled wanly and tried to look bashfully pleased by the praise. "Thank you."

"I sent my code to your tablet. Call me when you move here for that job. I want to see you again. You won't disappoint me, little boy, will you?"

His gorge rising, Nico shook his head emphatically. He'd inadvertently put himself in an even more perilous position. Littlewood now saw Nico as the ideal victim for an ongoing association. He'd pleased the secretary *too* well.

"I know your parents live out of state. You have any other family anywhere nearby?"

Nico's gut clenched at the question. Was Littlewood asking if he had anyone who would miss him, or was the man merely making conversation?

It didn't matter. Nico had absolutely no intention of ever being alone and within arm's reach of Littlewood again. He tried to brighten his responses a little, matching the secretary's ebullient mood and maintaining the fiction that he wasn't going to protest what Littlewood had done.

Besides, Littlewood didn't realize it, but he'd just given Nico an opening.

"Just a brother. He's on deployment, fighting over in Russia. I worry about him."

"Where does he live when he's not on deployment? Is he involved in your life? Protective big brother?"

Translation: would the fictional brother prove an impediment to Littlewood's desire to establish a brutally abusive, long-term relationship with Nico?

Nico shook his head. "No, we've never been close, really. We just kind of live our own lives. Still, I wouldn't want anything to happen to him."

"Well." Littlewood ran a tender finger over the bruise on Nico's cheek, his smile almost doting. "I'll see what I can do about keeping him safe. But you'll owe me a lot of favors for it. Don't forget to call, or I'll come looking for you. You don't want me to have to do that."

"I understand," Nico whispered with a shudder, cold, animal terror swelling in his chest despite knowing he would never again put himself at this man's mercy. "I'll call."

Littlewood seemed thrilled by Nico's fear, his face alight. "Good." He kissed Nico on the forehead and left.

Nico sat there on the bed in a defensive ball for what seemed to be hours, his knees drawn to his bare chest like a shield. Shivers racked his aching body. He could feel the wetness of the sheets beneath him, soaked with more than cum. A slight tang of iron underpinned the musk of semen and sweat. When he moistened his upper lip, he dislodged a flake of blood from beneath his nose.

Finally certain Littlewood was long gone, he rose from the bed and crossed to the control console on the wall, calling down to the front desk.

"Concierge. How may I help you, Mr. Fernández?"

"Do you have a medic on call?"

"Of course." Most high-end hotels kept a nurse practitioner or physician's assistant on staff should important guests suffer a mishap and their families get litigious.

"Please send them to my room in, say, a half hour. And have housekeeping come freshen the room and change the linens while I'm in the shower."

"Yes, Mr. Fernández." Not so much as a lilt of surprise in the concierge's voice, no indication this was anything other than a routine request. Nico had been in the business long enough to know it actually *was* routine.

After he ended the call, Nico took a long moment to inventory his injuries, shaking his head ruefully at what his impulsive decision to take McClosky's job had gotten him. Some escorts demanded top dollar to endure what he had spent the night suffering, and worse. A few years ago, the FBI had broken up an international snuff ring, where a service arranged contracts with desperately impoverished people who agreed to being sexually murdered by wealthy perverts in exchange for a generous payment to their families.

Of course, Littlewood wouldn't have wanted anyone who was willingly in the rough trade like that.

Nico's gut clenched again, and he dragged his aching body to the bathroom. After he was done shoving his finger down his throat to get rid of as much of Littlewood's spunk as he could, he douched to get rid of the rest, which felt like passing shards of ground glass. He dug in his toiletry kit for the empty hypodermic syringe he used when clients got a little too enthusiastic. Sticking it into the worst of his bruises, he aspirated some of the blood beneath the skin to help them fade faster. Then he climbed into the shower to wash away the last traces, and let the hot water sooth some of his soreness.

The bed was freshly made, the soiled linens gone, when he emerged from the shower. A soft rap came at his door, and Nico crossed the room to let in the medic. She lifted an eyebrow at the bruises peeking out from under Nico's robe and asked dutifully if she should call the police.

"There's no crime to report here," Nico said with a brusque

shake of his head. He sat still, letting her apply first aid to the places where Littlewood had drawn blood. She left him with a full course of broad-spectrum antibiotics and antivirals, as well as a medicated ointment for his anal tears.

When she was gone, Nico sank gingerly into a chair and reached for his tablet to make one final call.

"General Logan McClosky's home." Nico recognized the butler's punctilious voice.

"Peter, this is Nicolás Fernández. The general said you would be expecting me today?"

"Yes, Mr. Fernández. We're looking forward to having you stay with us, as always."

"Thank you. I'm afraid there's been a change of plans. I'm not really able to drive out there as I intended to."

"Would you like me to arrange for a car to pick you up, sir?"

Nico closed his eyes, rubbing his forehead. He didn't really want McClosky seeing him in this shape, but returning to his mother before he had healed up a bit was out of the question, and he desperately didn't want to be alone. "Yes, Peter, thank you. That would be perfect. Send it to my hotel around noon?"

"I'll do that, sir."

Once he disconnected the call, Nico refreshed the THC oil in the diffuser, complete with its special additive, and made a voice recording of the mantra he'd been chanting in his head all night, trying to offset as much of the psychological trauma from his ordeal as he could.

I have power. I am free. I am safe. I choose my own trials and my own destiny. Littlewood is an insignificant blip on the chart of my life, and nothing he has done matters. I am not his victim.

He set the recording to play on a loop and crawled between the fresh, clean sheets. The cannabis oil calmed him, and he willed his brain to absorb the programming. Lying there, he closed his eyes and listened to his breath as he meditated, sinking into a hypnosis-like trance and finally drifting to sleep.

4

DEFIANCE

"Father wants to see you in his study."

Zach blinked, pulling his wandering thoughts back to the here and now. The itinerary he'd ostensibly been perusing swam back into view before he looked up at his brother.

"What, now?"

"Yes, of course, *now*." Jacob rolled his eyes. "I don't know why you even pretend to work for him anymore."

Zach considered arguing, but Jacob had a point. He wasn't sure why he still worked for his father, either. He looked back down at the itinerary, unwilling to let Jacob know just how astute his statement was. In the three months leading up to their father declaring his candidacy—the press conference was scheduled for next week, and it would be followed by a grueling whistle-stop tour—Zach had become less and less a part of the reverend's campaign. Now he was little more than a glorified gofer.

Working downtown at the shelter had become his refuge, and he'd been letting matters with the campaign slide to make time for it. Even now, the thought of leaving town to accompany his father on the press tour was making pain spike behind his eyes.

He turned his back and shrugged off Jacob's needling. From the family room, he could hear his sisters—Mary, Naomi, and Rebecca —watching a vid. His mother was in the kitchen, telling the cook who would be attending tonight's dinner and what their require- ments were.

It was so cliché and antiquated an arrangement that Zach could have vomited. Nothing about the Houtmans' lifestyle had anything to do with the reality most Americans faced. How on earth did his father believe he could represent the public?

It had become a reflex to straighten his clothing before entering his father's presence. Zach wasn't sure why he bothered with that anymore, either. He certainly wasn't going to win any approval, and it was impossible for him to remain silent when the reverend's dogma got out of hand. Their arguments had been getting increas- ingly explosive, usually resulting in a headache and Zach yielding the field when it wasn't worth pressing his point.

Jacob appeared behind him in the hallway mirror as Zach checked his reflection. "He said I can go on tour with you next week," Jacob announced with a gloating smile.

Zach fought to keep the grimace off his face. "Don't you have school?"

"He's arranged with the principal to let me take my finals early."

"Then shouldn't you be studying?"

Jacob smirked. "Father made it clear he isn't paying my tuition and donating to the school to have them fail me."

Zach blinked and did a double take before he could stop himself, and Jacob's expression grew even smugger. Had their father seriously threatened to withdraw his support from the West Have- land Bible Academy if they didn't give Jacob a passing grade?

He shook his head and fumbled in his pocket for his prescrip- tion bottle, then checked his watch after he'd taken the tablet to see how long he had until he could leave for tonight's shift at the shelter. This was how his days often went: trying to hold his own against the reverend and Jacob, and then waiting impatiently for his chance to escape.

From the sound of it, his father was on a vid call with the door cracked open. Zach hesitated outside, torn between appearing as instructed and interrupting.

"I don't give a damn how impatient your people are, Dennis. You'll sit on them until after my press conference."

"Move the press conference forward." The voice on the other end sounded familiar, but Zach couldn't place it. "I'm telling you, Maurice, this opportunity is too good to pass up. The midsummer party—"

"That wasn't the plan. We talked about the campaign head-quarters."

"But this is better. If you can time your conference so it's just before the party, stir people up a little—"

Zach knocked without waiting to hear any more. To hell with interrupting. If he had to listen to one more person encouraging his father's misguided and frankly unchristian rhetoric, he'd scream.

"Hold on, Dennis." The reverend blanked the display and muted the sound quickly when Zach pushed the door open.

"You wanted to see me, Father?"

"Have a seat." His father gestured toward one of the chairs opposite his desk. It was a rigid, uncomfortable thing. The reverend's office wasn't about working with others; it was about authority. If he called someone in here, he wanted them at attention, even when he made a pretense of telling them to settle in. Zach had endured any number of dressing-downs sitting in those miserable chairs, and his backside had met the business end of his father's belt more than once as he braced his hands on that desk.

It occurred to him—not for the first time—that all his efforts to make himself acceptable to the reverend had failed. At first he'd tried because filial obedience had been drilled into his head from the time he could talk. Then he'd tried because he sensed that his father considered him a deficient son, and Zach had wanted to correct whatever it was he lacked. That drive had eventually been replaced by pure guilt. All his life, each time he dissented with his father, he pushed the blasphemy down with a sense of shame and redoubled his efforts. But it had never worked. Maybe he was born flawed, or maybe his father just couldn't be pleased.

Now, though, he recognized the futility of it all. He was tired of trying to convince himself that his own judgment was wrong and his father's was always right. He didn't even *want* to be the son the reverend wanted—unquestioning of his dictates, pandering to his sense of self-importance. Jacob was good at it, but even watching Jacob do it made Zach feel dirty. He wasn't about to try to emulate his younger brother.

Where did that leave him, though?

The reverend resumed his call, leaving it on voice-only as if he didn't want Zach to see whom he was speaking to. "Dennis, I'll get back to you. You make some good points about the midsummer events. I'll see what I can do about rescheduling."

Zach frowned as his father disconnected. "What's this about midsummer?"

Something—distress? annoyance? guilt?—flickered in the reverend's eyes. He wouldn't quite meet Zach's gaze when he answered. "Some of my advisers think it would be a good idea to formally declare my intent to run as a counter to the midsummer paganism, since it's such a tenet of my platform to highlight the way our society has drifted away from God."

Zach rubbed his temple. He should let it slide, but technically it was still his job to manage his father's campaign. "The midsummer celebrations are largely secular. They have no more to do with whatever rites they originated from than Christmas or Easter do."

"If we tolerate any hint of paganism, it will make us look weak," the reverend insisted. "Besides, there is a lot of media attention focused on the midsummer affairs. We can capture some of that vid-news time and capitalize on it."

"If you're looking to turn off potential voters, then go right ahead," Zach grated. "Or perhaps we could try to understand and acknowledge that Christmas became too expensive for many to cele-brate. The retail and industrial tenant workers needed another holi-day, something where the emphasis wasn't on buying presents or traveling to be with family. If you try to take that away from them—"

"It's not your concern, Zacharias." His father gave him a with-ering look. "We know what we're doing. Besides, most of the tenant workers give their proxy votes to their residence managers. *They're* the ones we need to impress, and they're the ones who have to clean up the mess when the celebrations get out of hand in the tenements."

Zach bit his tongue on another torrent of protests.

"If you didn't want my advice as your campaign manager, what did you want to see me about?" Zach finally asked, surrendering the urge to argue in favor of ending this conference as soon as possible.

The reverend grimaced again at Zach's informal tone. He wasn't sure when he'd stopped using the more deferential "sir" when addressing his father, but he was determined not to pander any longer.

"I called you in here to tell you that you are to stop volunteering downtown."

"I beg your pardon?"

"You're mingling with the wrong sort of people at those shelters. If word gets out about where you spend your time—"

"No."

"What?"

"No, I won't stop volunteering." He tried to soften the refusal by appealing to his father's ambition. "Charity work always looks good for a candidate, especially one espousing Christian values, and you'll be too busy to do it yourself. If I'm perceived as your representative there—"

"And will you also be perceived as my representative when you're dispensing aid and counsel to sodomites?"

The trap snapped shut around him, and everything inside Zach went cold. "I— Is that what this is about? Bryan Mitchell's court case?" He narrowed his eyes. "I don't even want to know how you know about that."

"It's my business to know what my *representatives* are up to." The reverend drummed his fingers on his desk, looking utterly unconcerned about having his son spied upon. "I've built my entire campaign on bringing morality back to this nation. You should know, you helped me build it."

"*No*. I helped you build a campaign based on bringing the Lord's word back to this nation. His *true* word. Christ's message of love and mercy. Not this warped, sensationalist excuse for hate- and fearmongering that your consultants and advisers are pushing on you."

Zach shook his head. "What happened to you, Father? You were always a little too judgmental at your pulpit, but never to this extent. Are you so fixated on your ambition that you've completely forgotten what Jesus taught us?"

"Don't presume to teach me God's word." There was something cold and vicious in the reverend's voice, and Zach hugged himself before he could stop the defensive gesture. "The bottom line is, you cannot be seen helping a faggot. It looks bad."

"What I'm doing for Bryan has nothing to do with his sexuality. His husband was murdered a year ago by the guards in the tenements while trying to prevent his little brother from being mugged, and when Bryan tried to protest the cover-up, he was fired and evicted. I just want to help him find justice—if there even *is* such a thing anymore—and an opportunity to get out of the shelter."

"Whatever the excuse, it ends now," the reverend decreed. "Now go."

"*No.*" Adrenaline surged through Zach in a sickening, gut-twisting rush, and he folded his hands together to hide their trembling. Never had he outright defied his father like this. He forced himself to hold the reverend's gaze without flinching. "I promised my help, and I'll give it."

His father's face flushed an ugly shade, and his voice grew even colder. "Zacharias, I would advise you to think very, *very* carefully before you flout my authority. Our ministry and political donors have provided for us generously. We live well here. What employment prospects do you think you'll have as a failed political adviser who parted on bad terms with his candidate? You never went to seminary, and you can be certain no congregation Houtman Ministries is affiliated with will offer you a job if you abandon us. Are you willing to join your street-trash friends living in the tenements, working for one of the retail or industrial corps?"

Zach blinked slowly. "Are you honestly saying you would throw me out simply for helping the less fortunate?"

The reverend sighed tragically. "It would be with a heavy heart, but I won't let you damage my campaign."

Zach rose on shaky legs, turned, and walked carefully to the open door. Jacob scurried away outside in the hallway, pretending he hadn't been eavesdropping. Zach looked over his shoulder at his father.

"So your campaign is more important than doing what's right. More important than your own son. Nothing you're doing here has anything to do with God," he said softly. "None of it."

He closed the office door behind him and met Jacob's smirk.

"At least Father still has one son he can rely on," Jacob gloated before he pushed past Zach to let himself into the office without knocking.

To hell with waiting for his scheduled time. Clenching his fists, Zach reached for the nearest comm panel and called for a car to take him to the shelter.

5

MIDSUMMER

Costas Companions always hosted a midsummer bonfire at Silvia's New Jersey estate. Even celebrities vied for invitations, which were generally only extended to favored clientele. Logan McClosky had been attending for more than twenty years.

The moment Nico saw the general walk into the reception under the pavilion, he knew something wasn't right. He glanced at his mother, whose eyes had narrowed. She gave McClosky a venomous look, and Nico took a step toward the general.

Silvia caught his wrist and stopped him. "I need to have a word with Logan," she said with ice in her tone. "Go see to the other guests."

Before Nico could argue, she strode across the pavilion alone, the jet accents on her sleek pantsuit glinting and flashing. Nico grimaced, then followed her.

"I don't recall sending you an invitation," she said without even a greeting. It was a small mercy that she pitched her voice low enough that the other guests couldn't hear. Anyone observant enough to notice the way her fists were clenched at her sides, however, would pick up on the tension.

McClosky flicked a look toward Nico, who was hanging back, close enough to overhear without Silvia realizing he'd followed her. It had been about three months since the general had returned home to find Nico covered in bruises from his job with Secretary Littlewood. Aching, Nico had attempted a lopsided smile for McClosky and had muttered, *"Someday that asshole's going to kill someone."*

"How is he?" McClosky asked, turning back to Silvia.

"As if you care," she snapped. The general steadily met her angry eyes. "How *dare* you send one of my employees—*any* of my employees—into such a situation? I've trusted you with my people for years, Logan. Don't tell me you didn't know what that man would do to him. Your information is always far too thorough for me to buy it."

"Silvia, I swear to you that there was nothing in his dossier to suggest he would go as far as he did."

Her chin lifted. "And if there had been, would you still have sent one of my employees to him, much less my son?"

McClosky opened his mouth only to close it again, his face neutral.

Silvia stared at him for a moment, then gave a jerky nod. "That's what I thought. While we thank you for your years of loyal patronage, General McClosky, I regret to inform you that Costas Companions will no longer be contracting with you."

"God willing, Silvia, I won't need to do it again."

"Good. If you do, find someone else. Feel free to stay and enjoy the celebration. Your hasty departure would be conspicuous. But when you leave, don't come back. Do not contact any of my people again, and do not ask my son to do any more jobs for you."

That was more than enough. Nico closed the discreet distance between himself and his mother, speaking over her shoulder. "I'll thank you to remember that *I* decide with whom I contract my services." She jumped when he spoke and looked back at him with an argument already forming on her lips. "If you don't like that, fire me. I'll go independent, and I'll take my client list with me. But don't carry on as though this is the general's fault. I've told you before: I could have removed myself from the situation and refused to carry out the job. I *chose* not to. When you blame him, you take away the validity of my choice and make me a *victim*, and no one does that to me, Mother, not even you."

Silvia's eye widened, and she gave him an entreating look. "Nicolás—"

Nico gentled his words with a smile and kissed her cheek. "Why don't we just enjoy the party, *Mamá*, okay?" He squeezed her hand and turned his soft smile to Logan. "Let's get you a drink, sir." Nico slipped his arm through McClosky's and led him away.

"What can I get you, General? Wine? Beer? Port? Vodka? Brandy? We don't have whiskey tonight, sorry. I really can't stand the smell of it just yet."

"Beer will be fine." McClosky frowned as if troubled that Nico was still so traumatized that he'd developed such an aversion. "How are you, Nico?"

"I'm fine, sir." At the general's sharp look, he smiled. "I mean that. I'm not just trying to be comforting. I won't say it's been easy or that I don't still flinch and have nightmares from time to time, but you hired me to do a job and I got it done. I did everything I could to take care of myself afterward. I started therapy as soon as I got home, and that's been good. It helps that I chose to go through with it, really. Knowing I had that much control matters. When I work on reprogramming the memories in therapy, that's what I hold on to. It was my choice."

McClosky accepted his beer and set it aside, fondly stroking a hand over the soft, dark waves of Nico's hair. "You're a remarkable man, Nicolás Fernández. I regret what happened, and I owe you a debt that goes far beyond money. I can't get into details, but what you did helped save a lot of lives. If there's anything you need, anything I can do . . ."

Nico grinned and sipped his champagne. "Sure there is. You can come back with me to my apartment tonight after the bonfire and fuck me through the mattress."

"I beg your pardon?" The general blinked, and Nico's grin widened.

"Even though my mother hasn't put me back on the list of active employees yet—not until we're confident I won't freak out with a client—my sex drive's doing just fine. I'm horny as hell, but it just hasn't seemed worth the bother to find someone. So what do you say? Help a guy out?"

McClosky looked genuinely caught off-balance, and after a moment, Nico realized he was blushing, of all the ridiculous things. That wasn't a reaction Nico had ever anticipated causing. "I think we've already established that your mother is quite irritated enough with me," the general argued.

"And I think we already established that I make my own choices. Don't you start trying to make me into a victim, either." Nico put some steel into his voice. "*I* know what's best for me. Respect me enough to honor that."

McClosky sighed and cupped a hand around the back of Nico's neck, brushing his lips in a light kiss. "All right, then. Find me after the bonfire. For now, though, I should let you get back to your guests."

Nico nodded enthusiastically, and he opened his mouth to reply.

That was when the world exploded around them and all hell broke loose.

⋀ ⋀ ⋀

Screams filled the air, and the scent of burning plastic was making Nico light-headed. Or maybe that was from hitting his head on a table as the explosion threw him. Thank God the bar had been at the very edge of the pavilion. He was lucky in that regard. The synthetic-silk blend of the large tent had caught fire and collapsed, melting and sticking like burning tar to everything it touched.

That was the cause of the screaming. Those who weren't shrieking were running away, around the house toward the gates and the street beyond. Some of them were calling the fire department and paramedics.

As Nico lay on his back, slowly shaking the fog of unconsciousness from his brain, he tried to make sense of the carnage and assess himself for injury. He had no idea where General McClosky was, but he only had a moment to wonder before people in dark clothing with face masks and guns were moving through the smoke and debris, shouting at each other.

"Find the madam! Get the cameras ready!"

Ice flushed through his veins in a surge of fear, and Nico went still as one of the figures began humming off-key as he nudged unconscious or dead bodies. The tune was a popular hymn, one whose lyrics had been spray-painted at the sites of most of the Righteous Action League bombings.

The hummer was so busy checking the broken forms littering the ground—pausing periodically to kick or spit on one here and there—that he fell behind his comrades. Or maybe this was his job, to give the coup de grâce to anyone who survived the explosion. Nico lay very still, hoping the tone-deaf terrorist would pass him by. He tried not to grunt as a booted foot connected with his ribs, but he must have winced because he *felt* the man's posture change as he took aim with his assault rifle.

Nico moved without thinking, flipping to wrap an arm around the man's legs and yank them out from underneath him. The attacker went down with a startled cry, with Nico already rolling to get above him, aiming an elbow for the front of his throat. While the man gagged, Nico wrested the rifle from his hands. He used the stock of the gun to smash the guy in the temple, and his coughing and writhing stopped.

Pushing to his feet, Nico stared at the weapon in his hands, trying to make sense of it. The self-defense classes he'd taken since he was a child had all been hand-to-hand. Unfortunately, a black belt or three couldn't stop bullets.

It would be in his way if he tried to fight hand-to-hand, but he didn't want to leave it where his would-be assassin could get his hands on it if he regained consciousness. Grimacing, Nico slung it over his shoulder by the strap. Billowing smoke and fumes burned his eyes, and he snatched the assassin's gas mask before he set off through the wreckage and groans, praying he'd reach his mother before their assailants did.

Suddenly voices crackled beside his ear, and Nico stopped where he stood. The mask had an open audio channel, a speaker nested in the strap that passed over his ears. Swallowing, he listened to the chatter.

"Any sign of her in the pavilion?"

"Negative. Our scout says he saw her head toward the house right before the bomb detonated."

Nico turned and made his way toward the house before the voice that seemed to be in charge gave the command to do so. He was tempted to break into a sprint and try to beat them there, but he didn't dare draw attention. In his black suit with a black shirt underneath, he could pass as one of them in all the smoke and confusion as long as no one got a good look at him.

The rest of the terrorists were heading into the house by the most direct route, up onto the deck and through the French patio doors. But Nico knew better than to look for his mother in the house. In all likelihood, if his mother was alive, she was helping direct her guests to safety. That meant she would be in front of the house, clearing the road and driveway for the emergency services. Would the assassins go after her when she was surrounded by innocents?

Nico snorted at his own foolishness. The RAL goons had just detonated a bomb in the middle of a midsummer party. Clearly they didn't care about innocent lives.

Ducking around the side of the house, Nico pulled his mask up over his head, debating if he should keep it to listen in on the attackers or get rid of it so they couldn't hear him. He couldn't find any switch or button to close the two-way audio channel, and he wasn't sure it was worth the risk.

He leaned against the outer wall of the garage and dug in his inner breast pocket for his mobile, breathing a sigh of relief to find it still working. He switched on the text messaging function and entered his mother's code.

Get away from the guests. The bombers are after you.

His blood rushed in his ears as he sat there and waited, blocking out the chatter over the audio link. He was vaguely aware of his head throbbing, but he didn't have attention to spare for that just now. He stared at his phone, praying his mother still had hers on her.

Apparently she did, because she answered right away.

Are you all right?

Yes. Get away from the crowd. RAL. They don't care who they hurt.

Emergency services are at least another five minutes out. People are injured.

Leave them or they'll be shot. RAL searching house for you now. Guest cottage?

Meet me there.

Nico shoved his mobile back into his pocket and began to pull his mask on again. Out of the corner of his eye, he caught a glimpse of a shadow moving and spun around. Too late to block the attack. A large body slammed him against the wall. Powerful hands seized his shoulders and pulled him forward, bending him in half to meet the knee that rammed into his solar plexus. Those same hands shoved him up against the fieldstone wall again, and one fist drew back for what promised to be a killing blow to his nose or throat. It stopped just short of its target, and Nico's gaze moved from it to Logan McClosky's startled eyes.

He slapped one hand over the general's mouth when he started to speak and stripped off the mask with the other, throwing it far away so it wouldn't pick up their conversation.

"Are you all right, Nicolás?" the general asked when Nico took his hand away from his mouth. He began patting Nico down as if checking for injury from their brief struggle.

Nico swallowed against a wave of nausea from the knee to the stomach, and nodded. "Fine. They're after my mother. I heard them talking about finding 'the madam.' I think they're RAL."

"I agree. Do you know where she is?"

"She's supposed to meet me at the guest cottage. I told her to get away from the house so no bystanders get hurt."

"Smart move. Let's go. You know how to handle that weapon?"

Nico shook his head, looking over his shoulder where the assault rifle dug into his back, all but forgotten. "No."

"Give it to me, then." As Nico shrugged the strap off his shoulder, the general reached inside his suit and pulled out a small handgun. "Don't try to shoot unless you're point-blank and absolutely have to."

Nico tucked the gun into his waistband, knowing he'd be far more effective using his fists if it came to that. They moved together through the darkness, hunched down and trying to keep to the shadows as they crossed the wooded lawn to the small guest bungalow. He swallowed a surge of bitter anger as he considered the poverty and prejudice his mother had overcome to obtain all this. She'd built an empire from nothing but her own charm and acumen in a world that did everything in its power to handicap her, and now these RAL assholes wanted to kill her for it.

The cottage was dark as they approached, and Nico could see no activity to indicate his mother had arrived yet. Silently, he and McClosky slipped in through the back door. If she was here, she would be someplace well hidden and defensible.

"There's a utility room between this hallway and the kitchen," Nico whispered, leaning close to the general's ear. "It has doors at both ends, so she wouldn't be trapped."

McClosky nodded, and Nico followed as the general went first. Nico didn't dare take the lead and come between McClosky and anyone he might aim that rifle at.

When they reached the door to the utility room, it was closed. McClosky gestured Nico over and against the wall, probably in case anything hostile lurked on the other side. Then McClosky opened it carefully.

Peering cautiously around the edge, Nico saw a glint of light off the jet beading of his mother's shadowed figure. She stood with her back to the wall at the far end of the room, beside the other door, which was also opening but with considerably less caution. Shots exploded in the stillness, driving McClosky back. Common sense fled as Nico imagined the attacker discovering his mother there, flattened against the wall he'd just charged past.

Nico broke cover, diving into the room in time to see his mother grab the assailant's outstretched gun arm. The snap of bone breaking and a startled masculine scream pierced the tense silence, and Silvia bent forward, using the leverage to throw her attacker over her shoulder. The floor vibrated with the impact. She kicked his gun away as he struggled to recover, then she dropped, her elbow drilling downward. Nico heard the crunch as the man's larynx collapsed.

For a moment, all he could do was stare at his mother, unable to grasp that he'd just watched her kill a man. Her dark eyes were wide and bulging. She had two more black belts than Nico did, and over the years she'd had to deter an abusive client once or twice. But never had she done anything like this.

He wasn't certain which of them was more astonished and horrified.

In the distance, sirens screamed. Help had arrived.

"Are you all right?" he asked his mother. He couldn't seem to rip his shocked gaze away from hers. She nodded, her bronze complexion gray and peaked, so Nico spoke over his shoulder. "General, we need to get her out of here in case there are any stragglers the police haven't—"

Ice crept into the pit of his gut as he heard only silence behind him. He turned to find McClosky lying on the hallway floor, blood wicking through the fabric of the white shirt under his suit jacket.

"Shit! General! *General!*"

6

CODES

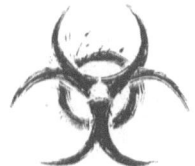

" . . . Today was the first court appearance for the Righteous Action League fundamentalists who bombed a midsummer celebration last month . . ."

Nico froze, his fingers poised midsentence. Almost against his will, his eyes moved to the projection on the hospital-room wall.

" . . . a number of guests were injured and killed in the explosion. One attacker was killed at the scene, and seven others apprehended. All have refused to answer questions and all have pleaded not guilty to multiple counts of murder, calling their actions justifiable. Families of the victims of the attack are calling it terrorism and have threatened a civil suit against the RAL."

He wanted to turn it off but couldn't quite break the compulsion to keep listening. The news was his window to the world as he might have experienced it if not for his mother's brilliance and determination. He'd been feeling more cut off from reality than usual since the bombing, having spent several weeks in protective custody after the RAL all but put a bounty on his and Silvia's heads, posting a series of vids urging their followers to complete the job the assailants at the party had failed to accomplish.

"In related news, Reverend Maurice Houtman, spokesman for

the Righteous Word Party and a newly declared candidate in next year's Senate election, posted a video update to RWP supporters this afternoon, protesting the ongoing investigation into any possible connection the RWP might have with the Righteous Action League or the so-called Midsummer Martyrs. He calls the inquiries 'persecution,' reiterating his party's commitment to returning the United States to its spiritual roots. The RWP exceeded their fundraising goals last quarter, championing Houtman's intended candidacy as a 'referendum on morality.'"

Nico snorted, then glanced at the sleeping form on the bed. After two surgeries to repair the damage to his heart, lungs, and aorta, General McClosky finally had come out of his medically induced coma the day before. This was the first chance Nico had to visit. Even now, there was an agent from a private security firm standing outside the hospital room, waiting to escort Nico home.

"News off," he murmured, pitching his voice low to avoid waking McClosky. He readjusted his HUD glasses and the typing rings on his hands and returned to working on his paper. An illusory keyboard appeared beneath the document in the field projected by the lenses. The rings controlled phantom fingers that hovered over the keys, interpreting each twitch of his fingers as a keystroke. The typing was archaic, and he received more than enough grief from his study partners for using it when voice recognition and eye-tracking technology was nearly flawless. But Nico retained information better if he physically wrote out the words.

He was absorbed in his work when a soft moan from the bed brought the world back into focus. With a flick of his thumb, he saved and turned off the projection, quickly removing the glasses and rings. He pulled his chair closer to the bedside.

"General?"

McClosky turned his head, blinking blearily at Nico for a confused moment. Then something seemed to click into place behind his eyes, and his gaze became more focused.

"Nicolás. You— I was shot."

"Yes, sir. I know the doctors talked to you yesterday, but you've been pretty heavily medicated so they weren't sure how much you'd retain."

"I think I recall the basics. You and your mother are all right?"

"We're both fine. Well, as fine as we can be with bounties on our heads, but yeah, we're okay."

"Is she still pissed off at me?"

Nico grinned. "No, sir. I think nearly getting killed at her party exonerates you of all wrongdoing, real or imagined."

The general managed a weak smile. "Can you please get me some water?"

Nico nodded and pushed up out of his chair. He fetched a sipper bottle from a nearby tray and filled it with ice water from a pitcher.

The general wet his mouth and cleared his throat. "Thank you. What's the date?"

"The twentieth of July, sir."

"Damn." McClosky closed his eyes. His head rolled back wearily for a moment before looking at Nico again. "All right, can you do me a favor? I know the staff here at the hospital has the codes for my emergency contacts. I need you to find the nurse and have someone notify Doctor Thanh at the Pentagon. Tell her I want her or her assistant here within the hour for a briefing."

Nico frowned. "Shouldn't you rest? Or clear it with your doctors first or something?"

McClosky shook his head, his expression so grave and concerned that Nico felt a moment of fear. "I've missed too much already. There were things I was— Of all the damned inconvenient times for this to happen. Please, just get Thanh here for me?"

"Yes, sir," Nico said as he packed up his equipment. He slung his bag over his shoulder. "Anything else I can get you? Food? Juice? Martini?"

The general laughed softly, his face drawn and tired. For the first time in all the years he'd known McClosky, it occurred to Nico that the general was nearly three times his age. And at that moment, he looked it.

"No. Just get me someone who can fill me in. And . . . thank you, Nicolás."

Nico gave him an encouraging smile. "You're welcome, sir."

7

AWAKENING

EARLY SEPTEMBER

"That's it, then." Zach dropped the file folder on the desk in the shelter administrator's office as Bryan's lawyer closed the door on her way out. He tried to catch Bryan's eyes, but Bryan was staring down at the white-knuckled hands clenched in his lap. "The case was thrown out. No recourse."

"Rochelle warned us it would be a long shot." Bryan's voice was muted and void of any inflection. "I'm just sorry the money you spent hiring her was wasted."

Zach waved off the words. "I don't care about that. At least the money my father paid me went to some good, in the end."

"Still, you might have needed it if he—"

"He hasn't spoken again about kicking me out. I think he's afraid of the scandal it would create if anyone found out." He sighed and rounded the desk to drop onto the sofa beside Bryan. "I'm sorry. I wish we could have done more."

"Don't. You did everything you could. I know Andrew would be so grateful."

"I just— I wish—" Zach's shoulders slumped in defeat. "I don't even know anymore. I don't."

"Hey." Bryan's hand settled on his wrist and squeezed. "It's okay.

Maybe at the end of the day, the important thing is that we didn't give up trying to get justice for him."

Zach forced a wan smile. "Maybe. Maybe I just need to have faith that God will see to dealing out justice." He met Bryan's hazel eyes, and he felt his own smile brighten into something more genuine. Working with Bryan these last months had both strengthened and shaken his faith, but they'd forged a friendship, the two of them. "So what's next for you? Have you had any luck with job prospects?"

Bryan snorted. "Excuse me if I don't spare your sensibilities when I say 'fuck no.'" They laughed together, and Bryan's thumb caressed the knob of his wrist joint idly. Zach blinked at it and looked away, which only made him that much more aware of the contact. Bryan was a touchy person, and probably just missed his husband's affection. He had no way of knowing that he was making a knot twist and tighten deep in Zach's gut. Something squirmy and uncomfortable that left him deeply uneasy.

Because it wasn't a *bad* feeling. Not at all.

"I don't know," Bryan said. "I couldn't find a job with a company that offered subsidized housing even if I wanted to, but what else is there for a tenement rat like me? I mean, I was motivated enough to spend a lot of time reading, so I'm better educated than a lot of the kids who grew up in the tenements, but still . . ."

Zach swallowed and laid his hand over Bryan's, stilling the stroking of that single digit. "I've been inquiring too, but all my contacts come through my father, and even if I weren't persona non grata there, those people aren't exactly trustworthy."

Since his last confrontation with his father, living in the reverend's house had become a very cold existence. Zach may not have been formally disowned, but he might as well have been living alone for all the companionship he found in his family home. His father acted as though Zach didn't exist, and each time his mother and sisters began to have a conversation with him, the reverend would appear with something that needed their attention *right now*. The only one who went out of his way to speak to Zach was Jacob, and that was to gloat at his favored place in their father's esteem.

Bryan shrugged. "I wouldn't want you to do that anyway. Actually, I have one small hope of an opportunity."

"Oh?"

"Yeah, um . . ." Was that a blush creeping up from under Bryan's collar? "There's a company based out of Princeton, New Jersey. Word circulated around the tenements that they were recruiting, and I think I might be qualified. It's not what I ever imagined myself doing, but it's a living, and I hear good things about the company."

"Really? What would you be doing?"

"Um . . ." Bryan cleared his throat and looked away. "Working as an escort."

"*What*?" Heat blossomed up Zach's neck and across his face. "You're joking."

Bryan gave Zach a tense look and pulled his hand out from under Zach's. "Actually, I'm not. At this point, it's either that or the military, and I just can't bring myself to . . . Look, I know what your beliefs are, and I respect them, but I don't share them. I think God would be a lot less unhappy with me working as a rentboy than if I were killing people for a living. I've heard terrible things about the corporate brothels, but if these ballot measures pass in November, a lot of jobs will be opening up in three different states for escorts who want to work as independent contractors. It's a chance, and those are pretty rare right now."

"I know, but Bryan—" Zach forced himself to close his mouth, shutting his eyes while he was at it, asking God for some guidance. He was just a man, human and thus fallible and in no way fit to be anyone's judge, but it was hard to remember that when everything inside him believed that what Bryan proposed to do was an outrage. "What about Andrew?" he asked at last.

Bryan looked away. "What about him? It's been over a year, and Andy would prefer for me to find work where and how I can than starve on the streets saving myself for his memory." He lifted his head and turned back to meet Zach's eyes. "Besides, some people, after a loss like this, they hurt too much to consider being with someone else, but I—" He shrugged, a helpless, befuddled gesture. "I just miss it. Andy and I made a lot of beautiful memories that way. I want that again."

Zach's flush grew hotter. "You're not going to find it working as a wh—an escort."

"Maybe not, but I'm definitely not going to find it here in the shelter." Bryan made a derisive sound. "It's a chance to get out, Zach. Don't you see that? To be something better than a tenement rat."

"I know! I just . . . I can't stand the thought of it."

Bryan smirked, a teasing glint in his eye. "Why, Zach, are you jealous?"

Oh Lord, his face was going to combust if he kept this up. "Don't be stupid. I'm—" His eyes widened, teasing and being teased forgotten as another thought occurred to him. "I'm afraid you could be hurt."

"*Afraid*? What do you mean? I've been told this service takes precautions against anyone hurting their employees . . ."

"Yeah, but—" Zach pressed his lips together, damming the suspicions that had been nagging at him since the beginning of summer. "Don't you remember those bombings?"

Those bombings the Righteous Action League had claimed responsibility for. Those bombings masterminded by a man named Dennis Adams, leader of the so-called Midsummer Martyrs, or so the prosecutors were trying to prove in court. Those bombings for which the Righteous Word Party had been investigated for possibly abetting.

The bombings had happened right after the reverend had announced his candidacy, which had been moved up to coincide with protests of the midsummer festivities, at the behest of a man his father had called Dennis . . .

He couldn't tell Bryan all that. Couldn't give those horrible suspicions a voice and lend them any more weight than they already had as wild flights of his imagination. Whatever he thought of his father's politics, he couldn't believe the reverend would actively conspire with terrorists and murderers.

"Zach . . ." Bryan's voice was full of tender fondness, touched with something sad. His hand closed over both of Zach's, which were twisting together in his lap, but Zach didn't dare look up, afraid of what he might give away. "Thank you for caring."

Lips gently brushed his cheek, and he jerked his head around to stare at Bryan in shock. He was so close, his hazel eyes huge and beautiful and filling Zach's vision. He could feel the whisper of his breath, and his stomach lurched, his heart taking off at a jackrabbit pace. There was something in Bryan's eyes, something that went beyond friendship and gratitude. Had it always been there? How was he only now noticing it? And then Bryan's mouth covered his, and thought and fear and reason all just melted away under an onslaught of *feeling*.

He'd kissed before. He'd had sex before. He'd had a girlfriend in high school and another in college. He'd been fond of them, tried to convince himself he loved them, even, though he'd never quite succeeded. He'd ended the first relationship because he'd felt guilty being with her and knowing she wasn't the woman he wanted to cleave to, as the Bible said he should. The second had ended when he'd graduated and returned home to work for his father. He'd been grateful for the excuse for the same reason he'd broken up with his high school sweetheart: something had been missing.

Zach had thought it was simply a product of his discontent over giving up his dreams of a ministry, but nothing seemed to be missing from Bryan's kiss. He tasted sweet—oh *Lord*, so sweet! He smelled earthy and inexplicably alluring, despite the must of his dingy, thirdhand suit and the odor of unwashed humanity that seemed to pervade the shelter. Zach wanted to breathe and taste him forever. He didn't even realize he'd pressed closer with a plaintive moan until Bryan's arms closed around him and his tongue advanced, teasing Zach's lips open.

And they did. God help him, he opened and let Bryan in. And it was good. So terribly good. His fingers somehow made their way into Bryan's ragged, slightly greasy hair, and he met that inviting tongue with his own, as if he would drink it down. Drink *Bryan* down. Inhale him. Absorb him into his very cells.

This must be it, he thought wildly. He could hear his father condemning him, imprecations of sin and evil ringing through his mind. Surely this was how damnation happens. Not with a feeling of guilt and wrongdoing, but with this terrible, *terrible* sense of rightness. This must be how Satan lured you in, by making it feel so good, so perfect, that it seemed wrong could never touch you, that sin could never have any relation to what you were doing.

Either that or everything he knew about sin and God and morality and *himself* was wrong, and always had been.

He tore himself from Bryan's mouth with something close to a sob, his breathing ragged. His tongue flicked against his lip, and he could *taste* Bryan there, and all he wanted to do was dive back in for more of that flavor.

"I can't!" he gasped, closing his eyes, trying to put the temptation behind him. But all he could feel was the heat of Bryan's body so near, the moist, warm breath still brushing his face, and he wanted it *back*, all of it.

"*Zach*—" He heard yearning and frustration in Bryan's voice, and sadness, as well. Finally Bryan pulled away, drawing himself to the other end of the sofa. "I'm sorry," he said, sounding defeated. "Apparently I read you all wrong."

"What?" Zach blinked at him, clenching his hands against the itching urge to reach out and draw Bryan back. "Read me wrong? I never—"

"Yeah, Zach, you did. I brushed against you once, just to see if you'd react, to try to get an idea of which way you swung, and ever since you've been putting yourself within reach of me, inviting me to touch you a little more each time."

"I—" Zach floundered for a rebuttal but couldn't manage one. Dear Lord, Bryan was right. After that first time, it had always been Zach placing himself in Bryan's personal space, seeking those subtle little caresses. Enjoying them. Denying that they meant anything at all, that it was just Bryan being touchy-feely. What in God's name had he been thinking?

"That's not who I am, Bryan," he said dully, knowing that he was lying. He'd wanted Bryan to push the issue, to make a move on him, to exonerate him of making the advance himself.

"You sure about that?" Bryan's voice hardened a little, sounding a bit bitter. "Because it felt a lot like you were kissing me back just now."

Zach covered his face with his hands, feeling the tingle of his lips beneath his palms. How had this happened?

He tried to envision telling his father and shrank away from the thought in terror. There it was. There was the shame he should have felt when Bryan had been kissing him.

"Maybe you're right," he said finally, his eyes burning with tears he didn't quite understand. "But I'm not ready, Bryan. If I am . . . what I am . . . I'm not ready for what that might mean."

"I know," Bryan murmured sadly, and Zach lowered his hands but stared down into his lap, unable to meet Bryan's eyes. After a moment, he felt Bryan's hand on his hair in an undemanding caress. "Take care, Zach. Thanks for everything."

He barely heard the door close, but when he looked up, Bryan was gone, and Zach knew he'd seen his only friend for the last time.

8

FREEZE

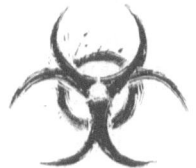

LATE NOVEMBER

"Have you any idea what this is about?"

Nico looked at his mother when she spoke. She was seated across from him in McClosky's limousine as it wound its way along the mountain highways toward the general's cabin. A heavy, wet snow lay on the ground between the dense trees, and the car's tires splashed over the slush on the roads.

"No." Nico shook his head. "To be honest, I'm trying not to think about it too much."

After the general's recovery, he and Nico had scheduled a contract for the weekend after Thanksgiving. But earlier in the month, McClosky had sent a very earnest—someone who knew him well might even say *urgent*—request for Silvia and Nico both to spend Thanksgiving at his cabin. That had thrown them both. They'd each had the general as a client at one time or another, and they both knew it. While Nico and his mother were fairly upfront about such matters, there was a certain amount of "out of sight, out of mind" they applied to the situation to keep it from feeling *too* incestuous. McClosky's invitation to them both—especially when he had booked *Nico's* time for the long weekend—had them off-balance and unsure of the general's intent.

Shrugging uncomfortably, Nico called up the news on the HUD and divided his attention between the broadcast and his mother. A medical alert logo appeared before the anchorwoman's sober face faded in.

"The Virginia Department of Health is now investigating what may be the first confirmed Virginian case of what appears to be a new strain of antibiotic-resistant, flesh-eating bacteria. The lethal infection was first documented in Maryland in September and resulted in the closure of Walter Reed National Military Medical Center, in Bethesda, for decontamination. Since then, at least two dozen other cases have been reported . . ."

Silvia shuddered. "Turn that off, Nicolás."

"Oh, don't tell me you're squeamish, Mother. I saw you kill someone with your bare hands this summer."

"Yes, well, that was in self-defense and didn't involve the words 'flesh-eating,' now did it?"

Nico snickered and shut off the HUD. He crossed the space between the opposing seats and sat beside her. "Are you all right, *Mamá*?"

She nodded, though her gaze darted rapidly past his face, refusing to settle on his eyes. "Of course. I suppose I'm looking forward to the new year. Between your being attacked and the bombing and threats, it seems this year has been more bad than good. I'll be glad to move on." She shrugged, clasping her hands together. "I don't know. Something about this doesn't sit right with me. Logan has been a client since before you were born, and I've never heard that tone from him. He's a good friend, but it seems as if he's accompanied all our misfortunes this year."

"Now you just sound superstitious." Nico smirked, trying to imagine the flinty general unnerved about anything. "Maybe he's just nervous about facing you again, even if you did forgive him."

Silvia forced a smile, patting Nico's hand. "Yes, I'm sure that's it."

They spent the rest of the ride in silence, though his mother's hand remained on his, stroking occasionally like she needed to touch him to reassure herself that he was there. Nico found himself staring down at it, trying to pinpoint the moment when it had begun to look like an older woman's hand. Slender and delicate boned, with dark-blue blood vessels snaking under thin bronze skin. Silvia hadn't tried to evade old age by surgical or pharmaceutical means and had instead opted to face it with grace and dignity, letting it ripen into a different sort of beauty.

Still, she had always seemed ageless to Nico. At least until now, when the years had begun to show in that frail hand.

The general welcomed them at the door to his cabin with all the warmth one would expect of family at the holidays. Not for the first time, Nico wondered why McClosky had no family of his own. It had always felt tactless to ask, but perhaps his mother knew.

"Let me show you to your rooms," the general offered, helping Silvia with her coat and greeting her with a restrained kiss on the cheek. "Thank you for coming."

"Well, I could hardly refuse such an invitation." She turned dark, slightly censorious eyes on him. "What is this about, Logan?"

"We'll talk over dinner." He clasped her hand in both of his and brought it up to his chest, an almost old-world gesture. There was something beseeching in his eyes, and Nico realized that he, too, seemed older than he had just a few months before. "I was about to pull it out of the oven."

McClosky showed them each to a guest room, which was out of the ordinary. Usually when the general had him to the cabin, Nico was ensconced in the master bedroom with his client. It seemed further evidence that, though McClosky had booked Nico's time as though it were any other assignation, he had something else in mind entirely.

They made subdued chitchat over their turkey, and Nico noticed his mother looking at McClosky almost as closely as he himself was doing. Finally, the general pushed away his barely touched plate and drained his glass of wine—his fourth that evening—leaning back in his chair.

"Silvia, Nicolás," he began, then paused, drawing a deep breath and releasing it in a sigh. "I'd like to speak to you about closing Costas Companions down for a while. At least until after the holidays. Preferably for the whole winter."

"What? Why?" they demanded, talking over each other. Nico

wasn't sure which of them spoke more sharply, but his mother nearly came to her feet with indignation.

"Why would you ask me to do such a thing?" she asked.

"Believe me, please, Silvia. I would not do so without a valid reason. I can't say more, but you will both be in danger if you continue working. In fact, it would be best for you both if you left public life altogether."

Silvia settled back into her chair. "Have there been more threats from the RAL that the FBI hasn't informed us of?" She grimaced. "I won't let those terrorists win. I won't. I run a legal business, and I do so ethically. They can't shut us down. I won't permit it."

"Silvia, it's not just you and Nicolás who are in danger. All your employees—"

"*I won't permit it!*" Nico startled as his mother sprang to her feet, her open palm smacking the tabletop with a rattle of cutlery and china. "How much will these people deny us before they are happy? These *upstanding people* who have such a problem with the morality of my business are the same people who would have sent my parents back to Guatemala to be forced into the labor camps when Soledad y de Santos took power. I will *not* have this!"

McClosky bowed his head, looking weary and heartsick.

"I promise you, this has nothing to do with the Righteous Action League," he said at last, releasing a long sigh. "I can't say more, Silvia. I'm sorry."

Nico looked from one to the other, the air heavy with the strain of their shared history, from their long-term friendship to their recent falling-out. The general's eyes pleaded with Silvia, but after a long pause, she shook her head and laid her napkin on the table.

"I'm sorry, Logan. I have hundreds of employees relying on me for their livelihoods. I won't put them out of work on someone's say-so. Not even yours." Another lengthy silence stretched out, and finally, Silvia dropped her gaze to the table. "I think perhaps it's best if you have the car return me to the city. If there is a danger, I must secure my business against it. Nicolás, are you coming?"

Nico swallowed and laid his own napkin aside, rising to take his mother's hands in both of his. He pressed a soft kiss to the knuckles of each. "I'm here under contract, *Mamá*. I'll keep to it and see you in a week."

Nico watched the general escort Silvia to the door, wishing he understood the stricken look in the general's eyes. But no matter what hypothetical disasters his mind offered him, he couldn't determine the reason for it.

⋀ ⋀ ⋀

Nico woke to a cold and empty bed, his muscles aching pleasantly. McClosky had been unusually vigorous once Nico had convinced him that he had no problems fulfilling their standing contract. The general hadn't been cruel or brutal, not like Littlewood, but there had been an undertone of urgency to his lovemaking each night that left Nico exhausted and collapsing in a dreamless slumber in the general's bed.

And he'd only gotten more intense once a travel advisory extended their holiday weekend well into the first week of December. The storm looked as if it would go on for at least another couple of days.

During the day, McClosky was courteously withdrawn, keeping Nico company for meals but excusing himself to his study to work for hours at a time, leaving Nico to entertain himself. And now he'd left him to wake up alone too. It wasn't the first time this week, either.

His concern for McClosky mounting, Nico threw back the covers, pulled on his silk shorts, and then reached for his robe. He wrapped it around himself before padding barefoot through the dark cabin to the general's study.

McClosky, absorbed in whatever he was doing, didn't seem to hear his approach as Nico entered behind him. It was the first time Nico had dared breach the sanctuary of the study, knowing the general often dealt with classified materials. He peered over McClosky's shoulder at a graph of some kind on the display. Nico wasn't close enough to read the labeling on the axes, but he could see it was charting the geometric growth of something that started small and quickly became huge.

"Can I ask what you're working on, sir? I thought you were supposed to be on holiday."

The general turned off the display and spun his chair around so quickly that Nico jumped. "You can't be in here, Nicolás. Go, now."

"General. *Logan*." Taking a deep breath, Nico knelt in front of McClosky, resting his hands on the general's knees. "You're my client, yes, but you've also been my friend. If I can help . . ."

McClosky's eyes searched his face for a long, troubled moment, and then he closed them with a sigh. "You and your mother are the oldest friends I've ever had. The only relationships I've been able to maintain these last thirty years. Did you know that?"

"I've always known you didn't have any family, sir. I wasn't sure about anything else."

"I should have fought harder to convince Silvia to stay, for your sake, if not my own. I'm sorry." When he opened them, his eyes were full of guilt and concern, but they held steady to Nico's. "I want you to promise you'll remain here with me. I have supplies, enough to last a year or more. They're in a hidden cellar beneath the cabin, and I have fuel cells for the generators, and we're away from the population centers. You'll be safe here."

"Safe from what? Is this about the RAL, still?" Nico saw the burgeoning graph from the display in his mind, its data exploding like a horizontal mushroom cloud. That didn't look like anything to do with the RAL.

McClosky shook his head. "If I tell you more, I'll be guilty of high treason."

Nico blew out an impatient breath. "Well, I'm not likely to report you. Is my mother in danger?"

"It may be too late for her now." The general looked away. "The national news sources have been conveying carefully doctored reports for months, but it's getting too big. A media blackout just went into effect. All communications satellite uplinks have been subject to censorship for weeks and are now completely shut down to unapproved traffic. The lid's about to come off."

"What are you talking about?" Nico gestured to the blank display. "What is it?"

"A juggernaut." McClosky's expression was bleak, and he turned on the display again. "Absolutely unstoppable. I want you to imagine how many people a single man—say, an orderly in a hospital—makes physical contact with over the course of three to six weeks. Perhaps a thousand? And how many people do those thousand each have contact with? Hundreds of thousands—possibly even millions—of people were infected before the first case even began to manifest symptoms, before any health authority was ever aware of what they were dealing with. It's all over the world by now. It is one hundred percent contagious and, as far as we can tell, one hundred percent lethal."

Nico's head spun, his stomach twisting. He thought he might actually vomit, but there was something more important to focus on, so he pushed the nausea aside and stood. "I have to call my mother. I have to get her away—"

"Did you hear what I said, Nicolás? It may be too late for her. How many Costas employees do you think could have it by now?"

"I have to *try* to—"

"*You can't get to her.*" McClosky caught Nico's wrist in a merciless grip. "The president and VP are dead; there's no telling how many in Congress and the cabinet have been infected. While you've been here, martial law has gone into effect. The official excuse is the megastorm that's hitting half the country. The highways have all been blockaded. The hospitals where cases have been reported have been cordoned off. Anyone trying to leave them is shot on sight. Armed patrols in hermetic suits are forcing people into quarantine in their houses, dropping off rations, killing anyone who resists. The only other information being broadcast anywhere is on approved channels." McClosky glanced away again, his eyes both merciless and remorseful when he looked back. "I'm sorry, Nicolás. I tried to protect you. Both of you."

"*Why did you let her leave?*" Quivering with rage, Nico shoved the general, pushing his rolling desk chair away. McClosky simply sat there, accepting it. "Why didn't you tell us before she left? She would have *stayed* if—"

"I couldn't, Nicolás. Not before the media blackout. Not before the martial law declaration. I shouldn't even be telling you *now*. I'm sorry."

"*Fuck* your sorry!" He shoved McClosky's chair again, tipping it dangerously before the general caught the edge of his desk to stop it. "Fuck your bullshit excuse! We *trusted* you!"

The general rubbed his forehead, as though overcome by a severe headache, and turned on several more HUDs. On one muted projection, a uniformed woman with a stiff smile was mouthing words, which the captions revealed were instructions for everyone to remain in their homes and wait for supply drops. On other displays there were rapidly scrolling reports of death and infection rates, as well as armed altercations between quarantine enforcement patrols and civilians.

Most horrifying, though, were the pictures of people staring sightlessly from agonized faces covered in suppurating lesions that mottled their skin like rotten fruit.

Nico watched it all with numbed disbelief, grabbing a wastepaper basket to spew into when the twisting of his stomach became too much to bear. When the heaves finally stopped, he wiped his mouth on his sleeve and grabbed McClosky's console. He entered his mother's code only to encounter a message that no signal was available.

"Call my mother for me. Get her now!"

The general stared at him a moment, then sighed and typed in codes and authorizations.

Silvia's face was drawn and worried when it appeared on the display. It was obvious she hadn't been sleeping. "Nicolás! Are you all right? I haven't been able to call out from the house for days!"

"I'm fine, *Mamá*. I'm here with the general still. Are you all right?"

"Yes, but they won't let me leave the yard. Men in suits threatened me with a gun when I tried to open the gate to go to work the day before yesterday. An applicant I was interviewing is stuck here with me, though, so at least I'm not lacking for company."

"That's good, *Mamá*. You need to stay there. Do you have food?"

"Yes, for now." Her eyes darted back and forth between him and the general. "Logan, do you know what this is about?"

"Just cooperate, Silvia. I'll make certain there are adequate rations delivered to you. Stay away from people for now. No one is safe to be around. Don't try to leave."

"What's happening here?" she asked.

"I'm sorry. We have to go. I'm not supposed to be making calls on this frequency except to work."

"No, please! Nicolás! You'll stay safe? I love you, *mijo*."

"I'll stay here where it's safe until I can come for you, *Mamá*, I swear. I love you too. I'll talk to you again as soon as I can."

When his mother's face was gone, all that was left on the projection displays were those horrific reports, all of which made it clear that the general's summation of the situation was an optimistic one. Nico took over the console again. Babyl-On and every other network he normally relied on to get word-of-mouth information were all offline. Each search he did came up with no results.

"You won't find anything," McClosky said heavily, after Nico slammed his hands against the console in frustration. "A few talented hackers will eventually find a way to access the old landlines and radio-wave transmitters, but that tech has been decaying and unmaintained for half a century or more. Even if they manage to get stories out there, very few people will be able to see them."

Nico grimaced. He'd always dismissed the posts fretting about the funneling of all data through the communication satellites as tinfoil-hat paranoia. People had been arguing for decades that relying solely on a satellite network controlled by the government would leave the public vulnerable to exactly this sort of blackout.

How long had the government been planning for such a contingency?

Nico sat on the floor, staring out the window as the winter sky transitioned steadily from black to gray. Coffee, and then breakfast, appeared beside him. Both went ignored.

It was past noon when he finally looked at McClosky again.

"You called it a 'juggernaut,'" he said, frowning as a vague connection began to form. "You've used that word before. It had something to do with the reason you sent me to Littlewood."

The general stared at him without affect; only his bleak, haunted eyes indicated anything might be amiss.

"Was this . . . Was this deliberate? Is it some sort of bio weapon? Germ warfare?"

McClosky continued to stare, but Nico thought he saw a wince.

"*Did you do this?*" he demanded, trembling. "Did I *help* you do this?"

The silence seemed eternal before McClosky murmured, "I'm sorry, Nicolás."

"Go to hell," he sneered before grabbing the wastebasket to vomit again.

9

ISOLATION

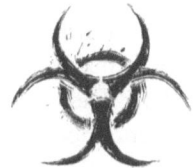

MID-JANUARY

"We have to find a way to get out of here," Zach muttered, pacing the floor of the snowbound Vermont rental. "We need to get to Mom and the girls."

"Mom and the girls are fine," Jacob said, and for once his tone was placating instead of antagonistic. "You heard what the guys delivering the rations said. Anyone breaking quarantine will be killed. Mom's holed up somewhere, just like we are. She's fine."

Zach whirled on him. "And how do you know that? We haven't been able to get a call or message through since we got here. Last thing we knew, they were supposed to be on their way to meet us. What if they got stranded somewhere?"

"Then they're getting ration deliveries, same as we are." Jacob shrugged, which made Zach want to punch him.

"How can you not be worried? Didn't you see that feed I managed to hack into?" The feed in question had been an underground signal, bringing reports of a staggering death toll and even more horrifying video footage of riots being suppressed, panicked people being gunned down for trying to escape quarantined hospitals. One especially hideous segment had focused on the tenement blocks, where the ration deliveries were reported to be inadequate, largely because the managers and private guards were hoarding the supplies.

Jacob frowned, though he still didn't look particularly concerned. "Father said it was just someone's idea of a sick joke."

Zach shook his head and resumed his pacing. "He's wrong."

"Care to say that to me personally, Zacharias?" The reverend sneered from the doorway, a glass of Scotch in his hand. "Go ahead, son. *Enlighten* us with your misguided conspiracy theories."

"I don't want to fight with you, Father." Zach turned away and rubbed his temple. How long had the reverend been drinking? Thankfully, it was a rare occurrence, but when it happened the results were volatile. He'd been livid over the disruption of his campaign, since they'd been stranded here just before Christmas. Over a month of forced seclusion with Jacob and their father had definitely given Zach a new appreciation for the concept of Hell.

He should never have agreed to come. Inviting him had been his mother's attempt at brokering peace between Zach and his father. She didn't often stand up to the reverend, but when she did, he wisely backed down. This year, she had drawn the line at not spending the holidays as a family.

Zach wasn't sure what made him go along with it. Perhaps it was a desire not to see his mother or sisters hurt by his falling-out with his father, but mostly he thought it was guilt. Guilt for what he'd almost done, for what he'd been *tempted* to do, for who he was increasingly coming to think he might be. He wanted to turn back time to before that moment with Bryan, when everything he thought he understood about himself and his beliefs had been called into question.

Or maybe he just hoped to remind himself just how wrong-headed the reverend was and reaffirm that those perfect, precious few moments with Bryan truly hadn't been a sin.

Why, when he knew his father to be wrong in so many other ways, did he keep feeling as though he'd done something deviant and illicit?

He taught me about God, he realized. *I have never questioned His existence a day in my life.* Maybe that was why he couldn't let go of his father's teachings. Because as long as he knew God to be true, he knew his father couldn't be entirely wrong?

Zach cast a furtive glance over his shoulder at his father, who had sat down beside Jacob and was once again perusing the now-defunct schedule of his January appearances. If the reverend kept that up, he'd work himself into a fury again.

"Look." Zach jumped at the sound of Jacob's voice next to his ear, so lost in his thoughts that he hadn't even heard him get off the sofa. "Even if the quarantine weren't an issue, have you looked outside? It's been five, six weeks of one winter storm after another, and they're not clearing the roads. We couldn't get to Mom and the girls even if we were allowed to. So just lay off Dad, would you?"

Zach closed his eyes, leaning his forehead against the cool wall. "For half an instant, you sounded like you were trying to be the voice of reason, Jacob," he said tiredly. "Our father doesn't need me bolstering him. He's got you for that. So I'll just leave you to it."

And no one stopped him leaving. When he was alone in his room, Zach tried to tap into the feed he'd managed to catch before. Each time a new vid played, the reporters seemed a little more desperate, both at the dire news they were conveying and at the authorities' increasingly dangerous attempts to track them down and silence them.

Perhaps the reverend was right. Perhaps it was all a hoax. Maybe this epidemic—whatever it was—wasn't the mass annihilation it appeared to be. But if not, why the quarantine? Why the media blackout? Why the military patrols?

Regardless, his mother and sisters—and yes, Bryan too—were out there somewhere, possibly sick or dead. Giving up on locating the rogue feed, Zach tried, without much real hope, to get a call through to Bryan's code. They'd stayed in touch through the autumn, but he hadn't been able to reach Bryan since the shutdown had begun. All the channels were still locked out.

Zach sighed, ready to give up for the night. He dimmed the lights, and then he crawled into his bed and curled into a ball, wondering what the world would look like when they were finally able to leave.

△△△

Nico spent the deep winter months haunting McClosky's study, listening in on the feeds the general received from various bases across the country and in other parts of the world. Those reports were torture, penance, killing another piece of him as the death toll mounted. Thousands became millions, which when added onto the global tally became billions.

And he'd helped it happen. He made himself eavesdrop on the reports as a form of self-flagellation for his prior obliviousness. He'd thought he was so clever, so informed, with his voyeuristic fixation on the news feeds. What a fucking ignorant, self-congratulatory dolt he'd been, not to question what his actions were putting into motion.

McClosky tried a number of times to explain what had led them to this point, but Nico refused to let him. The reasons and rationalizations for what they had wrought didn't matter. The reports he overheard, therefore, were disjointed and without greater context. The virus, he gathered, was codenamed Bane. It had something to do with troops who had been serving over in Russia, who seemed to be the test subjects of Project Juggernaut. The Rot was some sort of mutation, but it wasn't the only one.

The first reports of the plague mutating into a third strain were confused and disorganized, in large part because the sources from whom McClosky received his data feeds seemed to be dropping off one by one. *Ill, probably dead*, Nico figured. He sat out of sight of the video pickups while McClosky conferred with a virologist named Thanh, the same doctor McClosky had asked him to contact when in the hospital. The general said she was the most knowledgeable person in the world about the pandemic, but she was apparently stuck in a bunker somewhere, so all their information was second-hand, garnered from troops on the ground.

Almost all the hospitals had gone silent, which Nico interpreted to mean that there was no longer anyone alive within. The first report of a new mutation came from the guards outside one of the last "live" hospitals. A patient had emerged from the building covered in blood. When the troops on the other side of the barricade had instructed him over the loudspeaker to go back inside or face the use of deadly force, he had snarled at them—"like an animal," or so the report said—and charged. He'd moved so quickly the troops had been caught flat-footed. His speed had been described as "inhuman," and the first bullets to hit him barely slowed him down. He'd reached one of the guards and tore through the woman's suit, ripping at her throat with his teeth before a bullet to the head finally stopped him. The guard would have survived her injuries, but the odds of her being infected were one hundred percent, so she'd put a gun to her head before they could quarantine her for observation.

Since then, other reports had detailed similar events. People who were thought to be infected with the Beta strain were going mad, turning into feral, cannibalistic beings with incredible strength and speed. Some jackass had started calling them "revenants," making a joke about pandemic victims rising from the dead like zombies. Whoever that dubious wit was, Nico hoped he was now rotting away inside his own body.

Those reports had come in nearly a month ago. Now, there was nothing.

Nico hardly spoke to McClosky. Stuck together in the cabin, they were in a world by themselves.

And it was a *cold* world. As much as he despised McClosky for what he had done, what he had made Nico a party to, the general was all Nico had.

Which was why, as a fifth consecutive ice storm pummeled the cabin, Nico found himself in nothing but the underwear he slept in, standing in the doorway to McClosky's bedroom.

The general's eyes glittered in the almost nonexistent light, letting Nico know he wasn't asleep. He watched silently as Nico padded, barefoot and shivering, across the bedroom. Nico couldn't be sure why now, after nearly two months of giving McClosky the cold shoulder, he was seeking his bed, except that it felt like the world was dying outside and he desperately needed to touch someone, to remind himself that he was alive. How long that would remain the case, he wasn't certain. As soon as the weather permitted, he would attempt to get back to his mother's house, and he had no idea whether he'd survive that, either.

McClosky had been his first client; it was fitting, in a way, that he would be the last.

Nico pushed his underwear off his hips, his half-erect cock bobbing free, and crawled onto the bed. "I never knew I could hate anyone as much as I hate you," he hissed, and grabbed McClosky, crushing his mouth against his.

For all that McClosky had waited patiently and passively until Nico reached for him, those words brought the general to life. He was older, yes, but he was large where Nico was lithe. He gripped Nico with brutal force and tried to push him back on the bed, all the while launching a determined offensive with lips and teeth and tongue. But Nico wasn't in the mood to be accommodating. He fought, twisting one wrist free to punch McClosky in the face before diving in for another hate-filled, blood-flavored kiss.

The general grappled with Nico in return, trying to get him onto his back, using his weight to pin him to the bed. Nico made him pay for every inch of ground he gained. He made McClosky force him down, made him overpower him, and struggled to inflict as much pain as possible along the way.

And whatever McClosky's guilt, it didn't hold him back. He wrestled Nico onto the mattress and fought his way between Nico's struggling thighs as though he hated Nico every bit as much as Nico hated him. But even as they battered each other, Nico knew that wasn't true. Nico was just a stand-in for the true object of McClosky's loathing.

Himself.

The blunt tips of McClosky's fingers drilled bruises into Nico's biceps. His scalp ached where the general had caught him by the hair and dragged him back when Nico had nearly gained the upper hand. If McClosky had paused long enough to hunt down the lube, Nico would have bucked him to the floor and quite possibly turned this violent fucking into an actual, straightforward brawl.

Which was why there were only fingers, slick with spit, jabbing into Nico's ass and then curling forward to find his prostate, punishing him with intense pleasure as much as pain. McClosky didn't rush to replace those fingers with his cock, but instead he used them, driving into Nico until Nico was yelling, trapped between rapture and discomfort, and the fight began to bleed out of him. Only then did the general smear his dick with spittle and hook his arms under Nico's knees, bending Nico in half to breach him in one hard thrust.

It was good, and Nico *hated* that it was good, even though he'd known it would be. He wanted to find McClosky's lovemaking vile now that he understood who the man truly was. But his body knew the general, knew it with a familiarity he'd never established with any other client. It wasn't long until the way McClosky's cock pegged his prostate made spurts of cum puddle on Nico's belly. McClosky didn't stop, though. He swept his hand through it, tore his dick free to lube it with Nico's spunk, and then began fucking Nico again, harder than ever. It was too much, too soon after he'd come, but he didn't ask McClosky to stop, and McClosky didn't offer. He slammed into Nico again and again, until a second, weaker orgasm was pounded out of him. Nico's hateful snarls became shouts and cries and eventually sobs. Every muscle and bone ached by the time McClosky shuddered to a halt, gripping Nico hard and pulsing deep inside him.

When the general withdrew his cock, Nico could feel the trickle of semen seeping from his burning ass, and it only made him sob harder. He wasn't sure who or what he was even sobbing for, whether it was his own disillusionment and guilt, or the enormity of the tragedy he'd unwittingly helped give birth to. To his credit, McClosky made no effort to comfort him; Nico would probably have tried to kill him if he'd dared.

Nico curled into a fetal ball and let the grief and rage and hopelessness wash through him. He wanted to tell the general once more how much he despised him, but an exhausted slumber claimed him before he could get the words out.

10

DEPARTURE

Nico woke to find the muted daylight of the blizzard outside seeping between the louvered blinds. He was surrounded by the scent of McClosky, of sweat and cum and even blood from another night of violent sex. His split lip stung when he gingerly tested the damage with his tongue, and his ass twinged when he moved.

They did this every few days now, when everything became too much. Took their despair out on each other in the only way they knew. Nico wished he could say that returning to McClosky's bed meant that his loathing of the man was easing, but it wasn't. If the fucking wasn't full of rage, it was impersonal, an emotionless release with something a little more responsive than his own hand.

He was alone in the bed now, but McClosky was there, seated in a chair across the room and apparently lost in his own thoughts until Nico moved. The general had a bruise on his cheekbone, and one corner of his mouth was swollen.

That was when Nico noticed the ampule on the bedside table. It appeared to be some sort of nasal spray, the sort he used to get for allergies when he was younger. The words on the label were chemical mumbo jumbo, none of it sounding familiar.

"What is this?" His voice cracked, breaking off on a hoarse croak, and he had to clear his throat and try again.

"I want you to have it." McClosky looked grave. "It's . . . immunity to the pandemic, after a fashion."

"What the fuck does that mean?"

"What's happening out there—" McClosky waved a hand at the window "—what people are calling the Rot, is the mutated Beta strain of the virus contained in that ampule. The Alpha virus is nonfatal and will make you immune to the secondary and tertiary strains."

"And you've been *sitting* on this?" Nico shot out of bed in a new rush of fury. Only a tiny voice of self-preservation kept him from flinging the ampule at McClosky's head or making it shatter against the wall. "Why aren't people being immunized?"

McClosky glanced away for a moment. "Because even if we had enough—which we don't—we have no data on whether or not the mutation is also sexually transmissible or what effect it will have on gestating people and their fetuses. Believe it or not, there's more hope resting with whoever manages to survive this first outbreak of Beta."

"That doesn't make any fucking sense!"

"The Alpha virus is a weapon, Nicolás!" McClosky barked. "Anyone who is infected with it can spread Beta. It mutates when someone infected with the Alpha strain is wounded, their blood exposed to the air. If you had even a small cut in the presence of an uninfected person, you would infect them with Beta. We had a vaccine, of course, but it doesn't work against the mutated form of the virus, and even if it did, it was too late once we discovered the contagion was spreading in the United States."

Nico rubbed his gritty eyes and sat back down on the edge of the bed. "Explain this to me. From the beginning."

It was a request he hadn't made of McClosky before. He hadn't wanted to give the general a chance to justify himself. But if Nico was going to use the ampule, he needed to understand it.

McClosky scratched his lined, grizzled cheek, as though mulling over how much more to reveal, then nodded and spoke. "The Alpha virus was a means to deliver a genetically engineered payload into the RNA of a battalion of test troops. Once infected, certain portions of their DNA affecting strength, muscle and bone density, cellular regeneration, reflex reaction speed, and so forth would be overwritten. It would make them stronger, faster, more durable, and able to heal more effectively."

"You were engineering supersoldiers?" Nico blinked. "That's what this is about?"

"That was the first phase, yes. You have to understand, we were facing a recruitment crisis. We needed more effective troops to make up the numbers disparity on the ground in Russia."

Nico rolled his eyes. "You mean because it never occurred to you to, say, not invade the country and take over the Deep Siberian mineral mines?"

"Like they weren't invading eastern Europe to gain control of the mines there?" McClosky shot back. "Should we have let them get a stranglehold on worldwide fuel cell production?" Nico glared and the general waved his hand dismissively. "I'm not going to debate the politics behind the war with you. It's irrelevant now."

"Fine," Nico ground out. "What was the second phase?"

"The second phase was intended to weaken their forces—a massive epidemic that would spread quickly and quietly, no one realizing they were infected until everyone got sick in numbers." He held up his hands to forestall Nico's outrage. "*It wasn't meant to be deadly.* If the Beta strain had performed as designed, it would have made the population drastically ill for roughly two months. Their troops would be unable to fight. Their productivity would come to a screeching halt. Their economy would collapse. Every other nation —the few that hadn't already done so once Russia had adopted their aggressive expansion policies, that is—would implement travel embargoes. While they were unable to mount a resistance, we'd seize control of all their military assets using troops immune to the contagion. By the time they recovered, the war would be over. Nicolás . . . we were trying to *save* lives. To make the war nearly bloodless."

"But this other strain—the Beta strain—didn't work? It turned out to be the Rot instead?"

"While I was recovering from my bullet wound this summer, the

Juggernaut battalion had their first engagement with Russian troops. They performed exactly as they were meant to, and soldiers who were wounded in the engagement got close enough to enemy forces for the Beta strain to infect them." McClosky drew a deep, shuddering breath. "If I hadn't been in a coma, perhaps I could have prevented what happened next. Certain members of the various oversight committees, and the cabinet, had assumed the casualty rate for the Juggernaut troops would be virtually zero, and when it wasn't, they wanted the wounded troops brought back to the States for debriefing to figure out what had gone wrong. They were meant to recuperate in full quarantine, but instead, they were flown into Bethesda, where the proper precautions were not taken. One of the soldiers ripped out some stitches and exposed an orderly to his blood." He lifted bleak, grief-filled eyes to meet Nico's. "By the time we knew the Beta strain had mutated into something deadly, it was too late, and the vaccine we had was ineffective against the mutation."

The general frowned and looked down at his hands in his lap. "Perhaps if it hadn't been designed to spread so quickly and silently, we might have had time to research it more, but now most of the people who could find a cure are dead. Our only hope rests with those who've managed to remain uninfected."

"So why are you offering it to me?"

"Because I would see you survive by whatever means possible, and I'd rather not leave it up to chance whether you are exposed to Beta or not. If you have the Alpha strain, you'll be safe to get to your mother as soon as the weather permits. But you must understand: if you're infected with Alpha, you will be dangerous. Your blood will be deadly."

"Jesus." Nico's legs went limp, and he staggered back to the bed. "How can I possibly choose? What about my mother?"

"I have a dose for you to take to her if it's not too late. If you want to use it, you should do so now. It can take several weeks to manifest, and I imagine within another month or so, you'll be able to leave."

"Have you done it? Infected yourself with the . . . Alpha whatever?"

McClosky looked away. "I . . . have one for myself. I haven't used it yet."

Nico lifted an eyebrow, but he didn't ask the obvious question. He found he wasn't all that concerned with what McClosky did or why. All he could see were the images on the projection displays in McClosky's office, of people rotting away like moldy fruit and the reports of human beings becoming maddened animals, tearing one another apart with their teeth.

McClosky had done that. And he'd made Nico a party to it.

Feeling hollow inside, Nico cracked open the ampule, thrust it into his nose, and inhaled.

Λ Λ Λ

LATE MARCH

If not for the cabin's fuel cells keeping the computers running, Nico would have lost all track of time. McClosky was still getting infrequent reports from bunker-bound caches of high-ranking politicians and military personnel. Some of the bunkers had been running low on supplies, and the survivors within had announced their intention to relocate. As many officials as possible were gathering at Cheyenne Mountain in Colorado, in the underground facility that had once housed NORAD. According to McClosky, martial law was still in effect, which actually made him one of the highest-ranking government officials alive. As soon as it was deemed safe, a helicopter would be sent to transport him to Colorado Springs to help with the reconstruction.

"You can come with me," he offered, watching Nico gravely.

"What about my mother?"

McClosky looked away. "We haven't been able to contact her in nearly two months, Nicolás. She might be—"

"Don't say it." Nico narrowed his eyes at the general. "The last time we spoke, she said the house's fuel cells were running low. She probably took the unnecessary systems offline to conserve power for heat."

"I understand that. What concerns me is that since then, Silvia has made no attempt to sign onto her comm system, even momentarily. The personnel responsible for the ration drops are dead or unaccounted for. It's possible she may have had to leave the estate to find supplies—"

"If she did, she'll be back. She'll wait for me there." Nico shook his head sharply. "I'm not going anywhere without finding her first. I'll take your lightcar, since you won't need it. That'll help me get past the impassible roads, not to mention keep me away from any of the, um—"

"The Gamma victims."

"Yeah." Nico nodded tightly. The revenants. It was hard to even conceptualize that people were now wandering around cannibalizing what was left of the population like rabid animals. "I'll leave as soon as I've excavated the garage door."

Though the garage was buried by ice and wind-driven debris, the task wasn't as tiring as it should have been. Mostly it felt good to get out of the cabin after so long with only McClosky for company and a toning machine and old-fashioned calisthenics for activity. Clearly the improvised exercise had done some good for him, though, since Nico found the mass easy to move.

Making certain the repulsion-driven lightcar was in working order was another matter. Mechanics and navigation electronics had never been part of his studies. Low-mass, surface-skimming vehicles with sophisticated gravity-repulsion turbines that allowed them to hover above the ground were available only to the very wealthy or important. A lightcar wasn't navigable in severe weather that limited visibility, but it could get one past unplowed or weather-damaged stretches of road or massive pileups.

"It's running, then?" McClosky asked, coming up behind Nico without warning. Nico nearly hit his head on the hood as he checked over the systems with an amateur eye and then turned to glower at McClosky. In the natural light of the sunny spring day, the general looked alarmingly old, even frail. Strange, he hadn't felt that way in bed, though it had been weeks since Nico had sought him out. McClosky's admonishment about the possible sexual transmissibility of the virus Nico now carried had seen to that, even if Nico's revulsion toward McClosky hadn't.

He wished he could still look at McClosky and see the client of whom he'd been so fond instead of the man responsible for the deaths of untold millions—*billions?*—of people. He wished he could have something left that would enable him to look back on the general without horror and regret, but it was impossible. Where once he'd seen a mentor, now he saw a manipulator who had used him.

"Yeah, as far as I can tell, it's working. Of course, for all I know, I could get it a mile down the mountain and then it could drop me twenty feet to the ground to be crushed to death in a pile of blazing slag." He wiped his hands on his pants and grimaced at McClosky. "The nav-sat link seems to be functioning too, so I won't end up in Topeka instead of Princeton. I'm going to raid your supplies. Fuel cells, rations, anything I can pack in the car. If we're both taking off, you won't need them here."

McClosky could have argued, but he just nodded. "Of course. I'll help you pack."

Nico's chest began to ache as they worked in silent tandem, stuffing every spare inch of the car full of supplies. He and McClosky might never see each other again. And however much he loathed the general, something about that idea hurt. Not the loss of McClosky, perhaps, but the loss of the *idea* of him. Of the valiant, patriotic soldier whose efforts Nico had aided, thinking he was on the right side. Of the kindly, older man with whom Nico had always been a little infatuated, even if he hadn't loved him.

Some of the melancholy eased, though, when McClosky opened what turned out to be a weapons' safe and began sorting through the firearms, choosing guns that would be best suited to Nico and his mother.

"I told you last summer, I don't know how to use those," Nico protested, but McClosky was insistent.

"Then we'll spend the afternoon practicing, and you can leave tomorrow. I admire your competency in hand-to-hand, Nicolás, but you're going to be up against two threats once you leave. The Gamma victims are one. You might be immune, but they're still dangerous. Perhaps even more so are the people still alive. They're holed up now, in places where the revenants can't get to them.

They're hoarding their supplies and shooting on sight anyone who looks like they might be poaching. Or they might be looters trying to rob you. You may also—" Nico saw the general's Adam's apple bob before he continued. "You might come across Beta victims who are still alive. And suffering. Take the guns."

The reminder of those horrific deaths was enough to eradicate the last of Nico's sentimentality. He nodded grimly and spent the afternoon learning to sight, aim, and care for the cache of weapons and ammo McClosky was sending with him.

The sun was beginning to set when McClosky opened another lockbox. It held two ampules like the one he'd given Nico. "For your mother," he said somberly, handing one over. He didn't bother locking the box again.

"You still haven't used yours?"

"No."

"Why not?"

McClosky shook his head, and a sad smile tilted one corner of his mouth. "Would you believe guilt? Shame? Fear?"

Nico chewed his cheek a long moment, staring at the general dispassionately. "No," he answered, and walked away.

That night he lay awake in the guest room, every instinct screaming for him to get to his mother as soon as possible. McClosky's cautionary words about looters echoed in his head; surely his mother's estate would appear an ideal target to someone foraging for supplies. He itched with the need to take action.

He looked at the one gun he hadn't packed in the lightcar, sitting in its holster on his dresser, and thought of McClosky in the room down the hall. For just an instant, the temptation was strong to take the weapon and pass summary judgment on the man responsible for all of this. He could think of it coldly like that; he wasn't angry anymore. McClosky was responsible for more deaths than any war criminal in the history of the world, and soon he would be in a position of power in the military government establishing itself within Cheyenne Mountain. There would never be a trial. No one would ever hold him accountable. Only Nico knew of his guilt.

At one point, Nico even went so far as to get out of bed, to lay his hand on the butt of the sidearm. But he couldn't do it. Even now, he didn't have it within him to murder the general in cold blood. Perhaps it was his history with McClosky, or perhaps it was just the fact that he was a human being.

When the first gray hint of dawn touched the sky, Nico crept down the hall in his socks to McClosky's study. The bank of projection displays above the desk was dark, the feeds that had run on them continuously since December long since silent. Swallowing the eerie feeling, he opened the door to the storeroom McClosky had helped him raid earlier and lifted the lid on the small lockbox that held the last ampule of the Alpha virus. The one McClosky hasn't used for himself yet.

Nico stared at it for a long moment, his hand shaking, then he pocketed the ampule and slipped out the door into the frosty predawn stillness.

11

THE NEW WORLD

Twenty feet off the ground was just far enough to confirm how much everything had changed in the months Nico had been sequestered in the mountains. He kept his altitude low, as lightcars were most efficient when close to the gravity well. He didn't dare cruise higher, even though he wished everything were so small that he couldn't see the scars where fires had broken out. According to the early reports he'd listened to, there had been a lot of those as people tried to heat their homes after the grid collapsed.

Scraps of yellow barricade tape flapped around the hospitals and tenements that had been cordoned off by the National Guard. Nico had nearly lost his mind when he'd heard about that order on McClosky's news feeds. The measures taken to battle the pandemic had been as cold-blooded and callous as they had been belated and futile. Many of those buildings were burned-out ruins, as well, though he wasn't sure if that had been due to the National Guard or the people trapped inside.

By the time he was hovering over the gates to his mother's neighborhood, he'd seen more than enough to convince him that the devolution of the world he knew—a process that had been a grimly abstract nightmare from the safety of McClosky's cabin—was worse than anything he had imagined. He'd seen desperate people, drawn by the whining of his repulsion turbines, frantically trying to flag him down, but he couldn't stop for them. McClosky had advised him to park on rooftops when he needed to change the lightcar's fuel cell, and the one time Nico hadn't listened, one of the Bane Gamma victims had charged him as he was getting back in the car. Nico had gotten off the ground but not before the unfortunate man had managed to tear off a portion of the lightcar's front quarter panel.

He had to focus on his goal: get his mother out of harm's way. God knew when she'd last had anything to eat or who was scavenging in the area and could stumble upon her at any time.

Unable to find a flat expanse of roof to land on, Nico lowered it to the ground behind the garage, hoping no one saw where he'd parked. His mother was running from the house before he even had the door halfway open, flinging herself at him.

"Nico! Oh, thank God! *Mijo*! You're all right!"

"I'm all right, *Mamá*." He crushed her to him, unconcerned with the fact that she smelled of old sweat and something coppery and putrid. "Are you hurt?" He pushed her back, frowning at the rusty-brown stains on her clothing. "Whose blood is this?"

"Not mine. Not mine." She shook her head adamantly, looking dazed and feverish. "Come with me. Hurry! He's sick. I think I'm losing him."

"Who? *Mamá*, you can't go near—" But she was already out of Nico's arms and dashing toward the house.

The stench was stronger inside and intensified as he followed Silvia's voice toward her bedroom. Nico had to stop in the doorway, fighting a rising gorge as he saw the man from whom the odor was emanating.

"Get away from him!" Nico snapped.

"I have to help him. This is Bryan. I was interviewing him at the office when the announcement came that everyone was to return to their homes and quarantine themselves. He had nowhere to go, so I brought him with me." She stroked hair back from the man's deathly pale face. "He was attacked by someone a few weeks ago while looking for supplies. Did you bring medicine?"

Nico could tell by the way she touched the man, the way she spoke of him, that Silvia and this Bryan had spent the long, horrifying winter taking comfort in one another every way they could.

The man's face was mostly unmarked, but Nico knew what he would find if he looked beneath Bryan's bedclothes. He was already catatonic, staring blankly up at the ceiling.

"He has the Rot. There's no medicine that can help him. He's dying. Please, you need to stop touching him. We have to go."

"We can't just leave him!"

"We can't take him with us!" Nico scrubbed a hand through his hair. "He's dying, and it's not safe to stay here. People will have seen the lightcar pass overhead, and they'll be after it and looking for our supplies. Please!"

She shook her head. Not quickly, as if in denial, but slowly, as though dazed. Her brow furrowed, and her eyes unfocused for a long moment. She was so different from his sharply focused mother that Nico placed a palm on her forehead, checking for fever.

"Mother?"

She blinked, looking startled. "All right. All right, *mijo*." Silvia clung to the man's hand, though, drawing away from him reluctantly.

Nico cleared his throat. What McClosky had said about encountering dying people came back to him, and with reluctance, he said, "I . . . I have a gun in the car. Should I get it?"

"What? Why would you—" Her eyes widened. "Nico! How can you even think such a thing!"

"The general said—" Even as he spoke the words, though, Nico bowed his head, unable to finish the thought. He needed to stop considering McClosky's words to be gospel. The general might be the sort of heartless bastard who could kill people and call it mercy, but Nico didn't have to be like him. He wasn't a murderer.

"No," Silvia said, her eyes losing focus again.

Shock? Terror? What had these months been like, here?

She kissed the back of Bryan's hand and laid it across his chest. "No. He's resting peacefully. We'll leave him as he is."

To Nico's eye, there was nothing peaceful in the way the poor bastard lay there with his eyes open and his face frozen. His lips were bloodless and cracked, the whites of his eyes a sickly yellow. Only the shallow movements of his chest and the rattle of his breath said he was still alive.

Was McClosky right? Would it be a kindness to end the man's life?

It seemed like Silvia should have known the answer to that. She was a pragmatic, logical woman. The fact that she wasn't acting that way was a stark indication of just how traumatized she was.

"All right, *Mamá*. We'll leave him. Come on, please. We have to go."

Tears traced down Silvia's cheeks, and Nico noticed how much more silver there was now in her dark hair, how lines were carved around her mouth and eyes. Or perhaps it was merely the unaccustomed absence of cosmetics making her seem older. Nico grabbed a garment bag out of her closet and loaded it with her clothes, though nothing smelled as if it had been washed, except perhaps in the swimming pool. At least his own clothes were clean when he packed another bag with his things to supplement the handful of outfits he'd taken with him when he'd gone to fulfill his contract with McClosky. Then he wrapped an arm around his mother's waist, half supporting her weight as he led her to the lightcar.

"Where are we going?" she asked when they stepped into the daylight.

"Colorado. Logan says they're convening anyone from the government still alive and healthy at the underground facility in Cheyenne Mountain. There will be people there who can help us, keep us safe."

"Colorado." Her accent was thick, her voice slurred. God, she must be exhausted. "Fine. We'll go."

"Here. First, you need to use this." Nico dug in his pocket and pulled out one of the two ampules he'd brought with him from McClosky's cabin. "It's a nasal spray. Inhale it."

She stared at it as though it might bite her. "What is it for?"

"It'll keep you safe from the Rot. It's another version of the virus. A nonlethal version. It won't hurt you." He'd explain it all to her later, when she was less shaky.

"You're sure?"

"Yes. I've already taken it myself. The general gave it to me. Please. I don't know how long you have until it's too late." Jesus, if her companion had been infected weeks ago, it might already be too late. But he couldn't even contemplate that. "Take it."

Her hand was trembling, but she accepted the ampule and inhaled its contents. Nico enfolded her in another tight hug. "Good. That's good. You look tired. Let's get you into the car. I have food, and you can rest while I drive, okay?"

"Okay, Nico." She cast a hollow-eyed gaze back at the house. "Let's go."

∧ ∧ ∧

HIS MOTHER SLEPT like the dead while Nico drove, keeping the car high enough to be out of range of any looters who might try to take a shot at them but low enough to make an emergency landing if necessary. As the hours passed and Silvia slept without stirring, Nico tried to assure himself that she was merely exhausted. Caring for a dying man for weeks on end with no help, no hope of getting away. It must have been horrific. No wonder she was drained.

They were about halfway across Pennsylvania when his own exhaustion compelled him to find a place to land. He chose a high-rise office building, settling the car right up against the roof-access door to prevent anyone from coming through it. Then, with his gun loaded and lying in his lap, he closed his eyes.

Silvia was still asleep when he woke up hours later, the sun beginning to rise over the Allegheny Mountains. Nico tucked the gun in the waistband of his trousers, opened the door, and stepped out into the chilly morning. After relieving himself over the edge of the building, he opened the back hatch of the car to dig through their rations.

"Nico?" his mother called, and he looked up to see her climbing across the front seat to get out the driver's-side door, since her own was against the building.

"Back here, *Mamá*. How are you feeling?"

"My head hurts, and my back aches. Do we have any food?" He blinked at her querulous tone, then shook his head. She was exhausted and traumatized, and she'd just awoken in a strange place. What else should he expect?

"Yes, plenty. The general stocked us up. Why don't you stretch your legs and grab something while I check the fuel cells? Then we'll need to get going. We shouldn't stay in one place too long."

"Why are we on top of a building? You know I don't like heights!"

Nico clamped his lips against a sigh. "I'm sorry, Mother. I didn't want to park where someone might get to us. There are looters everywhere. I'll try to find somewhere rural next time, but this was the best I could do last night."

Silvia made a dissatisfied sound but didn't say any more, and Nico rounded the front of the lightcar to open the hood and check the cells. By the time he was finished, she was climbing back over to the passenger side.

"I'm hungry, Nico. What do we have to eat?"

The trunk of the car was still open, just like he'd left it for her, but she hadn't helped herself as he'd suggested. He looked at it and frowned.

"Here." He handed her a two protein bars and a vacpack of dried fruit before closing the compartment. "We need to get moving again."

He got into the driver's side and shut the door. As he started the turbines, Silvia stared at the rations he'd handed her in distaste, which he couldn't really blame her for. The initial lift generated by the repulsion engines made his stomach lurch too.

Silvia grudgingly unwrapped one of the protein bars and bit into it, making a face he caught out of the corner of his eye. "Don't we have any meat, Nico?"

What? He eased the car over the edge of the roof and into the air. "You almost never eat meat, Mother. You're practically a vegetarian."

"Yes, well, that was before I spent several months surviving without fresh groceries," she muttered, eating with more vigor. "Right now I can't imagine anything that would taste better."

Could the Alpha strain be affecting her already? His own appetite had easily doubled when he began to feel the effects of the virus, but it had taken weeks.

"I'll get some jerky out of the back for you next time we stop," he promised, patting her knee.

He tried not to frown when she flinched away from the touch. Even though she'd just been outside and it was a crisp March morning, a bead of sweat ran down her temple, and he could see the fabric of her shirt was darker under the arms and between her breasts.

Night sweats? No doubt she hadn't had her estrogen supplements in months.

It certainly couldn't be the Rot. Those people became lethargic until they slipped into catatonia. Now that she was awake, Silvia was about as far from lethargic as a person could get. She was practically vibrating with energy, her legs and hands twitching, her eyes bright.

She didn't go back to sleep, but she didn't try to make conversation, either. She didn't ask about McClosky or about Nico's journey from the cabin until he'd gotten to her. Every time he tried to talk to her, to ask her about how she'd passed the winter, or about the man he'd found her with, or any of it, the discussion devolved into Silvia snapping at him until he quit trying.

"I'm hungry," she complained again when they were on the Ohio-Indiana border. "Can't we stop to eat?"

"Sure, *Mamá*. There are some fields up ahead. I'll set down in one of them." The cornfields were a little too close to their respective farmhouses for his comfort, but he wouldn't irritate her further by setting the car down on top of another building.

"Get back in the car," he instructed when she followed him back to the trunk. "We need to get moving again. You can eat as we go."

As if she hadn't even heard him, Silvia began devouring the strips of jerky he offered her, tearing into them and grousing all the while.

"This is revolting," she muttered between bites. "I want a steak."

"Could you be anemic? Did they not bring you any iron supplements with your ration drops?"

She didn't answer, ripping open another package. Then they both jumped at the sound of a shotgun blast, and Silvia dropped her jerky.

"We don't want to kill you," a feminine voice called from the other side of a nearby irrigation ditch. "Just leave the car and the supplies, and go."

Silvia growled. The sound was so deep and furious that Nico's first instinct was to stare at her, but he couldn't turn his attention away from their assailants.

"Not taking our food," she hissed.

"It's okay," Nico told her. "I won't let them." He raised his voice and called back, "Don't come near us! We've both been exposed to the Rot. You need to walk away."

"Gee, isn't that awfully convenient for you?" the woman yelled. "But if you're dying, you don't need those provisions. Get moving, or you'll die a lot sooner."

"I'm not bluffing! We've got nothing to lose. Do you?" Jesus, he didn't want these people's deaths on his conscience, but there was no way he was leaving the car and their supplies. "Go ahead and shoot us! You'll just infect yourselves. Is stealing our supplies worth it?"

"We'll take our chances." The woman popped up out of the irrigation ditch with a rifle on her shoulder, and in his peripheral vision, Nico could see two men rise also, spread out about five yards from either side of her. They had Nico and Silvia in their sights from every angle. He kept his handgun aimed at the woman, though he knew it was useless. Even if he shot her, he'd be dead before he could get the other two.

Silvia made another enraged noise. She jostled Nico as she charged forward, her hands curled into claws. Staggering, he dropped his gun and sprung, catching her with an arm across the chest before she could get herself shot.

"Oh shit! *Don't shoot!*" the woman yelled, backpedalling quickly as her rifle fell from her hands. "Get back! Don't shoot!"

A chorus of curses echoed hers, and Nico watched as the three of them began to run, leaving behind the woman's rifle. Silvia quivered with anger as Nico held her in place, though she seemed to be calming.

"Are you all right, Mother?" he asked cautiously. He kept hearing the woman's startled cry. What had she seen that made her panic that way?

"Fine," Silvia snarled, jerking away from him. "Fine."

Nico nodded slowly and let go of her. She wasn't an animal he had to soothe.

Still, he kept his voice low. "It's okay. We're okay. Let's get you another piece of jerky, and we'll head out again."

Despite the fact that their would-be robbers were far in the distance now, Silvia stood rooted to the spot. Nico tugged at her sleeve as she stared after the fleeing figures as though she wanted to give chase. She was quivering with tension, her nostrils flaring with each heavy breath. Finally she let Nico nudge her toward the car, but she kept peering back over her shoulder, and the feverish look in her eyes chilled him.

△ △ △

THEY HADN'T BEEN off the ground more than an hour when Silvia started twisting around in her seat, trying to reach into the back of the car.

"What do you need, *Mamá*?" Nico asked as she bumped and jostled him, fighting with her harness.

Whatever she grunted in response was unintelligible. She tried to climb back between the seats, crushing Nico against the door. It was a good thing the navigation was performed by computers with satellite links or he would have crashed.

"Wait. Stop. It's in the trunk, you can't—" She began tearing through the packages of blankets and medical supplies in the backseat, and he grabbed her around the waist, attempting to pull her into the front again. "Damn it. Get back in your seat! Let me land the car!"

Silvia snarled and kicked at him, her foot slamming into the control console. It blared an alarm. Nico released her to turn his attention back to the navigation controls, trying to command the car to land. It lurched when Silvia kicked the panel again, and an error message chittered.

"Invalid input. Please try again."

"Mother, please, stop! Just let me—" When he tried to grab her again, to still her flailing legs, she screamed with rage. She jerked back from the tight space between the seats and turned on him, her teeth bared and her eyes blazing. It was like staring at a feral animal wearing his mother's face.

No. Oh God, please, no . . .

"*Mam—*" He barely had a chance to get his hands up to shield himself before she dove for his throat, teeth gnashing and guttural growls rising, punctuating her heavy breaths. "God, please, no! *Mamá*, please, don't do this!"

The cabin of the car was too cramped for a struggle. Silvia slammed into the console when Nico tried to push her back. Behind her grunts and snarls, Nico could hear the computer talking to him.

"Invalid input. You have fifteen seconds to enter a valid command or voice override code, or automatic navigator will initiate emergency landing. Fifteen . . . Fourteen . . . Thirteen . . ."

"Yes, land, damn you!" he shouted, catching Silvia's clawed hands to keep them from his eyes and pressing back against his door to evade her teeth. He wedged his knee between their bodies to try to force her back. The less success she had getting to him, the more desperate her struggles became. Spittle splashed her lips with each explosive breath, and one of her hands twisted out of his grasp, raking burning furrows down the side of his face.

"Eight . . . Seven . . . Six . . ."

"Land the damn car!" he yelled at the computer when Silvia's body thrashed against the console once more. His gorge rose as he felt the car begin to descend, but then it lurched again, alarms screaming as conflicting protocols jerked the turbines from one sequence to another. The engines howled in protest.

"Invalid input. Please wait for turbines to respond before entering another command. Do you wish to terminate landing procedure?"

"No! Land! Land now!" His stomach twisted as the car dropped altitude again, descending quickly. A scream of metal and another lurch said it had scraped something on its way down, and he caught a glimpse of a building sliding by.

Silvia managed to brace her feet against the passenger door and use the push to drive herself toward Nico, sinking her teeth into his shoulder just inches from his dangerously vulnerable throat. He howled, pinned beneath her thrashing.

And then the car struck something, and the entire world turned upside down.

12

SANCTUARY

"*M amá?*" Everything hurt. His shoulder throbbed hotly, and his shirt felt sticky with blood. Parallel lines of fire ran down the side of his face, and the sharp pain he felt with each breath suggested he'd cracked some ribs. He whimpered, despair crushing him almost as much as the pain and the crumpled cabin of the car were. "*Mamá*, please, answer me."

She was silent. In the thin slivers of light that managed to slip through whatever the car had crashed into, he could see her slumped against the passenger seat, a stream of crimson trickling from her brow.

Tears spilled from his eyes. "It's okay, *Mamá*," he whispered. Her chest was moving rapidly, her breath quick and shallow. He unclipped his harness and leaned over to reach her, running cautious hands around her body, checking for injuries.

Which was fucking ridiculous. How the hell did he know what injuries she might have?

He bit back a sob and tipped his head down, resting it against her shoulder. He swore he could still smell the perfume she'd used to wear, even despite the odor of her living so long without running water.

"It's okay," he crooned, biting his lip against another sob. He closed his eyes, and another tear slipped down his cheek. "You'll be okay."

How long he lay there, crying softly on her shoulder, he didn't know. But eventually he pulled himself together, testing his door handle. "I'll get us out of here. We'll be all right."

She's not going to be all right ever again.

He shut out the insidious voice, gritting his teeth against the pain as he shoved at the door with his shoulder. It squealed and gave an inch. His ribs screamed, as if he were being skewered, but he pushed harder. It opened another few inches, then stuck.

You've got to get out of here before she wakes up.

I'm not leaving her behind.

His mind and heart waged war with each other as Nico sat shuddering, gasping, trying to steel his nerves for another go at the door.

She's a revenant. That's what they were running from.

No. She's just traumatized. She can't be sick.

She's infected. You have the gun. Do it now, while she's unconscious.

No!

Before he could lose his courage, he threw his weight at the door, crying out in pain when it gave suddenly and poured him out into muddy sod and shredded grass. He staggered to his feet and looked into the destroyed interior of the car. A cold rain pelted him, a rain he didn't remember falling before they crashed. How long had they been out?

How long would Silvia remain out?

The car was a wreck; it wouldn't be taking them anywhere again. He was somewhere in Indiana, in the cold March rain, injured. He had ample supplies but no way to carry them.

She'll try to kill you again when she wakes up.

I can't. Please. I can't!

Then you'd better run, or you'll have to.

The wet polymer panel of the rear driver's-side door squeaked as Nico slid down it, his knees buckling beneath him. He gathered them to his chest, huddling there in a fetal ball as rain mingled with the tears on his face.

What am I going to do?

He wasn't sure exactly how long he sat there. Awareness of time and place kept fading in and out like waves lapping at his consciousness. It was long enough for his backside to ache from the contact with the cold, wet ground. Long enough for his clothes to cling to his skin, saturated by the drizzle. Long enough to have the disorienting sense that he'd passed out or lost time when he finally opened his eyes to stare at the leaden sky.

He startled when he thought he heard a moan from inside the car.

Get the gun. Do it now.

I can't!

"I'm sorry, *Mamá*," he whispered, his voice breaking under another torrent of tears. "I'm so sorry!"

Clutching an arm around his ribs, he dragged himself off the ground and around to the back of the car. The rain was freezing, and he was shivering desperately, his coat doing nothing to keep out the cold. The trunk hatch had popped open during the crash, and their provisions were strewn all over the field. Nico grabbed a rucksack and began stuffing it full of whatever he could reach—food, medical supplies, extra clips and magazines of ammunition. The fuel cells were heavy, but he made himself haul one of those, as well. He gasped as each movement sent another bolt of agony through his chest, and his sobs weren't making it any better, but he couldn't stop them. Each time he caught a glimpse of Silvia, who was growling softly even while she was unconscious, they wracked him again.

Reaching through the car to grab a blanket out of the backseat was nothing short of hell. He'd be lucky if his cracked rib didn't lacerate his lung. He draped the blanket around himself like a cloak, then shrugged into the straps of the backpack, using it to secure the blanket in place. He fastened the handgun in its holster around his hips, hung an assault rifle over his shoulder, then slumped against the car, shuddering.

He was sweating, and the pain was making him nauseated. Another quiet animal sound from inside the car drew his unwilling gaze, and Silvia stirred, moaning and grunting.

Do it. Give her at least that much dignity. You know she wouldn't want to live like this.

I can't! I'm sorry, Mamá. I just can't.

He broke into a hitching run before he could see her open her eyes.

△ △ △

IF ZACH HAD FOUND his family home lonely before, it was now downright desolate without his mother and sisters, without power and the constant bustle of activity from so many people living in a single building.

The journey from their holiday rental in Vermont back to Indiana had been fraught with danger. The car had been bulletproof, thanks to the fact that Reverend Houtman had been paranoid about his theological and political opposition for years. While Zach always considered the bulletproofing to be a testament to his father's ego, he'd been grateful for it as they crossed New England and rounded the Great Lakes. The highways hadn't been nearly as congested as he'd feared, either, courtesy of the home quarantine order. Still, there had been other survivors, some of whom had taken shots at them, no doubt after the car or whatever supplies they thought Zach and his family might have.

When they hadn't been attempting to evade human contact in the heavily populated areas they passed through, Zach had been appalled at how derelict the world suddenly was. Everything was still and empty, buildings dark, no traffic on the streets, no lights or signs flashing. Weeds were everywhere, and windows were broken in buildings where looters had attacked. Some houses and buildings were burnt-out husks with no sign of reconstruction. Everywhere they passed felt like a ghost town.

In the end, they may as well not have bothered to make the trip, as his mother and sisters were not there. For the first time, Zach began to accept that he might never see them again. That they might have been infected and died, or that they couldn't escape quarantine elsewhere to return home. If they were still alive, perhaps they were safer where they were.

How could so much have changed in just a few months? Everything was different now, and nothing that mattered before seemed to matter anymore.

Was Bryan one of the multitudes of dead too? Zach had been such an idiot, panicking over that kiss, rejecting what Bryan had offered. God had shown him a truth about himself that day, and he'd refused to see it for the gift of understanding it was. He'd been too enmeshed in all his father's lies and expectations. That moment with Bryan had been an opportunity for salvation, a chance to break away from all his father's hypocrisy and begin to think for himself and be who he truly was.

And he'd rejected it.

Now he was stuck with his father and Jacob because he knew, without a doubt, that there was safety in numbers. Safety in finding someplace well stocked and isolated.

Would God ever offer him another chance at freedom?

The house in Indiana was well provisioned, at least, since his mother had always worried about blizzards and the fact that they lived out in the country. They had fuel cells, lights, and enough canned and dried foods to make it until summer if they were frugal. Zach had retreated to his room and resolved to pass the time as peacefully as he could. He had avoided Jacob and his father, closeting himself with a lantern and his collection of books. Since he didn't talk to anyone, he didn't argue with anyone. At least not until the reverend began insisting upon twice-daily prayer meetings.

Zach had willingly attended the first one, for all of five minutes. But when his father began blaming the pandemic upon "fornicators and sodomites," calling it God's work to cleanse the world of wickedness, and thanking God for sparing the righteous, Zach had walked out.

"Zacharias! Get back in here!" the reverend had shouted, catching him in the hallway and snatching at his biceps with a clawed hand.

"The Lord isn't interested in your tired, self-serving bullshit, Father." Zach jerked his arm away. "*He's* not one of your easily diverted constituents, and in case you didn't notice, there's no offices to run for anymore. Everyone's *dead*, and you're only interested in patting yourself on the back for some imagined measure of moral superiority. That's not faith; it's vanity. I'll pray my own way, thanks."

Zach had turned to retreat to his room, but the reverend grabbed him again, the back of his other hand connecting sharply with Zach's cheekbone when he spun around.

"I have had enough," his father panted, his eyes blazing furiously, "of your disrespect and insolence."

Zach rolled his eyes, sneering. "What are you going to do? Toss me out? Write me off the way you did Mom and the girls?"

The reverend's mouth had curled up into a cruel smile. "Each day you refuse to obey will be a day you don't eat."

Zach's heart hammered in his chest. He was poised on a precipice, about to take a step off into the abyss. Drawing a breath and ignoring the smarting in his cheek that made his eye water, he had leaned close and hissed, "You and your petty tyranny can go to hell. Unless you plan to shoot me, this is *my* home too, and I'll eat what I want, *when* I want. And I'll pray how I choose, when I choose."

Since then, Zach avoided his father and brother as much as possible. If he ventured out for food, he took it back to his room, not lingering in the kitchen. What the two of them did to pass the time, he couldn't say. Sometimes he heard their voices coming from other parts of the eerily silent house, but he did his best not to listen to the words.

He spent his time thinking about Bryan, and how much of a coward he had been not to pursue what had been between them when he'd had the chance. He understood how little he'd lived and how much he'd sacrificed, enslaving himself to his father's will and ambitions. Now he knew, but it was too late to go back and claim the life he should have had before. Too late for everything.

He looked toward the window. The light coming through seemed different now. How long had he been off in his head? Had he lost hours?

No, the clouds had only thickened, and the drizzle that had been brushing the window before had turned into pelting splashes of sleet. March was late for this sort of weather, but it figured that even nature would conspire to keep Zach pinned in the house with Jacob and the reverend. The temperature must have dropped too; he could see transparent sheets of ice encasing the tree branches outside his window. Zach lost himself in the shifting weather, his mind wandering over everything and nothing, while the wind died down and the sleet turned to snow.

He didn't notice the shadowy form moving out by the shed, some twenty yards from the house, until he heard his father yell for Jacob to bring the shotgun, followed by a scramble of activity from the main level of the house. By the time Zach made it downstairs, the patio door was open and the reverend was shouting at someone.

"Get the hell off our property, or I'll shoot!"

Oh hell. Zach had no interest in supporting his father and brother, but he wasn't going to leave them vulnerable to looters who would steal their precious supplies. He changed course to swing by the gun cabinet in his father's study before stepping outside with another rifle.

"Please," someone called from inside the shed. A man's voice, though it cracked and broke. Was he just cold, or sick, or was he panicked or sobbing over something? Whatever it was, he sounded desperate. "Please don't come any closer. I was . . . attacked by someone a couple days ago. I don't know if she was infected or not, but I wouldn't want to risk your safety."

"Then you'll move on right now," the reverend snapped.

"I *can't.*" The voice quavered, as if its owner was trembling too hard to speak. Which made sense considering the wind chill. "Look, I'm begging you. Let me get out of the wind and heal up for a few days. I broke some ribs when my car crashed, and I can't walk any farther. I've got my own provisions; I just need some shelter and some rest, that's all."

"And if we take that chance, you can kill us in our sleep for the house and food stores," his father sneered. "This is your last warning. Get moving!"

"No!" Zach raised his voice to be heard over the wind, keeping the rifle to his shoulder and stepping back to aim it at his father. "No, Father. We're not going to drive off someone who is just asking for the use of our *shed*, for crying out loud! What's he going to steal, our pool net? A gardening rake? He'll freeze to death if his injuries don't kill him first, and I won't have that on my conscience. Leave him alone."

"Zacharias!" Through the haze of snow flurries, Zach could see the reverend's face flushing dark red. "Put that rifle down or so help me—"

"You'll what? Make *me* sleep in the shed? Think you'll still be able to call yourself a godly man when you've driven out one of your two surviving children to be murdered by looters, or eaten by revenants, or to die of the Rot? If we can't show one iota of compassion or mercy, then we may as well have died with the rest of the population." He shook his head fervently. "*No.* This is not how it's going to be, Father."

The look on his father's face was so ugly and full of hatred, Zach almost thought the reverend might actually consider killing him. Whether he was or not, Zach was well aware that he had escalated their uneasy armistice into outright warfare. His father lowered the shotgun and stormed past him.

Zach would need to tread very carefully until it was safe for him to strike out on his own. Assuming it ever would be again.

◬◬◬

THAT NIGHT, after the reverend and Jacob went to sleep, Zach sneaked down into his father's study and emptied all the ammunition from the weapons in the gun rack. He collected the boxes of spare cartridges and bullets and slipped into Naomi's bedroom, where none of them had gone since returning home. With his pocketknife, he cut a small slit along the side-seam of her mattress on the edge closet to the wall and hid everything within it, then carefully fitted the bottom sheet around it again. Then he went to the bedroom that Mary and Rebecca had shared and gathered the blankets off their beds, rolling them and stuffing them into garbage bags.

The snow had let up after night had fallen, leaving the sky clear and the moonlight reflecting off the sheets of white on the ground. He stopped a good ten yards from the shed and called softly, "Hello?"

"Y-y-yeah?" The voice from inside was weak, and breathy, and punctuated by a worrisome cough.

"I've brought some blankets. I apologize for my father and

brother. They've forgotten that the Lord told us to love and care for one another."

"D-don't come any c-closer. I m-m-meant what I s-said about not w-w-wanting to risk i-i-infecting you."

"I won't. I'll leave them out here. You can collect them after I've gone. Is there anything else I can get for you?"

"G-g-g-got any h-homemade chicken soup?"

Zach stared a moment, then chuckled softly, answering the raspy laugh from inside the shed. "No, sorry. We're on dried rations, just like I'm sure you are. Um, I think we might have some jars of stewed tomatoes left, though. If I can sneak it tomorrow, I'll try to heat some up for you. It's not quite soup, but it will help keep you warm."

"No. I d-don't want to take any of your s-supplies. I'll be okay once I get warm. M-m-maybe if you get a chance, c-could I have a sp-spare sheet to tear into b-bandages? I s-should try to b-bind my ribs."

"I can do that. I'll bring it out in the morning and leave it here by the patio steps where I'm leaving the blankets."

"Th-thanks."

"You're welcome. Try to rest."

"Y-y-you too. Good night."

Zach returned to the house shivering, but with a warm feeling in his chest that told him that maybe, just maybe, he was finally being the man God wanted him to be.

13

ENMITY

Ablow to the side of his head jerked Zach out of a sound sleep.
"Where is it, you little bastard?" his father snarled. Zach
had barely opened his eyes when the sight of another hand heading
toward his face made him close them again. The open-palmed clout
was not exactly a slap, but neither was it a punch. Still, it caught his
ear and made his head ring. "Where did you put it?"

"It's gone, so you can't harm anyone with it!" Zach managed to
get his arms up to shield his head and face, struggling to untangle
himself from his blankets as the blows continued to fall.

"You'll tell me where it is if I have to beat it out of you!"

A belt buckle jingled, and his efforts to get out of the bed grew
more frantic. Finally free of the blankets, he scrambled away while
the reverend was still jerking his belt out of its loops.

"Father? What's going on?" A sleepy Jacob appeared in the doorway, blocking Zach's exit.

"Hold him, Jacob!" The first stroke of the belt was wild and
uncontrolled, catching Zach on the upper arm as he tried to bolt
past his father. Jacob reached for him, and while Zach was trying to
evade the grip, another strike slashed down his back, making
him yell.

"No!" Larger than Jacob—though not by much—Zach shoved
him back, sending him stumbling into the hallway, then whirled on

his father. The belt returned, wrapping around Zach's forearm like a band of fire. Suddenly furious in a way he'd never been before, he grabbed the lash, and ripped it out of the reverend's hands. "*No!*"

His father's face was nearly purple with rage. "I want him *out of here!*"

It wasn't hard to guess who the reverend meant. It had been nearly two weeks of almost nonstop arguments over what to do with the man recuperating in their shed. The ice storm had passed and spring had returned, but Zach had invited Nico to stay where he was until his ribs healed well enough for him to travel again.

"He's not harming us!" Zach shouted, throwing the belt across the room. The buckle smacked the mirror on his dresser with an alarming *crack*, but no breaking glass followed. "Are you so lost to God's love that you can't even spare an injured man a few square feet of space in our *shed?*"

"He could infect us!"

"He's taking care to stay far away from us to avoid exactly that, Father, and you know it. We're not in any danger!" The stripes where the belt had struck him burned, but it was nothing compared to the despair that took root in Zach's heart, crushing his will to fight. Every day it just got worse. Was this to be the rest of his life—the endless strife, the enmity that poured out of his father every waking moment? "Can you really be so selfish? So completely without mercy?"

"Where's the ammunition?" The reverend growled, his hands clenched at his sides.

Zach swallowed hard. "I destroyed it."

"Bullshit. There's no way you could have."

Zach allowed himself a bitter, gloating smile. "For all the good it's going to do you, I might as well have."

"You've left us no way to defend ourselves, you idiot!"

"If I thought you had any interest in actually *defending* us, I wouldn't have taken it." Zach shook his head sadly. "You're full of hatred and violence, Father. Until you push that out of your heart, you can't be trusted. If necessary, *I'll* defend us. *All of us.* But I won't let you hurt people just because you've turned your back on God."

Silence fell, punctuated only by the irregular slashing of the reverend's infuriated breath. Finally, he shoved Zach aside and strode toward the door, bellowing, "Jacob! I want you to tear this house apart and help me find it. Now!"

He slammed the door shut behind him, and Zach slumped against the wall, covering his face with his hands.

Lord, please give me the strength to get through this. Please let me do Your will.

Even that small, simple prayer comforted him, filled him with the peace of God's love and grace. When he was arguing with his father, sometimes he lost that sense of surety that he was doing the right thing, the Godly thing. But in these moments of quiet, it returned.

Pulling himself together, Zach made his way into the bathroom attached to his bedroom. He winced as he stripped off his shirt to inspect the welts his father's belt had left on his skin. The thick lines were an angry red, already shifting toward purple as bruising set in. The brush of his clothing hurt, as did any effort to move the arm the belt had wrapped around. Sighing, he plugged the sink and filled it with water to bathe, since they had agreed not to use the showers to avoid depleting the fuel cell powering the water pump from the well. Once he'd sponged off, he submerged his forearm in the sink, hoping the cold water would lessen the pain and bruising.

His battered soul proved much harder to soothe.

⚠ ⚠ ⚠

HIS FATHER and Jacob had done exactly what the reverend had said they would do, and now the house was in shambles. Furniture was overturned, the contents dragged out of closets and strewn everywhere. The mattress where Zach had hidden the ammunition had been flipped over and searched under, but clearly no one had thought to strip off the sheet and look inside the thing. Now it was tossed haphazardly back onto Naomi's bed frame, its contents still secret.

Zach moved around the wreckage trailing through the whole house, making his way to the door. He opened it and crept out onto patio. "Nico?" he called from the steps, where he always stood when he checked in on their guest in the evenings. "You still in there?"

"Yeah, I'm here." Nico's voice sounded wryly amused as he pulled the shed door open a crack. "Not like I really have anywhere else to go. You all right?"

"Sure, why wouldn't I be?"

"I heard shouting. Again. I thought I heard you scream."

Shame seared through Zach. He didn't know why, but he desperately didn't want to tell Zach that his father had beat him.

"I'm okay. Just the usual stuff."

"That's usual?" Skepticism rode heavily on Nico's gentle tone.

"These days, yeah." Zach sat down on the steps and pulled his knees up to his chest, trying to stifle the sniffle that came when his eyes began to burn. He laid his forehead on his knees and let the despair wash over him again. "I don't know how all this happened."

"What do you mean?" Nico's voice was a little clearer, and Zach looked up to see the hint of a leg lying across the narrow opening of the shed door. Nico must be sitting right there, just inside the threshold. It was his first sight of any part of Nico; he'd always stayed well away from view.

It should feel dangerous, not knowing whether Nico was infected with the Rot. Zach should be afraid that they were becoming too lax in keeping a safe distance between them. But it didn't and he wasn't. Perhaps it was naive of him, but he couldn't reconcile the notion that Nico could possibly pose any danger.

"Things with Jacob and my father," Zach answered. "I can't understand how they got so bad. I mean, I can, but it doesn't seem real."

"I should probably be moving on." Weariness hung heavy in Nico's words, and Zach ached to hear it. "I'm making things worse for you, staying here."

"No, you're not. They were already getting bad before you came." Zach sighed and buried his face against his knees again. "We're all safer if we stick together. But how can I live like this?"

Nico cleared his throat. "I'm— Um, when I leave, I'm going to be heading to Colorado Springs. I understand a bunch of survivors are gathering there, outside the military installation at Cheyenne

Mountain. They wanted to take shelter underground. You could come with me. I mean, if you need to get away from your dad and brother."

"I can't leave them. They're family."

"Maybe you could talk them into going too?"

Zach smiled at the reluctance in Nico's voice as he floated that offer. "Maybe. Our supplies aren't going to hold out forever here. Only a few more months. We'll have to do *something*." He shrugged. "I don't know. Maybe if I get my father away from here, away from the place where he feels like he controls everything, he'll stop acting like such a despot."

"Well, you let me know."

Silence fell, and Zach looked out across their property, watching the sun descend. "When will you go?" he asked at last. "I mean, once you're sure you're not infected?"

"I'm not." He heard Nico clear his throat. "I lied about that. To keep your father and brother at a distance."

Something about his voice sharpened Zach's focus, and he found himself staring at that dark opening at the doorway of the shed as if he could study Nico through it. "No, you didn't. I heard your voice that night. You were genuinely concerned for our safety. But you're lying to me now about it. Why?"

"Zach . . ." Nico groaned softly. "You wouldn't believe me if I told you."

"Try me."

"No." Pain. That was what he was hearing in Nico's voice now, an undercurrent running beneath the words. "I'm not a danger to you, I promise. But I can't really talk about it."

Zach had heard that sort of guilty tone before, in the youth he'd counseled before he'd had to give up his ministry, in some of the unfortunate souls in the shelter. It was the sort of self-condemnation that came when an otherwise good person was convinced they'd done something terrible.

"All right," he murmured gently. "If you don't want to tell me, I won't make you. But if you do, I promise I will listen and I won't judge."

"Right. Because you true believers are big on not judging."

He refused to let himself rise to that bait. He'd heard that sort of bitterness before too. People like his father and brother made it difficult for others to understand that not all Christians were the same.

"The Lord tells us not to judge if we don't want to be judged ourselves," he said calmly. "The reverend may have lost sight of that, but I haven't. The God I worship is a God of love and mercy. And that love and mercy is unconditional."

There was a long beat of silence before Nico said softly, "I wish I could believe that."

"I'd like to pray for you tonight, if you don't mind. I'll ask God to help you begin to heal from whatever burden you're carrying. Don't worry—" He cut off the protest rising from within the shed. "I'm not trying to convert you. I've always thought someone's faith would have to be pretty weak and insecure to be threatened by someone who doesn't share it. But if I can help you find peace, I would like to do so."

"Sure, go ahead, if it'll make you feel better." The resounding lack of enthusiasm in Nico's words made Zach smile.

"Thank you for your permission. I should probably get inside now. It's going to be dark soon, and I'm not sure I'd put it past my father not to lock me out of the house."

"Okay. Look . . . if my being here creates too much trouble for you, I'll go, okay? Promise me you'll let me know if it gets to that point?"

The voice coming from that dark aperture in the shed was so unsure of itself that something moved in Zach's chest, gravitating toward it. "I will, Nico. Good night."

14

EXODUS

A furtive thump near his bedroom door woke Zach, bringing alertness rushing in with the screaming instinct that something was wrong. He lay still, keeping his eyes closed, and soon there was another soft sound. His door was closed and no one was barging in, but whatever his father or Jacob were doing out there, it couldn't be good.

Trying to remain quiet, he slipped out from under the covers and tiptoed toward the door, placing his hand on the knob. It turned, but his door wouldn't move.

Oh God. He jerked at the knob, pulling harder, but while the door rattled in its jamb, it remained stubbornly closed. He pounded on it.

"Father! Jacob! Open the door! Open it now!"

His father's voice was so near he had to be standing right outside. "Until you repent of your defiance, Zacharias, you will remain in your room without rations. I recommend you think very hard about where your loyalties lie. The Bible commands you to be an obedient son."

"What does the Bible say about imprisoning and starving your children, you damned hypocrite?" he shouted, wrenching on the door with all his strength. When it failed to give, he returned to banging on it until his palms stung.

"You've forgotten your duty." The calm in his father's—and Zach wondered how he could bear to think of him that way anymore—voice was terrifying. Zach could deal with the reverend when he was enraged, but now Maurice spoke with absolute confidence, a peaceful surety that he was right and he would win. "Once you tell me where the ammunition is, we're leaving this place. We need to go somewhere isolated, where we can establish the sort of faithful society God means for us to have. I know of a place in the Northwest. A retreat for men of God. There will be supplies there and room for us and any others we might bring. A new Eden."

"A faithful society with you in charge, I suppose?" Zach scoffed. "Sounds like you're buying into your own self-serving bullshit. You've been playing the role of the zealot so long to thrill crowds that you've started to believe it. Do you even *hear* yourself?"

"Perhaps after you've fasted and prayed awhile, the Lord's plan will be clearer to you," the reverend said with the sort of pretentious, long-suffering benevolence Zach had always despised. "I'll check on you in the morning."

"Father! *Father*! Let me out of here!"

There was silence from the other side of the door. Zach pummeled it with a flurry of angry kicks and blows, but it was useless. Panting, he slid down the panel to sit on the floor, thudding the back of his head against the door in frustration. The bars on the windows—another testament to Maurice's vanity and paranoia, considering how far out in the country they lived—painted stripes across the floor in the rising sunlight. No help there. He'd have to take the hinges off the door once his panic calmed. He closed his eyes, willing his heart to be still.

Lord, please help me. Please show me how to live in peace with him.

The serenity that normally filled Zach when he prayed was nowhere to be found. Just emptiness and despair. No matter how he begged God for guidance regarding his father, he got no answer.

Or is that what I'm not getting? We can't live in peace. Is it Your will for me to leave him behind?

There it was. *There.* That spark in his chest. Hope. Grace.

The man he'd been struggling against the whole winter—since

last year, really—wasn't his father anymore. It was time to let go of filial obedience and listen to the guidance of his own soul.

He remained there and lost himself in prayer. He didn't know how long he sat there on the floor. He simply listened to that sense of rightness until he was sure of what he had to do.

Voices from the backyard pulled him out of his meditation, and he looked out his window to see his father standing on the patio steps, holding a baseball bat. Jacob stood at his shoulder with a golf club.

"Come out of there! Come out of there right now!" Maurice shouted at the shed.

Slowly, the door opened, and Nico stepped out, one hand held behind his back. Zach's breath caught at his first sight of the man he'd known only by voice for weeks. Nico's clothes were filthy and his hair stringy. Weeks' worth of beard covered the lower half of his face, and he was thin, nearly gaunt. But still, he was beautiful. Sober, dark-fringed brown eyes peered out from a light-brown face, and Zach felt that rightness in his chest again.

He wasn't meant to be with his father and Jacob. Whether or not they could be saved and brought back to God wasn't a task the Lord meant for Zach to take on. He was meant to go with Nico.

As Zach watched, something dawned on Nico's face.

Recognition?

"Reverend Maurice Houtman. Wow. Well, that just fucking figures." Nico shook his head, his tone both bitter and amused. "Of all the yards for me to wind up in."

"How do you know me?" the reverend snarled suspiciously. "Did someone send you here?"

"I recognize you from the vids. I could never watch anything on Sundays without seeing you running your mouth on some pundit's show or another. Then, of course, there's also the fact that your RAL goon squad tried to murder my mother."

Zach wanted to reject the accusation. He didn't want to believe his father was capable of being behind the RAL's actions. But he couldn't. Not anymore. He'd overheard his father's conversation the previous summer, the one that had coincided all too well with everything Zach knew about the RAL's attack on that midsummer bonfire.

Maurice tightened his grip on the bat, shifting his defensive stance. "Who are you?"

"Nicolás Fernández. Or maybe you'd recognize my working name, Octavio *Costas.*"

"The faggot son of the whore," he sneered. "Get out of here before I finish the job God's soldiers failed to do."

"Try it and you'll be dead before you can finish swinging." Nico lifted his chin defiantly, raising the hand he'd been hiding to aim a handgun at Maurice. "I won't let you murder me. Where's Zach?"

"Zacharias is praying and repenting. Now it makes sense, his disobedience. You are Satan's own emissary, sent here to tempt him away from the Lord. But I won't allow it. Once my son knows what you are—a sodomite and a whore—he'll finally see his error."

Nico's eyes flickered at that, doubt crossing his face. "If that's true, fine. I want to hear it from him. I'm able to travel now, so I'll leave, but I want to see that he's all right first."

The reverend shook his head. "He'll be better once you're gone. We'll go away, somewhere that your kind can never reach us again."

"Still trying to elevate yourself to a position of authority?" Nico smirked. "Your whole self-serving, power-hungry dogma would be a lot more convincing if I didn't know just who your campaign contributors were, back before the pandemic."

"You think the opinion of someone who gained his notoriety by selling his body matters to me?"

"I may have been a hustler, but at least I was never a hypocrite," Nico said with a shrug. "Where's Zach? And spare me the whole repentance bullshit, because I know he's no bigger fan of your fire-and-brimstone idiocy than I am."

"Zacharias is none of your concern. Get off my property!"

"I swear I will go *through you* if I have to, and if I do, it's going to be very bad for you."

Zach was tempted to open the window and call down, but he worried that if he distracted Nico from his standoff with Maurice and Jacob, they might manage a blitz attack and get ahold of the handgun. Swearing, Zach rushed over to his desk and ripped the drawer out, spilling its contents on the floor to find something he could use on the hinges of the door.

He worked frantically, aware of his father's incensed and increasingly less coherent shouting. Using the flathead screwdriver he'd found as a lever, he lifted the pins out of the hinges, then wedged his fingers into the gap at the bottom of the door to pull it open, despite the hook latch his father had installed on the other side.

Then Zach dug in his closet for the duffel bag he'd traveled with when they'd been stuck in quarantine over the holidays and stuffed two changes of clothes, several pairs of socks and underwear, and an extra pair of shoes inside. He hesitated a moment before adding his Bible, as well. Not the one his parents had given him for his confirmation, but the secret one he kept tucked away.

Storming down the hall to Naomi's bedroom, he flipped the mattress over and dug out the boxes of shells and spare rounds. From the gun cabinet downstairs, he loaded one handgun and stuck it into his waistband, threw another into the duffel, and slung a shotgun over his shoulder, leaving the other behind. He couldn't leave them completely defenseless.

The bag was heavy, dragging on one shoulder, pulling him off-balance. Sooner or later he'd have to replace it with a rucksack, but for now it would have to do.

Jacob spotted Zach first, giving him a startled look as he came through the patio door. Zach drew the handgun from his waistband. He held it at his side, but the safety was off, and if either of them looked ready to use their clubs, he'd use it. A warning shot, first, and then to wound only if he had to.

"Put down the bat." Zach's voice was calm. *He* was calm. The terrible fear and impotent rage he'd always felt when confronting Maurice before was gone. The anger was there, but it was a steady, purposeful, *righteous* anger. He'd never been more sure of himself. "I'm leaving. *We're* leaving."

Maurice spun, staring at Zach in astonishment for a moment, before looking back and forth between him and Nico, or rather, the guns they each held.

"You'd choose some wetback faggot whore over your own family,

Zacharias?" the reverend demanded, his eyes burning with fury. "Go, then. Get out of my sight. I no longer have an elder son."

"You've lost your way, Father. And you're leading Jacob down the same wrong path." Zach turned his eyes to his younger brother, who was watching him with a disdainful expression. Only eighteen and so full of avarice and warped ideas. "You can come with us, you know. You don't have to be like him."

"Why would he follow you when he could come with me to find God's remaining chosen? With a new Eve, we'll begin to populate the world. Like his namesake, Jacob will beget a nation."

"Don't let him do this to you, Jacob," Zach pleaded, praying to see something other than contempt in his brother's eyes. "Listen to him. This is insanity, and he'll take you down with him. Come with us."

He thought he saw the briefest flicker of doubt in Jacob's eyes, but it disappeared in an instant, replaced by that gloating smirk he always wore when the reverend favored him over Zach.

"You heard my father," he said haughtily. "Go. Go on with your faggot boyfriend. We don't need you."

Zach closed his eyes for a long moment, then nodded once before tucking his gun away. "I left you one shotgun. You'll find the shells in Naomi's mattress."

The reverend stared impassively, gesturing at them to get a move on with an imperious jerk of his chin.

"I'll pray for you both," Zach whispered, his throat thick, and turned away.

△ △ △

ZACH STOOD guard while Nico gathered his gear from inside the shed, in case his father or brother got any ideas. But Jacob and the reverend were content to stand together on the deck and watch until they were certain Nico and Zach had left the property.

They didn't speak. Nico seemed to respect the enormity of what Zach had just done, severing his ties with his last surviving family. How many others out there were in the same situation? How many people had lost everyone and were now alone in the world? Were there families, anymore? Or were they all just the straggling remnants of humanity, too foolish to die with the rest of their species?

Zach stopped on the road that ran through what had once been acres of corn adjacent to the Houtmans' property to set down his duffel and rotate his aching shoulder. His arm felt like it would fall off.

"Here. Trade me." Nico shrugged off his rucksack and grabbed Zach's duffel before he could protest, then took off, apparently to forestall any argument.

Zach scrambled to get the rucksack on his shoulders and catch up. "What, you think your arm's not going to get as tired as mine?" he asked curtly, grimacing at the sound of his own petulance. It seemed easier to snap at Nico than to let the weight of the morning's events settle in and crush him. Now that they no longer had a yard and a wall between them, it seemed he had forgotten how to talk.

Nico shrugged, not meeting Zach's eyes. "I'm stronger than I look."

Zach took a moment to take in Nico's lithe stature. He didn't have the build of someone who could haul a heavy duffel for miles. "Is it true what you said back there?"

Nico glanced at him out of the corner of his eye. "Which part?"

"What you did before the pandemic. Were you—"

"An escort? Prostitute? Whore? Rentboy? Hustler?" Nico snorted. "Yeah, I was. And yes, most of my clients were men, and I was more than happy with that situation. Is that going to be a problem?"

His demeanor was so defensive that Zach immediately regretted what might have, on the surface, seemed like a very judgmental question. "No, not . . . not for the reasons you assume. I was just wondering what sort of survival skills that particular career path came with."

"More than you'd think." Relaxing, Nico flashed him a grin. "I've got black belts in tae kwon do and tang soo do. My mother made sure all her employees were able to defend themselves. As for guns, well, I'm not at my best there, but I know the basics."

"That's a relief. Hand-to-hand fighting isn't going to do you much good against revenants. Not unless you want to end up infected anyway."

"I won't get infected."

"That's pretty cocky of you."

"Would you believe I'm immune?"

"Nobody's immune."

"Trust me. I am."

Nico picked up the pace, making it difficult for Zach to keep up even though he was carrying the more portable load, much less demand an explanation for his outrageous claim. He ended up trotting to try to match Nico's apparently inexhaustible strides.

"Fine! You've proven your point. Please, slow down." He came to a halt and bent forward, panting to catch his breath. When he looked up, Nico seemed startled.

"I'm sorry," he stammered, his rich-brown complexion growing ruddy. "I didn't mean to do that."

"You mean you weren't trying to rub my nose in the fact that I doubted you could handle yourself?"

Nico shook his head, looking troubled. "No. I'm sorry. I just didn't realize that I was— It didn't feel like I was going that fast."

"I bet it didn't. You're not even winded."

"I'm sorry." Nico shuffled his feet, kicking at an old, picked-over cob lying on the ground. He turned in a circle and glanced around. "Do you have *anything* in this state besides corn?"

"Besides soy? I'm sure we do, but at the moment, I can't think of a thing." Zach looked at his duffel and laughed. The sound was harsh and nearly hysterical. "I didn't bring food. Oh God. I packed clothes and guns, but no food."

As if the strength suddenly drained from his legs, he dropped to sit on the road and covered his face with shaking hands, praying. He hadn't even eaten breakfast.

"It's okay. We'll manage." He felt the weight of Nico's hand on his shoulder, squeezing gently, and the pressure bolstered him. "You know, once I figure out where we're going."

"Yeah. Of course. I'm sure we'll find what we need. Sorry. Didn't mean to fall apart. It's been a hell of a morning." There was that hysterical laugh again.

"Sounded like it. What happened in there?"

Zach shook his head. "Doesn't matter." He drew a deep breath and blew it out slowly. "Okay. Let's figure this out. You still want to head to Colorado Springs?"

"I don't know where else to go, honestly." Nico dropped the duffel and sat on the road beside him. "It's the only place I know survivors are gathered, and I figure there's safety in numbers, right? And there's a government and military presence there. It's where they quarantined the last surviving cabinet and Congress members over the winter."

"How do you know this?" Zach turned his head to study Nico, getting his first close-up look at the man who had suddenly become his traveling companion.

"I spent the winter with a general from the Pentagon. He had power and information feeds." Nico's scowl warned him off asking any more about that particular situation.

"All right. I guess we just need to figure out food, then? And how we're going to find shelter at night. And transportation. And how to avoid the revenants, and—"

"Breathe, Zach. Just breathe."

He took Nico's advice, resting his forehead on his knees. The spring breeze was cool, too cool really for the shirt he was wearing. God. He hadn't grabbed a coat, either.

"I figure our best chance of avoiding the revenants is to stay away from the cities," Nico started. "That's where the most people were, so that's where they'll mostly be, right?"

Zach nodded, his brow rubbing against the fabric of his jeans. "Right."

Nico hesitated. Then he seemed to come to a decision and blurted, as if plunging into deep water, "As for supplies, I guess the best thing to do, for now, would be to try to find my lightcar. It's wrecked, but it was packed with supplies. If no one saw it crash and looted it already, that is. The question is, how to transport it all."

"Looted. Oh Lord. Everything will have been looted by now, won't it?" Zach closed his eyes and began to pray silently again, seeking God's presence to ameliorate his panic.

"Maybe, maybe not?" Nico's tone was the verbal equivalent of a shrug. "By the time the ration drops stopped, it was full winter. The roads weren't cleared, even if people had dared to leave their houses, and by spring . . ."

"Everyone was already dead," Zach finished bleakly, lifting his head to look around.

Nico nodded. "Yeah. So here in the north and in the plains states, it won't be so bad. Probably worse in the warmer regions where people weren't snowed in. Maybe. Hell, I don't know. I could be talking out my ass."

"If you had information feeds over the winter, you've got a better idea of what was going on than I do. That's good enough for me." Zach closed his eyes for a moment, bracing himself more mentally than physically before rising. "Okay. I know there's a farm a few miles down the road, where they used to sell preserves and canned goods at a roadside stand. Maybe . . . maybe they still have some stores we can eat while we figure everything out."

15

REFUGE

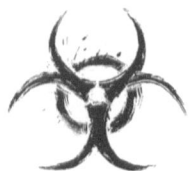

"A few miles" turned out to be something of an understatement. The sun was beginning to set when they finally reached the farmhouse. The roadside produce stand at the end of the driveway had clearly already been looted by someone now long gone. The chickens and animals running loose in the yard seemed untended, several of them dead, and no one had appeared with a gun to warn them away from the property.

"Wait out here." Nico deposited his bags under a tree and drew the gun holstered at his hip. "I'll check inside, make sure there's no one there."

Zach frowned at the derelict building. "What if there are bodies of people who died from the Rot? Could they still be contagious?"

"I told you, I'm immune."

"You're insane. And even if you are immune, I'm *not*."

"Which is why I'm going to check it out and you're staying here. If there are bodies inside, I'll burn them or we'll stay in the barn or *something*." Nico met his eyes levelly. "Trust me."

Zach seemed fretful, but he nodded reluctantly and let Nico go.

There were bodies, two of them. They looked like they might have been an elderly couple, though it was hard to be certain with the damage the Rot had done. They lay together in a bed upstairs. The smell was indescribable, and Nico clamped a hand over his nose, vomiting into a corner. He left quickly, closing the door behind him.

He emerged trying not to appear as queasy as he felt. "Looks like we're sleeping in the barn, unless you want to risk going in as far as the kitchen. It's on the other end of the house and they're upstairs, so it might be far enough away to be safe. Tomorrow we'll torch the house to burn the bodies."

Zach swallowed. "I think I'll take the barn, thanks."

Nico nodded. "Good choice. It doesn't smell very pleasant in there."

Though, to be honest, the barn wasn't a terrific alternative. The animals had been left untended for too long. The horse stuck in one of the stalls was dead, its ribs showing through its hide, and there was evidence of a rat infestation. But it was better ventilated, at least, and the circulating air had taken care of the worst of the odor.

Once they'd dropped their bags inside, Nico stood in the doorway, staring at the chickens, goats, and pigs in the yard. "Don't suppose you know anything about killing and butchering animals?"

"A little. My father's late brothers all hunted deer. He made me go with them once when I was fourteen. I know enough not to damage the intestines and taint the meat."

"We're low on protein." Nico turned to face Zach, lifting his shirt and pulling the waistband of his trousers away from his body to reveal a significant gap. "My metabolism is fucked up. I need more calories than I'm getting. Do you think we might be able to butcher one of these goats or pigs? Even a chicken will get us by for tonight, but I was hoping we could take something with us."

"We could try." Zach seemed to be having trouble tearing his eyes away from the expanse of midriff Nico had uncovered, so he dropped his shirt. Zach shook himself and lifted his gaze to nod, focusing on the subject. "It's more preserving the meat that would be a problem. Without refrigeration, the most it will last us is a few days."

"That's fine. We just need something to live off until we can figure out how to carry what was in my car. Or find a store that hasn't been looted. Or a restaurant. Or, I don't know, *someplace*."

"Then let's do it." Zach gave the animals a speculative look. They were tame enough; they had flocked around Zach and Nico, hoping to be fed, when they had approached the house. "You go inside and find me a butcher knife from the kitchen, then start gathering wood for a fire. I'll deal with the animals."

Nico was scavenging for cooking implements and almost dropped a pot on his foot when he heard the gunshot in the yard. When he came out, Zach was kneeling over one of the goats, which had been shot cleanly between the eyes. While he butchered the carcass, Nico built a fire. They rigged a crude spit for slices of the goat meat, which cooked unevenly, but Nico tore into it while it was still rare, groaning at the flavor.

Zach was hardly any more decorous. Nico wasn't sure what sort of food stores Zach's family had maintained, but he probably hadn't had much in the way of fresh meat in recent months, either.

They both seemed more emotionally stable by the time they were done eating. It was hard to be distraught with a full belly. They sat companionably on opposite sides of the fire, cooking strips of chevron that they would wrap in foil and take with them when they went.

For all that, though, Nico noticed they both had their handguns lying on the ground beside them, ready to use if anything approached.

"I suppose you want some explanations." He gave Zach a reluctant look, but he made himself face the fact that he was going to have to address this.

Zach snorted. "I'd say that's an understatement. I don't know what the hell is going on, but if we're going to be traveling together —assuming I'm not, in fact, going to die—then I need to know."

"It's a pretty incredible story. I need you to trust me enough to believe that it's the absolute truth, or at least as much of the truth as I know." Nico swallowed and poked the fire with a stick. "I swear to you, I'll be completely honest, but you have to take some of it on faith."

Zach hesitated longer than Nico would have liked, mulling that over, but he finally nodded. "Fine. Tell me."

So Nico told him. Everything. How he knew General McClosky. His contract to entertain Secretary Littlewood. All that McClosky had told him about Project Juggernaut and the Bane virus. There were points where Zach had looked dubious, but he hadn't interrupted with any incredulous protests.

"You blame yourself," was his only observation when Nico finally reached the end of his story.

"Yes. No. Shit, I don't know. I keep going back and forth." Nico began snapping the stick he was holding into small pieces, throwing them on the fire. "I couldn't have known what McClosky was asking me to do, but maybe that's where I fucked up. Maybe I should have been questioning more instead of enjoying the subterfuge. Thought I was Mata fucking Hari or something."

"You were used, Nico." The understanding in Zach's voice was almost too much to bear. "He used you."

"I know," Nico said bleakly, swallowing around the lump in his throat. "If I hadn't had so many other issues with what happened that night I was with Littlewood, it might not feel so awful."

"What do you mean?"

"Secretary Littlewood was— Well, let's just say the world's a better place if he died in the pandemic. God, I hope he died, because the thought of him surviving is fucking terrifying." Nico shuddered. "I spent months in therapy processing what I had to do that night. I *chose* to do the job, even once I realized what a monster Littlewood was. But learning what they had done, what it had all been for . . . That was the first time I actually felt powerless about it. Victimized."

Zach didn't say anything; he simply watched Nico with those gentle, sympathetic eyes. Nico glanced around, checking to make sure there was nothing sneaking up on them, but all the animals in the yard were calm.

"Maybe I'm just looking for someone to blame," Nico said with a philosophical shrug. "There's plenty of it to go around. McClosky answered to the politicians whose wars he needed to find a way to fight. And hell, if those RAL goons hadn't tried to kill my mother, McClosky wouldn't have been shot. He could have stopped them from bringing the wounded Juggernaut troops back to the US."

"The RAL—" Zach gave him an astonished stare, and then he began to laugh. Long, uncontrollable peels of hysterical laughter that made Nico look around nervously, afraid someone or something would overhear. Zach flopped over onto his side, wiping at his eyes, but each time his giggles died down, a new wave would start up again.

"I'm sorry. I'm sorry!" he gasped. "It's not funny, it's absolutely tragic, but—" Another fit of hilarity followed, until Nico was ready to poke him with a burning stick to get him to knock it off. "The RAL. Oh my God!"

"Care to share with the rest of the class?" Nico groused.

Zach guffawed but managed to hold himself together enough to choke out, "All these months—" *snicker* "—my father's been blaming—" *gasp* "—people like you for the pandemic. 'Fornicators and sodomites,' he keeps ranting. But it was the RAL's so-called soldiers for God that caused it all along!"

Then he was off again, but the longer it went on, the less it sounded like laughter and the more it sounded like sobbing. Nico stared helplessly, finally crawling around to Zach's side of the fire and petting him like he would a child, until he calmed down.

"I'm sorry. I'm sorry."

"It's okay. Take your time."

Zach pushed away, wiping at his face, and Nico let him go. "It's just . . . I suspected my father knew what the RAL was up to. I even heard him having a conversation with someone that—after the fact, at least—sounded like he knew about the RAL planning to bomb that midsummer party. I guess if you're partly to blame for what you helped McClosky do, maybe I am too. I never said anything. I told myself I was making it up."

Nico waited silently. Finally, Zach licked his lips and said, "So, you were going to tell me how this all means you're immune to the Rot?"

"I have the Alpha strain." There didn't seem to be any subtle way of putting it.

"You *what*? But you weren't a soldier."

"Nope. I'm still a whore." He gave Zach a wry half grin. "McClosky had some ampules of the Alpha virus, and he gave one to me. Well, two, actually, and I stole the third because I didn't want that asshole getting immunity to the pandemic he created." Pain lanced through his chest as he admitted, "I gave one to my mother, but it was too late."

"What do you mean?"

Nico clenched his fists against his thighs. "The, um, the woman I told you about. The one who attacked me before I wound up in your shed. It was her. That's why we crashed. She'd been exposed a few weeks before I got to her."

"Oh Lord." Zach closed his eyes, and his lips moved almost imperceptibly for a moment. Was he *praying*? "I'm so sorry. She was a revenant?"

"Is." He clenched his hands tightly together. "She . . . she was knocked unconscious in the crash, but I *couldn't*—"

Now it was Nico's turn to fall apart, and Zach rubbed a soothing hand up and down his back, murmuring in his ear. He didn't try to chastise Nico for all the deaths he might have inadvertently caused by not killing his mother when he'd had the chance. Maybe he knew Nico had already been torturing himself with those thoughts.

"She wouldn't want to live like that. I know it. She wouldn't want to hurt anyone. But I couldn't do it. I *couldn't*."

Zach's eyes and voice were full of empathy. "Of course you couldn't."

It was insane, confiding all this, letting Zach comfort him. They were total strangers. He was a whore, and Zach was a Bible-beater, even if he seemed to be a fairly decent one. But it didn't matter after those evenings they'd spent talking anonymously across the yard to each other. What mattered was that Zach was the first sympathetic ear he'd had since this whole nightmare had begun.

His confessor.

"I'm so afraid of going back to that car, that we might come across her. I'm going to be looking for her everywhere, and I don't know what I'm going to do."

"If we find her, do you want me to . . . do what needs to be done?" Zach asked gently.

"You can't." Nico raised his face, startled to see how close Zach's bright eyes were. "You can't go near her. I don't want you infected. If we come across any revs, or anyone with the Rot, you need to stay away. Let me take care of it. I'll— If it's her, I'll do what I have to do. Somehow."

Zach's arm around his shoulders squeezed. "I'll pray for you to find the strength, if it comes to that. And for the Lord to give you solace."

The part of Nico that had been at odds with bigots like the Reverend Houtman his whole life wanted to tell Zach to take his prayers and shove them someplace biblical, but he was so sweetly earnest that Nico couldn't do it. Zach hadn't said a single thing about the state of Nico's soul or where he might be destined in the afterlife. He'd just listened and understood and offered Nico reassurance from the same place he found it himself.

When would the other side of Zach emerge? The sanctimonious, judgmental side? When would he reveal his disdain for Nico's previous occupation, for his preference for men, for his lack of religious faith?

"You need to heal, emotionally as much as physically," Zach said softly, and Nico was startled to realize he'd been on the verge of dozing off with his head on Zach's shoulder. "We should bank the fire and get some sleep."

"You go. There were some afghans in the living room that were far enough from the bedroom to be safe. I put them in the barn. Go wrap yourself up to keep warm, and I'll stand first watch. I'll wake you up in, what, four hours?"

Zach lifted one eyebrow ever so slightly, his lips twitching. "You will, huh? Just how much sleep have you been getting the past couple weeks on the cold floor of our shed?" He nudged Nico up with a push on his shoulder. "At least I've had a bed. I'll take first watch. You get some rest."

He was too tired to protest. He helped Zach bank the fire and wrap the last cooling strips of goat meat in foil before finding a place where he was sheltered from the wind and where the stale straw in the barn wasn't too dank. His last glimpse of Zach before he lay down and closed his eyes was of his new companion sitting with his head bowed by the fire, a book that looked suspiciously like a Bible closed on his knee.

16

DAYBREAK

Nico opened his eyes to find the first hints of daylight seeping into the barn. He sat up with a gasp, throwing back the blankets to rush out into the chilly gray dawn, terrified that something had happened to Zach while he'd slept.

But Zach still sat by the fire, a blanket wrapped around his shoulders, reading. He must've sensed Nico's presence, as he looked back over his shoulder and smiled a greeting. Nico slumped against the wall of the barn, willing his heart to stop hammering.

"You didn't wake me up," he accused, crossing to join Zach by the fire.

Zach shrugged. "Seemed like you needed the sleep more than I did. You should go get a blanket or a jacket or something. It's too cold to be out here in just a shirt. I found some canned soup in the kitchen to warm for us."

"Thanks." Shivering too much to argue, Nico ducked into the barn to grab his jacket and went out to the fire, where Zach scooped steaming soup into mugs.

"It's not coffee, but it will have to do."

"Oh Jesus. Don't mention coffee. You'll make me cry." Nico sipped the hot broth, slurping up noodles and chunks of chicken before he tore into one of the strips of cold meat they had cooked the night before.

Zach blinked, watching him stuff his face. "Is this what you meant about your metabolism?"

"I think so." It took an effort not to rip another chunk of meat off with his teeth and speak with his mouth full. If only the clients who had paid a thousand dollars or more an hour to wine and dine him at the finest restaurants on the East Coast could see him now. "I think it's part of the virus. I'm always hungry, and being on such lean rations, the weight has just been dropping off me."

"And still you're able to walk miles carrying heavy bags without breaking a sweat." Zach chuckled softly. His eyes passed down Nico's body from head to toe in a rather unmistakable appraisal. "If I were the insecure type, I'd feel inadequate."

Nico smirked, then shook his head. "It's not all great. I probably should have mentioned this last night . . . I told you the Rot came from when people infected with the Alpha virus were wounded and others were exposed to their blood, right?" At Zach's nod, he continued. "If I ever start to bleed, you need to stay the hell away from me. Don't try to save me. Don't administer first aid. Let me die if you have to, but don't come near me."

Something dawned on Zach's face, as if he'd just solved a mystery. "So that's why you were so afraid for us that first day you came to our shed. You were wounded."

Nico nodded. "I mean it, Zach. I don't know you well, but I don't want to be responsible for your death, okay? I've caused too many deaths already. Unless—" He dug in the inner pocket of his jacket and pulled out the third ampule. "You could use this. It's the last ampule of the Alpha virus, the one I stole from McClosky. Then you'd be able to keep up with me. And you'd be safe from the Rot, or becoming a revenant."

Zach took the ampule from Nico's hand, staring at it as if mesmerized. "I'd be strong and fast. Superhuman. And you're just offering it to me like it's nothing."

"I don't care what happens to it. I'd rather see you safe."

Zach closed his eyes and bowed his head, his brow wrinkled in concentration and his lips moving. Praying again? It was something he seemed to do a lot. When he looked up, his brow was smoothed and his eyes were calm. He offered the ampule back to Nico. "No. I don't want it."

Nico hesitated, and Zach shoved the ampule at him more firmly. "You're sure?" Nico frowned.

Zach nodded, a decisive jerk of his head that brooked no argument. "I'm sure. Whatever God has in store for me, I don't think being a superhuman with toxic blood is part of it."

Nico bit back an argument and dropped the ampule back inside his pocket. The silence stretched out between them, threatening to become uncomfortable, until Nico gestured to the Bible that Zach was absently caressing.

"How many times have you read that?"

Zach held it up. "This? Never."

"What? Seriously?"

"Well, I mean, I've read the Bible before. Several times, in fact. This is just the first time I've read this particular version of it."

"What's different about it?"

Zach smiled his gentle smile, his thumb stroking the gilt letters on the cover. "It's annotated with linguistic analyses of passages that have historically stirred up controversy because of questionable and possibly biased or politically motivated interpretations. For example, the word for 'young girl' being interpreted as 'virgin' when referring to Mary."

Nico snorted. "I bet your dad loved you reading that."

"Oh, he never knew I had it. He would have thrown a fit." Zach's smile turned a little edgier, as if he relished the thought of seeing his father blow a gasket over it. "I bought it last year, when I was helping out a man at a shelter where I volunteered. He was the first homosexual or bisexual man I'd ever knowingly become closely acquainted with. I had to decide how I felt about that and what the Bible had to say about it outside my father's narrow interpretation of cherry-picked passages. Especially when I realized I was attracted to him."

"Oh?" Nico's eyebrows shot up. Instinct finely honed by his profession had left him a decent judge of where other people stood on the issue of sexual preference. He'd picked up on the fact that Zach had an inclination toward men almost immediately, but he hadn't expected Zach to be comfortable admitting it so openly. "So what does it say?"

"Well, we could be here all day discussing that." Zach smiled wryly. "There are a lot of places in the Bible where the original text might have several viable translations, and at times it's possible those translations were made to suit the biases of the interpreters at the time. It's hard to mistake the relationship between David and Jonathan, though some people will try. But then there are more debatable passages, such as Jesus healing the 'honored servant' of a Roman centurion. When you look at the cultural and linguistic intricacies of the words used to describe the servant, there's a strong indication that he might have actually been the centurion's male lover. If you accept that interpretation, the question then becomes whether or not Jesus condoned or even blessed the relationship by rewarding the centurion's faith and healing the servant."

Nico gave him a dazed smile. The existence of such interpretations of the Bible was nothing new to him; they were used all the time by activists to counter fundamentalist dogma. He just would never have expected to hear the son of Maurice Houtman, spokesman for the extreme Christian fundamentalist renaissance, considering them.

Zach blushed under Nico's stare, and continued. "Just now I was reading about Ruth and Naomi, who the original text seems to indicate were quite likely life partners. Their story was speaking to me fairly strongly today."

Intrigued, Nico let the rest of his chevron drop into his lap. "Why is that?"

Zach shrugged. "I'm not sure. Maybe because one of my sisters was named Naomi and I miss her. I'll almost certainly never see her again, or even know if she's alive. Or maybe I'm feeling just a bit like Ruth right now."

"How so?"

"All common sense says Ruth was destined to go hungry and unprotected unless she returned to her father's house after she was widowed. But she chose to endure danger and hardship with Naomi rather than take advantage of the security of her father's care." Zach lifted his eyes, meeting Nico's squarely. "I defied my father. I threatened him with a gun—twice. I left a reasonably secure, well-armed house stocked with provisions and walked straight into uncertainty. With you."

Nico squirmed. "So, I'm Naomi in this scenario?"

"Not necessarily. I don't know. That's why I was reading, trying to figure out where God is leading me in all this. Do you just happen to be going in the direction in which He wants me to go? Or is He leading me toward *you*, for some reason I haven't come to understand yet?"

The soft huff of laughter Nico gave felt forced, and he broke away from the intensity of Zach's regard, wrapping up the remainder of his uneaten meat. "Well, if you figure it out, be sure to clue me in, because I have no idea what the fuck I'm doing. If God wants to weigh in on it, sure, why not?"

Zach rose as Nico came to his feet. "Thanks."

"For what?"

"Not shutting me down when I talk about my faith. I realize you don't share it, but you respect the fact that it's important to me." Zach smiled and turned away, beginning to pack away his Bible and other belongings in his duffel.

Nico shrugged. "Just respect that I have no interest in being converted, and that it doesn't make you any better a person than me, and we'll be just fine." He ducked into the barn to gather up his clothes and bedding from the night before. He lashed the rolled blankets to the rucksack with a cord.

Zach appeared in the doorway of the barn. "What do you think the chances are that these folks' truck still works?" He gestured toward the driveway, where the vehicle in question looked like it had been sitting all winter.

Nico stared at it thoughtfully. He'd had noticed it the previous evening, but he'd been more concerned with the prospect of fresh meat. "If the fuel cell is dead, I have a replacement in my pack, and more in my car, if we can find where it crashed. Start raiding the pantry and load it up while I get it running.

Once they were certain the truck would run and they'd denuded the farmhouse of every provision they could reasonably carry, Nico splashed kerosene he'd salvaged from emergency lanterns in the pantry around the baseboards and set a match to it. Flames began to lick up the walls of the house, and Nico backed quickly out the door, watching until he was sure the fire was going to continue to burn. He forced himself not to think about the couple on the bed upstairs as people who had suffered and died a horrible death.

"There. Now no one will stumble over the corpses and manage to get infected." He wiped eyes that were burning from the smoke as he joined Zach. They loaded their accumulated baggage behind the front seat of the truck. The heavier rucksack. Zach's clumsy duffel. The assault rifle he placed between them within easy reach.

"Look at me," Nico complained as he climbed into the driver's seat. "This time last year, famous people booked me months in advance and spent thousands for a few hours of my time. I was well on my way to my master's degree and only a few years off from taking over the most successful escort service in the country. And now—" He swept a hand up and down his body. "Well, at least I make refugee chic look good."

Zach snorted. "Oh, poor baby," he scoffed, though he gave Nico a wicked grin that made Nico's heart beat a little faster and, surprisingly, tugged on things south of his belt. He was a good-looking guy, this preacher's son, with his dark reddish-brown hair that hadn't seen a barber in six months, his sparkling aqua eyes, and cheekbones sharp enough to cut glass. But then Nico sobered as he pulled out of the driveway, remembering where they were heading.

"I think the car crashed somewhere east of your property. I *think*. I limped around for a few hours before I found your place."

"All right. Take a left when we get out to the highway. I'll get you to the country road that passes east of our house, and we can begin searching from there."

Finding the crash site took all morning, since it had been deep into a soy field, far off the road. Nico gripped the steering wheel tighter with each mile.

"You have to swear to me you'll stay in the truck," he muttered to Zach when they finally saw the wreckage. "Let me gather everything up. Shoot anyone who approaches."

"We'll be in and out faster if we both—"

"No!" The steering column creaked in his hands, and Nico

made himself loosen his grasp. His chest felt too tight, like he was trying to breathe with a hundred-pound weight sitting on his sternum. He shuddered, blinking away the burning in his eyes. "*Please,* Zach—"

Zach laid a hand on Nico's wrist. "It's okay," he said gently. "You're all right. We'll be okay."

"Sure." He couldn't meet that concerned aquamarine gaze. Not unless he wanted to fall completely apart, and with the balls Zach had demonstrated in doing what he'd done the day before, he didn't need Nico turning into a wreck on him.

"You're shaking." Zach kept his hold on Nico's arm, studying him with a frown. "And sweating."

"Sorry." Nico didn't know what else to say.

"Let's just find the provisions and get out of here as quickly as we can," Zach suggested. The brisk note of confident determination sounded a little forced, but Nico appreciated the effort.

Despite Nico's plea that he remain in the truck, Zach proposed a better idea. He hauled himself up onto the roof of the cab with the shotgun, where he said he could practically see for miles in every direction. Nico couldn't argue with that logic, especially since the flatness of the fields worked in their favor.

Luck was with them in that apparently no one had found the wreck and raided the supplies, at least. The meat products had all been torn apart—though whether by animals or his mother, Nico wasn't certain—but the water and the rest of the rations, in their sturdy, scent-proof packaging, remained untouched.

The stressful part was how long it took to gather everything up and walk it back across the field to where the truck was parked on the road. The ground was too soggy to risk pulling the truck any closer. The back-and-forth trips took forever when he was hauling everything one armful at a time, but it was a relief not to have to leave all the fuel cells and extra weapons behind. By the time Nico was done loading the truck, the bed was packed. He hoped no one decided the full bed made them a prime target.

Despite the fact that Zach never sent up the alarm and that gathering up and transferring all the scattered supplies wasn't very heavy labor, Nico's shirt was soaked through at the armpits and down his spine when he finally dropped into the passenger's seat with a gusty sigh.

"You okay?" Zach asked softly, and Nico nodded.

"Yeah, let's just get out of here. The whole afternoon is gone already." He looked at the distant wreck of the lightcar with a strange sense of hopelessness. His mind kept playing images of his mother emerging from the debris or approaching from across the field, smiling and lucid and completely herself. It felt so real he wanted to cling to it, convince himself that it might still happen. But it *wouldn't*, and if he didn't accept that, he'd never be able to do what he needed to if he happened to cross her path again. His eyes burned and blurred, and he ground his palms against them before the moisture could spill over. "Just go."

Zach pulled back onto the road without another word.

Silence settled between them, until Nico finally released a shuddering breath and murmured, "I should have shot her. It would have been the responsible thing to do. The kind thing to do."

Zach flicked a glance at him before returning his eyes to the road. "You're not that man."

"Yeah, well, I need to *become* that man. We all do." He wrapped his arms around himself, shivering despite the warmth of the truck's heater. "I need to stop pretending the world hasn't really changed. How many people could die because I left her alive?"

"Nico—" Zach's gentle hand closed over his knee. "She was your *mother*. Right or wrong, wise or unwise doesn't factor into it. We're still *people*, or I certainly hope we are or humanity truly is dead. Cold pragmatism is a good theory, but the Lord put love and compassion in our hearts for a reason. And I'd like to think, more often than not, love steers us in the right direction. Look at my father. The coldly pragmatic solution would have been to do what he intended to do and kill you preemptively when you yourself said you feared infecting us, but I stopped him. And even if that decision does end up putting me in danger, I don't regret it."

"I know, but—" His voice broke, and his eyes stung again. It felt like he was moments away from completely cracking. "I'm not sure I can live in this world."

"We'll find our way," Zach said warmly, squeezing his knee again. "And you won't be alone."

Nico managed a grateful smile and closed his eyes, pressing his face against the window until the nausea and despair passed. "I think what's eating me is that I'm never going to have a chance to undo that decision. She's gone, and unless I try to hunt her down, I can never correct my mistake. The rest of my life, I'll know she's out there and that I didn't have the balls to do what she would have wanted me to do."

He peered at Zach, who was nodding thoughtfully, though not judgmentally. "I can only pray that you'll find a way to make peace with that. If it's any consolation, though, she was injured and without spare clothing or shelter in the middle of an ice storm and subfreezing temperatures that lasted for nearly a week." The corner of Zach's mouth lifted the smallest bit, and his expression went a little softer. "Maybe your inability to act when you think you should have was actually the Lord telling you to let Him handle it."

He said it with such simple, heartfelt conviction that Nico couldn't bring himself to remind Zach that he didn't share his beliefs. "Thank you. That's a . . . That's a nice thought."

He was damned if that incandescent peace Zach seemed to exude wasn't contagious, though. Nico grew calmer. The choice he had made would haunt him, he was sure of it, but right now, it felt like something he could live with.

Since Zach knew the area, Nico was glad to let him handle the driving for now. But gradually the mood in the truck shifted, tension creeping in. Zach's profile became stiffer, the corner of his mouth drawn down.

"What's the matter?"

"Oh, nothing." Zach pressed his lips together until they whitened, then sighed. "The only road that won't take us any closer to more populated areas is going to go past my—our—my former house."

"Sorry." Nico wasn't sure what to say for a moment. He wished he could offer Zach the sort of comfort Zach had offered him, but he couldn't. "You don't think they'll take a shot at us, do you?" he offered instead, grinning to let Zach know he was only joking.

Zach scowled, but it gradually morphed into a smile as he caught on that Nico was teasing him. "I think by the time they realize they're hearing a truck drive past and get the gun, we'll be out of range."

Nico gnawed his lip. "Have I thanked you for standing up to your dad for me?"

"It was long past time." Zach shut his mouth with a snap, staring fixedly forward, cutting off any more discussion on that subject.

Nico fell into an uncomfortable silence, peering west to try to determine how much longer they had until sunset. Rather than becoming more at ease with his decision to part ways with his father and brother, Zach seemed to be going in the other direction. What would he do if Zach wanted to go back? Would he have to make the trip all alone?

"Are you changing your mind?" Nico demanded finally, as the sun was getting low in the sky and the shadows lengthening.

"What? No." Zach at least looked startled by the question, as if the idea had never crossed his mind. That was reassuring. "I'm just— I'm angry, all right?" he snapped. "Angry at my father for being such a hypocritical tyrant and angry at myself for putting up with it for so long. And I'm trying not to take that out on you, because it's not your fault that I couldn't see what was going on. But I don't know what's going to happen tonight, or tomorrow when we're on the road, or once we get to Colorado Springs, and—"

"And you're scared."

"Yeah," Zach breathed. "I've been trying to pray all afternoon because normally that calms me down, but I keep getting distracted by other thoughts."

"'Other thoughts,' huh?" Nico loaded the question with as much innuendo as he could. Zach seemed to respond well to being distracted with teasing. He blushed, and Nico grinned, finding himself suddenly on very familiar ground, indeed. This was too delicious to pass up. He slipped into flirtation like a comfortable pair of shoes. It was the first time in two weeks he felt something other than fear and worry and grief for his mother. "You should have said something. We could have spent last night having some fun."

"What? I— No, I— I wasn't—"

"You weren't?" He leaned close to Zach's ear, letting his lips brush it as he spoke. "Why not? You already told me you've been attracted to at least one other man. And I'm *awfully* pretty."

"I'm not— I mean, I wouldn't— I hardly know you?"

The note of uncertainty at the end was so desperate that Nico cracked. Laughing, he shook his head and pulled away. "Relax, choirboy. I'm teasing. You go ahead and think whatever *other thoughts* you're comfortable with. You decide you want to act on them, well, we can figure that out when and if it happens."

The crestfallen expression and conflicted yearning in Zach's eyes when he glanced sideways at Nico stopped the laughter.

"Sorry. I didn't mean to make fun of you. Why don't you let me drive and you can get some sleep? You sat up all night last night."

Zach narrowed his eyes at Nico for a moment, as though looking for a trap, then shook his head, gesturing to the sun, already low in the western sky. "It's only a couple hours until sunset. I'm okay."

"Suit yourself." Nico leaned back in the seat and closed his own eyes.

"Showers," Zach said after a moment.

Nico opened his eyes and looked dubiously at the clear sky. "Um, I doubt it."

"Not rain. Baths."

"What about them?"

"You slept in a barn last night, after sleeping in a shed for two weeks. Might want to think about that next time, before you tease me about how pretty you are."

Nico gawked at him for a moment, then burst into laughter again. "Touché, man. Touché."

17

REVELATION

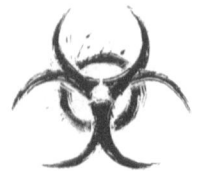

"They're gone!" Zach stomped on the brakes, bringing the truck to a standstill in the middle of the road. The driveway to the left was as empty as the pit of his stomach.

Nico jerked in the passenger seat, where he'd clearly been dozing. "Did they pull the car into the garage?"

Zach shook his head. "The garage door wasn't on any of the circuits powered by the emergency generator. It was only wired up for the essentials. They're gone."

"Are you sure?"

"Yeah." He stared at the shadowy form on his childhood home, trying to decide how he felt about that. The last of his family had hardly even waited a day on the chance he might return to reconcile. It made no sense to feel hurt about that, because he certainly *hadn't* considered returning, and yet— "Guess they figured they might as well leave, once they wrote me off. Father kept talking about some-place in the northwest. I just didn't realize he actually was going to go, much less so soon."

"Well." Nico sucked in a deep breath and released it, his shoulders slumped. "It's okay. Doesn't change anything we're doing, right? Look, it's only a couple hours until dark. Let's sleep here, if the house really is empty. Then we won't have to search for somewhere safe to stay."

"I don't want to leave our supplies outside unattended, even this far out in the country."

Nico snorted in the darkness behind him and clapped him on the shoulder. "Don't worry. I'll get the garage open."

For no reason that made sense, his father had locked the house, and Nico had to break the back door down to get them in. Zach called out, announcing their presence, but no one appeared, armed or otherwise, to confront them.

They really had left him behind.

"They couldn't have taken the generator. I'm sure they took the last fuel cells, but if you've got one of yours, we can have a little bit of light and hot water."

"Point the way."

They kept only a couple of low lights on to conserve power but risked turning on the hot-water heater. Zach looked around in the semidarkness. The house was still in shambles from the ransacking after he had hidden the munitions, but now it was even worse. Clearly, his father and Jacob had been determined to take everything they could possibly carry that might be useful.

"What happened here?" Nico asked as Zach led the way to his bedroom, where the door was still propped against the wall, sans hinges.

"Jailbreak. Father thought he could lock me up and starve compliance into me." The drawers of his dresser had all been pulled out and emptied. "Damn. I only took two changes of clothes when I left. I was hoping I could take more now, but Jacob must have pillaged it all." Zach gestured for Nico to follow again. "Here, this way. You can use my parents' room. It has the best shower. I'll use my bathroom, and then we can turn off the water heater."

He left Nico standing in the tastefully decorated master bedroom and retreated down the hall to his own room. How could Nico bear going so long without bathing? His father, brother, and he had cut back their showers to twice a week, leaving the water heater off when not in use. But they'd slept indoors; there hadn't been much opportunity to get dirty or sweaty. Now, after only a couple of days of living rough, Zach felt absolutely wretched. That should probably tell him something about how fortunate he'd been to have a well-supplied house to take refuge in.

He bathed as quickly as possible, dressed, and went looking for Nico, who had turned on all the bathroom lights and was standing at the sink in the master bathroom with a towel around his hips. He'd just finished shaving the growth of black beard from his jaw and was splashing water on his face to rinse away the soap.

The sight of so much bare skin was downright startling. When was the last time he'd seen someone nude, or nearly so? In the Houtman household, one did not leave one's bedroom any less than fully dressed. It had been more than three years since his last relationship, and even longer since he'd spent any time in the locker room at school.

His eyes drank in all that exposed flesh, satisfying a thirst he'd never realized he'd had. He wasn't even sure that hunger was sexual, so much as it was just awing to be in the presence of someone who clearly felt there was nothing awkward or shameful or sinful about his own body. It felt *honest*.

Which wasn't to say Zach didn't have the predictable reaction, to his chagrin. It took him a moment to remember how to make words. "R-razor."

"Hmm?" Nico turned an inquiring look in his direction, and Zach cleared his throat, trying to keep his eyes above Nico's shoulders.

"I'm surprised Father and Jacob left any razors in the house."

"I had this one in my pack. Call it wishful thinking."

Nico hadn't been exaggerating about how pretty he was. Zach swallowed and looked away from that lean, bare chest, waiting half in eagerness and half in dread for Nico to make a move. Which he inevitably would, of course. Right? He'd already flirted with Zach, after all, and now he was standing here mostly naked. Considering his former occupation, it wasn't like he could possibly have any reservations about sex. What would Zach do if Nico did make a move? What should he . . .?

Nico brushed past him into the bedroom, where the clothes he'd brought from the truck sat in a pile on the bed. Zach hovered behind him, trying to make sense of his own confusion. With an utter lack of self-consciousness, Nico hung his towel around his neck and bent over to step into a pair of underwear.

Zach averted his eyes, glancing around the barely lit space of his parents' bedroom. It felt like there was a poison in this room, and while it shouldn't be any stronger than the toxic presence his father had exerted on the rest of the household, Zach felt it more intensely here.

Three of his four siblings had been conceived in this room. Rebecca should have been the last. After that birth had turned out to be so hazardous, his parents had been advised not to have any more children. But of course, his father would never consider contraception—much less sterilization—and Zach's mother had been brainwashed only too well to be an unquestioningly obedient wife. So Jacob had happened. Their mother had been hospitalized for the last three months of the pregnancy, and Zach now understood that if Jacob's birth hadn't resulted in her having an emergency hysterectomy, eventually there would have been a sixth child, which—if the emphatic worry of her doctors was to be believed—would have undoubtedly killed her. Maurice would rather have seen his own wife die than admit there was a fault in his philosophy.

Considering how his brother had turned out, Zach had to wonder if the selfishness that had led to Jacob's conception had been imprinted on Jacob's soul.

How had he come to these understandings so late in his life? Why had he not seen years earlier how vain and misguided his father's dogma was, how he'd hurt them all over the years?

In willful defiance of Maurice's lingering presence, determined to exorcize it lest it cling to him and follow him away from here when he left for good, Zach strode across the room and wrapped a hand around Nico's solidly muscled biceps.

Nico went still, and then he turned calm, expectant eyes to Zach. Waiting. Why wouldn't he take the lead? Surely, he knew better than Zach what to do? But he just *waited*. Zach's hand shook as he laid it along Nico's bare jaw and leaned in, covering Nico's mouth with his own.

If he thought the kiss he'd shared with Bryan months ago had been a revelation, it was nothing compared to the moment when

Nico's lips parted beneath his. It was so, so very *right*. God was offering him another chance; he knew it. Another chance to be the man he was born to be, to understand that God's truth had nothing to do with the indoctrination he'd received his whole life. This wasn't the damnation he'd feared before. It was the opposite. It was his salvation.

Nico willingly stepped closer and pressed his bare body against Zach's. The house was still cold enough that his drying skin had grown chilled, and Zach closed his arms around him, offering him warmth. Beneath his fingers, the naked plane of Nico's lean back awakened something deep inside Zach, a craving he'd never suspected himself to be capable of. His blunted fingertips dug in, kneading the muscle to still their own trembling. They stretched the skin, dragging down the curve of Nico's spine to the elastic band around his hips.

Nico drew back with a small smile, giving Zach a slow, scrutinizing look. How could he be so calm?

Of course, he would be. For him, this was nothing new. But for Zach, it was taking the final step over the threshold into a whole new world.

Nico trailed a finger down the front of Zach's sweater, from his neck to just above the waistband of his trousers. "Not that I'm opposed to this, but before we go much further, I just need to make sure you're not going to have second thoughts. Because I really don't want to try to travel across the country alone."

"I'm not." Zach swallowed hard and shook his head. He ventured a nervous smile. "I can't think of a better way to send my father a big 'screw you.'"

The attempt at levity fell flat when Nico pulled away, his eyes hardening. He turned around and grabbed his shirt, jerking it on, before whirling on Zach with a sneer. "Yeah, no thanks. The only people who get to use me pay for the privilege first, and sorry, sweetheart, but your money just isn't worth much these days. You'll have to find another way to deal with your daddy issues."

Damn. Zach closed his eyes, desperation rising up in him. "No, I'm sorry, that's not what I meant to—"

Nico jerked his head toward the door. "*Good night.*"

"Right. Good night." Zach sighed and turned away, kicking himself for his stupidity. He stopped in the doorway, speaking over his shoulder. "Imagine spending your whole life so caught up in lies that it took you more than twenty-four years to even begin questioning, much less see the truth." He took a shuddering breath. "About the only good thing I can see in all that's happened to this world is that I finally have a chance to start living honestly. I guess I'm not sure how to handle that. I didn't mean to insult you. I'm sorry."

He retreated before Nico had a chance to answer.

⋀ ⋀ ⋀

ZACH SPENT the night in the room he'd slept in his whole life, staring at the empty doorway as though willing Nico to appear in it and give him another chance. But two days of tumult and nearly no sleep caught up with him just before dawn.

The sun was high when he finally opened his eyes again, and the house was silent. Zach spent a moment orienting himself, recalling that he wouldn't hear the sounds of his father's and brother's voices carrying through the walls. But neither could he hear any sound of Nico moving around. He bolted out of bed, panic surging within him. Had he insulted Nico so badly that he had decided to risk the journey alone?

Then he heard steps on the stairs and sank onto the bed, weak with relief. Nico appeared in the doorway.

"You're still here," Zach said stupidly.

Nico frowned, but then his face grew softer, and he rubbed the back of his neck. "I'm sorry. I . . . overreacted. Knowing who you are . . . who raised you, what you were taught to believe . . . I keep waiting for some hint that you think you're better than me, and after all you've done, that's not fair to you."

"I don't. I swear I don't."

"I know." Nico stepped through the doorway, peeling his long-sleeved shirt over his head. Zach froze, his eyes devouring Nico's skin as it appeared, but he didn't move, didn't touch. He waited. Nico met his gaze and, deliberately maintaining the eye contact, stood between Zach's feet, bending over and pulling him up into a kiss.

Oh. Heaven. Nico smelled perfect, *tasted* perfect, and Zach wouldn't say a damned word if it meant not screwing this up again. Nico teased his lips, coaxing Zach to open for him, which he did gladly. The caress of Nico's tongue against his own was sweeter and more sensual than anything he'd ever known, and he wanted more.

It didn't matter that he'd only known Nico for mere days, at least as anything more than a stranger's voice coming from a dark shed. It didn't matter that he had no idea whether or not they'd have any sort of future together. Zach was the furthest thing from a casual-sex type of guy, but this didn't *feel* casual, no matter what Nico's past life had been like. This felt affirming and so very *necessary*. If God didn't exactly approve, Zach knew He would at least understand.

He didn't think it was casual for Nico, either. Nico's eyes were too sober, his expression questioning as he pulled away to tug at Zach's shirt. When it was gone, Nico dropped to his knees beside the bed, running his hands over Zach's shoulders and chest.

The feel of Nico's palms gliding over his skin was magic. It was as though Zach had never felt the touch of another person before, as if his nerve endings had just suddenly come to life after years of nothingness. Nico pushed Zach onto his back and slid his fingers over the twitchy skin of Zach's lower abdomen, under the waistband of his underwear and pajama bottoms. With a moan, Zach lifted his hips and let Nico shimmy them down.

Then those talented hands wrapped around his shaft and drew upward. Zach melted into the mattress, groaning a desperate plea for . . . he wasn't sure what, so long as it didn't stop.

The heat of Nico's mouth replaced his hands, and all Zach could do was grasp Nico's curls and beg for more. He propped himself up with his other elbow, unable to bear the thought of not seeing what Nico was doing to him.

"Nico . . ." he panted, his fingers curling against Nico's scalp in an effort not to grip his head and hold him while he pumped up into that wet heat.

Nico slid back, releasing the suction on Zach's cock with a *pop*. He dipped his head and began nuzzling the crease of Zach's groin. When Zach spread his legs wider to offer Nico better access, Nico ducked under his jutting dick and began to suck on Zach's balls.

Nico looked up from beneath Zach's cock, his dark, heavy lashes sweeping upward. "Two things," he said. "First: I'm here because I want to be, but the moment you even think of treating me like a whore, I'm gone. Second: As long as we're both comfortable with what is going on, there are no rules. Leave anything you've been taught at the door. Just let me know what you don't like, let me know when you want more of what you do, and I'll do the same. Forget about what's appropriate, or sinful, or what anyone ever said you *should* want or do."

Zach gasped and writhed as Nico's hand slid up and down his shaft, jacking him in a slow, steady rhythm. "Pretty sure that's . . . not gonna be a problem . . . Oh God, Nico . . ."

That twist thing Nico was adding to the end of each stroke was going to be the death of him, he was sure of it. He'd lost control of his hips, seeking more. Nico obliged. Did he know his touches were like a banquet for the proverbial starving man? Zach liked that idea better than thinking it was all professional skill that made what Nico was doing with his fingers and lips and teeth so incredible.

It wasn't just the feeling of his hand and mouth on Zach's cock, either. It was the way his fingers slid up Zach's chest to pinch his nipples while he sucked leisurely on just the head. It was the way he peppered biting kisses around Zach's belly and groin and even the ridges of his hips when he eased Zach back from the edge. It was the way he rolled Zach's balls before gripping his ass and squeezing, pulling Zach's hips forward, urging him to follow the instinct to thrust.

It was the way his soft, brown eyes fluttered open and met Zach's, crinkling at the corners in an encouraging smile.

Zach had never felt anything like it. He didn't know if he ever would again, so he would take it all and relish it for as long as it lasted.

"Nico!" His hand smacked weakly at Nico's shoulder, trying to warn him. Either Nico didn't get the message or didn't care, and seconds later Zach was too far gone for it to matter. His world shorted out, his senses overloading in a cataclysm of pleasure.

By the time he managed to pry his eyes open again, Nico had sat back on his heels, his lips wet and shining. He looked pleased with himself, but there was something else creeping into his eyes, cagey and evasive.

"I'll go gather up my stuff. We should get on the road," he said with a tight smile, shoving to his feet. Beneath his trousers, the rigid line of his cock was obvious.

Zach reached for him, trying to draw him into another embrace, but Nico sidestepped.

"Come back when you're done?" he asked, feeling ridiculously shy about pointing out that Nico hadn't come yet. Zach wanted to offer to remedy that situation, to try to bring Nico the same pleasure Nico had brought him, but the words froze on his tongue.

Nico seemed to stare at something just past Zach's left ear, because he certainly wasn't meeting Zach's eyes. "We really need to get going. We have a long trip ahead of us. Who knows what we'll come across."

"Uh . . . okay?" Zach sat up, folding his hands over his flaccid cock. He glanced away, composing himself and trying not to make an issue of Nico's strange withdrawal. Nico *had* to want . . . something more? Zach cleared his throat and forced himself to speak. "You don't need . . .?"

"No." Nico shook his head a little too quickly, and his smile seemed forced. "I'm good. See you down by the truck."

Zach dropped his gaze to the floor and nodded. When he looked up again, Nico was gone.

He didn't have time to figure out what had just happened. Drawing and releasing a long, slow breath, Zach kicked off the pajamas Nico had left wrapped around one ankle and dressed, then started searching the house to see what his father and brother had left behind that might be scavenge-worthy.

He took all the bedding he could find, wrapped them into tight rolls, and tied them with twine. Wherever they ended up, there was no guarantee they would have adequate shelter or blankets. In the rafters above the garage was the camping equipment they had saved from when Zach and his siblings had spent weeks at Bible camp in the summer. He set all that out, as well, relieved that it hadn't occurred to his father or Jacob to take it with them.

An ax and saw for firewood. Utility gloves to keep them from getting blisters that could get infected, for which they would have no medicine. Should he bring any gardening equipment? They couldn't rely on the military installation at Cheyenne Mountain to supply them with all the food they would need. How many other survivors were there? Eventually they would have to find a way to become self-sufficient, wouldn't they? Where would they get seeds?

Joining Nico, he worked on loading it into the truck. They labored largely in silence, but it was easy, companionable. Nothing like the quiet of the last several months Zach had spent in the company of his father and brother. And if Nico felt any discomfort or resentment from that morning, he gave no sign of it. They dug conservatively into their rations, finishing off the foil-wrapped chevron they'd cooked two nights prior, along with some of the dehydrated fruit Nico carried.

"Ready to go?" Nico asked when they were done. Looking out the window, Zach saw the day was already aging; they'd be racing the sun to make progress and still find someplace secure to stop for the night.

He took one last look around his childhood home and nodded grimly. There was nothing left of the life he'd lived here.

"Let's go."

18

OBSTACLES

Much to Nico's frustration, it took them hours to find their way around the Indianapolis metropolitan area. They were trying to stay outside the city limits, but the truck's navigational system—no doubt detecting a complete absence of traffic from the satellites and thus no reason to avoid the main thoroughfares—kept trying to reroute them onto the shortest-distance course through the city. Finally, they stopped so that Zach could find the computer's auto-routing program and disable it, hopefully without turning the truck into a lawn ornament.

"Next time we come across a reasonably small town, someplace with a really low population, I want to stop at a pharmacy," Nico announced once they'd managed to skirt Indianapolis.

Zach nodded, accepting it without question. First aid supplies were the one thing they weren't very well equipped with, after all, even if it wasn't Nico's primary concern just now. They stopped along a deserted stretch of road to eat lunch and swap drivers, and Nico watched Zach assess each passing town to find the smallest one that would still boast a pharmacy.

"Thanks," Nico muttered when Zach pulled into the parking lot. So far, so good. The place looked completely deserted. Nonetheless, he grabbed the assault rifle and reached in back for the shotgun.

"Mind getting up on the roof again to play lookout while I run inside?"

Nico took a moment to admire the length of belly that was exposed when Zach scrambled up to stand on the roof of the truck, then walked away.

The store had already been looted, so he didn't have to break down the door. No doubt the drugs behind the counter were long gone, but Nico wasn't after pharmaceuticals. Even if it would be nice to have some antibiotics on hand, just in case.

Holding a flashlight between his shoulder and jaw, Nico snatched up a bag and began filling it with whatever he could find among the jumbled mess on the floor and shelves. The looters had been sloppy, as looters tended to be. He grabbed bandages and gauze, ointments, antihistamines—anything of use that had been left behind. Even the condoms had been scavenged, though, thank God, not completely. He was stuffing a couple of large boxes into his bag when he heard the thunderous report of the shotgun, followed by Zach's bellow.

The glass door shattered, along with the window, when Nico burst through it, his bag left behind on the littered floor of the pharmacy. A second shotgun blast nearly deafened him. Out of the corner of his eye, he could see Zach still atop the truck, apparently unscathed. One body lay in the road some thirty yards away, but another human form was pelting toward them with inhuman speed.

Nico charged before it could get any closer. The matted hair and ragged, half-absent clothing, and the bestial snarl on the revenant's face only registered as an afterthought. He just knew he had to intercept her. If the woman was moving that fast, she wasn't anyone he wanted within breathing distance of Zach.

He slammed into her, driving her backward before she could get closer than ten yards from the truck. She crashed onto the ground, her clawed hands already coming up to shred him as she screamed in animalistic rage. He couldn't let her cut him any more than he could let her get close to Zach. Without thinking, he did what he'd seen his mother do the previous summer and drove his elbow down into her throat. There was a crunching, shattering sound—louder and more grotesque than he remembered—and then she died, convulsing beneath him, struggling for a breath she would never take.

It took a long moment for the red haze to fade from his vision. Zach's voice crept into Nico's awareness, getting closer. He quickly thrust a hand up. "Stay back! I don't know if she clawed me."

He couldn't feel the burn of any scratches, but then, he couldn't feel much of anything just now. His face and extremities were numb as the surge of fury and fear that had propelled him through the door and into the path of the oncoming revenant faded. He spun to face Zach, devouring him with his eyes, needing to assure himself that Zach was all right.

He was pale and his aquamarine eyes were bulging, but he was unscathed, staring at Nico from a safe distance.

"You're not bleeding," he said, speaking gently, as if trying to soothe an agitated animal. "Nico? You're okay. You're not bleeding."

That was all he needed to hear. With another rush of energy, he closed the distance between them and drove Zach against the truck, his open mouth hungry on Zach's. His heart was still racing, his mouth still had an odd, metallic taste on the back of his tongue, and every impulse felt too big for his body to contain, like the need to act was going to erupt through his skin, shattering him like the peak of a volcano.

Zach was trembling in his arms and his grasp on Nico felt weak, but it didn't matter. Nico spun him so that Zach was facing the truck, his ass pressing into Nico's unexpected erection. Nico gnawed and sucked at his neck, gripping him hard, spurred by the need to seize and bite and fuck and claim.

Zach's moan was a plaintive sound that barely registered as Nico's searching hand found Zach hard beneath the fly of his trousers. He ripped the zipper down and thrust his fingers inside to grasp Zach, jerking him roughly as he ground hard against his ass. Zach came with a startled cry, and Nico humped against him, needing that release, needing to do something with the fire and passion and violence welling inside him. Needed—

He tore himself away from Zach, hunched over with the pain of the stymied orgasm swelling his cock and clutching his balls. "Fuck. I can't."

Panting, Zach was slumped against the car, but he managed to gasp, "Nico?"

He couldn't do it. He couldn't remember *why* he couldn't do it, because nothing was making sense right now, but he couldn't do it. He had to stop.

"Gimme a minute," he muttered, cupping his aching groin. "I feel— Something's not right. Just gimme a minute. I can't think. Get back up on the roof. Stay there."

He staggered away before Zach could question him, striding down the length of strip mall that housed the pharmacy and rounding the corner of the building, putting plenty of distance between him and Zach. When he was sure Zach wouldn't follow him, he opened his fly and jerked himself to completion against the wall of the building, then slumped beside the mess and tried to make sense of the chaos in his brain.

It seemed to take forever for his scrambled thoughts to organize themselves, for his pulse and breathing to slow to the point where he felt sane and human again. Even after his orgasm, the urgent, violent *need* didn't fade, at least not right away, and he had to stop himself from returning to Zach to finish what he'd started. What the fuck was wrong with him?

He slowly walked back around the building to find Zach sitting on the roof of the truck as Nico had ordered him to. And what was that about, anyway? What made him think he had any right to just bark orders at Zach and walk away, especially after manhandling him the way he had?

Zach didn't look very alert. In fact, if something else had tried to attack, it would be on top of them before Zach even noticed. His face was drawn, his wet eyes unfocused and absolutely devastated.

"Oh God," Nico whispered, reaching up to help him down. "I'm sorry, Zach. I'm so sorry. Did I hurt you?"

"What? No." Zach blinked at him and then shook his head, slipping off the roof into Nico's arms. He made a strangled sound. "I killed someone. Oh, my God. *I killed someone!*"

Zach fell apart, sobbing into Nico's shoulder. Nico held him, murmuring soothing nonsense. "Shh. It's okay. We both did. We had to. It's gonna be all right."

Strange that it was only now occurring to him that he'd murdered someone as well. It hadn't seemed important during those strange, fugue-like moments of rage and lust. He could barely remember now what he'd done, except that it had seemed absolutely necessary and absolutely right at the time.

He hadn't felt that way when Silvia had attacked him. But then, he'd been focused on getting the lightcar to land and then he'd been unconscious. If she'd still attempted to attack him once they were on the ground, would he have reacted the same way he just had? Was this part of the Alpha strain? Even during the bombing at the midsummer party, he didn't remember feeling that same bestial need to destroy any and all threats when he fought.

"Are *you* okay?" Zach finally asked, drawing back and wiping his face. He still looked pale and shocked, but his eyes were focused again. "What happened?"

"I don't know. I'm okay; I just—" Nico spread his hands with a helpless shrug. "I don't know. Maybe it will sink in later."

"Nico, was it . . . was it *her*?"

Nico turned to look at the body he'd left lying on the ground. The hair was entirely the wrong color and length, the skin far too pale, the breasts too large.

"No." He wasn't sure if he was feeling relief or regret that he hadn't had a chance to correct his mistake, and he didn't want to examine it. "If she's still alive, she's miles from here. Let's get out of here. Just . . . get the stuff we need and go."

"What about them?" Zach jerked his chin toward the bodies. "Should we bury them? Burn them?"

Nico pressed his lips together and shook his head. "No. I know it's the right thing to do, and part of me wants to, but the longer we stay here, the longer something else has to come after us. You can't go near them, and if I touch the one you shot, I'll be covered in blood and that won't be safe for you, either. I'm not risking you again."

Without giving Zach a chance to argue, he hurried into the pharmacy to grab the bag he'd dropped, then rushed out and stuffed it into his rucksack in the back. Zach was already in the driver's seat with the engine running, and at Nico's muttered command, he sped away as fast as he could safely manage.

▲ ▲ ▲

THERE WAS no possible way to completely bypass St. Louis. Eventually they would need to approach a more heavily populated area to cross the river. Nico really didn't want to be stuck trying to find their way around the city in the dark, so they agreed to give up on finding a country road that wouldn't get them hopelessly lost and would just try to get through the metro area as quickly as they could.

Derelict suburbs with overgrown lawns—the crumbling remnants of a middle class that had ceased to exist long before the pandemic—quickly gave way to rising walls of apartment buildings lining either side of the freeway. The windows in those buildings were dark; some had been shot out or broken. He'd managed to mostly miss that element of this new world in the lightcar; it hadn't seemed quite so empty and haunted from an aerial view.

Despite the emptiness of the outskirts of the city, their progress was slow. Debris was scattered across the roads, though whether from riots or accidents, Nico wasn't certain. He didn't want to risk damage to the tires or the undercarriage of the truck by driving over something sharp, so he stayed as far from it as he could. Periodically there were abandoned cars they had to drive around, and on the other side of the freeway, they passed a number of leftover police and National Guard barricades apparently intended to keep people from leaving the city.

Nico shook his head at the futility of it all. It was one thing to force an in-house quarantine on those in the suburbs and country, but to do it to the people packed into the urban areas had been tantamount to sentencing them all to death. Survival had favored the wealthy, and no doubt the white.

The closer they came to the inner city, the more decrepit the buildings were. Factories and warehouses that had been defunct for years or decades added to the tableau of ruin. Occasionally, they would pass one of the urban renewal areas, where gentrification had driven out the indigent people in favor of renovations that only the very wealthy could afford.

If anyone was still alive inside those overpriced condos now, it didn't show.

I helped make this happen.

The thought ate at Nico, though he knew his role was tangential and insignificant at best. If it hadn't been him, it would have been another escort hired by McClosky.

Zach didn't seem as amazed by the silence and stillness as Nico did, but then, he wouldn't, would he? He had already passed through it before, when he and his father and brother had left Vermont to return to Indiana. He was solemn, and several times Nico thought he saw Zach's lips moving in silent prayer. Was he praying for the souls of all those who were lost, or simply that he and Nico would make it through unscathed?

Perhaps he was praying for forgiveness. For Nico, if not for himself.

It took Nico a moment to realize what the large, uneven mass on the road in the distance was. Another roadblock. But not one of the official cordons the cops or military had put in place. Instead, it was a jumble of furniture, and even cars, forming a barricade across their side of the highway.

"Shit," he muttered.

Beside him, Zach asked, "Who do you think left that there?"

"I'm not sure I want to know." He stopped the car a good fifty yards from the obstruction, not turning off the engine. No one appeared to be manning the roadblock, unless they were waiting for him to drive closer so they could come up behind and box him in. There were no nearby exits, no easy way to get off the freeway and choose another route. But perhaps whoever had constructed the thing was gone now, their efforts to prey on hapless passersby failing due to lack of hapless passersby.

"Get back up on the truck." Trying to see out every window at once for any signs of habitation, Nico reached blindly into the back for the assault rifle. "I'll check it out and see if I can clear things out of the way if there's no one around. *Do not* come down."

The edges of Zach's tense lips were white as he, too, kept darting his gaze around in every direction. His reloaded shotgun had been propped between them, and he grabbed the handgun off the dash. "What if someone attacks you?"

"If they do, take the truck and get the hell out of here." Nico's shoulders twitched as if he could feel predatory eyes upon him. Which he wasn't sure he did, but he didn't think he could be blamed for being a little paranoid. "We won't know if they're infected or not, so you stay away from them. If I can take care of them myself, great. If I can't, though, I'll probably be injured badly enough that you'll need to keep clear of me too."

"I'm not going to *abandon* you!"

"*You don't have a choice!*" He glared at Zach. "I *do not* want you getting infected, so just get your fucking ass in the truck and get out of here if you need to."

To avoid giving Zach a chance to argue further, Nico flung himself out of the truck and slammed the door behind him. The empty highway and abandoned buildings were quiet all around him. *Jesus, so quiet.* It shouldn't be like this. The silence could drive him mad.

Nico held his gun at the ready and cautiously approached the barricade, incessantly scanning his surroundings for any hint of who might be lurking there. Damn it, they didn't have time for this. It was already late afternoon, and he desperately needed to get Zach out of the city before nightfall.

Finally, it came down to a choice between standing there waiting for something to attack or putting his gun down and trying to clear enough room for the car to get through. Or would they be better off turning around and trying to find another way to go? He took a deep breath. Either whoever had built this thing was incredibly patient or they were long gone themselves. His hands shook with adrenaline as he slung the assault rifle across his back and began testing the construction of the roadblock.

The furniture was easy to move. The sofas and chairs were musty and rank; obviously they'd been sitting out for weeks or even months. He heaved them across the concrete median where they thumped onto the other side of the road, sometimes with a snap of cracking wood.

The cars were another matter. Whoever had rolled them into place to form the foundation of the roadblock hadn't left enough of their operating computers intact for Nico to gain access and drive them out of the way. Instead, he had to push them to the shoulder of the highway, struggling against their flat, locked tires the entire time.

He was grunting and panting so loudly, his heart pounding in his ears, that he didn't hear the first growl until he paused to wipe the sweat from his eyes. The low, animal sound was deafening in the unnerving silence, and a chorus of others joined it. Nico froze and straightened very slowly, his eyes quickly finding the pack of ragged, dirty dogs that were milling around the truck.

Some were sniffing at the doors and tires, or looking up at Zach, who was out of their reach. Others had their attention on Nico. Even at this distance, he could see Zach was pale and terrified. The dogs were rail-thin, starving, and obviously feral. Cautiously, Nico began fumbling behind his back, trying to bring his weapon around. There were seven—*no, wait, eight*—dogs, and if they charged him en masse, there was no way he could gun them down before they were on him. Worse, he'd be firing in Zach's direction, and he wasn't great with a gun.

Fuck. If they bit him, he was going to bleed, and if that happened, there was no way he could continue traveling with Zach.

Several of the largest dogs had sunk low, prowling forward with their hackles up and those bass growls rumbling from their throats. Shaking, Nico tried to steady himself enough to release a short spray of bullets at the nearest one, a mutt with dingy, scraggly gray fur. His aim was off, and he hit the ground beside it. Chips of concrete flew, and the dog leaped away, yelping loudly.

It was enough to give the other dogs pause, though. They crouched lower, their growls even more alarming. Another quivered on the brink of pouncing, but as his haunches tensed to spring, the short, sharp bark of Zach's handgun thundered through the quiet, and the dog dropped where it had stood with a truncated howl, blood pooling beneath it.

Zach's face transformed from grim determination to alarm as his gun came up, as if he were taking aim at Nico. "Nico, *get down!*"

Nico started to turn to see what Zach saw when something slammed into him, sending him flying. His head cracked against one of the cars still forming the barricade with an explosion of agony and white light. His skull made a sickening sound knocking against the pavement as the human figure drove him the rest of the way down. Panic sliced through the pain, knowing that had been a bad hit. He swore he could feel his brain bounce around his skull.

He wavered at the edge of consciousness, trying to fend off the body on top of him. It stank to high heaven, just like the woman outside the pharmacy had. Its putrid breath hit him like a noxious wall of fumes as he brought up his arms to try to keep the gnashing teeth at bay. And its eyes . . . There was nothing human in them. They burned with pure, inhuman hunger.

Nico tried to shout at Zach to run, but he wasn't sure he actually managed to make any sound. A dark form flew at the man—*thing*— on top of Nico, striking from the side in a blur of filthy fur. The revenant threw the dog off with a snarl, twisting as he rose from Nico's body and sprang to his feet to face the attacking pack. The dogs were darting toward him one after the other, trying to flank and hamstring him, sometimes dodging his attempts to strike back, other times catching the blows and being knocked aside.

It was impossible to tell which growls were revenant and which were canine.

Nico wanted to fall back on the ground and let unconsciousness claim him. His head throbbed, and everything looked blurry and just *off*. But the dogs and revenant wouldn't keep each other occupied forever. Either the revenant would drive the dogs away and then kill Nico or the dogs would kill the revenant and then come after Nico. If they wounded the revenant, its blood might get on him, making it unsafe to be near Zach.

Desperately, Nico dragged himself down the freeway toward the truck, pulling with his arms since his legs didn't seem to want to move and fighting off the waves of blackness threatening to tow him under. He could hear the savage battle between the dogs and the revenant behind him growing more frenzied, and all he could think was that he needed to get Zach away from it before someone started bleeding.

Unless he was bleeding already. Nico stopped and put a hand on the side of his head where it had hit the first time. He felt the tender lump there, and his hair was wet with sweat, but there was no blood on his fingers when he pulled them away from his scalp. Grit and gravel were tangled in his hair from the concrete, but again, no blood.

He staggered to his feet and ignored the pain and nausea that tried to overwhelm him as he broke into a limping jog toward the truck.

"Oh God. Get in, get in, *get in*!" Zach pleaded, his face pinched and pale. He'd already thrown open the passenger-side door, and Nico flung himself into the seat. He barely managed to slam the door closed behind himself before Zach put the car in motion, the tires squealing as he reversed at a dangerous speed, putting distance between them and the feral creatures fighting by the roadblock.

Then he hit the brakes and swung the car around in a sharp turn. It threw Nico against the door, and another wave of excruciating pain crashed through his skull. He was aware of the force of Zach's acceleration pinning him to the seat, and then he lost his grip on consciousness.

19

RECOVERY

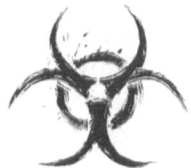

When Nico opened his eyes for the first time since they'd sped away from the barricade, night had fallen. The world outside was so dark he had no way of knowing where they were. He only knew that Zach was driving very carefully, his hands clenching the wheel in a white-knuckled grip and his eyes intent on the road. He wasn't even trying to be silent as he muttered a prayer for God to get them through without crashing into something in the darkness.

Sickened by the pain in his skull, Nico closed his eyes and left Zach to it.

Dawn was spreading tendrils of pink into an inky-gray sky when he woke up again. "Where're we?" he slurred, blinking.

Zach's eyes flicked over at him in an uncertain glance before he turned his attention back to the road. "I'm not sure. Somewhere in Missouri still? I keep seeing signs for Kansas City, but I have no idea how we're going to get around it."

Nico started groping urgently for the door handle. "*Pull over.*"

Zach barely managed to come to a stop before Nico flung the door open and leaned out of the car, retching out the meager contents of his stomach. He would have tumbled out into the small pool of his own spew if Zach hadn't caught hold of his shirt and kept him from falling.

"This is not good," Nico panted when the dry heaves subsided.

His throat burned from the acid backwash, and he could feel his own skin covered in a clammy, cold sweat. The pain in his head was blinding even in the dim, predawn light.

"I saw you hit your head." Zach's voice was tight with emotion, sounding as worried as Nico felt. "I even heard it. For a moment, I thought— I wasn't sure you could have survived that. It sounded like a melon breaking open."

"Sorry." Nico wasn't sure why he was apologizing, except that Zach seemed afraid and he couldn't stand to be the cause of that fear. He struggled to get himself back upright in his seat. It took several attempts to get the car door closed because any exertion came with a fresh explosion of pain in his skull, but eventually he succeeded. "Have to keep going."

"You sure? I'm trying to find someplace safe to stop."

"Need sleep?"

Zach scoffed, but it was shaky, like he was trying to laugh and couldn't quite pull it off. "I'm too afraid to sleep. You're injured, and I don't know what to do for you."

"Don' worry 'bout me." Nico could see his hand trembling as he lifted it and laid it on Zach's arm. "Do what's safe f'you. Stop if y'have t'sleep."

"God, knock it off!" Nico winced when Zach's raised voice cracked. Zach shot him an angry look before turning back to the road. "I'm not the only person in this car. Quit acting like only one of us needs to be protected."

"Ow. Please don't yell." Nico sank down in his seat, closing his eyes as the sky brightened with the day.

"Sorry." Zach hardly even whispered the word, and when Nico ventured to slit an eye open, Zach was staring at the road with the sort of fixed concentration people acquired when they had to focus on something or else fall completely apart. "Don't suppose *you* know what to do for head injuries?" he asked after a moment, one corner of his mouth lifting with just the barest amount of wry humor.

Nico swallowed against another wave of nausea. He tried shaking his head, but then thought better of it. "'Fraid not. Guess I'm just going to have to pass out here and hope for the best. Pull off and get some sleep if you need to."

THE DAY PASSED in sporadic bursts of painful consciousness, punctuated by sweet oblivion. Nico had no appetite and couldn't make himself eat, even though he knew that whatever the Bane Alpha virus was doing to his body, it required far more fuel than it was getting. Whenever he woke up, Zach would force water down his throat, which he usually vomited right back up. He wasn't sure he should be sleeping so much, but he didn't seem to have much of a choice in the matter.

He had the feeling it had been another day of slow travel as Zach tried to find routes around Kansas City, Wichita, and God only knew what other cities they had passed by now. It was too dark around the truck for Nico to tell where Zach had eventually pulled over that night.

Zach was snoring behind the driver's console, his seat reclined and his face turned toward Nico, slack with sleep. Nico stared at him, not quite praying—certainly not the way Zach did—but hoping with all his heart that he could find a way to protect him. Just this one guy. He didn't delude himself into thinking he could do anything to stem the destruction he'd unwittingly helped unleash upon the world, but this one man, this one life. This decent, sincere, kind person who would hold a gun on his own father to protect a stranger. Maybe if Nico could just preserve that, it wouldn't have all been a waste.

Zach's eyes blinked open in the moonlight, and he shot upright, immediately on full alert when he saw Nico. "You okay?"

"Head still hurts like a bitch, but I think I might live." Nico rubbed the tender knots on his scalp cautiously. "Go back to sleep. I'm sure you need to rest."

"Yeah, okay." Zach twisted and tried to stretch in the confines of the driver's seat, then settled back in. "You too. Wake me up if you need anything."

Zach's eyes drifted closed, but Nico found he wasn't sleepy. He was in too much pain to think very hard about anything, but he couldn't stop staring at Zach, as if he could make all this turn out all right if he kept watch over him.

Zach's eyes didn't open, and his voice was soft sometime later when he murmured, "You still awake?"

"Yeah."

"Can I ask you something?"

"Sure."

"What happened with us before? In my bedroom, and then in the parking lot. Why did you . . .? I mean, why *didn't* you . . .? Did I do something wrong?"

"No." Now Zach looked at him, and Nico found himself glancing away to avoid that searching gaze. "You didn't do anything wrong. It was great. I wanted more. A lot more."

"Then why did you run off?" Zach's fingers crossed the distance between the seats to brush the back of Nico's hand.

He sighed. "This virus . . . the one it mutates into when I bleed. I'm just not sure if it's *only* in my blood, you know? I didn't want to risk you getting the Rot if I came with you nearby."

"Oh." There was a note of relief in Zach's voice. "Then, it wasn't because you didn't want—"

"To feel you jerk me off? To blow my load all over you?" Nico smirked. It was too dark to tell if Zach was blushing, but he'd swear he could feel the heat radiating from Zach's face. "Believe me, I *definitely* wanted. I can't remember the last time I wanted it that badly."

"Oh." Zach closed his eyes, frowning slightly, then looked at Nico again. "I suppose, considering your profession, it sort of, um, loses its shine?"

Nico pressed his lips together. That hurt. He knew Zach wasn't trying to pass judgment, but it still stung.

"Is that what you think? That I'm jaded? That I've been fucked so many times, by so many people, I don't feel anything anymore?" He shook his head. "It wasn't like that."

"*Oh.*" Nico was starting to hate that syllable, particularly for the hesitant silence that followed it. "I'm sorry. I want to understand. What was it like, then?"

Nico licked his lips, pulling his thoughts together as he tried to come down from his knee-jerk irritation. He was so primed for Zach to turn judgmental on him that he was ready take offense at anything.

At least talking gave him something to focus on other than his headache.

"Well, when my mother started tricking, her claim to fame, as it were, was that she tried to emulate the *cortigiana onesta* of the Italian Renaissance. They weren't simply whores. They were intellectuals. Poets. Entertainers. Musicians. Women with the freedom to pursue an education and a relative degree of ownership of their own bodies. Being with them wasn't just a matter of money for sex; it was an *experience.*"

Zach blinked at him, and Nico could tell he wasn't getting it yet. "How?"

"The men who employed them sought a companion who was witty and graceful and entertaining. Yes, sex was part of the deal, but sometimes men would contract my mother just to have a date whose company they knew they would enjoy. And when she began hiring other escorts, she looked for that same level of engagement from them." Zach's eyes widened at that, and Nico nodded emphatically. "And when it came to sex, that sort of dynamic meant that a connection was often formed. It wasn't just a commercial exchange, money for orgasms. With the exception of the sort of jobs we sometimes did for General McClosky, we usually knew our clients. Frequently, we even liked them. Enjoyed their company. And, yes, enjoyed having sex with them. The sex was very rarely something we just gritted our teeth and endured because it was what we were being paid to do."

He let Zach absorb that for a while. He looked a little dubious about the idea, and Nico sighed again.

"Look, I'm not saying it's like that for every sex worker. The abuses of the corporate brothels are fairly well-known. Sure, they put the pimps out of business, but they replaced them with something even worse—a legally sanctioned *something* at that." Nico grimaced. "Brothel workers aren't given the option of turning down customers, and they make so little, it's straight-up wage slavery. Human trafficking by another name. But my mother—she started tricking to *get away* from a man with that endgame, so she took what he wanted and expanded it, packaged and sold it on her own terms. I respect the work she did. And the work I did as her employee."

Zach looked a little pained at that. "I'm sorry. It's just . . . the idea of a mother employing her son to do . . . *that* . . ."

"Yeah, I'm sure it seems a little warped to you." Nico smiled sadly, longing for his mother, grief for her loss spearing him through the chest. "But she wasn't ashamed of who she was or what she did or what she had built. If she wasn't ashamed of it, why would she discourage me from following in her footsteps? And if I wasn't ashamed of her, why wouldn't I do it myself?"

"So you honestly never felt jaded about it?"

"Well, I can't say I always felt the same degree of pleasure with every client, but it never became something rote that I had no feelings about."

"Did you ever . . . *date*? Have relationships outside work?"

"Sometimes." Nico shrugged. "Hard to date when I was so busy with school and work. Relationships were a little harder, for obvious reasons."

Zach nodded understandingly. "Did it feel different?"

"What?"

"Making love with someone you weren't . . . *seeing* on a professional basis?"

Nico chuckled. "You're so diplomatic."

"Don't laugh at me."

"I'm not. I just— I'm not sure how to answer that." He shook his head. "I mean, I'm not cut out for celibacy. I need what I get from sex. I'm not talking about orgasms, either. I need . . ."

"What?" Zach's face was sober in the faint silvery hint of moonlight and his eyes shockingly pale. He seemed to be hanging on to Nico's every word.

"Touch." Nico dropped his gaze, staring down at his hands. It felt like weakness to admit that. He'd never said it to anyone before. "Connection. Having someone's skin on my skin. The smell of another person. The taste. The feeling of their hands on me. I crave it. I can't seem to go long without it."

Which was why he'd gone back to McClosky's bed over and over during the winter, despite the fact that he'd come to loathe the man. He didn't confess that to Zach.

"So I guess, in answer to your question, it was different but it wasn't. For me, it was always about making that contact, whether I picked someone up at a club or they were paying me for the night."

And I never knew it could be more than that until you put your hands on me and I felt someone who needed to touch me as badly as I needed to be touched.

Nico looked up when Zach's hand settled over his. Of its own volition, Nico's wrist rotated, turning his palm up so that his fingers could lace between Zach's.

Even that. Even that little touch awoke a longing in his chest, making him ache for more.

"What about you?" he rasped. "No guilt? No penance? No little angels or demons on your shoulders, telling you how badly you sinned with me the other day?"

Zach's lips quirked up into a small smile, and he shook his head. "No. You know, it was my first hint that my beliefs were different from my father's when I realized I didn't buy into the idea that God was some dirty old voyeur peeking in people's bedroom windows to judge what they were doing in there and with whom."

Nick tutted. "Dangerous, radical thought, there."

"I *know*. Scandalous blasphemy, isn't it?" Zach gave a self-effacing shrug. "Don't get me wrong. I think God ultimately wants people to marry or form committed, lifelong relationships. To establish stable families and communities. I think He unreservedly sanctions sex within the context of those relationships. I just think that for those who have sex without that bond, it's at worst a minor infraction against God's plan for us. Not the heinous sin a lot of people would make it out to be."

"So we're not going to Hell because you're not wearing my ring yet?"

Nico could have bit his tongue off at the last word, which had slipped past his lips without any thought. It implied all kinds of possibilities of a future that Nico had no business even thinking of. But either Zach didn't notice or he chose to let it pass unremarked.

"No. I think He has other concerns right now." Zach's small smile faded, his eyes growing large and soft. The look on his face was so sweet and earnest, it made something in Nico's chest ache. "If you weren't injured, I'd want to do it again. Except—"

"What?" The pounding of his head negated the possibility of Nico's cock taking much active interest in whatever Zach was saying, but Nico could feel his libido sitting up in the background, perking its ears curiously.

"I'm, um, not sure I'm comfortable continuing that if you're not getting anything out of it." Zach frowned and looked away. "Doesn't feel fair."

"Hey." He reached out and caught Zach's jaw, compelling him to face Nico again. "Who says I don't get anything out of it?"

"But you didn't— You won't—"

"Just because I didn't finish while I was in your company doesn't mean I didn't enjoy myself." Nico cocked his head, smiling slowly. He turned on seduction with instinctive ease, and he saw the way Zach's lips parted before he licked them, the way his pupils dilated and his breath quickened. Now Nico's libido was definitely in the game, even if his body had to sit this one out. "I liked kissing you. Touching you. Tasting you. Knowing I was the first man ever to do that for you. It was sexy. I can't wait to do it again."

Zach closed his eyes and shuddered. He shifted in his seat enough that Nico had a pretty good idea of what was happening in the shadows below his chest. He wished there were more light so he could appreciate the bulge in Zach's lap and the beauty of his long, thick dick.

"And just because I'm not really up for playing myself right now doesn't mean you can't have some fun." Zach's eyes shot open at that, and Nico grinned, feeling absolutely predatory. "I want to see you get yourself off."

"What?" An uncertain smile lifted Zach's lips and wavered there, as though he wasn't sure whether Nico was being serious or not.

Nico reached across the space between them and ran his fingertips down the tented front of Zach's trousers. "I do. Will you put on a show for me?"

Zach licked his lips again, nervousness combatting desire in his eyes. "I don't— I mean, it's not that I'm opposed, but—"

"You don't have to," Nico reassured him gently. He covered the bulge he'd been teasing as if protecting it, then withdrew his hand. "Not if you don't want to. Not if you don't feel comfortable. But if you do, I'd really love to see what you look like when you're plea-suring yourself."

Zach stared at him for a long, indecisive moment, and then he reached down, and Nico heard the unmistakable sound of a zipper sliding down.

"Where's our flashlight?" Nico whispered.

Zach reached into the back, fishing one out of the supplies stacked there. Nico turned it on and laid it on the console between them, not aiming it at Zach's crotch like a spotlight, but using it to shed enough light for him to see what was happening down there.

"Beautiful," he murmured, spying the tip of Zach's cock protruding from the waistband of his underwear. "Will you push everything down so I can see better?"

Another moment of hesitation, and then Zach levered himself up and shoved his trousers and underwear down his thighs, letting his bare ass sink back onto the seat. He gave Nico time to indulge in the sight of him before he licked his palm and reached down to wrap his hand around his dick.

"Like this?" he asked, panting softly after the first gasp of contact had faded.

"God, yes. Just like that." Despite his headache, the tightness of arousal tugged at Nico's balls, filling his cock. It didn't matter. It was a pleasant sensation, but not something he felt any need to do anything about. He watched Zach's face as his hand made that first slow slide up the length of his cock, watched Zach's head fall back and his throat vibrate as he groaned. "That's it. Keep going."

It was magical. It was a show Nico had put on for people before, but he'd never seen it done for his own enjoyment. And the way Zach gave himself over to it was so pure and unreserved that it took Nico's breath away. Once engaged, Zach didn't hold back anything.

"Talk to me," Nico whispered. "Does it feel good?"

"Yes." Zach nodded emphatically, and Nico could see the sheen of sweat on his forehead. He could hear the quaver in his voice. "So good. Just . . . wish it were you . . . touching me . . ."

"Then slow down. If it were me jerking you off right now, I'd take my time with it." Zach immediately obeyed. The pumping of his fist slowed to an easy glide, and some of the edgy tension in his body relaxed. "Good. That's it. Make love to yourself. Let me see you do it."

Zach's eyes opened again, a flicker of self-consciousness and indecision there. And then he closed them and very deliberately pushed his shirt up with his other hand, using his fingers to toy with his nipple. "Oh God!" he gasped as he pinched himself lightly, and Nico echoed his groan.

"Fuck, yeah. God, that's sexy. You're so damn beautiful."

Silence punctuated by moans and pants filled the space between them. The windows fogged up, and the air in the close confines was so thick with the essence of aroused male that Nico could damn near taste Zach's musk on his tongue. He could see Zach unraveling, the helpless way the pace of his stroking increased and became more erratic, the uncontrolled noises he made. Unable to stop himself, Nico reached out and laid his fingertips on the hand pumping up and down Zach's dick. The touch triggered something in Zach, and he cried out, jerking, his cum spurting over the top of his fist in a hot, slick torrent to dribble down his hand and coat Nico's fingertips.

"Yesss . . ." Nico closed his eyes and sighed, breathing in the scent of Zach's spunk and sweat. He brought Zach's hand to his mouth and sucked his fingers clean, opening his eyes to see Zach watching him, enraptured.

"Thank you," Zach whispered, looking boneless slumped there in his seat.

Nico smiled. "What are you thanking me for?"

Zach's gaze wavered, his slack, sated expression softening into vulnerability. "I'm not sure. I guess we haven't done much. So why is it that—"

Nico waited, but Zach didn't finish the thought. He instead began hunting around for something to wipe his hand on, finally settling on his shirt. He mopped his forehead with the back of his arm and turned on the truck to open the window and let cool air flood in, driving away the musky scent.

"What?" Nico prompted.

"Why should what we've done be the most incredible experiences I've ever had?" Zach demanded suddenly, twisting and shuffling to straighten his clothing while still seated.

"I don't know." Nico turned to lie on his side as best he could. "Maybe because you're free for the first time? You can be who you are and enjoy what you want without worrying about what anyone else is going to say or do about it?"

Zach processed that for a moment. "I guess that makes sense." He met Nico's eyes again with a tremulous smile.

That vulnerable look was going to get him far.

"Don't worry about it." Nico reached over and laced his fingers with Zach's again, which was really the best he could offer as far as physical closeness went just now. "Let's just get some more rest. If my head is doing better tomorrow, we'll see if I can drive for a while."

Zach nodded and tried to make himself comfortable as well, writhing around for several minutes before he mirrored Nico's position, lying somewhat on his side facing Nico. Once he was settled, he caught Nico's hand and held on, brushing a kiss across Nico's fingers before his breathing evened out once more.

Nico closed his eyes, but it would be hours before that terrifying ache in his chest that blossomed again at the gentle touch of Zach's lips would let him sleep.

20

ARRIVAL

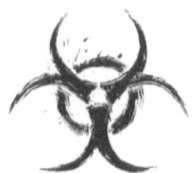

"Nico. Wake up. There are people in hermetic suits with guns blocking the road ahead."

It looked like something out of a vid about some far-fetched and horrific dystopian future. Zach had to close his eyes against the sight for a moment.

This is it. This is our reality now. Oh Lord, what are we going to do?

He stopped a good hundred yards or more from them, waiting. They were spread across the road, facing the truck, their weapons ready.

He'd let Nico sleep as long as possible on the final leg of the journey to Colorado Springs because he honestly had no idea what to expect once they got there. Even four days after his injury, Nico was still struggling with blinding headaches and periods of disorientation. He and Zach probably could have made the trip in half the time if they'd both been healthy.

When Nico didn't respond, Zach glanced over at him in alarm. "Nico?"

His eyes fluttered and slowly opened, then he immediately winced and closed them again. "Yeah?"

"There are people in suits with guns on the road. Should I keep going?"

"Um . . ." Nico shook his head slowly as if to clear it and opened his eyes again. It seemed to take him a moment to actually see the suited figures blocking the road ahead. Zach bit his tongue, holding in a concerned inquiry. The second night after Nico's injury, Zach had thought Nico was on the mend, but he seemed to be alternatively improving, then backsliding. "Are we still in Kansas?"

"No. We've been in Colorado all day. We're close to Colorado Springs, now. I think these people may be military."

"We're there?" Nico blew out a slow breath. "Guess we don't have much choice but to talk to them, do we?"

Zach sighed, giving the suited figures a dubious look. "I guess not." He put the truck in motion again, approaching the roadblock at a crawl and stopping when he was close enough to hear the people in the suits shouting at them.

"Stop the truck, and get out with your hands up! Leave any weapons in the vehicle! *Do it now!*"

Exchanging wary glances, he and Nico did as they were bidden, leaving their guns behind as they carefully and slowly emerged from the truck.

"Names?" A female voice demanded from one of the shorter-suited forms.

"Zacharias Houtman"

"Nicolás Fernández."

"What are you doing here?" she asked.

Zach let Nico speak for them. "We understand that this is where survivors are gathering, that people are getting shelter from the plague in the mountain complex."

"Who told you that?" The voice sounded suspicious and far from welcoming.

Nico made an impatient sound. "Does it matter? Is it true or not?"

"No one gets into Cheyenne Mountain except critical military and government personnel. You'll be processed and assigned an isolation pen in the quarantine camps."

"Isolation pen?" Zach burst out. He stepped forward but quickly retreated as the guns swung toward him.

The guard who appeared to be in charge turned her hooded head toward him. He couldn't make out her features behind the coppery sheen of her mask. "Would you rather gamble on whether or not any of your neighbors have been exposed?" There was a definite note of *you idiot* tacked on the end, there.

The tone apparently didn't set well with Nico because he clenched his fists at his sides. "What the fuck is an isolation pen?"

"You'll be assigned to a tent in a fenced-off area, with enough space between you and your neighbors to avoid airborne contagion. You'll be there for three months, long enough to be certain you haven't been infected, then you'll be processed for entry into the Clean Zone, assigned housing and work on the reconstruction, security, or agriculture and livestock crews." She looked down at a data pad embedded in her sleeve. "Register Zachary Horton as detainee number thirty-seven hundred forty-six, and—"

"Um, that's Zacharias Houtman," Zach corrected, but she wasn't listening.

"And Nicholas Hernandez as detainee number thirty-seven hundred forty-seven."

Nico, already gray skinned and unwell, seemed to go even paler. "Thirty-seven hundred? That's all there is?"

The cock of the guard's shrouded head looked distinctly impatient. "Plus twelve hundred surviving military and government personnel, yes. Did you think you were taking a trip to Disney Universe? Everyone's fucking dead, okay?"

"You think I don't *know* that?" Nico snarled, taking a stride forward. The guns swung in his direction now. But no sooner had they moved than Nico staggered, swaying dizzily. As quickly as they had turned their guns on him, the guards scrambled back as a single mob.

"What's wrong with him?" the leader demanded. "Has he been exposed?"

"What? No!" Zach quickly put himself between Nico and the suited security forces. "He hit his head the other day. We were attacked by wild dogs in St. Louis. They knocked him down, and his head slammed on the ground." He decided to leave out the addition of the revenant Nico had scuffled with. He didn't think much of their chances of not being shot immediately if they admitted to having had contact with anyone who was infected. "He needs medical help."

He could feel the suspicion behind the masked faces, and he trembled as Nico moaned softly behind him.

"It's okay," Nico said. Zach wasn't sure if he was trying to reassure the guards or Zach himself. "It's just this fucking headache. I'll be okay."

They didn't lower their guns. Zach stared at them, overcome by the horrifying notion that they might just preemptively kill him and Nico and dump their bodies in some unmarked pit. They wouldn't do that, right? These people in the suits, they were here to help the survivors and rebuild everything, not kill people out of hand.

Weren't they?

Finally, the leader lowered her gun, and the others did the same. "Put them in Priority One containment. Have the medics add their pen to the rounds."

Zach shivered. He wished that decision sounded more reassuring than it had. "What does that mean?"

She snorted behind her mask. "It means we'll be keeping an eye on you. And if we have even the slightest reason to believe you've been infected, you'll be euthanized. For the safety of the other survivors."

She walked away before he could protest, and one of the other guards gestured Zach into motion with his gun. "Sorry, man," he muttered, and his voice was a little kinder and less rigid than hers. "I know it seems harsh, but you gotta understand. We don't have a choice. If we let someone with the Rot through, *everyone* who's left will die. Get it?"

"We get it," Nico answered for them, sounding subdued. He still looked like he might fall over, and Zach finally dared go to him, stationing himself by Nico's side to catch him if he staggered again.

"Great. We'll give you a moment to grab some clothes."

Zach glanced at the car. "What about our truck and food supplies?"

"Anything you bring with you to the Clean Zone gets added to the stores to be redistributed among the population," another guard replied as they escorted Nico and Zach to the bed of the truck to watch them open it and dig out their duffel and rucksack. "The truck will be kept for use by emergency-response personnel."

"You can't do that!" Zach protested.

The guard who had spoken kindly shrugged and shook his hooded head. "Like I said, we don't have a choice. We can't let people starve while others who were fortunate enough to get their hands on a stockpile do just fine. And we're having difficulty right now with transporting military and medical personnel between Cheyenne Mountain and the quarantine camps. That truck of yours might make all the difference when it comes to one of our medics making it on time to save someone having a dangerous birth or a kid with an appendix about to rupture."

"Let it go, Zach," Nico muttered, leaning on him as they left the truck behind and shuffled along surrounded by guards. "We'll be okay."

"No, we won't. They can't just steal our supplies. Your . . . *metabolic problem*—"

Nico shook his head sharply. "Don't."

"What metabolic problem?" The sympathetic guard looked back at them. "If you have distinct medical needs, those can be taken into account. We just need to have the medics examine you and document it."

"It's not necessary," Nico ground out. "I'm *fine*."

Zach swallowed and held his tongue, finally understanding the reason for Nico's reticence. They could not tell the medics that Nico was infected with the Bane virus. Zach couldn't say with any certainty that the Clean Zone military forces wouldn't just preemptively kill Nico.

The sense of being in a horror vid grew as they watched their own truck drive past them, taking their guns, food, and spare fuel cells with it. Now they had literally nothing but the clothes they wore and their packs. A mile or so down the road, ten-foot-tall fences topped with razor wire began to line the sides of the highway. They stopped at three different gates, each one manned by armed and suited personnel who grilled the team accompanying Zach and Nico with what sounded like coded questions and answers.

"Trying to make sure we didn't kill the guards and take their suits, I guess?" Nico theorized, rubbing his forehead. His brow was furrowed with pain. "Not sure that would accomplish anything, except maybe giving us access to the underground complex inside the mountain."

"Where is the mountain?" Zach asked, looking around. They seemed to be smack in the middle of suburban hell. Beyond the fences were empty houses and apartment buildings, derelict strip malls and shopping centers.

"Other side of the city, to the southwest, if I recall correctly." Nico didn't seem very concerned. "Makes sense they wouldn't keep the refugee encampments too close to the place housing the government personnel and military forces."

At the final checkpoint, a repurposed, battery-powered trolley—the open-sided sort that might have once hauled loads of tourists around a zoo or amusement park—waited for them. Which was reassuring. They'd been walking for nearly two hours at that point from checkpoint to checkpoint, and there was still no sign of these quarantine "pens" the guards had spoken of. The transport carried them past another checkpoint to a field that looked like it might once have been a fairground or perhaps a small airport. Then Zach understood what the guards meant by "pens."

Each unit was roughly ten by ten yards, with another ten yards separating it from its neighbor. They were made up of chain-link fencing topped with razor wire, with only a single gate leading into each pen. Pipes carrying what Zach assumed to be water traveled from one pen to the other, and tracks in the reddish mud created rough roads, separating the pens into neat rows.

The guard Zach only knew as the "kinder" one called over his shoulder from the front passenger seat. "We have to keep each group who comes in separate from every other group who comes in, see? Otherwise everyone could get infected. The hot zone for airborne contamination with the Rot is about ten, fifteen feet, but don't worry. There's thirty feet and two fences between you and your neighbors. You'll be safe so long as everyone stays in their own units."

"For three months, you said?" Nico asked.

The guard nodded. "If you were exposed yesterday, it would take three to six weeks for you to start showing symptoms. We make it three months, just to make sure everyone is safe. And because there's a backlog getting houses ready for people in the Clean Zone."

Zach grimaced at the sight of small tents within the pens and a rough shed that looked like a possible latrine in the back corner. "There's no power or sewage?"

"Sorry. This is the best we could do on short notice. We only began building the camps a few months ago. Before that, everyone was assigned a unit in a repurposed tenement near downtown." The guard cleared his throat, the sound rasping and rattling the amplifier in his mask. "Someone went rev, broke down their door, started a panic. Everyone was exposed. We had to burn it out."

Nico went rigid beside him. "With everyone still inside?"

The guard groaned softly. "Look, you gotta understand, man, we're doing the best we can here, and we have to follow orders. We gassed the building first to try to knock everyone unconscious so they wouldn't suffer, but . . . We had no choice. We just didn't."

Nico scrubbed a hand over his mouth, his grayish pallor suggesting he might just start vomiting. "That's why you're using tents instead of all the derelict houses. You don't want to have to burn existing buildings."

"That, and the houses are too close together. And we couldn't keep water going to them."

Zach linked his fingers with Nico's and tilted his head back, grateful to be in the open-sided trolley where the fresh air could blow away some of his own nausea.

Apparently, the guard who was driving had enough of his friendly comrade's chatter. "If you're found outside your unit, you'll be shot on sight and your corpse burned for the safety of the other detainees. Ration deliveries will be made every other day. Since it's just about planting season, we're trying to equip each pen with gardening tools and seeds so you can help stretch out the rations. By winter they'll be getting pretty low. We have wind turbines pressurizing the water pipes. Water's suitable for washing, but the treatment facility is offline so I wouldn't recommend drinking or cooking with it unless you boil it first. Ration deliveries will include enough firewood for you to boil a gallon or two every couple days, and you'll find a fire pit outside the tent."

"What are we going to do about climate control?" Zach asked. April had just begun, a fact he wouldn't have known without the computer system in their truck. He wondered how long it would take him to lose track of the date now that they didn't even have that. "Summer's coming up. It's going to be too hot for everyone here in the desert to be without shade during the day, especially with so little water."

The guards fell silent. Clearly no one had worked out the logistics for that, yet.

The kinder one cleared his throat again. "You're just going to have to do the best you can. I'm sorry."

The sight of the fenced-in enclosure where they would be expected to reside for the next three months was no better than any of the others had been. A sick, sinking feeling weighed down Zach's chest as he shouldered his bag and approached the gate the guards were unlocking. He had a distinct sympathy for criminals approaching the place of their incarceration on their own power, knowing their freedom was gone.

He couldn't seem to pick up his feet; they shuffled through the rusty-red mud, resisting his efforts to propel himself forward. He flinched when the gate clanged shut behind him.

"I don't know why I'm being such a coward about this." He sighed and dropped his bag by the entrance to the tent. The wind shifted, carrying the odor of the latrine toward them for a moment before shifting back the way it had been blowing.

Great.

"After being stuck with my father and Jacob all winter, a tent in the open for three months should be a holiday in comparison."

Nico grunted but didn't reply as he ducked under the flap of the tent. It wasn't a reassuring sound. What did it mean? Was Nico's injury so bad that he couldn't be bothered to talk? Or did he have an issue with the way Zach was behaving?

Zach followed him inside. "Are you all right?"

"I shouldn't be here."

"*What?*"

"I'm putting everyone at risk. I don't know what the fuck I was thinking." Nico sank down to sit cross-legged on a cot inside the tent, rubbing his temples. "They can't ever let me past the quarantine here. *Never.*"

"Don't be stupid. We just have to be careful—"

"How careful do we have to be to ensure I never have an accident, Zach?" Nico's voice cracked, and he looked up at Zach with shimmering eyes. "How can I avoid getting a blister from a gardening tool that breaks open and bleeds? Or falling and skinning my knees? Or—" He broke off, wiping his face brusquely. "No. I just need to tell the medics what's going on and let them know that they either need to send me on my way or keep me away from the rest of the people here."

"You can't! Did you *see* how they were behaving back there? They would have put a bullet in your head and burned your body on a bonfire!"

"I doubt they'd shoot me. Too dangerous." Nico smiled bitterly and let his hands fall back into his lap. "Poison, maybe? Or suffocation?"

"Stop it!" Zach dropped to a squat before Nico's cot, laying his hands on Nico's thighs. "Don't talk like that. I'm not going to let that happen. Besides," he offered Nico a weak smile, "they might shoot me too, just for being with you."

"You don't need to remind me that I'm dangerous for you too. Don't you get that, *cariño*?" Nico's eyes swam again. "I shouldn't be with you, either. I should be alone."

"You won't make it alone." Zach's hands began their own journey over every part of Nico that he could reach, especially where the skin was exposed, feeding the hunger for touch he now understood as a part of who Nico was. The idea of this beautiful, sensual man in isolation, where he could never get the contact he so desperately craved . . . It was horrifying. He thought of tales of Hell being a place not full of fire and torment, but of endless, empty cold, cut off from God's comforting presence and grace. Surely seclusion, without the chance to touch or be touched, would be such an existence for Nico. "And I won't let you leave me behind."

"Then take the last ampule, Zach." Nico's dark eyes pleaded with him. "Be like me so I don't have to worry about hurting you. Then we'll leave here together."

It was tempting. Lord, so tempting. To be strong and able to defend himself. To erase that fear from Nico's eyes. Why did everything in Zach clench up in an adamant refusal to truly entertain the notion beyond a passing, *What if. . .?*

He was shaking his head before the no even fully formed on his lips. "That's not who I want to be."

Nico bowed his head. His hands shook where he clenched them in his lap, until Zach reached for him and pulled his hands apart, holding them snugly. Nico stared at their joined hands for a moment, then laced his fingers with Zach's. "I don't know what to do here."

Zach leaned in and brushed a kiss on the corner of Nico's mouth. "Rest. How can you be expected to think clearly with a head injury like this?" He reached for the buttons on Nico's synth-cotton shirt and carefully opened it, easing it down his shoulders. Part of Zach was tempted to do it seductively, to turn on flirtation the way Nico could, like throwing a switch, but he didn't think Nico was in any condition to appreciate it. But Nico did tip his face up and seek out Zach's mouth, parting his lips and letting their tongues slide together.

By the time they separated, Zach was the one whose hands were shaking. He had to ball them into fists to keep from pushing Nico to do more than he was clearly physically capable of handling. Lord, had it been less than a week since they'd been in his bedroom together, and Nico's mouth had been on him, and—

"Rest," Zach choked out, and gently shoved Nico down on the cot, then helped remove his trousers. He looked sideways at the other cot, but he couldn't bring himself to move to it. Instead, he dug his Bible out of his duffel and urged Nico to sit up until Zach could slip behind him, serving as a pillow. "I'll wake you up when they bring us some rations, or when the medics arrive, or . . . I don't know. Just rest."

Nico didn't argue. He turned on his side, his face pressed to Zach's belly, so temptingly close to Zach's aching groin. He was asleep almost immediately.

Is it just touch for you? Would anyone do? Zach ignored his Bible, delicately brushing his fingers over Nico's shaggy hair. *Am I the only one feeling more?*

Was he feeling more? Or had he simply imprinted on Nico because they were alone in the world and because being with Nico felt like the first honest and blessed thing Zach had done in his adult life?

Does it matter? We're together now. And I'm where God wants me to be—with him. I know that without a doubt.

Sighing, Zach leaned down and pressed a kiss to Nico's temple.

We'll take care of each other. That's all we need to do right now. What happens later is in the Lord's hands.

21

SOWING

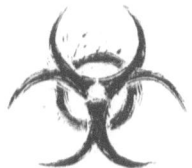

T he sun was already oppressively warm by midmorning on the seventh day of Zach and Nico's quarantine. Zach had spent most of the week pampering Nico as he rested and healed. Nico didn't even put up a fight since they had nothing else to do, a fact that had them both ready to climb the fencing around their enclosure within a matter of days.

Fortunately, the military personnel in charge of ration deliveries had come through on their promise to provide gardening tools the day before. They even went one better and delivered a few young pine trees with their roots intact, which they recommended the detainees plant southwest of their tents to provide more shade for their lodgings in the midday and afternoon sun.

"Christmas trees. Can you believe it? We've got reclamation teams scouring the whole county for shit like this. Any random thing people can put to use," the soldier—who was unmistakably the same kind guard from their arrival—explained while he unlocked the gate and delivered the supplies. As he did so, another guard told Zach to keep his distance and reinforced the command with a gun.

"A couple guys keep lookout for revs while the rest scavenge anything they think we can use," the kind guard continued.

"Thanks, um . . . I didn't get your name?" Zach ventured uncertainly.

"Gillett Morris." The suited soldier bobbed his head with what Zach imagined was a shy smile under his mask.

"Thanks, Gillett." Zach pictured a fairly young man behind the mask, from the voice and the tendency to babble. Perhaps still a teenager. Had he enlisted straight out of school? Perhaps he was even one of the vocational training recruits. Kids as young as fifteen, desperate to escape the tenements, received early diplomas and full-time incomes by enlisting in the armed services, so long as they weren't assigned combat roles until they turned eighteen. In that case, being helpful was pretty much Gillett's entire job description.

"Have you thought about having the detainees help raise live-stock?" Zach asked, just to keep the conversation going as the guard propped the trees up and shovels in a corner of the pen near the latrine. Even though he had Nico for company, it was nice to have other people to talk to. "We have enough space for a goat, and the milk would be good since Nico needs more calories. And if you got us feed and something to build a coop with, I bet a lot of the detainees could take care of some chickens, harvest the eggs for another way to supplement the rations. And it would give people something to do."

Gillett's head bobbed again. "I'll pass that along to my CO, sir. But can I ask . . . more calories? We don't have orders for an extra ration drop for this pen. Did your partner discuss it with the medics?"

Damn. He'd forgotten that Nico didn't want to make an issue of his dietary needs because then he'd have to explain why.

"Oh, it's not a big—"

"If there's an issue, sir, the medics will accommodate him, as best they can. We're not that low on rations just yet."

Zach pasted on a bland smile and nodded. What tests would the medics need do to confirm Nico had an issue? Would they need to draw blood? "I'll be sure to let him know."

Gillett and his comrade left, and Zach turned to relieving his boredom by digging holes for the trees. It was nearly mid-April now, and the heat was already rising, an alarming forewarning of the summer to come, and the shade would be a welcome friend.

"Something interesting about that hole?"

"Huh?" Zach jerked, realizing he'd been staring at the ground where he'd been digging, resting on his shovel, for . . . he wasn't sure how long. He looked over his shoulder to see Nico standing at the flap of their tent, shirtless. The distinct protrusion of his ribs canceled out Zach's immediate and very visceral reaction to the sight of his bare flesh. "Oh. Guess I got lost in my thoughts."

Nico stepped out into the sunlight. "What were you thinking about?"

"The super-spore farms." He gestured to the saplings. "They brought us these trees for shade, and then I started thinking about how hot it's going to get soon. I wonder if the Atmosphere Repair Project is offline now or if the farms can operate without someone attending them. Is this all for nothing?"

Nico frowned thoughtfully. "What, trying to survive?"

"Yeah. I guess?" Zach shrugged and wiped away the sweat streaming down his face. "I don't know. We're so caught up in these minute details about how we're going to get by from one day to the next now. Ration deliveries, and avoiding infection, and how to find enough shade so we don't keel over from heat stroke. But not all our big, global problems from before the pandemic went away when everyone died. If the farms go offline, then we're back on the countdown timer until the planet becomes uninhabitable anyway. Just delaying the inevitable."

"Maybe we are," Nico said after a reflective pause. "Should we stop trying?"

". . . No. Of course not." Zach scoffed at his lapse into pessimism. Maybe the spore farms would continue to thrive unattended. Maybe by the time the solar-powered drones that spread a haze of contrails across the sky to keep the effects of global warming in check failed, the spores would have cleaned the atmosphere and repaired the ozone enough that the drones wouldn't even be needed.

Yeah, that felt like the proper way to look at it. The idea brought a lightness to Zach's heart, the feeling that God was stroking his hair and saying, *It's all right, child, I'll take care of that for you.*

There was enough to worry about without considering all the things that they had no hope of controlling or influencing. Zach had to leave it in His hands.

"So," Nico said after a moment. "Trees?"

Zach shrugged. "Seems like they're trying." He propped the shovel against the chain-link fence and gave his aching hands a rueful look. By the end of the day, he was pretty sure he'd have blisters. Which meant Nico's fears about not being able to pitch in much with the gardening work were well-founded. He'd have to see if they could requisition some gloves, at least. "How're you feeling?"

Nico's eyes got a distant look, as if he were performing a mental inventory, before he shrugged. "Better, I think. My head is still hurting, but I suspect it's mostly because that fucking cot is killing my neck."

Zach ducked his head, scuffing his toe against tufts of patchy grass in the red soil. "Guess those things are limited in all kinds of ways." His face heated up, and he ventured a glance at Nico from under his lashes.

Nico chuckled. "If my head is still doing all right tonight, we're going to fold the damn things away and just lay our blankets on the bottom of the tent."

"Are we?" Zach's heart took off racing in his chest. The last week had allowed for some more sexual exploration between the two of them, but it had been rendered logistically difficult by cots that were barely large enough for one person, much less two, and tempered by Nico's blinding headaches and need to sleep them off. He'd grumbled bitterly over having to take a rain check on Zach's offer to attempt his first blowjob for just that reason. They'd managed some relatively satisfying groping but not much beyond that.

"Hell yeah, we are." Nico licked his lips, and his grin grew downright sinful. "You know how good you look, standing there all sweaty and panting? I've got my very own *Lady Chatterley's Lover* gardener fantasy locked in this cage with me."

"I'm dusty, and I smell," Zach demurred, but Nico was slinking toward him. His hands settled on Zach's hips, jerking him forward until their crotches bumped. The contact wrenched a gasp from

Zach's lungs, and the heat in Nico's eyes seemed to sear away any air that might have replaced it.

"I'm not complaining." His tongue traced the sweat-beaded rim of Zach's upper lip before slipping inside his mouth. Zach let him in with a needy moan, his gritty arms sliding around Nico to bring their bodies into fuller contact. Just like that, he was on fire, incinerating from the inside out. The feeling kept getting stronger the longer they were together. He needed more. More of everything Nico was and everything Nico had to offer. He set something loose inside Zach, something he hadn't known was trapped until it finally took flight, and all he wanted to do was soar with it.

He was stuck in a damn cage, and he'd never felt freer.

"Know what?" Nico murmured, tipping his head back when Zach's lips sought out his throat. A low groan vibrated against his lips as Zach nibbled and sucked every inch of warm skin he could reach.

"Hmm?"

"I'm not going to wait and give that fucking headache a chance to return. Come on."

He linked his fingers with Zach's and started tugging him toward the tent, but Zach refused to move. "I need to wash up."

Nico made a dismayed sound, then sighed. "Fine. I'll stow the cots; you get the water. *Hurry*."

A thrill shivered through Zach to know that Nico was so eager for him. Nico, who had immeasurable sexual experience. Who had made a study of the art of pleasure. Who had *no* reason whatsoever to think much of Zach as a lover, or potential lover, or whatever he was at this point. Nico wanted him badly enough to be impatient. It was a heady feeling, to be wanted that way.

Zach grabbed the water bucket from outside the tent flap and went to fill it. Under the intense sun and in the conveniently private space between the newly planted trees and the tent, he shucked his dusty trousers and began washing as best he could with the cold water. He watched the runoff trickle away to hydrate the roots of the transplanted evergreens, scrubbing at his skin with one of their scavenged washcloths.

Another bucket joined the one by his feet, and Nico's shadow merged with his.

"Hey," Nico murmured. His voice was like liquid sex sliding along Zach's nerve endings, making them tingle and burn. "Need some help with your back?"

Zach glanced around as if someone might be standing beside their fence, peering down the alley between the trees and the tent. Then he ducked his head and shrugged. "Sure."

He kept his eyes on the ground, afraid to look up lest self-consciousness at being even this far in the open overwhelm him. Cool water dribbled from the washcloth in his hand, down his belly, trickling droplets kissing his cock, which had no qualms about the privacy issue.

Nico swirled a cloth of his own in the fresh water bucket. A moment later, Zach shivered as Nico wrung the chilly water over his shoulders. Nico followed its path with his cloth, wiping with soft, slow, sensual strokes. The thumb of his other hand came after, gently kneading the muscles beneath the wet skin.

"Feels good," Zach whispered, closing his eyes.

"Good," Nico breathed against Zach's ear, and then his lips trailed after that gently massaging thumb, before his tongue went right down the gully of Zach's spine. "You'll tell me if I do something you're not comfortable with, right?"

"Uh-huh." How was it possible for Zach to be panting already?

"Perfect." Another splash as the cloth swished in the bucket again. Another cool surge of water, this one starting lower, at mid-back. More soft scrubbing, more massaging, more kisses that ended in tender nibbles at Zach's hips, just above his backside.

If Zach didn't finish washing and get into the tent soon, there would be nothing left to do inside the tent. He went back to work, cleaning his stiff cock and tight balls with considerably less finesse than Nico was demonstrating.

Then more water, right at the small of his back, flowing down the crack of his ass and followed by Nico's cloth.

Zach gasped. "Oh God."

"Lean forward a little," Nico coaxed, and Zach obeyed. It felt obscene to stick his rear out that way, but Nico took advantage of the way it opened him to bathe him there as well. Then he gripped Zach's buttocks in both hands, pulling them apart with his thumbs, and his breath warmed Zach's crevice.

Zach yelped at the first brush of Nico's tongue on something he'd had no idea could be so very sensitive. "Th-the tent," he panted, craving that seeking tongue even as he was terrified of what it might do to his minimal self-control. "Please?"

"Of course." Nico trailed light, damp fingertips up and down Zach's thighs in soothing circles for a moment before pressing a kiss to his buttock and standing. "Let's go."

The air inside the tent was warm and still, enough to be stifling. For a moment, Zach wished they could have stayed outside in the spring breeze, but he wanted the privacy to be able to feel absolutely unreserved with Nico. He dropped to the pallet on the ground without hesitation, turning to catch Nico as he flung himself down on top of Zach. His mouth was hard and hungry, and Zach yielded to the demand of the kiss.

"Yes." He hissed at the press of Nico's body against his water-slick skin, pushing him down onto the blankets. The way he fitted their bodies so perfectly together, getting every inch of skin-on-skin contact he could, made Zach understand that Nico hadn't exaggerated his need for touch in the slightest. If anything, he'd downplayed it. It felt like Nico would have crawled right inside Zach if he could.

And Zach was glad to give Nico everything he needed. His hands were restless, skimming over Nico's flesh, trying to explore every part of him at once. He wanted the next kiss more than he wanted air. When Nico began pushing down his loose, drawstring sleep pants, Zach happily aided the endeavor, until their cocks were slotted together, alongside one another between their bellies, giving them just that much more contact.

"*Yes,*" he whispered again as Nico rocked against him, a sheen of new sweat and leftover water lubricating the way. He reached down and grabbed Nico's butt without shame, creating more pressure, more friction. He could come just knowing that it was Nico's lean abs and satiny dick he was rubbing off against.

"Yeah?" Nico broke the kiss to raise his head, searching Zach's eyes. He gave another thrust and grinned an absolutely wicked grin when Zach groaned. "Like that?"

Zach nodded emphatically, torn between sucking that smile right off Nico's face and holding the contact with those beautiful dark eyes.

Nico's rocking slowed, and his smile grew softer, fonder. "Think you might want to fuck me today?"

"Can I?" Zach licked his lips, staring up at Nico as his body surged with another rush of pure, physical *need*.

Nico nodded, looking pleased. "Yeah. But first I want you to turn over so I can finish what I started outside."

Zach was in motion before he even managed to whisper, "Okay."

The first touch of Nico's tongue on the rim of his anus was electric. Like nothing he'd ever imagined he could feel. Nibbles and flicks. Long, broad strokes. Short, poking jabs. And when it pushed inside . . .

Zach lost all sense of shame. Forgot he'd ever even known shame. He writhed and scrambled, biting the blankets and moaning so loudly he was sure they could hear him ten pens away. Every nerve in his body was centered on that small, clenching ring of muscle, igniting with more pleasure than he'd ever thought possible.

"Please. Nico. Not sure how much longer I can—"

"Okay. Hold on." Nico's weight disappeared from Zach's legs, and Zach rolled over to see Nico rummaging through his rucksack, fishing out a bottle of lubricant and condoms to toss on the blankets. "Normally I don't mind things a little rougher, but under the circumstances, we're gonna take this slow. Make sure I don't get any tears. Understand?"

Zach nodded, sitting up as Nico got down on his hands and knees and reached behind himself with lube-coated fingers. Zach swallowed hard to see Nico's body take them inside, the seemingly impossible stretch of that tight ring. Especially when Nico's low moan joined the picture.

After a moment of watching Nico work his fingers in and out, the urge to feel the grip of those muscles grabbed hold of Zach and pushed him to blurt, "May I?" He brushed his own fingertips over

Nico's knuckles where they were pressed against the globe of his buttock.

Nico gave a huffing laugh. "Let me see your fingers." Zach obligingly presented his hand, and Nico studied it for a moment before placing a kiss on the back of it. "We'll trim your nails and you can do it next time, okay?"

"Right. Okay." Zach nodded slowly and fell silent again as Nico continued to stretch himself. After a moment, Nico rolled over, lifting his leg and working his hand under it to continue penetrating himself with those thrusting fingers.

"Get the condoms," he urged. Zach obeyed, rolling a sheath down his own cock with shaking hands. "Put one on me too."

Zach blinked, sobering as he realized what it was Nico was truly trying to protect them against. He pushed the thought away, unwilling to let that cloud of ever-present concern overshadow the wonder of what they were about to share. He unwrapped another condom and worked it down Nico's rigid dick. Nico smiled and withdrew his fingers, handing Zach the lube. "Good. Now, use plenty."

He wasn't sure he could stand it, the exquisite glide of his own hand slicking his cock up and down. Especially with Nico lying spread out in front of him, watching Zach stroke himself with a hungry look in his warm brown eyes. Nico's arms and legs welcomed him, forming a cradle for his shoulders and hips when Zach finally crawled over him.

"Stay there," Nico whispered, reaching down to take Zach's slippery cock in his hand and guide it to where it needed to be. Then Nico's legs tightened against Zach's waist, and he pushed himself onto Zach's cock.

"Oh God," Zach groaned, his eyes snapping shut at that first impossibly tight grasp of Nico's body. He pried them open again immediately, unwilling to miss a moment of Nico's enraptured expression. It hovered somewhere between pain and pleasure, intense with effort and concentration. Sweat beaded and pooled in the notch of Nico's clavicle, and Zach couldn't help but lean down to lick it off. "This is amazing. You're amazing."

A little of the tension in Nico's face relaxed as he smiled. He was being so painstakingly careful that it saddened Zach, because he could sense Nico was holding something back, a desire for abandon that he didn't dare give rein to.

Zach leaned down and captured Nico's mouth in a hard, urgent kiss, hoping to coax him to let go, if only just a little more. Nico returned it eagerly, moving beneath Zach in little rocks and shoves that eased Zach's cock a little deeper into Nico with each shift.

Finally, Nico broke away with a moan, and his head fell back onto the blankets, a gentle, almost drunken smile curling his lips. "Stay there a moment," he said. "This is my favorite part."

"You're so beautiful." Zach took the opportunity to drink in the sight of him, the sort of intense stare he was embarrassed to be caught in when Nico was paying attention. The scrutiny kept him distracted from that incredible pressure surrounding his cock and the fact that if he wasn't careful, this was going to be over all too soon. "What's so good about this, right now?"

"It's . . ." Nico's throat bobbed as he swallowed, and he licked his lips. "This moment when the sting is fading and it's just *intense*, and soon I'll want you to *move*, to go deep and hard, but right now it's all anticipation and just . . ." He shook his head, opening his eyes to peer up at Zach wryly. "I can't explain it."

"You don't have to." Zach realized he was shaking as he dropped another kiss on Nico's mouth. "As long as you keep smiling like that, I'll do anything you want me to."

Nico's smile broadened, and the way his body tightened as he chuckled softly tore a gasping groan from Zach's lungs. "You're too fucking sweet to be real. Okay, enough of this. Move now, Zach."

"Like this?" He gave an experimental push with his hips, and the result was electric for both of them. That tight clench engulfed Zach's cock more fully, on top of the sliding friction along his length, and he couldn't imagine anything ever feeling so incredible.

"Oh *fuck*. Yeah. Like that." Nico nodded eagerly, panting. "Go with it. Do what feels good. Just go."

Zach went. He let go of everything, every fear, every doubt, every vestige of restraint, and dove headlong into the yearning he felt, the desire to be as deep inside Nico as he could possibly get, until there was no possible way to separate them. *This.* This was the connection he'd never felt with the two women he'd dated and made love to. It wasn't just physical. This was a *spiritual* experience, a merging in the truest sense. His eyes burned with the intensity of his new understanding. It was hunger and intimacy, and there was so much *power* behind it that it left Zach awestruck and humbled.

Thank you, Lord, for letting me know this.

Looking down, he could see the hazy nitrile of Nico's condom had grown transparent with moisture. Zach caught himself before he could act on the mad impulse to strip that sheath away and taste the salty droplets he knew were collecting underneath it.

He worked in and out of Nico's gripping body until they were both drenched with sweat, until his muscles began to ache and his limbs trembled. The only thing that kept him from spilling over the edge was the desperate need to never let this end.

When his climax finally did come, it struck with devastating force, driving unrestrained cries from Zach with each thrust. It was heat flashing through his veins, and blinding light, and the roar of his own pulse in his ears. He felt the bite of Nico's fingernails against his shoulders, heard Nico's moans and pleas, but he was lost in his own torrent of devastating pleasure as he pumped into Nico over and over before he finally went still and shuddered.

He gasped something into Nico's ear, but he was too lost to even care that he'd just confessed his love to a man he barely knew.

When he became aware of the world again, his weight was draped over Nico, who was pushing up against his belly, trying to wedge a hand between them.

"Let me," Zach rasped, and gripped Nico's sheathed cock, watching his face as he tried to find the right pressure and rhythm to satisfy that need in Nico's eyes.

"Careful not to—"

"Hush. I won't." He pressed a kiss to Nico's stubbled jaw and made sure his strokes weren't dislodging the condom. "Trust me. Relax."

Nico nodded, and the anxious furrow between his dense black brows eased. Zach watched the play of pleasure and emotion on Nico's face as he worked to jerk him off, the way his face would soften with relief when Zach did something just right, or tighten with dismay when he needed something a little different. It was a visible process, the ebb and flow of pleasure, the way it mounted in steps and bounds and finally, *finally* crested. The condom under Zach's hand grew hot and soft with the milky fluid filling it, and Zach wished it were spurting over his fingers instead.

Almost immediately, Nico gripped the base of the condom and pushed Zach's hand away. "Careful," he admonished fretfully. He shoved Zach up gently with a hand on his chest, making a sharp, uncomfortable sound when Zach slid out of him. "I'll be right back."

Zach sighed and removed his own condom as Nico hurried from the tent, presumably heading for the latrine before there was any chance that Zach would be exposed to his fluids. It was a stilted ending to what had been the most intense, intimate experience of his life, especially after Zach's unintended declaration. He couldn't help but resent the worry and anxiety that dragged Nico from his arms when they should have been twined together, basking.

But when Nico came back, there was no awkwardness on his face. He was warm and open, dropping to his knees at the edge of the pallet and crawling across it to where Zach reclined. His smile flashed between kiss-swollen lips, easy and relaxed. "Thank you for that."

Zach snorted, unable to resist grinning back. He opened his arms to Nico and was gratified that Nico slipped right into them, settling onto him for a leisurely kiss. "*You're* thanking *me?*"

"Yeah, I am." He nuzzled behind Zach's ear. If he felt any alarm or embarrassment over what Zach had so gracelessly blurted out at the worst possible moment, he didn't let on. "Everything just feels so *good* with you. Just . . . like this is the way it's supposed to be. So thanks."

It wasn't exactly a reciprocal exchange of sentiment, but it was close enough. Zach wrapped himself around Nico and gave a contented sigh, drifting off in postorgasmic lassitude.

If this was how he had to spend the next three months, he'd be okay.

22

RECKONING

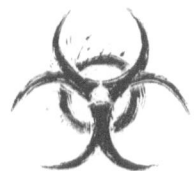

Nico paused in weeding the garden to watch a troop of suited guards stomping down the lane between their pen and the one directly west of them. He'd been watching the activity around that enclosure all morning. The medics doing their rounds earlier had scurried out of there as soon as they were done. Now they were back, with a full complement of guards in tow. The soldiers unlocked the gate to the pen, and a woman ran out of the tent with a child in her arms.

"Please!" she sobbed, but at this distance the stiff breeze snatched away any other coherent words, much less the guards' lower-pitched and muffled responses. But the way they leveled their weapons at her when she became increasingly hysterical spoke volumes.

One suited form—another medic, probably, since he or she wasn't carrying a weapon—came forward and spoke to the woman inaudibly, offering her something.

Nico didn't realize Zach had come up behind him until he felt a hand between his shoulder blades.

"I heard screaming," Zach said, eyeing the activity across in the other pen. "What's going on?"

Nico swallowed the surge of nausea twisting in his stomach. "I think the people she came in with—her husband and whoever else she's with in the tent—are sick. The medics came this morning and left in a hurry, but now they're back again. With reinforcements."

Zach blinked and fell silent, watching the urgent back-and-forth exchanges, the medic continuing to proffer whatever he was holding while the soldiers' mere presence offered its own threat.

"Please tell me they aren't giving them a choice between killing themselves or being shot," Zach said sickly.

"I think that's *exactly* what they're doing."

The toddler the woman held wasn't responding to the activity, and she was clearly fighting with the weight of the child. Finally, she sank to her knees with a wail, hugging the child fiercely as she wept. She nodded tightly, and the medic disappeared into the tent. When he emerged, her sobs redoubled, and she lifted one of the toddler's limp arms. The medic injected the child with something, and then stuck the syringe into the woman's arm, as well. Heaving herself and the baby up, she staggered into the tent.

The soldiers waited. When five minutes or so had passed, the medic went into the tent and then returned a moment later, nodding.

The soldiers erupted into a flurry of bustling activity. They carried a stretcher into the tent and emerged with a plastic-wrapped body on it, carrying it to the trolley. It was followed by three more, two of them child-sized. A moment later, smoke started billowing as the tent and everything the people inhabiting it had possessed was set aflame.

The trolley rolled past. Nico watched it soberly, grief pulling at his chest. Those people had only arrived at the quarantine camp a couple of weeks ago. Just the day before he'd seen the children running around the pen, playing. How could they be dead today?

He didn't hesitate to turn to wrap himself around Zach, only to be wrapped up in return. Over a month into their quarantine now, he and Zach had fallen into a comfortable, tender intimacy that Nico had never suspected he'd longed for until he finally had it.

"Those people were *fine* yesterday," he muttered against Zach's neck. He was shaking, despite the scorching heat of the late-May afternoon. "Jesus, Zach, this damn virus scares me so much."

"I know." Zach pressed his lips against Nico's temple. "I just don't see how they all could have fallen sick in a single day."

"That's part of what's so fucking terrifying. Not just the virus but the way we're responding to it. You heard what they did to the people quarantined in the tenement." Nico drew back to meet Zach's eyes. "McClosky used to tell me about how the virus worked. It can take a different amount of time for each person. I'm afraid that—" He swallowed and licked his lips. "I think one or two of those people fell ill, and the soldiers just *killed* the rest. Killed people who weren't even sick yet. Like that woman."

Zach whispered a gentle curse. "That's an *insane* policy. What if they weren't going to get sick? What if some of them were immune?"

"McClosky said that, as far as they know, no one is immune."

Zach's face twisted. "Yeah, and as far as he knew, the virus was harmless too."

"Ouch."

"You know I'm right. How will they ever know unless they give people the chance to live?"

"Yeah, I know." Nico sighed. "Between the military government killing people out of hand, people killing each other for supplies or because they're afraid of being exposed, revenants hunting people, supply shortages, the heat and the cold . . ." He shook his head. "There's no way to tell how many people have died who might have actually survived the pandemic."

He pressed himself against Zach again, silently begging to be held. Their days were numbered. The events of the morning had made that clear. He was putting Zach in danger, not only from himself, but from the people who might kill him out of hand if they suspected he might have been exposed. He had to put some distance between them.

Anything to protect Zach. Anything.

If that's true, then why are you still here? Why haven't you demanded to be quarantined separately? his conscience nudged him.

The answer to that was easy. Nico could feel it in the pressure steadily hardening against the point where Zach's crotch rubbed against his hip, seeking comfort and distraction from their gruesome reality. He could feel it in those warm, soft hands that covered his back and slid slowly downward to hover at his hips in silent inquiry. He could feel it in the full, moist lips that tasted the salty sweat the midday sun was cooking onto Nico's skin.

Tomorrow, he promised himself, letting Zach lead him into the tent. *I'll do it tomorrow.*

◭ ◭ ◭

SILVIA HUNCHED in the passenger seat of the lightcar, growling softly even while she was unconscious. Each time she twitched and snarled, Nico jumped as though she might leap at him.

"Come on, come on, come on,*" he muttered, hurrying Zach along, but Zach refused to be rushed. He took his time picking through the scattered supplies that had spilled from the car when it crashed.*

"It's all right." Zach paused in his pillaging to give Nico his tender smile. "I'm safe with you."

Nico's heart melted. Everything within him went warm and soft, an ache forming in his chest that could only be assuaged by wrapping his arms around Zach and holding tight. He stepped forward to do just that when a dark form charged him, shoving him aside and sending him flying.

"Zach!" The cry came out with a pained yell as he crashed into the ground, rocks and sharp, prickly weeds gouging him through his clothing, drawing blood. Nico fumbled for the handgun at his hip and pushed himself to his feet, staggering. Warm blood trickled down his palms and shins. He tried to take aim at the dark, unruly mass of hair on the head of the attacker, but it was a blur to him. He couldn't get a clear shot.

Then his gaze flicked down to Zach, and everything went still. Dark, oozing patches of putrefying skin had set in on Zach's face and neck. His eyes were hazy and empty, and they seemed to stare at Nico with a plea.

Then the dark shape hovering over Zach turned, and Nico stared into the feral face of the creature who had infected Zach.

His own features stared back at him. His own eyes gleamed triumphantly at the sight of the gun he held on himself.

"What are you waiting for?" the other Nico taunted.

Nico woke with a scream.

Zach was there in an instant, his hands and lips already soothing away Nico's terror. "Another dream?"

"Yeah." Nico scrubbed his hands over his sweat-and-tear-damp face and looked up at the sky. The heat of the night was so stifling they'd elected to sleep outside the tent once they'd finished making love, though it was scarcely better out in the open. Nico's balls still ached with unreleased arousal. With both of them needing to use a condom every time, they were running low, and he hadn't had the energy to go to the latrine and finish himself off after Zach had come. Zach hadn't been pleased with the refusal, especially since they'd already argued over whether Nico would use one of their few remaining condoms or save them for Zach to use when Zach fucked him.

"I'd rather just stay here with you," Nico had said, willing his erection to subside. It wasn't hard to do when he considered the possibilities of what might happen if he came near Zach.

Zach had given a frustrated grunt. "It's bad enough that you have to disappear and I can't get you off or see you come, but now you're not even going to do it for yourself?" He raked his fingers through his hair. "I don't like this. It's supposed to be about sharing, isn't it? Not me getting what I need and leaving you—"

"With the immeasurable satisfaction of having watched you. Who says that isn't sharing?" Nico had cut him off with a kiss. "Relax. I don't do quid pro quo. Blue balls won't kill me."

"Yeah, well, maybe *I* want to watch *you*," Zach had grumbled, but he'd settled in Nico's arms and fallen asleep.

Now they lay together under the canopy of the sky, stars sparkling impossibly bright against an indigo backdrop. Somewhere in the distance, a child cried and— Was that a woman screaming, her voice rising and falling in wails, or was it just Nico's imagination playing back what he'd heard that morning? Had someone in one of the distant pens died? Was it the Rot, or had another detainee succumbed to heat stroke?

"Nico?" Zach's voice dragged his mind back from its wanderings.

"Sorry. Yeah. Bad dream."

Zach propped himself up on an elbow to gaze down at Nico. "That's been happening a lot lately."

"Yeah." Nico rolled away, unwilling to let Zach get a good view of his face. He suspected he looked like hell. Zach's concerned expression whenever Nico took off his clothes was a pretty good indicator of what so many weeks on a drastically insufficient diet was doing to his body. If his face was anywhere near as gaunt as the rest of him, he probably appeared downright ghoulish, especially in the moonlight.

"Nico . . ." Zach's voice held a pleading note, and his fingers brushed down the xylophone of Nico's ribs. Nico shivered and hugged himself.

"I don't want to talk about it."

"I love you," Zach whispered, trailing kisses atop his shoulder.

"I know you do." And he did. There was no doubt in Nico's mind that Zach loved him. It didn't matter how long they'd known each other or what influence their dire situation might be having on their emotional states. Zach was too open, too pure a soul to question the sincerity of his feelings. And really, who cared if it *was* a product of the stress and trauma and fear they were under? In a world of straw houses, those feelings felt like brick. "I love you too."

Nico turned back to face Zach, letting him drape himself over top of him. His weight felt good, reassuring. And like something Nico would miss far too much when it was gone.

He wouldn't mention that, though. Instead, he kissed Zach slowly until they both hovered on that precipice of being too turned on to go back to sleep. But the mood wasn't exactly right. Instead, Zach slid off to the side and drew Nico in close, and Nico let himself be surrounded by Zach's nurturing love as he drifted off again.

⋀ ⋀ ⋀

WHEN THE GUARDS came the next morning with the rations, Nico was ready. He waved Zach off to continue tending their little garden and greeted the suited guards himself.

"Look, I need you guys to do me a favor," he said, pitching his voice low. His chest ached and his eyes burned, but he made himself issue the request he'd been procrastinating on for over a month. "I need to talk to General McClosky."

The suited heads turned toward each other. "General McClosky?" one of them asked.

"He's here, isn't he? There was supposed to be a helicopter that picked him up from his cabin in Virginia and brought him here a couple months ago."

They nodded. "He's here. But how do you know him?"

"Does it matter?"

"If you want me to bother him with some possible Rot case out in high-priority quarantine, it does."

"He's an old friend of the family. He knew my mother, and he's known me since I was a kid. Just tell him Nicolás Fernández needs to speak with him. He'll know what it's about."

They didn't seem to know what to make of that and stepped back to murmur to each other a moment.

"We'll pass it along to our CO," one of them finally said, shoving Nico and Zach's box of rations at him. "No promises."

"Of course," Nico muttered, and watched them leave.

When he turned back toward the enclosure, Zach had paused to squint through the morning sunlight at him. He dropped their box of rations outside the tent to cross their pen and grab Zach's hand. He pulled the hoe from his grasp and tossed it aside, dragging Zach close and kissing him hard.

Zach responded with all the sweetness Nico had come to expect of him, giving Nico a quirky smile when they finally came up for air. "Not that I'm complaining, but what was that about?"

"Nothing." Nico shook his head, letting his eyes devour the sight of Zach's swollen lips and flushed cheeks and sparkling eyes. "Just— Let's go inside. I need you. I can't wait."

Zach blinked and frowned, like he wanted to push, but in the end he said nothing and let Nico lead him into the tent.

Days passed with no further word on whether or not Nico's message had been delivered. Nico couldn't keep his hands off Zach, spending the time trying to pack every touch and taste and sound into his memory until the afternoon when a whole truckload of guards appeared, armed to the teeth, and surrounded the gate to Nico and Zach's pen.

They formed up around another suited figure, keeping their distance in a way that suggested this one was different. Nico and Zach stood shoulder to shoulder, waiting to find out what was going on.

"Nicolás?" the general's familiar voice asked, tinny and slurred through the mask of his suit. "You made it."

"Logan," Nico said coolly, nodding once.

"Why didn't you tell them to let me know you had arrived when you got here?" McClosky demanded.

"I think you know why." Nico pressed his lips together tightly, then shook himself. "Besides, we needed to go into quarantine."

McClosky's mask angled slightly, just enough for Nico to get the idea that he was perusing Zach. "And you've been here . . .?"

"Nearly six weeks, General," one of the guards supplied. "So far no sign of the Rot."

"Of course not." McClosky sighed. "Nicolás, you're going to need to come with us. You can't stay here."

Zach started. "What? No!" He put himself between Nico and McClosky, then turned to Nico with a plea in his eyes. "Nico, you can't."

"I don't have a choice, Zach." Nico closed his eyes. He'd known this would be difficult, but now that the moment was here, he wished it had never occurred to him to do it. How could he possibly go through with this? He looked at the mask where McClosky's face should be. "Please. Give us a minute?"

There was a pause, and none of the people with guns seemed happy about it, but McClosky nodded, and Nico led Zach into the tent.

"You contacted him!" Zach accused when the flap closed behind him.

Nico swallowed, blinking rapidly to try to dispel the sting in his eyes. "I can't go into the Clean Zone, Zach. We were kidding ourselves to think I could."

"Then we'll go away! We don't need to stay here. The house in Indiana . . . hell, anywhere!"

Nico took Zach's face between his hands, silencing his spluttering, desperate protests. "I don't think they'd let us do that. Right now they're trying to stop the spread of the pandemic, no matter how brutal they have to be about it. I don't think they'd let anyone just walk out of quarantine. Especially me."

Zach shook his head frantically. "They can't keep you prisoner!"

"I think they can do whatever they think they have to right now." He pressed his brow against Zach's, swallowing hard. "I'd do anything to keep you safe. Anything. Which means I need to be as far away from you as I can get."

"Nico, *please*!" Zach pulled back, his eyes swimming with tears, and his voice cracked. The moisture spilled down his cheeks, and Zach didn't even bother to try to check it. "I don't want to lose you too."

"I'm sorry, *cariño*." Nico pressed a hard kiss to Zach's brow, then ripped himself away from Zach's clutching hands, rushing from the tent only to be halted by the sound of weapons being readied. He froze and glanced around to see the guards all taking aim at him. A tear of his own slipped down his face, and he peered over his shoulder, where Zach stood by the flap. "I'm so sorry."

"Nico!" Zach sobbed, but Nico couldn't bring himself to look at him again. He turned to McClosky and nodded once, not even bothering to ask to take any of his belongings with him. One of the guards gestured him toward the truck with the barrel of his gun, and Nico began walking.

If there was any pity on McClosky's face behind the mask, he didn't want to see it.

⋀ ⋀ ⋀

Nico wasn't sure where they would take him. An empty house within view of Cheyenne Mountain would certainly not have been his first guess.

"What is this?" he demanded of McClosky when the truck came to a stop. The house, which looked hastily erected, was surrounded by fencing just as the pens had been.

"Did you think I'd simply tell our troops to execute you, Nicolás?" McClosky replied, leading the way through the gate.

"I have no idea what I expected. I just want to know what the fuck is going on."

McClosky didn't reply until the door had shut behind them, leaving them inside the house with only a single armed guard, the others stationed outside. "I assume you and the young man you were quarantined with were close?" he asked.

"Fuck you. Zach is none of your business."

He could practically feel the censuring look McClosky gave him. "He is if he's been exposed, Nicolás."

"He hasn't."

"Are you sure?"

"Yes, I'm sure! Do you think I would risk him, after what you just saw?"

"You care about him."

"Oh, go to hell, old man. You don't get to play the kindly, concerned patron now."

McClosky sighed, the sound rattling the speaker of his suit. "Your companion will need to stay in quarantine several weeks longer, now. Until he's been out of your presence at least six weeks."

"Oh, sure, because you couldn't possibly take my word for it." There was no answer from McClosky this time except for a shrug of those bulky shoulders. Nico took petty consolation in the thought of what the inside of that suit must smell and feel like on a scorching day like today. "What's the matter, General? Didn't you have another dose of the Alpha virus for yourself? Is that why you have to hide inside a suit now?"

"You of all people should know there were no other doses of the Alpha virus," McClosky said chidingly. "What did you do with it? Did you give it to your friend?"

Nico shook his head. "I offered. He didn't want it, so I destroyed it." That much was a lie, and he had to work at giving McClosky his frankest, least-guilty stare.

"Destroyed it how?"

"Threw it on a fire somewhere in Missouri, I think. Buried it with the coals the next morning."

"And the dose you took for Silvia?"

Nico looked away. "She used it, but it was too late. She'd been caring for a guy with the Rot for weeks before I found her."

That hooded head bowed, the shoulders slumped, and Nico could almost believe that McClosky truly grieved for a woman who had been one of his oldest—and perhaps only—friends. "I'm sorry, Nicolás," he murmured gruffly.

"Damn right you are." Nico folded his arms over his chest and glared. "So now what?"

"Now we spend some of the very valuable and limited fuel we have remaining to fly you to the CDC in Atlanta, where the rest of the Juggernaut troops are quarantined." McClosky sighed again. "It's too dangerous, keeping you here among the uninfected population."

Oh God. They were sending him away. It was worse than he'd imagined when he thought they might just imprison or kill him.

Zach, what have I done?

"What will I do there?"

"Same thing the rest of the troops are doing. The surviving staff and guards at the CDC and the Juggernaut troops are establishing a settlement, a plague colony, if you'd like." *No, I wouldn't like, you son of a bitch.* Nico swallowed the urge to snarl. "We can't bring them here to join the rest of the population, and just like us, they won't have enough rations to get by indefinitely. So they're learning how to provide for themselves."

Nico gulped. "And there's . . . no chance I can ever return? Can I at least—I don't know—write letters or something?"

"Fuel cells are being conserved for only top-priority communication between us and the CDC," McClosky answered with a shake of his head. "I'm sorry, Nicolás. You need to let it go."

"Easy for you to say." He turned his back, unwilling to let McClosky see what the knowledge that he'd never see Zach again was doing to him. "Get out."

"Nicolás—"

"*I said get out!*"

The suited soldier with the gun had it tucked against his shoulder and aimed at Nico before he finished shouting, and Nico sneered at him.

"Go ahead, asshole. Shoot me! Unless you blow my head off, I'm betting there's a good chance I can rip the general's mask off before I die."

McClosky held up a stilling hand. "That won't be necessary." He paused a long moment, as though he were taking Nico in, tempted to say something, but then his shoulders sank a fraction of an inch, and he turned away. "Take care, Nicolás. I'm glad you made it through alive."

Nico managed to hold back his tears until the general and the guard had left.

23

SEASONS

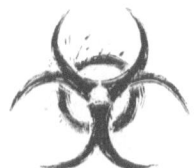

I t wasn't hard to figure out why they kept Zach in quarantine longer than the prescribed three months. He was fortunate that they hadn't decided to kill him as a precautionary measure. Instead, he had to sit through hours of grilling by suited personnel demanding to know everything about his time with Nico, including details of their sex lives. How often did they have sex? Who was the penetrative partner when they had intercourse? Did Nico ejaculate in his presence? Did Nico ejaculate in his mouth? In his rectum? What did Nico do with the condoms he discarded? Was Zach sure he used one every time? Had Zach noticed any differences in his level of appetite? In his strength or endurance?

Sometimes, when the aching solitude and longing for Nico were unbearable, and the utter mortification of having such sacred, cherished memories invaded so crudely was at its strongest, being shot seemed like it might have been preferable.

He was being melodramatic, of course. Once Nico had been taken away, the isolation and fear had just become too crushing, and Zach had sunk into a melancholy unlike anything he'd ever known. Some days he felt too disheartened to even pray. It didn't seem as though God were listening to him, anyway, if Zach had lost the one thing in this whole nightmare that had given him solace.

Had they killed Nico? Or did they have him imprisoned somewhere even lonelier than the pen where Zach now lived by himself? Nico, who so desperately needed human contact and physical touch; he would be wretched living that way.

He wanted to resent Nico for leaving him behind, for not fighting harder for the two of them to stay together, but he couldn't. He understood all too well the fear that had driven Nico's choice; he might have done the same if the situations were reversed.

But knowing that didn't help the loneliness.

When Zach could find it within himself to pray, those prayers were full of more questions than he'd ever had before. He'd never been one to doubt God's will or plan for him, but now all he had were doubts.

Why give me someone to love, Lord, someone who loves me without reservation, if we can't be together? Why put me in Nico's path? Why show me how it feels to finally be complete only to take it all away?

Surely Zach simply wasn't seeing the greater purpose to it all.

Or was he?

Sitting alone and sleepless under the stars, Zach looked back toward the tent where Nico's pack sat in a corner exactly where he had left it. Within one of the pockets, he knew, was the final ampule of the Alpha virus that Nico had offered him twice.

Is that it, Lord? Am I meant to take this gift?

If Nico were still alive, it would mean that Zach could be with him, wherever he was. In refusing to accept the Alpha strain, was Zach standing in the way of God's plan for him? He was reminded of the tale of the Christian man in the flood, who kept rejecting all rescuers who came along because he knew God would save him, never seeing that the rescuers were God's attempt to do just that until it was too late.

Maybe God meant for him to become one of the so-called Juggernauts.

The thought haunted him through the night, which was far too hot for sleeping. Finally, as the first gray hint of predawn light stretched across the sky, Zach left his blanket on the ground and went into the tent. The ampule was exactly where he'd last seen Nico tuck it away. It was lighter in Zach's palm than it seemed like it should be. Shouldn't an object of such magnitude be heavier?

He could take it. He could be with Nico. Yes, he would be a plague-bringer, his blood deadly to anyone he might ever go near, but at least he could be with Nico.

And he'd be *powerful*. Strong. Fast. Resilient. He wouldn't have to be afraid of anyone or anything, ever again.

Except . . . that didn't feel like God whispering in his ear, urging him along the right path. It felt like the voice of temptation, guiding him in the direction his own unadulterated self-interest wanted him to go. He knew the peace and certainty that came when he was acting in accordance with God's will. He'd felt it when he'd begun standing up to his father, when he'd helped Bryan, when he'd kept the reverend from killing Nico, when he'd left his family behind and tied his destiny to Nico's. Each step of that journey, he'd felt God's hand on his shoulder, offering comfort and reassurance that yes, this was the right thing to do.

Looking at the ampule, his shoulder was cold in the absence of that encouraging weight. Only the selfish desire of his own lonely heart urged him to crack open the nasal spray and inhale.

Clutching it in his fist, Zach stirred up the fire he used to boil his drinking water and threw the ampule on it, then got as far away from the fire as he could within the confines of the pen. He heard the pop of the ampule rupturing and prayed that it meant the heat was incinerating the virus within, rather than dispersing it on a cloud of smoke. Huddled in one corner of the pen, he waited for hours until the fire died down.

Once the sun rose, Zach grabbed a shovel and dug a small, deep hole at the roots of one of the pine trees he'd planted. He shoveled the ashes from the fire into it, stamping the dirt firmly on top of them.

His heart ached, but his shoulder felt warm again. Or maybe it was just the intense heat of the morning sun. Either way, when the guards arrived that afternoon and told him his quarantine was over and he would be allowed to join the growing community inside the Clean Zone, he left willingly, and he didn't look back at the tightly packed dirt beneath the pines.

ΛΛΛ

"I THINK you should start leading prayer meetings," Chantal said as Zach helped immobilize the man's shifting bones so she could splint his leg. He'd been injured falling off a leaky roof he'd been trying to repair. The man was lucky the injury hadn't been worse. "You can't spend all day every day working here."

"Why not?" Zach snorted, keeping his eyes on the patient. "You do."

Aiding the few doctors and nurses who had made it to the Clean Zone so far had been a grim and eye-opening experience these last few months. There was talk of whether or not it would be possible for the Clean Zone to establish a viable gene pool with the current mortality rates. The coming winter didn't look very promising, particularly for those still living in tents in the quarantine pens.

The statistics of detainees and Clean Zone denizens who had succumbed to the summer heat were astronomical. Now, with the advent of the autumn rains, the water supply had become tainted for some quarantine pens and homes inside the Clean Zone, or perhaps the people had simply failed to boil it sufficiently. And that wasn't the only problem. Shocking numbers of people were dying from other causes, as well.

The pyres didn't just burn for pandemic victims these days.

"Zach, did you hear me?"

He shook himself and looked across the legs of the groaning man at Chantal. "No, actually. I tuned you out. I'm not a minister, and I've come to realize I don't actually want to be one."

She blinked and frowned, but didn't reply until the splint was secured and one of the other volunteer medical assistants was walking—well, hobbling—the man through the process of requisitioning a pair of scavenged crutches from the communal storehouse.

"*You* don't want to be a minister? Since when?" she demanded, sweeping back wisps of gray-streaked blonde hair that had escaped her bun. Chantal was one of two MDs who had made it to the Clean Zone so far. It wasn't likely that there would be many more. Medical personnel on the whole had been especially obliterated by exposure to the pandemic. Chantal had only evaded infection because she had already been homebound when the pandemic started spreading, recovering from cancer treatments that had compromised her immune system. "I thought your dream had been to go to seminary once upon a time?"

Zach shrugged, digging in the box of nutrition bars they kept in the break room of the "clinic." It had actually once been a boarded-up secondhand clothing store that had gone out of business, but since most medical facilities were off-limits due to fear that they might be contaminated, the government had begun repurposing other buildings, particularly those that hadn't been inhabited at the time of the pandemic.

"I was a lot younger then," he finally replied. "I thought I wanted to be like my father and have my own ministry, but these days I'm more inclined to heed Christ's words about praying silently and worshipping in private."

Not that he was worshipping much these days. More like floundering desperately in the darkness, hoping against hope to accidentally brush against the grace that had once reassured and comforted him.

"Zach . . ." Chantal gave him a worried look. "I've heard you with the patients. You're respectful of the ones who don't share your beliefs, but for the ones who do, they take a lot of comfort when you pray with them."

"And I'll happily continue doing that." The protein bar was dry in his mouth, but Zach didn't feel like choking down flat, boiled water at the moment. "Working here with you is very rewarding for me, especially when I can give people in need spiritual support, as well. But that's all I want."

Chantal sighed. "Look, I'm just saying, it's not only people's bodies that need healing right now. Everyone is scared and lost. Everyone is grieving. For friends and family and spouses and children. Maybe it wouldn't be a bad idea to offer them something to help heal their souls."

"That may be, but I'm not sure it would be good for *my* soul." He wiped the crumbs from his hands and discarded the wrapper. "My only example of how to run a ministry involved a great deal of hypocrisy and dogmatic bludgeoning. I don't ever want to get to a place where I think my voice is God's. Just let me help you patch people up. Their souls will find their way to God on their own."

A crash in the outer room of the clinic startled both of them before Chantal could come up with another argument. Three rain-soaked men, one of whom was a uniformed member of the Clean Zone security force, came charging in; the other two carried a boy who couldn't have been more than sixteen, or perhaps an under-nourished and underdeveloped eighteen.

"We've got another one," the soldier—whose face Zach recognized, though he couldn't place a name to it—gasped as the civilians laid the boy carefully on the examination table. He was nude and covered in bruises, like just like the twenty-year-old man who had been found behind a derelict house last month. This boy was shivering, though from shock or the rain, Nico couldn't be certain.

"Where did you find him?" Chantal demanded, leaping into action. Zach wrapped the boy in blankets as she checked his pulse and blood pressure, shone a light at his pupils, and listened to his heart and lungs.

"Another empty property. Complete other side of the Clean Zone from the last one," the soldier replied. His eyes kept skating away from the boy on the table, as if he were unwilling to really see the mess someone had made of him. Both the boy's eyes were swollen shut, his lips puffy and split. From the swelling of his face, it looked like one of his cheekbones might have been fractured, and the whimpers and moans he made whenever they tried to move him —even while unconscious—weren't promising.

"He's, um, bleeding too." One of the civilians who had helped transport the boy gestured to the pinkish stains on his wet shirt. "Not just his face, if you know what I mean."

Zach swallowed as Chantal grabbed one of their carefully rationed examination gloves. "Help me get his legs up, okay, Zach?"

He nodded, feeling ill, but he did as she asked. Like the soldier, he couldn't look at the boy. He couldn't see that ruined face while helping Chantal check for the sort of trauma she was checking for.

Already, a small but spreading crimson stain was coloring the sheet of the examination table beneath the boy. Zach saw it as he helped bend the boy's legs and spread them so that Chantal could examine him.

"Fuck," she muttered. "This much blood is more than just anal trauma. He's bleeding internally. And there's no trace of semen here. My guess is he was raped with a foreign object, with enough force to perforate his colon." She looked up at Zach with bleak eyes, then turned to the civilians who had brought the boy in. "Does anyone know his name? Does he have any people? Family, or anyone he traveled with to get to the Clean Zone?"

They all shook their heads, looking sickened.

Chantal turned to the guard. "I'm going to need you to go to the population registrar and see if you can track down who he is and if he has anyone who'll want to say good-bye to him. And I want you to do it fast. Even if I had the surgical skills to repair the damage to his colon, he's going to die of peritonitis, and it's going to be painful. You've got maybe a couple hours, and then I'll euthanize him. Go now. Every minute we waste, he's suffering."

Once the soldier had gone, Chantal mustered a reassuring smile for the civilians and thanked them for helping transport the boy. She told them to go back to the work they'd been doing, or to go hug their own people, and they took their leave as if they couldn't wait to get out the door, abandoning Chantal and Zach to sit a deathwatch.

"You'd think they would have stayed to at least be here for the kid, in case no one else shows up," Zach muttered, watching their departing backs.

Chantal shook her head, wiping a tear from her face as she caressed the boy's muddy hair with her other hand. "I don't blame them. No one wants to be close to something this horrific. God, Zach, what have we come to? As if enough people weren't dying, we have someone here in the Clean Zone doing *this* to the survivors?"

"You think it's the same person who raped that man last month?"

She shrugged. "I don't know. But the fact that the only two really violent rapes we've had so far with damage to this extent have both been committed against men who were of a similar age suggests the possibility of a connection."

"The other man survived," Zach pointed out, his stomach

twisting as he took note of the crescent-shaped bite marks all over the boy's chest, shoulders, and neck. "It wasn't this bad."

"Which means, if it's the same person, he's becoming more aggressive," she said bleakly.

The soldier never returned. Which wasn't surprising, unfortunately. He had seemed like a decent guy, but the population registrar was, quite frankly, a sanctimonious asshole who resented being asked to do any work unless his superior officers commanded him to do it. And whoever the guard's CO was, he might have decided there were more pressing duties than running an errand of mercy for Chantal.

So she and Zach were still alone with the victim when she opened her chest of medical supplies and withdrew a 50 cc syringe. Zach took the boy's hand in his and began murmuring a prayer.

"Lord, be with this young man, to help ease his suffering and find his way into Your eternal grace. Comfort any survivors he may leave behind who love him, and will miss him, and will be bereft of the joy he no doubt brought into their lives. Protect the rest of us from becoming the next victim, dear Lord, and help us find whoever is guilty of this heinous deed and mete justice upon them for the sake of this boy and any of Your other children he may have already harmed. In Jesus's name, Amen."

She waited for Zach to finish and echoed his "Amen" before she slid the needle into the boy's carotid artery just beneath his ear. She depressed the plunger slowly, injecting a bolus of air. Zach startled when the boy convulsed, his damaged face contorting and twitching, and the hand Zach held spasmed painfully around his own.

It wasn't an immediate death. He and Chantal somberly waited out the stroke until, deprived of blood to his brain, the boy died.

Chantal covered him with a sheet and wiped her eyes. "Zach, will you go find someone on patrol to come collect the remains to take to the crematorium, please? Then you can go ahead and call it a night. I'll finish up here. I think I'd like to be alone awhile."

"Sure," Zach whispered, and did as she asked. Walking through the eerily empty streets toward the reclaimed house he'd been assigned to, Zach found he envied Chantal her tears. She hated them, grumbling bitterly that she'd lost all professional detachment with the knowledge of how precious few people had survived the pandemic. Zach's own eyes were hot and dry. The grief over that young man's senseless and violent death was pent up in his chest like magma pooling beneath a volcano.

He wondered if he'd ever be able to cry again, and if he'd survive the eruption if he did.

24

HOPELESSNESS

"That's all of them." Nico dropped the bushel basket full of squashes at the end of the row. "I don't think we're going to get any more out of this harvest."

"Great. Can you start putting away the stuff we've already finished canning in the storehouse?" Marc asked, eyeballing the baskets.

"No, I'm pretty sure that's outside the realm of my capabilities. Unlike the rest of you, I didn't go through basic training, and thus, I'm woefully underqualified for fetching, carrying, and menial kitchen labor." Nico tossed Marc a jaunty grin and crossed the industrial kitchen to begin loading jars of stewed squash into crates.

Nearby, other Jugs worked industriously to preserve the last yields of the harvest. Out in the gardens and fields, almost all of the plants were bare and beginning to die. Heaving a crate up onto his shoulder, Nico paused by Marc, who was acting as Sierra Company's supply officer. "Any word on whether we're going to get permission to go out scavenging for more livestock?"

"We're working on it," Marc said softly, and gestured Nico to continue on his way.

Nico pressed his lips together at the dismissal. He'd been at the repurposed prison the CDC was using for a quarantine facility for almost five weeks now, and very few people had warmed to him.

Marc was coming around, but most of the Jugs were still acting like he was a spy. Upon his arrival, Nico had spent days being questioned by high-ranking personnel—not from the CDC, but from the 1st Juggernaut Battalion itself—all of whom wanted to know how he'd come to be infected with the Alpha strain and why he'd been sent to Atlanta.

Nico hadn't bothered lying. He had nothing to hide. He'd told them everything he knew about McClosky, and everything McClosky had told him about Project Juggernaut. He'd confessed his role in getting the operation green-lit, and about the ampule McClosky had given him.

He wasn't sure if they believed him, but they'd eventually assigned him to Sierra Company and put him to work. That didn't mean the others had welcomed him with open arms, however. The overwhelming sense he got from the Jugs was that they were a tight-knit group whose morale was incredibly low. There had been several suicides since Nico had arrived—hanging being the preferred method, since it was bloodless and put no one at risk—and he'd overheard enough to make it clear that these were just the tail end of a rash of suicides that had swept through the battalion after news of what the Beta strain was doing to the world had reached the Jugs.

Nico couldn't exactly blame them. The Army hadn't explained to them, when it administered the Alpha strain of the Bane virus, that they would never be allowed to return to civilian life once their enlistment ended. They would never be allowed to retire. Their families were almost certainly dead, and even if they had surviving family, they'd never be able to live with them for the same reason Nico couldn't live with Zach. The only options they had now were death or quarantine. The ones who didn't choose the former kept occupied with 1st Juggernaut's massive provisioning requirements, where Nico worked alongside them, trying to find his place.

A great deal of the land surrounding the prison had been cultivated and planted the previous spring. Huge farms made the gardens in the pens at Colorado Springs look pathetic. As a result, Nico finally had sufficient rations and was rebuilding some of the body mass he'd lost during his months quarantined with Zach. There was a push to gather more livestock for milk, eggs, and meat, but they had to receive permission from their COs to leave the quarantine facility to scavenge, and that was being doled out sparingly.

Why, Nico had no idea. It wasn't like there was anyone left to infect.

The storehouse Marc had sent him to was a massive building in the middle of the various cellblocks. Thick brick walls and semi-underground construction kept it nicely climate controlled with a minimal use of the CDC's fuel cells. The Jugs had done as much as they possibly could with what they had available. They were keenly focused on provisioning, even beyond what seemed necessary for the upcoming winter.

When Nico reached the bottom of the steps leading into the underground storehouse, a crash from somewhere deep inside made him nearly drop his crate. He heard the unmistakable sound of glass shattering.

Fuck! The supplies! He set his crate off to the side and broke into a sprint, searching for the source of the devastation before they lost any more desperately needed rations.

He had expected to find shelves collapsing or unbalanced stacks of jars. But as he rounded the end of a row of shelves, an agonized shriek made him jump out of his skin, followed by a torrent of harsh, painful-sounding sobs.

At the other end of the aisle, he found a woman who looked to be of Mediterranean descent, dressed in the same jumpsuit everyone in quarantine here wore and restraining another woman, who had freckles, a pale complexion, and titian hair. The redhead was strug-gling as if she wanted to do more damage. The evidence of her rampage was scattered around her, but she calmed as Nico watched, slumping to the concrete floor and weeping. It was a noise Nico had become used to in Colorado Springs, the sound of someone who had just lost a loved one. But he'd always heard it from a distance before, from one of the other pens. He'd never been slapped in the face with such savage and immediate grief.

The olive-skinned woman with the long braid wrapped her arms around the redhead, murmuring disjointed words of comfort. She looked shaken herself, but her dark eyes were dry when she opened them and saw Nico standing there.

"Can I help?" he asked as softly and unobtrusively as he could.

"Go out to the fields. Look for a Hawaiian man named Kaleo. He's with Delta Company. Tell him Xolani says Schuyler needs him. Tell him Hope is dying this afternoon."

It took Nico a moment to realize that Hope was a name and not a concept, but he nodded and took off for the fields.

Locating Kaleo wasn't difficult. What was harder was seeing the way his face turned gray when Nico quoted the message the woman had given him. The way his eyes flashed with tears. The way every other member of Delta Company in the fields formed up behind him like an escort as he took off for the storehouse at a sprint. Unsure what to do with himself after delivering his message, Nico followed in their wake.

The group stopped outside and let Kaleo proceed alone. The half dozen or so men and women who had left the fields were grimly silent. One of them, a solidly built person whose collar was embroidered with a small transgender symbol, indicating he identified as male, looked like he was on the verge of tears himself.

"Hey, Jamie." A short, wiry man made his way through the small crowd to stand at the distressed man's side, squeezing his shoulder. "It's okay, dude."

Jamie shrugged and wiped his face. "I guess. At least we found out *before* you donated for me, huh?"

"You'll still get to have the family you want, man. We'll find a way. Maybe when we get out of here, you can adopt—"

"Adopt *who*?" Jamie scoffed. "Everyone out there's dead."

The shorter man shot a look in Nico's direction, and Jamie followed suit, as if they only just realized whose company they were in. "You're the new guy, aren't you?" he asked. "I'm Toby."

"Nico." He wiped his hand on his jumpsuit and accepted Toby's proffered handshake. "And yeah, I guess I'm the new guy."

Toby nodded an acknowledgment. "Cool. This is Jamie. And those people over there are Luis, Darius, Gina, and Titus. You saw Kaleo, and I'll venture a guess that you ran into Schuyler and Xolani down in the storehouse."

Nico made note of the others' names and faces, but they were either off in their own thoughts or conferring softly with their heads together, taking no notice of him. "Um, do you mind if I ask . . . what's going on? Is everything— Well, I mean, obviously everything's not okay, but—"

Before he could stop stammering and complete the thought, the doors to the storehouse opened. Kaleo and Xolani appeared, Schuyler leaning heavily on Kaleo between them. Both their faces were wet. Kaleo escorted Schuyler toward the infirmary while Xolani paused to speak with the men Toby had identified as Darius and Luis.

"It's confirmed. The Alpha antibodies didn't pass through the placental barrier. Hope started showing a rash this morning, which turned to lesions after a couple hours." She kept her voice low, but they were all clustered closely enough to overhear. The three of them, who seemed to be the leaders, fell into step, heading in the direction of the infirmary after Schuyler and Kaleo. The rest of the Delta Company Jugs, plus Nico, followed suit.

Nico's belly churned. "Hope's their *baby*?" he asked Toby, keeping his voice as soft as he could manage.

Toby nodded, his eyes shining and his lashes spiky. Jamie looked just as grief stricken. "She was born four weeks ago. We knew this could happen, but we were hoping— Well, hence her name."

"How did she get infected?" Nico inquired. He remembered McClosky remarking that they had no idea what effect being infected with Alpha would have on pregnant women.

"Didn't have the surgical equipment for a bloodless C-section," Jamie answered in Toby's stead. His voice was hollow, and his face bleak. "She was exposed the moment she was born. Which means, thanks to what those fuckers at the Pentagon did to us, any of us who ever wanted kids are shit out of luck."

"Obviously, Jamie here is one of those," Toby added with a nod. "But Schuyler . . . She was only a few months away from getting out of the Army when they transferred us to the Juggernaut Battalion, and all she could talk about was how she was going to settle down and have a house full of babies. None of us knew when they gave us that damn virus that it meant we were never getting out."

The grim vigil the group had begun at the storehouse continued outside the infirmary for the next hour. Nico wondered if he should excuse himself, but he felt like turning his back on this—especially after the part he'd played in making it happen—would be uncaring. More and more members of Delta Company joined their comrades, trickling in in small groups. There were dozens of them standing with their heads bowed, some with tears on their cheeks, when Kaleo and Schuyler finally reappeared, clinging to each other, devastation clear on their faces.

That night, almost the entire two-thousand-troop Juggernaut Battalion gathered in the exercise yard. They carried every piece of wood they could find—broken furniture from the warden's office, shattered crates, deadfall from a nearby greenbelt past the fields—and they built a pyre, unconcerned with the scavenged kerosene they wasted to ignite it. Schuyler herself laid the tiny, blanket-wrapped bundle atop it, and Kaleo lit the match.

Delta Company stood nearest to the fire, with Schuyler at the middle. She still looked grief stricken but also absolutely livid. Fury burned deep within her eyes, and the reflection of the flames only made it that much more intense. Part of Nico wanted to go to her and beg her forgiveness for the minor and unwitting part he'd played in her tragedy, but he didn't dare.

NICO RAN into Kaleo a lot after that. He hadn't ever noticed him before, but they worked together frequently in the kitchens and fields. At first, Kaleo was withdrawn and quiet, but as weeks passed, what emerged was a generally jovial guy with an irrepressible grin and an eagerness to find the absurdity in everything. He responded warmly to Nico's hesitant attempts to strike up conversation.

Other than Kaleo, most of Nico's contact with the Jugs was contained to Sierra Company. They were good people but still standoffish. Nico wondered if it was his involvement with McClosky and the origins of Project Juggernaut that kept them from welcoming him, because no matter what he did, there was always an undercurrent of suspicion and resentment in their attitudes. Or maybe they just didn't know what to make of a civilian who had somehow become infected with the Alpha strain.

"They need to start fucking training you, for one thing," Kaleo had snorted when Nico mentioned feeling like he had no place with the Jugs. Nico opened his mouth to mention his extensive self-defense training, but Kaleo didn't allow him to get a word in. That was how conversations tended to go with Kaleo. "Doesn't matter how you ended up becoming one of us. You're here now, and we've got to deal with that. Next time you don't have anything to do, come out to the yard and we'll work out. I'll start teaching you some basics."

For obvious reasons, the Jugs didn't have weapons, but those who weren't struggling with depression—and some who were fighting to overcome it—worked hard to keep fit, a large part of which involved hand-to-hand sparring. The following afternoon, Nico joined them. Straight-faced, he nodded as Kaleo walked him through a proper fighting stance.

"Don't worry," Kaleo said reassuringly. "I won't go all out on you yet. Just try to attack me."

Nico nodded and waited for Kaleo's signal, then feinted at Kaleo's head. While Kaleo was blocking that, Nico swept his feet out from underneath him. Kaleo went down with a curse, staring up in astonishment as Nico paused over him with a fist drawn back, ready to drive it into his face. The action in the courtyard came to a complete stop. Until Kaleo laughed, Nico half feared they were going to attack him for dropping one of their own, especially Kaleo.

"Holy fuck!" Kaleo hooted, and everyone relaxed. Nico had the sense that they indulged Kaleo's tolerance of him only in the interest of permitting Kaleo anything that might lessen his grief over the loss of his and Schuyler's daughter. "What were you before the pandemic?"

Nico grinned and offered him a hand up. "A rentboy."

Kaleo laughed at that and quickly gave up teaching Nico the basics. Though the element of surprise was on his side for that first attack, Nico was desperately out of practice and out of shape, and he and Kaleo settled in to sparring companionably. The workout felt good, though Nico's muscles soon started protesting.

"So," Kaleo panted when they flopped down onto the lawn for a breather. "Turns out what you actually need is weapons practice. Which we can't really give you."

"I learned a little this spring." Nico shrugged awkwardly. "Maybe not enough to really consider myself qualified, but what does it matter? Even if we had weapons, who would we use them against?"

Kaleo's omnipresent grin faded, and his eyes flicked toward the walls surrounding the yard for an instant. Which were always absent of guards, a fact Nico found bizarre. He'd seen very little indication that anyone was around to actually enforce the Jugs' quarantine, with the exception of the CDC researchers working on a vaccine. "Guess you never know."

Nico dropped his voice to a murmur. "What does that mean?"

Kaleo narrowed his eyes. "I don't think I'll answer that yet. I kinda like you. I'm not really keen to kill you just now."

After that, Nico spent a lot more time watching the interplay between the Jugs and the CDC personnel. There were obviously troops here who weren't Jugs, but it seemed like they were no longer acting as guards. Maybe they, too, had come to the conclusion that there was no reason to keep the Jugs prisoner when there was no one left for them to infect. Instead, they worked together to lay away provisions for the upcoming winter, which they would all need to survive, and the Jugs came and went as their COs commanded, voluntarily abiding by their quarantine.

The Jug COs and medics regularly conferred with the research and medical staff to make sure that the Juggernaut Battalion had everything they needed to stay healthy and active. As fall faded into winter, rumors circulated that the Jugs might be recalled to active duty, speculation that was met with a combination of excitement and consternation.

"Active duty doing *what*?" Nico demanded while he and Kaleo sparred, as they did every other day, regardless of the weather. "I mean, I guess I can see using us to clean up whatever's left of the cities. God, when we were crossing the country, Zach and I had to go through St. Louis. It was terrifying, and I'm not just talking about the revenants. Even the small towns—"

Kaleo was giving him that amused look he sometimes wore, like

Nico was missing something. "We're not going anywhere but Colorado," he said with finality.

"Colorado?" Nico ignored the pulse in his chest that might as well have screamed *Zach!* and tried to focus on what Kaleo was telling him, or not telling him. "Why would they bring us to Colorado?"

"Didn't say they were gonna bring us to Colorado." Kaleo launched into a dizzying combination of hits and kicks that landed Nico on his back in the mud. "I said that's the only place we're going. Now shut up and fight."

ΛΛΛ

NIGHTS WERE THE WORST. Especially in the winter when the weather was too inclement to go outside for long and the darkness seemed to last forever. Wild winter hurricanes battered them even this far inland, adding the constant sense of being under siege to the cabin fever.

After over a year in seclusion with one another, with no foreseeable opportunity to get out and especially knowing that most—if not all—of their partners and spouses were dead, the Jugs were pairing off. Some had settled into long-term relationships, like Kaleo and Schuyler. Others just hooked up for the night. With the disparity in numbers between Jug men and women, many of the men who would have been otherwise inclined had chosen the route of opportunist bisexuality. And thanks to the utter lack of privacy, none of them were shy about where they indulged their need for companionship.

Nico saw them with one another or heard their moans and grunts and the slapping of their flesh in the dark, and he ached for Zach. For the first time since puberty, he had no desire to partake in the sexual escapades of the people surrounding him. The loneliness and the need to touch someone and be touched was still there, and as the Jugs slowly began to warm toward him, Nico had offers to indulge it, especially once word about his former occupation got around. If he accepted those offers, the emptiness would ease for a while, but it wouldn't be the same as it had been with Zach. It would be a cheap, unsatisfactory substitute, and he couldn't find any motivation to act on the urge for even that superficial relief.

I'd understand if you did. You are as the Lord made you, Zach's voice whispered to him in the dark dormitory when other members of Sierra Company fumbled around on their narrow bunks around him. *I've known who and what you are all along, and what you need.*

They weren't words Zach had ever spoken to him; they'd never discussed this possibility. But if Nico did indulge, he had no doubt Zach would understand and forgive. Maybe he wouldn't even consider it a betrayal, since they had no realistic hope of ever seeing each other again. The sanest thing to do would be to move on and try to find happiness of another sort, but to *Nico* it felt like a betrayal. He had no idea what inside him had changed, to make the unapologetic whore into a monogamist dedicated to a man he could never hope to be with, but there it was.

Just over a year ago, Nico could have seen Zach every day, even with half the country separating them. They could have indulged in hours-long vid calls, talked dirty to each other until they both came all over their hands, and then signed off with an *I love you* and a smile. It wouldn't have been the touch he craved, but it would have been something.

Now he couldn't even send a letter. He'd managed to requisition a notebook and pencil—which had earned him a narrow-eyed look from the supply officer—to try releasing some of his loneliness and need for Zach by journaling. It felt woefully inadequate, the sentiments trite and clumsy. Zach had become the only thing that made surviving in this merciless new world worthwhile for Nico.

The Jugs had lost everything, even their freedom, but they still had one another, and the bonds of love and friendship, and even the lust they were forging together. But Nico could never really share in that. Not when his heart demanded he stay true to Zach, and when his conscience insisted that he was part of the chain of events that had ruined the Jugs' lives, taken away their families, their freedom, and their hope.

Swallowing back another wave of misery, he pulled the pillow over his head to block out the sounds around him.

25

SPIRAL

People kept telling Zach that just over a century ago, Colorado Springs had been known for its dry and relatively mild winters. It didn't seem possible after months of being lashed by violent monsoons. Purportedly, late summer had once been monsoon season, but the weather patterns had shifted, the summers becoming dryer and more scorching, and the winters colder and wetter. And longer. Much longer.

Now, the rain was half-frozen, pelting the windows of the clinic as if it would batter the place down, while he and Chantal hunkered inside, each in several layers of clothing, trying to stay warm with no heat in the building.

A violent rapping at the door startled them both in the gloomy silence.

"Shit. Is it that time again?" Chantal groaned.

"I'll get our suits." Zach slid off his stool and made his way to the back storage room, where they kept the hermetic suits they wore when making what the military police euphemistically referred to as "wellness visits" to the quarantine pens. The quarantine population had grown large enough that the medics weren't able to handle the load, so he and Chantal had been given suits and pressed into service. Fortunately, there had been very few cases of Bane requiring victims to be euthanized. There had, however, been an excess of cases of infected wounds, broken bones, tainted food, and contaminated water. Not to mention pneumonia, frostbite, and other exposure-related conditions whenever the temperatures dropped below freezing. Pregnant people were miscarrying courtesy of the inadequate diet or dealing with childbirth complications, including postpartum bacterial infections.

And suicide. "The Second Pandemic," as it was being called. No one could forget the suicide attempts. Or the fact that it was rumored to be another reason there were no longer enough military medics to handle the workload.

At the moment, it was only by virtue of the increase in new arrivals that the population of the Clean Zone was growing. The death rate still far outpaced the birthrate.

The tension in the quarantine camps was palpable, even through the miserable, icy downpour. The tents leaked, and their occupants coughed. The attitudes ranged from sullen to downright confrontational.

"When are we getting out of here, huh?" one woman demanded of their military escort while Chantal examined a wheezing child. "You said we'd be here three months, and it's been over four. Yeah, I've been keeping track. I can fucking count!"

"You'll be processed into the Clean Zone once we've found living quarters for you," the guard said. His hooded head didn't dip; he wasn't looking at her face, he was looking over her head.

"So when's that going to be?" she pressed. "There's a whole city full of empty buildings here!"

The guard sighed like she was being bothersome, which made Zach dislike him intensely. "The buildings that were occupied by possible pandemic victims have to be burned down and new housing built. At this point, there are no more quarters available within the Clean Zone perimeter, and construction has been slowed by the weather. We're working on scouting new neighborhoods with empty housing, but it will take time."

The woman threw up her hands. "So why can't you put us in a tent in the Clean Zone? Or quarter us with someone else? We've passed quarantine. There's no reason to keep us here!"

"How would that be any different from staying in your tent right here?" the guard asked snidely.

"Because at least there I wouldn't be locked in a cage, with someone only checking on us a couple times a week! I could get my son to the doctor when he starts sounding like he's drowning, instead of waiting for someone to make time to get to us!" She began gesticulating angrily with each word, stepping closer to the guard, then pitched forward, bending double as a racking cough took over.

He brought down his weapon. Not quite aiming it at her, but . . . "Step back. Now."

"Hey!" Chantal shot to her feet, advancing on him like she was driven by God's own wrath. "Don't you *dare* point that at her! You have absolutely no justification for even the threat of deadly force here."

"Then tell this bitch to get out of my face," the guard gritted out. Zach wasn't sure how his blank, copper-toned mask could look irate, but it did.

"How about *you* get out of my face and go requisition me some antibiotics and an albuterol inhaler for this child?" Chantal retorted, bracing her gloved hands on the hips of her suit.

The soldier's head moved emphatically back and forth. "No can do, Doc. New regs from inside the mountain. Pharmaceutical supplies are only for people who have passed quarantine. We can't waste meds on someone who might die from the Rot anyway."

Chantal went rigid with outrage. "What the fuck sort of regulation is that? Besides, you heard her. She's been here four months. She's passed quarantine."

"Not my call. I have orders. No drugs in the pens. Talk to the committee if you don't like it. Now, are we done here?"

Zach clenched his hands into fists inside his sweaty gloves. Chantal's posture suggested she wanted to punch the soldier in the throat too, but she eased back, her breath slashing through the filter in her mask. She knelt down beside the boy's cot, tucking his blankets around him. "You rest now, sweetie. I'll be back soon with medicine, okay?"

The boy's nod turned into a fit of violent coughing, and Chantal turned her masked face toward the woman. "I need to see what I can do about this medicine situation, or getting you out of quarantine and into the clinic in the Clean Zone."

The woman didn't look reassured. There was no more anger in her eyes as she looked at Chantal, only fear and doubt. Unable to contribute anything more useful, Zach closed his eyes while they spoke, muttering a prayer for the woman and boy softly enough that he thought it wouldn't be heard outside his suit.

He was wrong. "Who are you talking to?" the boy rasped from his cot.

"God." Zach tried to put a smile in his voice, to let the kid know this was a hopeful, good thing Zach was trying to do.

"Who's God?"

Zach shot a glance to the woman, who overheard the boy's question and managed a soft chuckle.

"His parents—my brother and sister-in-law—were atheists."

"Ah." Zach nodded and sidled past Chantal and the woman to squat beside the boy. "God is sort of a friend of mine. A really big, strong, powerful, kind, invisible friend. He's a good guy. He loves everyone, especially kids. And some people, like your mommy and daddy, don't believe in Him, and that's okay. He loves you, anyway."

The boy blinked. "Invisible friends aren't real. My brother said so when I was little."

Zach shrugged. "Did you ever have a teddy bear? Or a doll, or a blanket? Something you liked to hold on to that made you feel better?" The boy nodded. "Well, maybe that thing had a special power to make you feel better or maybe it didn't. Or maybe it only had that power because you *believed* it did. But it still *really* made you feel better when you held on to it, didn't it?"

The boy's feverish face scrunched as he thought this over. "I guess. Does talking to God make you feel better?"

"Sometimes." Zach stroked the boy's brow, feeling the warmth of his skin through the gloves. "And sometimes I ask Him for favors, like taking care of people who are sick or sad. I ask Him to help them feel better."

"Does it work?"

The innocent question went through Zach's heart like a dagger.

It was the question he kept coming back to, the question that had him feeling like his own faith stood on wobbling, constantly weakening legs. He couldn't possibly answer yes without being a liar. And lately the needless, endless death and terror around him made God's will seem very random and capricious, indeed. He didn't know how to reconcile that with the loving and merciful God he prayed to.

"Sometimes," he whispered, drawing his hand away and standing quickly. "But right now, medicine will work better, so I'll ask God to help us find a way to get you the medicine you need, okay? You get some rest while we work on that."

He hurried—or rather, *ran*—out of the tent before the little boy had another chance to ask him questions he wasn't sure he believed the answers to anymore.

$$\Lambda \Lambda \Lambda$$

PUBLIC SENTIMENT in the Clean Zone wasn't much more favorable than it was in the quarantine camps, especially after the government issued an edict that rations would be cut back by ten percent for the winter. It was becoming apparent that as the populations grew, the stockpiles held somewhere within the complex beneath Cheyenne Mountain were depleting at an alarming rate.

Gangs had formed among the population, running protection rackets in exchange for a portion of people's rations. Unfortunate things had a tendency to happen to people who didn't pony up, and no amount of complaining to the Clean Zone authorities seemed to alleviate the problem. The soldiers said they had no way to track down the extortionists, and the multitude of excuses for their failure to act had some people muttering that the soldiers were getting kickbacks out of the pilfered supplies.

Sexual crime was also running rampant within the Clean Zone. The "lone wolves," as Chantal called them—meaning unattached people, usually men, whose families had died in the pandemic, or who had never had family to begin with—were frequently too aggressive about trying to secure companionship. There was no official word on what the age of consent within the Clean Zone was, and rumor suggested this was due to concern that anyone above the age of puberty might need to contribute if the Clean Zone had any hope of establishing and maintaining a viable gene pool. It wasn't true, according to Chantal; the Clean Zone had a more than adequate gene pool. But since no one in power had asked her opinion, many of the youngest women were being bribed, coerced, or outright forced into relationships with sickening age disparities.

Some of those relationships were with the guards themselves, who had been granted permission to start families with the civilian population if they so desired.

Then there was the serial rapist, who seemed to have a preference for young men. Since the youth with the perforated colon, there had been no more deaths. It almost seemed as though the perpetrator had realized he'd gone too far. But by the end of February, there were three subsequent victims, all of whom had lived, but only one of whom could provide any useful details about his attack.

"He offered me food," Ross, the seventeen-year-old boy, had told Zach as he recuperated in the clinic. "I'd just been shaken down for my last rations. I hadn't eaten in a few days, so when he said he'd share his if I'd blow him, I figured why not?"

Zach had nodded sympathetically, doing as Chantal had instructed him, listening without judgment to anything Ross wanted to share.

"He couldn't get it up." Ross's voice broke, and a tear traced down his cheek. "That's when he started hitting me. Shit, I don't know, maybe I was bad at it. I've never blown anyone before. But he — It was like . . . he wasn't hitting me because I didn't do it right. He was hitting me to *try to turn himself on*. And when it didn't work, he made me suck him again, and then he'd hit me some more, and hit me harder, and then he used the belt, and—"

Ross dissolved into sobs at that point, but Zach had already heard him recite the rest of the story before, to Chantal and one of the guards. Unable to rouse himself by inflicting pain, the perpetrator—whose face Ross hadn't gotten a good look at because he'd been wearing a scarf when he picked Ross up on the streets before taking him into a darkened building—had become increasingly violent, finally sodomizing Ross with a cane when his own body wouldn't cooperate.

"Before he left . . . he said he wanted to see me again. Like we'd been on a fucking *date*! He told me to make sure he could find me when he came looking again. *Came looking*. Like he's just passing through town. Creepy, sick fucker." The brutalized boy broke down again, and all Zach could do was watch him weep.

Despite the information Ross had provided on when and where the attack took place, the guards' purported investigation turned up nothing. Given the attitude the guards were taking to most crime happening within the Clean Zone, Zach entertained the uncomfortable suspicion that the investigation had been minimal, at best.

Time seemed to pass in a weird sort of stasis. The situation in the Clean Zone was untenable, but there was no way to change it. Just like when he'd been in quarantine, and before that, when he'd been stuck with his father and brother. He was biding time, waiting for something to shake the new world out of this strange deadlock and make them all begin to live again rather than just exist.

It was coming up on the second spring since the pandemic had begun. Almost a year ago, he'd met Nico. How long would it take, if not to get back to normal, then to at least accept that the present reality *was* normal?

Zach entertained these mopey thoughts while he worked on cleaning the already-pristine clinic. Chantal was still back at her house sleeping, since she'd been up late assisting with a birth. They had moved in together so that Zach's house could go to someone still stuck in the pens but on the waiting list for the Clean Zone. His stomach growled, but he was getting used to ignoring it. Rations were lean enough that he never felt truly full anymore. If not for the emptiness in his heart, he could have been glad Nico wasn't here. He would surely have starved to death by now.

Did Nico at least have access to more sufficient rations wherever he was?

Sometimes that was the only thought that sustained Zach when the yearning to see Nico again became too keen—that Nico might be thriving better than he could have here. Zach refused to let himself think that Nico had been killed. Surely he was too valuable an asset for that, being one of these superhumans the Alpha created.

Zach paused in the middle of disinfecting a supply cabinet

inside and out when he heard shouting seeping through the walls from outside. Dropping his cloth in the bucket of bleach water he'd been using, he stripped off his gloves and wandered into the makeshift lobby. A crowd was gathering a block down, and smoke billowed through the rainy midmorning haze. Alarm tightened his shoulders, and Zach rushed out and down the street.

One of the houses at the end of the block was fully aflame, and the fire had clearly just spread to its neighbor. Bystanders were clustered on the other side of the street, watching the structures go up, while two men and a woman argued with the guards who had come to investigate.

"I'm telling you, I know who did it, so why are you still standing here with your thumbs up your asses and not dealing with this guy?" one of the men yelled, going toe-to-toe with the soldier. Zach had seen him around the neighborhood but couldn't recall his name. He was sporting the vestiges of a black eye. "Cole Leehan. White, sandy hair, brown eyes, six foot one, tattoos up both arms."

The guard looked almost bored. "You've been bitching about this Leehan guy for months. You've never been able to show a bit of evidence that he's running a protection racket, and everyone in his area of the Zone vouches for him."

"There's your fucking evidence!" the woman beside him—was her name Karla?—shouted, gesticulating wildly at the burning houses. "We've made sure he can't get to our rations anymore. We told you last week when he beat up Adam that he said he'd be back and something worse would happen if we didn't pay up. This is on *you*. You could have stopped it and you *didn't*!"

"Lady, we don't have the *resources* to chase down everyone you've got a beef with!"

This was met with another round of incoherent shouting, and Zach had to shoulder his way through the crowd to get to the participants in the argument.

"Excuse me, Private . . ." He trailed off invitingly, but the soldier refused to provide his name, leaving Zach standing there awkwardly. "Fine. Private whatever. If you haven't noticed, there are about a dozen more houses on this street downwind of the fire. I assume you've contacted your superiors about getting a fire engine out here?"

The soldier shook his head. "There's no sense wasting fuel cells activating one of the engines when the rain will take care of it."

"Has the rain taken care of it yet?" Zach arched his brows. "It's already spread to a second building, and that third there is starting to smolder. How many people are going to be out of a home tonight before the rain 'takes care of it?'"

"Maybe they should have been more careful with their fires, then."

Zach narrowed his eyes. The soldier looked well rested and well fed, the waterproof camouflage jacket of his fatigues fitting so snugly the zipper strained. Zach was willing to bet that if some of the guards were on the take, this one was one of them. "Would you like to explain to your CO why you didn't stop the blaze before it reached the only medical clinic serving this side of the Clean Zone?"

That got his attention. So far, the clinic had been exempt from the extortion rackets and other corruption seeping through the city. Even the crooks had the sense to realize it wasn't in their interest to deprive themselves of what sparse healthcare was available. In return, Chantal kept her head low and refrained from reporting a lot of suspicious injuries, making the clinic neutral ground.

If the clinic burned down, the medical care for hundreds of people would once again fall to the Army, who were trying to transfer as much of that burden as possible to Chantal and Zach and to the other clinic serving the far side of the Clean Zone.

Looking like he'd swallowed something nasty, the guard tipped his head to the side to mutter something to one of his comrades, who took off running.

An hour and two more burning houses later, a fire engine finally appeared, and then another. It might not have been enough if not for the fact that the rains turned heavy again. Nonetheless, there were four households without shelter that night. Chantal offered to let them sleep on the floor of the clinic temporarily. Thus, Zach was present for an impromptu community meeting after curfew had cleared the streets of the gawkers watching the remaining embers smolder.

"This can't go on," Mike, Adam's brother, declared. He'd been sharing the targeted house with Adam and Karla. "Someone has got to step in and do something."

Chantal frowned. "I agree, but you know how precarious my position is here. If I don't stay under the radar——"

"We know, Doc," Karla hastened to reassure her. "We know how important the clinic is. But the gangs are out of control and the guards aren't doing a fucking thing."

"Meanwhile, they're living nice and comfy in the complex in the mountains," Adam sneered. "How many of those precious fuel cells they refuse to part with are keeping that underground facility lit and powered while we've been out here freezing through the winter and unable to get a damn fire engine or ambulance when we need one?"

A woman whose name Zach didn't know threw up her hands. "No wonder they're not lifting a finger. Why mess with the status quo when it favors them?"

Mike nodded triumphantly. "Exactly. If they won't deal with the gangs, we have to."

One of the other neighbors, Drew, shook his head. "It's risky. I heard a woman who was trying to organize her block to resist the protection racket in the southwest quadrant turned up with a bullet between her eyes."

All faces turned to Chantal, who gave them a bleak look. "That's what I heard from Marie at the west-side clinic, as well."

Mike jumped to his feet. "They have fucking *guns* now, too?"

"How can they have guns? None of us has guns! They were all confiscated when we went through quarantine!" Zach didn't recognize the speaker who posed that question.

"Unless it was a guard who did the shooting," Karla murmured grimly. "Or provided the guns to the thugs who did."

"Fuck." Mike began pacing. His hands flailed in a way that eerily reminded Zach of Nico. "Look, I've already lost my husband to the pandemic, I'm not going to lose my brother and sister-in-law to a bunch of thieves who don't seem to get that we're all in this together!" He stormed past the curtains to the back and returned with a sheet, which he tore into wide shreds. He wrapped one of them around his face, creating a makeshift mask over his mouth and nose.

"If the guards are going to give the gangs weapons, I say we make them give us weapons too."

Chantal folded her arms over her chest. "You're insane. This is suicide."

"Better than sitting around waiting to be picked off by crooks!" Adam, Mike's brother, rose, as well, and claimed another strip. Once most of his face was covered, all that was left were their nearly identical eyes. "We start luring the guards off their patrols in less populated areas and get the drop on them. Knock 'em out, take their weapons, their rations, their power cells, all the shit they're holding out on us. And they won't be able to ID us."

"And what will the rest of us do when they start a manhunt?" Zach demanded, speaking up for the first time. "You know once you attack one of the guards, they're going to come down on *all* of us. They're going to search our houses and who knows what else. You'll make it worse for everyone!"

"Well, maybe then they'll finally locate the protection racket ringleaders!" someone snapped.

Karla scowled. "Worse, how? How does it possibly get any worse than watching my family and neighbors preyed upon by some wannabe crime lord?"

Zach caught Chantal's fretful eyes over the small cluster of people to see his own dread mirrored in her face. It was true that the current situation was utterly untenable, but if this went badly—and there didn't seem to be any way that it wouldn't—they were going to see even more people die. How were they supposed to go up against armed military forces? What would they use, shovels and clubs?

But then he saw Mike, his mask now hanging around his neck, talking animatedly to their neighbors, and he felt his own ambivalence giving way to something he hadn't felt in too long. *Hope.* For good or ill, what Mike and Adam were proposing—and what the other area residents were endorsing enthusiastically—would shake the status quo. *Finally*, they would break out of this powerless limbo and try to actually live rather than just get by.

He had a feeling if Nico were here, that would be his choice, as well. He'd be standing next to Mike, stirring the people up into a lather, urging them to take action. Zach had spent too much of his life standing by, permitting the intolerable, and here he was, doing it again. He couldn't participate in this guerrilla rebellion for the same reasons Chantal needed to remain neutral, of course. Too many people relied on the clinic for them to put themselves in the crosshairs. But somewhere deep inside, a spark kindled and a tiny flame smoldered. He couldn't take action, but if there was any way he could support their cause without endangering Chantal or the clinic, he'd do it.

Λ Λ Λ

IN THE PREDAWN hours of the next morning, Zach woke, his mind too restless to return to sleep. Tiptoeing, so as not to disturb what little slumber Chantal was able to snatch, he dressed and slipped down the alley to the clinic to pick up where he'd left off cleaning the day before.

This was where he spent his life. Except for Chantal, he had no friends. He had nothing but his work and his memories of Nico to get him through each day. Oh, he was on a first-name basis with many of their patients and neighbors, but he never socialized, never reached out to them in kinship.

But then, he never had made friends easily. Maybe something about the way his father's dogma and demands had isolated their family had set him apart, rendered him unable to connect with others. Maybe that had been why his instant attachment to Nico had hit him so hard and left him so devastated.

It was lonely. *He* was lonely.

"Can't sleep?"

The soft murmur made Zach jump, set his heart hammering in the examination cubicle he'd been scrubbing. He'd thought everyone in the clinic was asleep.

Mike stood in the part between the curtains, eyeing him with something that was uncomfortably close to understanding.

"Not for months," Zach answered, pitching his voice low to avoid disturbing the others.

"Who is she? Or he?"

"Huh?"

Mike smiled softly. "You get a look on your face sometimes like you're thinking of someone who isn't here. I recognize it because you look the way I feel when I remember Wade, my husband. So who are you missing?"

"His name's Nico." Zach braced both his hands on the examination table.

"Died in the pandemic?"

"No." Zach drew a deep breath, trying to figure out how to summarize the situation, then sighed and let his shoulders slump. "Not exactly. He could still be alive. It's difficult to explain."

"Not necessary. If you're not ready to let him go, you're not ready to let him go." Mike shrugged, an oddly diffident gesture considering the fury and determination he'd exhibited the night before. "It takes time. God knows I know that."

"I *know* I should give up hope of ever seeing him again, but I can't. It doesn't feel right. Like the Lord is telling me he and I aren't through yet. Not that it does me much good. It's not like I can go find him." Zach huffed a humorless laugh. "Why I still think the Lord is really telling me anything these days, I don't know."

"You'll move on when it's time." Mike fiddled with the curtain, running the fabric between his fingers. "I guess it would be harder without confirmation if he's alive or dead."

"You're sure about your husband?"

Mike's jaw flexed, and he nodded.

"If you don't mind me asking, how was it that he was infected but you and the rest of your family weren't?"

For a long moment, it seemed Mike wasn't going to answer. Then he sighed. "He worked at a naval hospital. I'd been out of town visiting Adam and Karla for a couple months, looking for a job near them because I wasn't having any luck where we lived." He filled his lungs with air and released the breath with an almost meditative slowness, giving Zach an idea of how hard he was struggling to keep calm. "When the National Guard cordoned off all the hospitals and refused to let anyone in or out, someone hacked into a communications frequency and Wade used it so we could talk a few times. He knew it was only a matter of time until he was infected. He vidded me one last time when he first started showing symptoms so we could say good-bye."

Zach swallowed. "God. I'm sorry."

"Hard to believe it's been sixteen months now." Mike shook his head. "I miss him. Which is probably going to make it seem pretty crass when I say what I've been meaning to say to you. Look, I'm not over my loss any more than you're over yours, but I'm pretty damn tired of sleeping alone and I've caught you looking at me a couple times. So, you know, if you ever just don't want to be alone . . ." He shrugged and sighed again, trailing off weakly. "I'd get that. I'd be okay with it just being that."

It surprised Zach to realize how tempting he found the offer. He'd thought he would reject it out of hand, but he couldn't. A part of him yearned in Mike's direction, reaching for what he offered.

What could it hurt? He would never see Nico again, and God help him, these days he almost understood Nico's need for contact, to touch and be touched. To not be alone in the world anymore.

But he couldn't.

Even if it didn't feel like adultery—which it did—Zach didn't care for the chances that when everything was said and done, he'd end up watching Mike die. Getting involved, however superficially, would be a colossal error.

Smiling gently, Zach stepped around the examination table to kiss Mike softly on the cheek. "Thanks for the offer, but I'm not ready for that, either."

Mike accepted the refusal with grace and a regretful smile. When he was gone, Zach closed his eyes and tipped his head back, turning his face skyward.

Lord, I don't know if You hear me anymore. I don't know if You've ever heard me. I've never wanted to demand that You prove Your presence to me, but please. Please, Father, I'm too weak to keep going on blind faith that Your will is being done. Show me . . . something. Just some indication that I'm on the right course. Please.

Silence answered him, as it always did. He was no longer sure if the lightness he felt in his chest after he prayed was God's answer to him or just wishful thinking. Disheartened anew, Zach packed the loneliness and despair deep down in his gut and went about his work.

△△△

IN RESPONSE to the guerrilla attacks on the guards, the Clean Zone curfew dropped by an hour. Then another. The patrols doubled. Zach watched a pair of fatigue-clad, assault-rifle-armed guards toss the clinic for the second time that spring, searching for stolen weapons stashed by the masked civilians who executed sneak attacks on patrols. There were no weapons to be found. No way would Chantal let them stow them here, but the guards' failure to locate the hidden cache only seemed to make them more determined to turn every stone.

God help everyone when it was uncovered.

Today's inspection was even worse than the first time. The soldier in charge was named Traverse, the same guard who had been indifferent when Adam, Mike, and Karla's house was torched by the gangs. The other one was clearly in a position of being forced to follow orders. He seemed reluctant to be conducting the search and hesitant to do so with the amount of—fully unwarranted, in Zach's opinion—aggression Traverse was using to throw his weight around. Zach stood back and let them get on with it until the subordinate guard got a good look at him, and his gray eyes widened in surprise.

"Zach, isn't it?" he asked.

His voice scratched the edge of Zach's memory, calling up memories of unexpected kindness and patience hidden behind a coppery mask. "Private Morris? Gillett?"

The soldier nodded, venturing a smile, but Traverse snapped at him. "Catch up on your own time, Morris. We're going to find who coldcocked Havarti, and we're going to give them some hurt."

Morris turned to him, a slow, steady pivot that suggested this wasn't the first time Traverse had tried his patience. "Aren't we supposed to be protecting the civilians, Traverse?" he asked blandly.

"How safe are they if we've got a gang arming up?"

Morris looked like he was going to protest, but Zach laid a hand on his biceps and shook his head. "It's okay, Gillett. Come hang out sometime when you're off duty."

He nodded and followed Traverse, who stormed out of the clinic as if its refusal to yield the stash of weapons were a personal offense.

Zach stepped over to the front windows and peered out, tracking their progress down the block. He went cold when they paused in front of Mike, Adam, and Karla's burned-out house. "Chantal!"

She came scurrying out of the back room, where they hoarded their precious allotment of medical supplies. After the first pair of soldiers had tossed the clinic looking for weapons, some of their meds had turned up missing, so Chantal had refused to let Traverse and Morris search unsupervised. "What is it?"

"They're poking around the burned-out houses," Zach murmured, trying to imbue the words with particular weight. He'd noticed after the last time a patrol had been attacked that Mike's clothes and hands had been stained by soot the following morning. He'd caught Chantal eyeing those stains as well, drawing the same conclusions.

She grimaced. "Mike and Adam are helping Viola plant her garden while she's off her feet on bed rest. One of us has to stay here in case someone comes in. Can you stroll down the street and see just how deep they're poking? If it looks like they're in danger of finding anything, run and let Mike and Adam know to hide."

His heart thundering, Zach nodded, pulling on his threadbare jacket. Affecting a casual attitude as he walked down the block, he craned his neck to get a look at where the guards had gone.

Morris's raised voice gave him something to follow.

"What do you mean, we're not reporting these to the CO? Goddamn it, Traverse, stop! You're messing with evidence here. We can use these to bait a trap, catch who's been carrying out the attacks. At the very least, we need to get them back to the armory!"

"Why? So the sheep can just steal them back? I know a better place they can go."

"Get that fucking gun off me!"

Zach moved without thinking, grabbing a charred piece of lumber. The sound of a gunshot and Morris's agonized scream cloaked his stumbling approach through the scattered debris, and

Zach raised the two-by-four over his head, intent on bringing it down on Traverse's skull with all his strength.

At the last instant, Traverse spun, his gun coming up as Zach's board came down. Something sizzled along Zach's ribs before the force of the wood crashing into Traverse's left shoulder vibrated up his arms, numbed his fingers, and wrenched a yell from the soldier.

Zach couldn't keep hold of the two-by-four when Traverse batted it from his hands, and then he was staring down Traverse's gun. His hands came up almost of their own accord, a gesture of harmlessness, surrender, which seemed singularly futile in the face of a man who had just shot his own comrade. Especially when Zach now knew, without a doubt, that Traverse was slipping weapons to the gangs. He was dead. It was just a matter of waiting for Traverse to pull the trigger.

But then Traverse jerked. A shadow rose over his shoulder, coalescing into Mike's grim face as Traverse's breath left him in an odd wheeze, followed by a trickle of blood that bubbled at his lips. Mike moved, and Zach registered the unfamiliar yet unmistakable sound of a blade sliding through clothing and flesh as Traverse jerked again. He dropped to the ground so suddenly that his spine must have been severed.

"Get out of here, Zach," Mike growled. The world seemed to be blurring around the edges, but he managed to look past Mike to see Adam looming over Morris, another knife in his hand.

"No!" He shoved Mike aside, aware of the chill of wet fabric against his side and hip, and launched himself at Adam. He almost ended up with Adam's knife embedded in his chest for his trouble, but Adam managed to jerk it back at the last instant. "Don't kill him!"

"We *have to*, Zach," Mike gritted. "He's seen us. He saw us kill this asshole!" He kicked Traverse's still body for emphasis.

"Traverse was trying to kill him. They're not in it together!"

"That doesn't mean he won't still report us!"

"I won't." Morris's voice was thready with pain, but he was gaining his feet. "Traverse was dirty. I can tell the CO that you saved me."

"And how do we know your CO isn't in on the corruption?"

Mike demanded. "You've got us penned in here like we were still in quarantine, and now you're taking our food, raping and kidnapping our women and boys, bleeding us dry."

"Not him!" Zach spun, pleading with Mike with his eyes. He ventured a cautious hand to his ribs and felt blood trickling sluggishly down his torso. "Please. Mike. I need to get him to Chantal. If he lives . . . he can work with us, okay? He's one of the good ones. He can help us bring them down."

Mike's paranoia blazed in his eyes, etched itself in the crumpled, uncertain lines of his face, but finally, he nodded. "Go. Take him with you. When he goes back to his CO, he never saw who attacked him and Traverse. He got shot, passed out, and when he woke up in the clinic, Traverse was gone. As far as his CO is concerned, he was Traverse's best friend. He learns anything about who's crooked on the inside, or comes up with any ideas how to help us, he brings that info to you and you get it to us."

Zach nodded eagerly and brushed past Adam to help Morris, staggering under his weight and feeling his own bleeding increase with the exertion. Chantal had clearly heard the shots and was running down the block from the clinic. Karla and a few other neighbors were approaching, as well, but they were all people who had been in the clinic the night they had discussed taking action against the crooked guards and the gangs. They could be trusted.

He stopped worrying about them and started worrying about getting Morris to Chantal before they both bled to death.

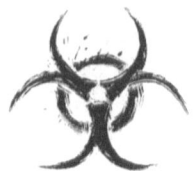

"Anyone know what this is about?" Nico asked as he stood next to Marc, surrounded by Jugs on all sides in the Sierra Company dormitory. They'd been pulled away from planting the first crops of spring to report for a last-minute briefing. Murmured speculation made the crowd buzz, and Nico's head ached with the din, his ears straining for an explanation.

"Listen up, people!" Captain Valentino, Sierra's CO, barked from the doorway of the dormitory. The soldiers fell silent with gratifying speed and snapped into as neat a standing order as they could manage, considering they were crowding between bunks. Nico tried to follow suit. Valentino rocked on the balls of his feet, a smirk lifting the corners of his mouth and his eyes glinting with something Nico couldn't understand, something eager that he would have called glee if it hadn't left him feeling vaguely afraid. "We've got marching orders," he drawled. "Seems the military government in Colorado Springs is having a little trouble providing security for the civilian population, and they've asked for our help."

Zach! A hundred questions flooded Nico's mind, all of them concerning what was happening in Colorado Springs and if it meant Zach was in trouble. But something about the captain's wry delivery electrified the crowd. Everyone felt it and grew a little stiller. Then they subtly started drawing away from Nico, and he felt their eyes flitting toward him.

"What?" he hissed to Marc, who—more than anyone in Sierra Company—had finally warmed to him. Marc looked anxious, his eyes flicking from the captain to Nico and back.

If Valentino caught the undercurrent, he gave it no heed. "Last spring, when we overthrew the guards and took over operations here at the CDC, the lieutenant colonel made a promise to all of us. He knew we had families we wanted to check on, to see if they'd survived, to make sure they were safe. He promised us if we held tight for a while, let them think we were still under their control, built up our supplies, waited for an opening, we'd get a chance not just to be free but to deal with the people who did this to us. Well, this is our chance."

Nico closed his eyes, resisting the urge to smack himself. Suddenly everything that seemed odd about the way the quarantine was being run made sense. The Jugs were only pretending the CDC was still in charge; no doubt they had control of all communications in and out of the quarantine facility. They wouldn't have let the government keep them imprisoned indefinitely.

No wonder they acted like he might be a spy.

No one's attention was on Nico now, though. As Valentino spoke, the tension in the barracks transformed to a rage that echoed the anger in the captain's voice. The whole company quivered with it.

But for all the fury under his words, Valentino spoke gently. "I'm not talking to you now as your CO. Let's face it. There ain't no Army anymore. Neither the lieutenant colonel nor I can *order* you to do anything here, any more than that *illegal* martial law committee running the show inside Cheyenne Mountain can give us orders. But I figure all of us stuck around for a reason when we could have taken our freedom and gone. We wanted our shot to handle the people who infected us without our permission, who unleashed this virus that's killed *billions of people*. Now we got a chance to see it through. Are you with us?"

The roar was deafening. Nico wanted to shout along with them. Finally, *finally* someone was going to do something to bring

McClosky and his cohorts to justice. But that sense of him being on the outside, of not being a part of the team, was stronger than ever. Why were they even allowing him to hear their plans? Didn't they still think he might act against them?

When the yelling and cheers subsided, Valentino's eyes settled on Nico. "There's someone here who knows what the picture on the ground is in Colorado Springs."

Nico froze.

"Rumor has it, you're not a big fan of McClosky and his ilk," Valentino said calmly, as if he'd never suspected Nico of being a plant or a spy. "What do you say? Want to go all in, help us take them down?"

Nico licked his lips and considered for a moment. When he pulled up images of Colorado Springs in his mind, what he saw were the intimidating, featureless masks of the armed and suited guards, whose authority over the quarantined population was as unassailable as it was terrifying. A part of him still felt that intimidation, still felt there was no hope for the people stuck in those pens against the people who kept them there.

If he helped the Jugs, he could be sending them to their deaths. Not only theirs, but possibly the deaths of the civilians in Colorado Springs. Even *Zach's*. All it would take is one wounded Jug, and it would be all over for everyone *except* the Jugs, who couldn't reproduce. Within a generation, humanity would be no more.

It was an unconscionable gamble.

So why did every part of him pulse with the need to tell them everything he knew?

Stupid question. If the Jugs scattered, he'd never see Zach again. Which he shouldn't even be contemplating doing, anyway, except— What was happening in the Clean Zone that was so bad the military government felt the need to bring the Jugs into the fray, and how was it affecting Zach? If Nico *didn't* help the Jugs, was it possible that he was leaving Zach to his own devices in a situation even worse than what they'd encountered in quarantine?

When he looked at it that way, it didn't seem to be much of a choice at all.

"I'd given up hope that anyone would ever try to bring

McClosky to justice." He pitched his voice so they could all hear, kept his attitude relaxed but intent. "But I was in quarantine most of the time I was there, so I'm not sure how much information I can give you. They didn't know until I'd been there for a couple months that I was like you."

It felt strange to say that, to claim a place among them. Even now, he couldn't call himself a Jug. Even if they hadn't suspected him, he didn't have the history they did, hadn't trained and served with them, hadn't been misled into accepting the Bane Alpha virus that would change his life and forever make him an outcast. They had an esprit de corps that only extended to him to a certain point.

And yet they were offering him that place, and he couldn't bring himself to reject it. Especially not now.

"I can speak to the conditions in quarantine, but I never saw the inside of the Clean Zone proper," Nico continued when he knew he had their attention. "I know they confiscated all our weapons when we arrived, and all our supplies, so Cheyenne Mountain has anyone who enters quarantine by the balls. I don't know how things have changed there since I left seven months ago. I suspect they've deteriorated heavily if the committee is calling in reinforcements with as much potential for disaster as we pose."

Valentino nodded. "Will you tell us what you can?" he prompted.

Nico grimaced and looked around, trying to catch as many eyes as he could.

"I'll tell you everything I know."

▲▲▲

THE JOURNEY through Tennessee and Missouri was miserable. The early spring heat wave was bad, but most of Nico's agony stemmed from knowing he might see Zach again. Maybe even touch him again. But what about the future beyond that?

Well, maybe he could lay at least one worry to rest.

He picked up his pace, moving up the column of double-timing soldiers to catch up with the member of Sierra Company he knew best. He'd be more comfortable talking to Kaleo about this, especially since he'd confided in Kaleo about Zach. But Kaleo was marching with Delta Company alongside Schuyler. They were both doing much better than they had been the day he'd first met them in the storehouse. It was obvious to anyone who saw them together how attached they were to one another. Kaleo was like a big, smitten puppy, and Schuyler regarded him with all the affection and occasional exasperation she might have shown an actual puppy.

"Hey, Marc?"

"Hmm?" he answered as Nico shouldered his way into formation next to him. The column shifted effortlessly to accommodate the change.

"Question for you. I know we can transmit the Beta strain in our blood. Does anyone know if we can transmit it in any other fluids?"

Marc gave him a sideways look, his eyebrows coming up. "You mean like, saliva or jizz?"

"Yeah."

"Why d'ya ask?"

Nico swallowed. "Well, if this works out, we're gonna be around a bunch of non-Jugs once we get to Colorado Springs, right? If someone were to get involved with one of them . . ." He let his voice trail off suggestively.

Marc snorted. "All winter, you've been turning down everyone who wants to get in your pants, and now you're thinking of boning a civvie? You got some sort of fetish?"

Nico sighed and shook his head. "Never mind. Forget I asked."

He was about to fall back when Marc said, "Talk to one of the medics. They got the full briefing. Being around civvies hasn't been an issue for us, yet, but now I suppose it's something we all ought to know."

"Right." Nico nodded. "Thanks."

That night, their progress was halted early by several roadblocks through Nashville they needed to deal with, and then a trio of revenants who'd been drawn by the noise, and later a clutch of survivors intent on killing anyone who entered what they considered to be their territory.

The Jugs looked sickened, though not as much as they had the first time they'd encountered revenants on the way out of Atlanta.

They were obviously deeply upset to see just how much destruction their lethal blood had wrought, even if they had been powerless to stop what had been done to them. Their anger and determination for a reckoning grew sharper, a little more vicious as they burned the revenant bodies. Their fury was keen enough that once they had subdued the civilians, they flat-out refused to travel any more that day and made camp.

When they were settled in for the night, Kaleo picked his way through the maze of bedrolls on the ground and plopped down next to Nico.

"Hey. Coming down okay?"

Nico blinked at him. "Coming down?"

"Our adrenal responses are all fucked up now. Part of the changes: once we go into fight or fli—well, there's really just fight for us, and then there's not one of us who's decent company for hours after." Kaleo gave a helpless shrug. "Fucking it out is a good way to let off the residual tension."

Nico laughed softly, remembering that day he and Zach had encountered the revs in the parking lot, and the bizarre, out-of-control lust that had followed. The way he'd ravished Zach against the truck in a maddened haze. "Yeah, I think I've experienced that. Good to know there's an actual reason for it."

Kaleo nodded. "Heard you were thinking of fucking a civvie," he segued gracelessly.

Nico rolled his eyes and sighed at the inevitability of gossip traveling between companies. "You know exactly who it is I'm thinking of, and why."

"Yeah, I do, which is why I took the liberty of feeling out Xolani on the subject for you."

Nico sat up a little straighter. "What did she say?"

Kaleo grinned. "That the magic ingredients to trigger the mutation from Alpha strain to Beta are air and the clotting factors of an open wound. Unless you're actually bleeding, you can't transmit Beta."

Thank you, God, Nico thought, unconcerned at the moment with his own agnosticism. "Thanks." He offered Kaleo a grateful smile. "I appreciate you asking for me."

Kaleo plucked at the grass. "Yeah, well, don't exactly thank me yet. She says Alpha isn't airborne, but no one knows if it can be transmitted in other fluids. I assume since you kissed your guy and he didn't become a Jug, that's safe, but I wouldn't recommend fucking him or letting him swallow unless he knows what he might be getting himself into."

Nico shook his head. "He doesn't want to be a Jug. I know that for sure."

"Well, then, guess now you know where to draw the line."

Nico closed his eyes after Kaleo had gone, sighing. *Not sure I'd say that, pal.*

⚠ ⚠ ⚠

THE JUGS WERE NOT PERMITTED entrance to the underground facility within Cheyenne Mountain. Those massive gates, large enough for huge trucks to pass through, remained tightly shut. Instead, they were quartered in a large hotel resort not far from the mountain.

The hotel had been emptied when the home quarantine went into effect at the first outbreak of the pandemic, so there were no dead bodies to be disposed of, and aside from dust and the musty smell of disuse, it was generally quite clean. It afforded more privacy than the dormitories in their previous prison had, as well. Apart from the fact that some of the Jugs were wearing CDC guard uniforms and patrolling the perimeter to maintain the appearance that the Jugs were under the CDC's authority and control, it almost would be easy to think that everything was normal.

No one had questioned the ruse, yet. As far as anyone was concerned, the Jugs were brainlessly following orders without the slightest qualm or hesitation. Which was exactly the way the Jugs wanted it.

The only problem now was how to actually get to the decision-makers inside the mountain.

At least, that was the only problem for the rest of the Jugs. Nico had another concern altogether. His entire being had begun pulsing with the need to find Zach the moment they had crossed the state line into Colorado. Where was he? Was he all right? Would they be able to find a way to see each other?

He tried not to sigh too loudly as he flipped in his bed in the hotel room he was sharing with Marc, who was presently snoring beside a guy from—was it Bravo Company?—named Paolo Chockly. They both came awake with a start when someone rapped softly on their hotel room door.

Apparently, Nico wasn't the only one on-edge.

Nico got up to answer, though whoever was standing outside could have just walked in. They'd had to break the latches off the hotel room doors when they'd set up their quarters, since the electronic locks no longer worked.

"Invite me in?" Captain Valentino's voice dripped seduction, and his eyes were intent on Nico's, compelling him to pick up on some unspoken message. He reached out to trail a hand up Nico's jawline and cup his face, leaning in close to breathe against Nico's ear, "Cheyenne Mountain guards at the end of the hallway. Pretend this is a social visit."

Ah. That made sense. Nico tamped down a surge of amusement and a wry comment about how his new life as a Jug was beginning to resemble his life from before the pandemic. Smiling as if the captain were a client he was focused on seducing, Nico slid his hands around either side of Valentino's waist and down to his hips, hooking his fingers through the belt loops to tug him forward. He walked backward, keeping them pressed groin-to-groin and nuzzling Valentino's neck until he kicked the door closed behind him.

He dropped back the moment he was sure they had privacy, gratified to know his skills hadn't gone entirely rusty. At least, not if the swell beneath the gray urban camouflage of the CO's fatigues was any indication.

"What's up, Captain?" Marc demanded, unconcerned with his own nudity or that of his companion as he crawled out of bed to dig through their mingled, discarded clothing.

"Chockly, I want you to get back to Bravo Company and help your CO spread the word that we're ordered to muster tomorrow at daybreak. We're gonna accompany the Clean Zone security forces inside the perimeter to confront some civvie insurgents they suspect of stealing and hoarding weapons." Marc's companion nodded briskly at the directive and began pulling on the clothing Marc had handed to him. Valentino gave him an approving look. "Try to make it look like you're playing musical beds when you spread the word. We want these fuckers thinking we're undisciplined and lazy after sitting in quarantine for almost eighteen months. Let everyone know their security forces will be wearing hermetic suits in case someone takes a shot at us. If the signal goes up, first order of business is to about-face and rip their masks off. They don't get a shot off at us without sacrificing their own, got it?"

"Got it." Nico, Marc, and Chockly all responded in unison, and Chockly left. Valentino waited in Nico and Marc's room, not quite looking like his nerves were on-edge but clearly lost in thought. For which Nico couldn't blame him. The Jugs had no time or opportunity to do recon or form a strategy. They needed to strike quickly, decisively, before anyone had a chance to suspect them, and definitely before they were forced into a confrontation that could endanger the civilian population.

Finally, after some minutes, the captain gave Marc a jerky nod. "Okay, you next. Go look like you're trolling for company and get the word out. I'm gonna keep up appearances here with Nico for a while."

Once Marc was gone, Nico leaned against the wall on the opposite side of the room from Valentino, who had his arms crossed over his chest and a frown pulling down the corners of his mouth.

"Captain, do you, um— Did they mention the names of any of the people we're going up against?"

Valentino shook his head. "We were told insurgents. Nothing more. They say these people have been getting the drop on patrols, stealing weapons and supplies, terrorizing their neighbors to keep quiet about their activities." The CO sighed. "I'd be a lot happier if we had a better picture of what's actually been going on down here."

Nico nodded in sympathy. He'd been racking his brain since they arrived, hoping to think of a way to get a message across to Zach, if he was even still— No, Zach was fine. Hopefully fine in a way that meant he was keeping his head down and he wouldn't be one of the people they were being sent up against tomorrow.

Valentino opened his mouth and drew a breath to add something else when a solid knock on the door made them both jump.

"Expecting someone?" the captain asked tersely, his hand dropping to his hip as if he was reaching for his sidearm, though no one had given them access to weapons yet. Nico shook his head, shrugging into a shirt he hadn't bothered with earlier, while Valentino slipped back into a shadowy corner behind the door.

Two people wearing hermetic suits stood in the corridor, and Nico swore he heard one of them gasp when he opened the door. Neither of them bore markings from the CDC, which meant they were from Cheyenne Mountain.

"Can I help you?" Nico asked.

Only one of the guards spoke, reaching back with a restraining hand as if to prevent the other from saying anything. "Nico? Maybe you recognize my voice? I'm Private Gillett Morris. I was one of the guards who checked you and Zach Houtman in when you arrived?"

Nico nodded cautiously. "I remember."

The guard looked both ways down the corridor, where at the ends, members of the Jugs' escort detachment were watching curiously. "We need to come in. I have orders from General McClosky to be here." Nico's back stiffened, but Morris dropped his voice as low as he could and still be heard through the mask. "*Or so your guards think.* Please."

Nico swallowed and stepped back to allow them through the door. Morris closed it carefully behind him, and the moment it was shut, the other quarantine guard with him began tearing at the latches securing the hood of his suit.

The tousled, dark-auburn hair that emerged, fringing stunning, anxious aqua eyes, drove the breath from Nico's lungs like a fist to his chest.

"Zach?"

The hood dropped to the floor with a *thunk*, and Nico's hands were grasping the sides of Zach's flushed face, fingers weaving into his sweat-damp hair. His body moved to Zach's like a magnet pulled to true north, heedless of the suit, only needing to *touch* and *kiss* and see for himself that Zach was truly there.

Hours could have passed before they broke apart if Morris hadn't interrupted them. "Zach. We need your suit. Sierra Company's CO and I are gonna brief on the situation in the Clean Zone in his room. You've got an hour."

Nico had been too focused on Zach to notice Valentino had already emerged from the corner to confront Morris, or to hear Morris's replies. But apparently Morris had told the captain something worth hearing. Valentino took Zach's suit so two suited figures entered the room and two suited figures exited. Then Zach and Nico were alone, each staring into the other's eyes in stunned disbelief that it had turned out to be so effortless for them to find each other. He wanted Zach so badly that he was almost hesitant to touch him again, too overwhelmed by the need to have all of him to even know where to begin.

"Nico—" Zach's voice fractured, and that was enough to break through the emotional and psychological deadlock that kept Nico standing back. "I didn't even know if you were still alive," he gasped between kisses. "But when Gillett came and told us the committee had called in something called Juggernaut, I'd *hoped*—"

Nico muttered something so unintelligible that not even he knew what he was saying, or meant to say. All he knew was that there were too damn many layers between his skin and Zach's, and they only had an hour. He worked to fix that problem with shaking fingers. They could talk or they could touch, and right now the answer to that particular dilemma was so self-fucking-evident it didn't bear considering.

Clothes gone with a minimum loss of contact between his mouth and Zach's, Nico got Zach on the bed beneath him and tried to glue every inch of his skin to every inch of Zach's. It was too damn much trouble to locate Marc's lube to get Zach inside him, and he didn't have to worry about Zach merely being in the presence of his semen anymore, so he urged Zach to grip his hips with his thighs and thrust against him in time to their urgent kisses. Sweat slicked their way, and grunts and moans provided a soundtrack to the frantic rutting. Zach's fingers dug into Nico's shoulders, careful to avoid even an edge of nail, until Nico wrenched his mouth from Zach's and buried his face against Zach's damp throat, shuddering and spilling, slick and hot, between their abdomens. A moment later, Zach followed suit, his cry sharp and choked off and his arms threatening to fracture Nico's ribs as they clamped around him.

"I love you. I love you. Oh God, love you so much," Zach whispered, the words a prayerful chant carried on panting breaths between kisses. Then his voice cracked, and he hid his face against Nico's shoulder. "I was so lonely without you."

Nico's eyes burned, and he rolled off Zach so that they could entwine facing each other on their sides. His blood still pulsed deafeningly in his ears, but he wiped away a tear that had rolled down Zach's temple. "I know, *cariño*. I know."

Nico could practically feel their precious, limited minutes ticking away, each one speeding by and bringing them closer to having to part. He still needed answers, as loath as he was to break the mood between them.

"Tell me what's been happening here."

Zach's arms tightened around Nico, and he shook his head as if he didn't want to speak. But eventually he raised his head and answered. Nico listened to his recitation with mounting rage. So few survivors of the pandemic, each one a precious, irreplaceable resource, and the military government was willing to risk them all by throwing the Jugs at them because they dared struggle against grift and corruption?

"More people are resisting paying the protection rackets," Zach said, winding down. "It's summer, so food isn't going to be quite as scarce. We've tripled the size of the community and yard gardens, and half the people in the Clean Zone are doing a crash course in food preservation. But we lost a lot of people to malnutrition over the winter, especially those who were already weakened by other illnesses."

Nico swallowed against the clench of fear in his chest. "How active are you with the, um, resistance?"

Zach's silence was its own terrifying answer. "I had to do *something*. I've stopped working in the clinic with Chantal because I don't want to compromise her neutrality, but after I saw Traverse try to *murder* Gillett . . ." He shrugged helplessly.

"I understand." Nico forced a smile, though he desperately

wanted to tell Zach to get his head down and keep it down. "How did you end up here? I mean, why did you and Morris come?"

"We took a gamble." Zach laced his fingers with Nico's, leaning his forehead on Nico's shoulder. "Gillett's position is still secure. He's been trying to feed us as much information as he can on the activities of the corrupt guards and what, if anything, the military government is doing about it. The answer is not a damn thing. Honestly, they seem to think their responsibilities begin and end with making sure no one who's infected gets through the perimeter, and overseeing the ration deliveries. And even that . . ." He heaved a troubled sigh. "I don't know if they're so much corrupt as they are clueless, or maybe guilty of a criminal level of self-interest. They're prioritizing the remaining government and military personnel for rations and medical supplies under the theory that they can't protect us if they're too sick or starved to function. It doesn't seem to register with them that we're not going to be able to build the population back up and carry on with reconstruction if people can't carry pregnancies to term or aren't healthy enough to work in the gardens. I don't think they realize the corruption of the gangs and the guards that protect them has become so widespread."

Nico nodded. "Okay. But that still doesn't explain why you came to see us."

"Gillett was promoted this year. He oversees a security patrol squadron now, so he's included in briefings. After the recent riots, they were told that the military government was bringing in reinforcements from Atlanta, a special ops battalion called Juggernaut. Gillett didn't know what it meant, but I did. I knew we were in trouble if people ended up fighting the Juggernaut soldiers, especially if they managed to wound one. So Gillett and I came here hoping to talk to the commanding officers and explain what really has been going on inside the Clean Zone." He gave a troubled grimace. "I don't know if it will make a difference, but if we could just keep them from hurting anyone or being put in a situation where one of them might be wounded around the civilian population—"

"Don't worry. The Jugs never had any intention of fighting the civilian population." Nico smiled tightly as Zach's head came up, his eyes widening. "I can't speak for what Valentino's going to tell Morris, but I suspect what he'll encourage is for you to spread the word for the civilians to keep their heads down and stay out of the way while we take care of the security forces and then move on the military government."

"The government?"

Nico nodded. "This doesn't go beyond you and me, but there's going to be an overthrow here. The martial law decree was never legal. The committee has no legitimate authority. There's no way the Jugs are letting the people who did this to them—to everyone—stay in power. Billions of people have died. Someone is going to answer for it, and a new constitution and civilian government needs to be formed. No military dictatorships, especially not by this military." He sat up and gave Zach a fierce look. "I mean it when I say to stay out of the way, Zach. You know what can happen if any of us is wounded. If there's another outbreak of the Beta strain—"

Zach's face was pinched, and his eyes shone wetly, but he nodded. "I know. I don't know how I'm supposed to just hole up somewhere while you're out there fighting or dying, but I'll do what I can to keep everyone else safe."

27

REVOLUTION

Zach missed working for the clinic. He stood outside it for the first time in months, not nearly as concerned with the wrong person seeing him and deciding the clinic was no longer a neutral entity as he was with disseminating his message as quickly as possible.

Inside, the building was packed. The privacy curtains were pulled aside, people seated on the examination tables and standing shoulder to shoulder with barely enough room to move. Chantal had arranged for them to be here, to hear what Zach had to say. Gillett stood beside him, and Mike, Adam, and Karla were in the front of the crowd, nearly vibrating with tension.

When Gillett held up a hand, they all fell silent. Some of them were still suspicious of him, but they trusted Zach, Mike, and Adam, who all vouched for Gillett.

"We have confirmation that the government has, indeed, called in reinforcements," he announced without preamble. "The soldiers they've brought in were being housed in Atlanta, known as the Juggernaut Battalion. I'm going to turn this over to Zach because he's the closest thing we have to an expert on what this means."

"Thanks, Gillett." Zach drew a deep breath and wiped beads of sweat from his upper lip. "I'm going to say to you what the person who told this to me said: This may all sound a little far-fetched. It may be hard to believe, but you know me. I've worked for you, tried to help you, and I swear to you now, on my own soul, that it's true to the best of my knowledge. It's absolutely critical for you to follow the instructions we're going to give you at the end of this meeting and to make sure all your neighbors do the same."

Consternation furrowed the brows of the men and women listening. Zach wasn't looking forward to the panic that was sure to follow.

"Two years ago, the United States armed forces were facing a recruitment crisis and an untenable personnel shortage on the ground in Russia. Their solution was to make their existing troops more effective, so they infected a battalion of soldiers with the Alpha strain of an experimental virus known as Bane."

A furor followed that announcement. People recognized the name of the virus; how it had become common knowledge, Zach wasn't sure. No doubt some word of it had spread on the hacked feeds during the in-house quarantine before everyone had started dying.

"That doesn't make sense!" someone shouted. "Why would they kill their own troops?"

Someone else called, "How do you know this? Where are you getting your information?"

Zach held up his hands until they all fell silent again. He proceeded to explain the different strains of the Bane virus, what their intended purposes had been, and how an unforeseen anomaly had led to billions of deaths.

The entire room erupted at that. Zach bowed his head, not acknowledging any of the questions that flew at him. Despite all the days and nights he and Nico had spent talking about what McClosky had told Nico about the virus, he was by no means an expert, and many of the questions—such as a demand to know how the mutation had occurred—required answers even McClosky had been unable to provide.

"Please!" Chantal had to yell to be heard over the uproar. "People, we don't have much time. We need to let Zach finish!"

Eventually, they calmed enough for him to continue. "I don't know the science behind what happened. All I know is what I've been told, what I've seen with my own eyes. The Alpha strain of the virus makes the Juggernaut Battalion immune to the fatal strains, but when an infected soldier bleeds, the virus becomes airborne and deadly. That's all I know. And really, that's beside the point. The only reason I told you this much is because I need you to understand the reasoning behind what we have to do."

The crowd grew even quieter with that, an expectant quiet. Zach closed his eyes and said a silent prayer in the space of time it took to blink, then opened them again.

"Like Gillett said, the Juggernaut Battalion has been called in to reinforce Clean Zone security. That would be very bad news for us, because even if they weren't stronger and faster than anything we can hope to match—and I've seen that personally, there is absolutely *no question* about their abilities—we couldn't fight back against them. We couldn't risk wounding them and infecting ourselves with the Rot. We'd be helpless."

They all sobered at that. They'd been so caught up in trying to understand the implications of all Zach was telling them that they'd forgotten what it might mean for their resistance. Nor had it occurred to them that the military government would risk exterminating them all by means of another outbreak of the Beta strain just to put down that resistance.

"But, here's the good news. The Jugs—as they call themselves—are no more pleased with the military who did this to them than we are. They won't risk killing the remaining uninfected population. And tomorrow, when they are sent into the Clean Zone to start 'ensuring the peace,' the Clean Zone security forces are going to find themselves facing something a hell of a lot more dangerous than a mob of barely armed and untrained civilians."

Savage, triumphant cheers concussed Zach's eardrums, making his head ache, but he answered them with his own victorious grin. Nico was back, and he had brought along salvation for them all and freedom from a corrupt and uncaring regime.

"What can we do to help?" Chantal asked, speaking loudly enough to be heard over the whooping and yelling. Everyone fell silent again, looking at Zach.

"Well, that's the bad news." He grimaced. "The most important thing for us to do right now is *stay out of the way.* It's too dangerous for us to be near the fighting. If the security forces wound any of the Jugs, we need to make sure we're nowhere near them. I know, I know!" He held up his hands again as protests started swelling. "It goes against the grain. We've fought against the gangs and the corrupt guards for months, and now the Jugs expect us to sit back and let them take over? It's not right. But it's our *only* choice. Of course we want to see this through to the end, but think about what's at stake. There are so few of us left. Will we really risk another outbreak after we've all survived this long? We have homes, families, *children.* Will we endanger them?"

He let them process that a moment, then continued gently, "Here's what the Jugs have asked us to do. Once the military government is deposed, we need to reinstate order as quickly as we can. We need a new civilian authority ready to step up with a new constitution ready to enforce. So while they're fighting and putting themselves on the line for us, we'll also be working. We'll be fielding nominations for a Clean Zone Congress to be elected as soon as we can take a vote. We'll be drafting a constitution so it's ready to be ratified the moment Congress is sworn in. We'll be laying plans for a more humane quarantine and rationing process, and coming up with ways to increase our food production and stores until no one is reliant on rations from a central depot any longer."

Zach looked around the room, trying to make eye contact with as many people as he could. Sober gazes full of worry, yes, but also purpose. "What was done to the Jugs was against their will. They didn't know what they were being given when they were infected with the Bane Alpha virus. And now their lives have been irrevocably altered. They can't have children, can't have normal lives, but they're willing to fight for us anyway. And this is all they've asked in return. So, can we do it? Can we give them that?"

⚠ ⚠ ⚠

THE WEIGHT of a weapon on Nico's back after so long without one was heavy, but not nearly as heavy as the knowledge that the military government was sending them armed to the teeth against civilians.

His one consolation was that it didn't appear to be an outright bid at genocide. Assuming things went the way the committee envisioned —which, of course, they wouldn't, but the committee didn't know that—the Jugs were commanded to apprehend anyone who resisted and ensure none of the insurgents returned to the uninfected population.

But accidents happened, and the appalling thing was that the committee clearly understood this, because the Jugs would be walking into the Clean Zone alongside security forces protected by hermetic suits. His own barely tamped outrage was reflected on the faces of the other Jugs. The callous disregard for the lives of the insurgents—and the risk to the public—cemented their determination to protect the people from the corruption of the Cheyenne Mountain Martial Law Committee.

The suburb enclosed by the Clean Zone perimeter was miles from Cheyenne Mountain. Nico supposed it said something that the military government had opted to set itself up somewhere that was virtually unreachable. No one knew who exactly was on the committee, or how decisions were being made, or what the command structure was inside the mountain. They were all being governed and commanded by an unseen, untouchable entity, and once the Jugs had secured the Clean Zone, changing that state of affairs would be the next order of business.

Even if it meant laying siege to the underground complex until they starved the military government out.

The streets were quiet and empty when the security patrols opened the checkpoint gates to let the combined ground forces through. No one was working in the yards or gardens. The Jugs had been expecting this, but the suited security forces had not. They all clutched their weapons nervously, too disconcerted by the silence and lack of resistance to pay much attention to the Jugs.

It was so subtle as to be unnoticeable, the way the Jugs slowly and steadily shifted their formation and placement so that they separated and surrounded each squadron of Clean Zone security forces. The numbers disparity was a fucking joke. There were nearly two thousand Jugs and only a few hundred Clean Zone troops. Nico watched the gradual rearranging of their forces until the Clean Zone perimeter gates closed behind them. That was their signal to take action. The Jugs moved with a speed and concert that Nico, even possessing the same abilities, marveled at. They each reached for the mask or hood of the suited guard nearest them and ripped it off.

It took seconds. Mere seconds for the noise of the hermetic suits being carelessly torn open to shift to startled shouts followed by the sound of safeties being released. Nico saw his own Sierra Company comrades pounce on the guards nearest them, and beyond that, Delta Company. The sun caught Schuyler's titian hair and made it blaze like polished copper, and her face was pure, savage fury as she wrestled a hoodless guard to his knees.

Then came the frantic bellows.

"Don't shoot! Don't shoot!"

Only one shot was fired, and it was—gratefully—discharged from an assault rifle that was knocked aside by a Jug so the round didn't hit anyone. None of the guards realized that at first, however. They heard the shot and screamed in panic. Some began sobbing.

"Oh God. God, please, no!"

"Put down your weapons!" the Jugs yelled at the few security forces who had managed to escape the initial onslaught and who stood several feet off, their guns trained on the Jugs. They all quivered with hesitation, however, as they took inventory of their captured, defenseless comrades. When the Jugs barked, "Drop 'em!" the guards obeyed and put up their hands.

"Echo, go!" At the order, the one company of Jugs who had held back from the initial assault burst into action, sprinting along the street they'd originally marched up. The guards at the checkpoint were unsuited; their only job was to wave the patrols through the gate and close it behind them. It was no contest. They stood by helplessly as Echo Company ripped the gate down and herded them out of the booths to join their comrades kneeling on the pavement.

Unfortunately, there was no way the checkpoint guards hadn't radioed the initial assault in to command inside Cheyenne Mountain. Which meant that by the time the Jugs got to the entrance of the underground facility, it would be sealed tight. Now they'd be dealing with a siege.

Nico's attention was pulled from the spectacle by Valentino's voice. "Nico! Go find Morris and check in with the resistance, then begin flushing out the gangs they told us about."

Since Nico had a "personal contact" within the resistance, he'd been earmarked to act as the Jugs' liaison, a job he was only too glad to embrace. Concerned that the civilians might be wary of the Jugs, each company had assigned one or two of their most charismatic and easygoing people as envoys to work with the civilians on hunting down the gangs. They would incarcerate the culprits—along with the guards who had aided and abetted them—pending trial once the civilian government was established.

Following that first bloodless attack in which the Jugs crippled the security forces, a strange lull took over the Clean Zone, at least with regards to the fighting. Companies of Jugs rotated a 24-7 watch outside the gates to the bunker under the mountain, while in the Clean Zone, a hastily pulled-together interim Congress started composing a constitution. Getting the Clean Zone back under civilian authority was priority one, even beyond the siege at the mountain.

In all other ways, the Clean Zone was more active than ever. The Jugs assumed responsibility for tending to the detainees in quarantine since there was no danger of them being infected. Seeing human faces instead of featureless masks went a long way toward pacifying the people in the pens. Food stores weren't an issue yet, either, as the Jugs had brought their own provisions. Hopefully by the time they ran low, the harvest would be coming in. To supplement, they scavenged every grocery store, pantry, wild field, and orchard the military hadn't yet managed to pick through all the way up to Denver.

The addition of the Jugs nearly doubled the Clean Zone population, but productivity increased exponentially. They demolished contaminated properties, raided lumberyards, and helped build new housing, moving in people who'd been in quarantine sometimes for months past their mandatory three-month stint.

As far as Nico was concerned, those assholes inside the mountain could never come out and he'd be perfectly happy. Because at the end of the day, after helping to get the Clean Zone's shit straightened out, he got to go home to Zach. It was hard to remember, spending night after night wrapped up together, that all the reasons why he'd walked away from Zach in the first place still applied. They were the same reasons why the Jugs didn't work side by side with the civilians. The Jugs set up their own district just outside the Clean Zone, and their own work crews, but their goal was the same.

At least until it came to drafting the Clean Zone Constitution.

"What the fuck is this?" Nico demanded as he sat in bed beside Zach, reading the latest draft the Congressional Committee had sent for him to take to the Jugs. "Mandatory segregation? Permits to enter unapproved areas? What, because we're not already being careful to segregate ourselves? Special penalties for anyone using their abilities as a Jug to 'intimidate, harass, or otherwise disrupt' the rule of law within the Clean Zone?"

Zach groaned. "I know. I'm sure Chantal's been trying to talk the rest of the committee down from those items. After all the Jugs have done to help us—"

"*Help* you? Like we're not a part of this? What, it's not our lives too? We're not citizens unlawfully detained under an illegal military regime, same as everyone else in the Clean Zone? We're different, right? Fucking typical." He snorted and flung himself out of bed, beginning to pace.

"Nico, please." Zach held out a hand. "You know I don't feel that way, and Chantal wouldn't, either. Their rationale is that they're afraid that the Jugs' physical superiority might cause them to resist arrest if they happen to break any laws, or to intimidate voters during elections."

Nico covered his face with his hands, a short, humorless chuff of pitiful laughter escaping his lungs. "Right. Sure, they're afraid of that. Same bullshit, different century."

"What's that mean?"

"You don't see it, do you?" He dropped his hands, fixing Zach with a stare. "Of course you don't. Zach, this whole fucking thing is going to spin into a referendum on race relations if someone doesn't make those assholes see what they're actually proposing."

Nico watched Zach do a mental inventory of the civilians and the Jugs, and then he groaned. "Oh God, how did I not see that before? It makes way too much sense."

"You're damn right it does. The survivors who have been making their way to the Clean Zone are the people who had their own houses, who were well-off enough not to have to live packed together in apartments. They had enough money to have food supplies and fuel cells stashed away to hold them over until the first wave of the pandemic had passed." Nico shook his head, resuming his pacing. "The people who died in the pandemic were the poor, the people crowded together in the cities, many of them brown or black or indigenous. Except for the Jugs, because the military was one of the best ways to avoid unemployment or the tenements. And now those white 'survivors' are afraid we're going to break their laws and fuck up their elections. And we sure as hell can't mingle in their neighborhoods. Jesus."

Zach hung his head. "Do you honestly think they mean it that way?"

The question speared Nico with something that felt almost like betrayal. He couldn't blame Zach for his upbringing and the resulting naïveté, but sometimes it was easy to forget that, as sweet and well-intentioned as Zach was, he had the luxury to be obtuse, and Nico didn't.

"Do you honestly think they *don't?*" He stared hard at the top of Zach's head until Zach finally looked up again. "Not that a single one of them will admit to it. Hell, I'll even be generous enough to concede that a lot of them don't realize what they're doing. But when it comes down to it, we're dancing to a centuries-old tune here. The fact that we're Jugs—and therefore, yes, there *is* a real reason to be afraid of us—just gives a veneer of legitimacy to prejudices that were in place long before the pandemic."

"I'm sorry, Nico." Zach began gathering the pages of the constitution Nico had flung aside. "I'll take this back and tell them there's no way the Jugs will ratify it."

Nico caught the sheath of papers. "No. Leave it. I want the Jugs to know what we're dealing with. And for my own part, I'm going to recommend we assign a delegate to the committee."

Zach's crestfallen face reflected just how much hope of success he thought that proposal would meet. He bowed his head again. "I'm sorry," he repeated.

"You're not the one who did it." Nico sighed and set the papers on top of the dresser, returning to bed to crawl across the sheets and straddle Zach. "I need you and Chantal to remind these people that we're Clean Zone citizens too. We're making our homes here. This is going to be *our* constitution as much as theirs."

"I won't let them forget." Zach moaned softly as Nico's weight settled on top of him, his mouth parting. The taste of his yielding was heady, and not for the first time, Nico regretted the circumstances that prevented him from ever knowing what it would feel like to be buried within Zach. If they could trust condoms, it would be another story, but after several seasons on dusty shelves, exposed to the extremes of winter and summer without any climate control, they couldn't risk it. Even though the Beta mutation didn't occur in the course of sexual contact, Kaleo's words of caution about whether or not he could infect Zach with the Alpha strain were always with him. Nico had offered to try to infect Zach with Alpha—if it was even possible, which most people seemed to think unlikely—after they'd reunited, but Zach had refused, and since he'd disposed of the ampule, that was the end of that.

But that pang of regret was short-lived as Zach's hand slid between Nico's straddling thighs, cupping and stroking his increasingly heavy cock through his fatigues. When Zach's fingers did *that* —oh God, yes, and *that*—he could forget all about the constitution. And the endless wait for the remaining personnel in Cheyenne Mountain to surrender. And his worries for his own future and that of the other Jugs here in the Clean Zone. He had Zach, and they had a home, and everything else was negotiable as long as they could keep touching each other, coming together at the end of the day.

28

STALEMATE

Now that they no longer had to worry about the gangs, Zach happily returned to working in the clinic. He was updating files from some scribbled notes when Chantal trudged through the door, her mouth pulled into a grimace.

"What happened?" She didn't make that face without damn good reason.

She shook her head. "Just got back from watching the civilian police interview that man who they detained trying to grab that girl last week. He says he wanted to force her to be his common-law wife. He's a rapist, all right, but he doesn't match the description we've gotten from the serial rapist victims. We're still not any closer to finding the guy."

"Did you seriously expect it to be him?" Zach's eyebrows shot up. From the moment they'd heard of the case out of the south quadrant, he'd doubted it had anything to do with the young men—and occasionally women—who had been brutalized in all the quadrants.

"Not really, but that's not what's bothering me." She hopped up onto the edge of the desk, facing him with her legs swinging restlessly. "There haven't been any more attacks by the serial rapist since the Jugs came."

"Yeah?" Zach almost tacked on the question, *What about it?*

when her meaning dawned on him. "You think it's someone inside the mountain."

Chantal nodded. "I do. The only other explanation is that it's one of the military guards the Jugs detained on accusations of corruption, but the description we've got is of someone closer to middle age than any of them are. And none of the victims indicated that the guy acted like a soldier."

"So it's someone fairly highly placed." He shuddered. "That's a grim thought."

"I could be wrong." Chantal ran a fingertip along the edge of the desk. "It could be that whoever it was just went to ground when security in the Clean Zone became less corrupt."

"Not sure if that's more or less encouraging. If that's the case, we may never flush him out."

"Not until he attacks again."

"What if he doesn't?"

Chantal made a face. "I'm not an expert, but don't these guys always go back for more, sooner or later?"

Zach tossed his pencil on the desk in disgust. "So now we're left hoping he'll victimize another person. Great."

"*Not* hoping." She slid off the desk and squeezed his shoulder. "Go on home. I'll finish the paperwork. And let the Jugs know the committee will have another draft for them by the end of the week."

"Any progress on getting them to accept a Jug delegate to the committee?"

Her eyes slid away from his, and her mouth tightened again. "It's being considered."

⋀ ⋀ ⋀

"This is *bullshit!*" Schuyler threw the papers down on the table of the apartment she and Kaleo shared in the Delta Company housing, glaring at Nico as though this were all his fault. Admittedly, he had been the one to drag her into it. He nominated Schuyler—who came from a long line of politicians and, as such, had studied political science before a falling-out with her family had driven her to enlist in the Army on a rash, rebellious impulse—to be the Jugs' delegate to the Congressional Committee. Which was why he was bringing her the latest drafts of the constitution while they debated whether or not to allow her in.

"I know it is," Nico said, his hands up in a mean-no-harm gesture. "Zach says Morris has resigned from the committee in protest. He says he's surprised Chantal hasn't done the same."

"So not only am I *not* allowed to act as our delegate to the committee—" she flipped the papers over again and skimmed them as if she might have missed something "—but they've added tighter restrictions on which parts of the Clean Zone Jugs with uteri are allowed access to? Are they fucking *serious*? Is this the Middle Ages? We already *know* we have to stay away from the civvies when we're menstruating!"

"Chantal told Zach it's because they're afraid you might start bleeding unexpectedly due to irregular cycles."

"I will fucking *give* them something to be afraid of and it won't have a goddamn thing to do with my *period*!" Her face was redder than her hair, her eyes snapping with fury. "Because I haven't lost enough to this motherfucking virus, now I'm going to be treated like a leper?"

Even good-natured Kaleo looked pissed off. "That takes some gall. We're eighty percent of the Clean Zone's productivity. We're good enough to help build their houses and dig their perimeter trench and hunt down the revs in a hundred-mile radius, but we can't have a say in the constitution?"

"I'm sorry," Nico murmured. "I don't know what to do. I wish I did. Zach's afraid they're going to start putting restrictions on fraternizing between the Jugs and the uninfected population. He's worried that if he speaks up any more, it's going to draw their attention to the fact that he's around us every day."

"You think they don't already know that? The moment they don't need you two as a conduit for communications anymore, they will shut that shit down." Kaleo sneered and began pacing. "I'm starting to think Charlie Company is right. We need to just get the fuck out of here, go start our own settlement. These assholes can just deal with being under military rule."

"*No!*" Schuyler whirled on him. "Not until the fuckers who did this to us answer for it. I want that bastard McClosky out of the mountain and in front of a firing squad." Her mouth twisted, like she was about to say something more, but then her shoulders dropped and she turned away, stalking toward the door. "*Then* I'll walk away, if they still can't treat me like I belong here, but not a moment before."

‹‹‹

BY THE TIME summer had passed, the Clean Zone had been transformed. A perimeter trench had been dug and seeded with razor wire and metal and wood spikes to keep revenants and potentially infected newcomers out. Adequate housing had been built, the agriculture and animal husbandry operations were in full production, ensuring everyone would have enough to eat come winter. Deaths due to illness, accident, and suicide were far fewer than before. And most importantly, live births were beginning to outnumber deaths for the first time since the pandemic.

Quarantine had become a more humane—though not necessarily pleasant or easy—process that was far less likely to kill the detainees than it once had. The quarantine zone was set up on the perimeter of the Clean Zone, with another trench circumscribing it. And beyond that was the neighborhood the Jugs had commandeered. Only Zach, Nico, and a handful of other Jugs ever passed along the causeway into the Clean Zone itself, and then only when absolutely necessary.

The Jugs still did what they could to make the Clean Zone habitable while they waited for the committee to surrender. What else were they going to do? Sit by and do nothing while the civilians struggled for survival? But it was with an undercurrent of resentment now. All progress on the constitution had halted because the Jugs flatly refused to ratify the document until it treated them as full citizens with equal rights.

Zach lived with Nico near the Jug housing, far enough away to be safe if one of their neighbors happened to be bleeding. He found and refurbished a bicycle too, because the walk was so long. The clinic was thriving, and Chantal now had two other assistants. If not for the contention over the constitution, he might have called the situation perfect. Until a new patient, just out of quarantine, arrived at the clinic.

"Not you," the father of the developmentally disabled preteen said, reaching out as if he was going to grab Zach to prevent him from helping the boy to the examination cubicle. "They told me about you. You're the one that lives with those infected soldiers. I'd like someone else to help us, thanks."

Zach blinked slowly, biting his tongue on the heated retort that sprang to his lips. He made himself smile reassuringly. "I appreciate your concern, sir, but I assure you, there's no danger. My husband would never risk infecting me." It didn't matter to Zach that they had never filed any papers or made any formal declarations of intent. He knew what Nico was to him.

The man regarded him flatly. "So you say, but I'm not taking any chances. Get someone else over here to help us."

"Sir . . ." Zach bowed his head and drew two long breaths before continuing. "I understand that you just got out of quarantine. It must be strange to be around people again. Maybe it leaves you feeling a little exposed and insecure. But we're all God's children, including the Jugs, and we're all citizens of the Clean Zone. We have to learn to live together and trust one another. If—"

"Zach, can I have your help back here a moment?" Chantal interrupted, stepping out of one of the exam rooms. "Mandy, take over for Zach?"

Frowning at the interruption, he nodded and left the patient and his father behind, following Chantal to the break room in the far rear of the clinic.

"Zach, as much as I know it hurts you to hear it, that man isn't wrong," she said, pitching her voice low. "I think it might be time for you to find some other place to work, away from the public. I don't want people refusing medical treatment because you're here."

For a moment it felt like she had punched him in the chest, his lungs burning with the need for oxygen as he gaped at her. "What? Chantal, are you *serious*?" He ran a strangely numb hand down his mouth, fingers scraping along the bristle on his jaw but not really feeling it. "You— You're a *doctor*. You've been working on the constitution, trying to get the committee to remove the discriminatory clauses against the Jugs."

"*No*, Zach. I support those clauses. I helped draft some of them. You thought I would try to have them removed because that's what *you* wanted, but it's my duty as a physician to be on guard against public health hazards. You assumed I felt the way you did, but I *don't*." She sighed, looking—of all things—frustrated with him. "I've been trying to tell you for months. You can't keep living with the Jugs and working here. You're putting us all at risk."

"I can't believe this. After everything they've done here—"

She folded her arms over her chest, squirming. "I don't dislike the Jugs. God knows they helped us when we needed them, and the Clean Zone is a much more stable and sustainable place thanks to them. But they are *dangerous*. It may not be their fault, but it's still because of them that billions of people have died. We've been telling you this all along, but *you won't listen*."

"*We?*"

"All your friends. Mike, Adam, Karla, me. About the only one who will be near you is Morris." Now she had the audacity to sneer. "Not that you'd notice, since you never make time to be here with us unless you're working."

"Oh, so now I'm, what? A *traitor* because in the evenings I want to go home to the man I love? *You* were the one who said I should be the liaison!"

Damn her for daring to act like she was being the reasonable one. She put on her best I'm-dealing-with-an-irrational-patient expression and asked softly, "Did Nico shave this morning?"

"What?"

"Just answer the question. Did Nico shave this morning?"

"Yes, of course he did."

"Were you there with him?"

Zach growled. "*Yes*, I was. We always get ready together in the morning. But he didn't cut—"

"What if he had?" Chantal stared at him without blinking.

"He *didn't*."

"But *what if he had*?" When Zach refused to answer, she prodded more insistently. "Zach? What if he had cut himself?"

"Fine. Then I'd be exposed, and there's no way I would have come into the Clean Zone today."

The mental image of that happening was like something out of a nightmare. The utter *devastation* Nico would feel if he accidentally infected Zach with the Beta strain. It was almost enough to make Zach regret discarding the ampule of the Alpha strain. Zach supposed it said something that he was less concerned for his own safety than he was for what it would do to Nico if that situation ever arose.

"How do *I* know that?" Chantal persisted, her arms still folded stubbornly across her chest while Zach was the one pacing and gesticulating. "How do I know you wouldn't still come into work?"

"Oh, good Lord, Chantal! *Because you know me!*"

"True. But I don't know Nico."

"What's that supposed to mean?"

"Are you absolutely certain he didn't cut himself this morning?" She lifted one eyebrow. "Maybe just a nick, when you weren't watching. Something he covered up?"

"He wouldn't do that. He knows the dangers better than anyone. All the Jugs do. Why do you think they've formed their own enclave *outside* the Clean Zone?"

Chantal shrugged. "People panic and make horrible decisions. Sometimes because they want to deny—maybe even can't accept—that there's a problem."

"Nico wouldn't do that."

"So you say, but am I supposed to risk my life on that? The lives of my patients?" Finally, she dropped her arms, and now she looked angry, and it awoke a similar fury in Zach because *how dare she?* "Nico has an accident, he can't make himself face the fact that he's killed you, so he hides it. Doesn't let you or anyone else know, and then all of us are dead. Just like that."

Zach gaped. "That is the most far-fetched, irrational piece of *bullshit* I've ever heard. I can't believe you're saying this."

"I admire your loyalty, Zach, but the fact is, they're *not human.* Not anymore."

He stared at her, horrified. "Chantal—"

Her eyes were sympathetic but merciless. "You need to decide where you belong, Zach." She turned away, stopping at the break-room door to speak over her shoulder. "Go out the back exit, away from the patients, please. And good luck, whatever you choose."

∧ ∧ ∧

NICO HAD awoken knowing in his gut something would happen that day. There was a charge in the air, leaving his skin prickling. He was antsy and distracted as he got dressed, had barely focused enough to kiss Zach good-bye, and had spent the day helping to clear a new field. New survivors were still trickling into the Clean Zone, and it wasn't likely that this year's production capacity was going to be sufficient for the number of survivors who would arrive next year.

Kaleo wasn't wrong. They had become the labor force for the jobs the civilians didn't have the physical strength to do. What else were they supposed to do? Leave the Clean Zone unlivable, sit around all day doing nothing? The Jugs lived here and needed those crops and supplies even more than the civilians did, and it made horrible sense for the Jugs to do the heavy labor that once could have been done by machines. They had the strength and endurance for it, and the civilians would only accomplish a fraction of the work in much more time. And they couldn't do only enough to take care of themselves and leave the civilians to starve; that would be tanta-mount to genocide. The civilians were the only people who could reproduce, who had any hope of ensuring the continuation of humanity.

So in that way, it was at least voluntary labor, but the dynamics of the whole situation were incredibly uncomfortable. Especially knowing now that they weren't going to get equal representation in any government the Clean Zone formed.

Nico's head came up when he realized the people around him had stopped working, their attention drawn to a commotion at the far end of the parking lot. He dropped his pickax and stripped off his gloves as he jogged over, finding a sweating Kaleo in the crowd.

"They're surrendering," Kaleo explained excitedly, catching him up on the news the messenger from Delta Company had reported.

"They sent a message out from Cheyenne Mountain today, asking for a list of demands from the civilian government. Foxtrot's going to deliver it when they relieve Bravo."

Cheers broke out, incredible whoops and shouts of triumph as the Jugs jumped and embraced and clapped one another on the backs. Nico laughed when a woman he didn't even know from Echo Company jumped up and wrapped her arms and legs around him in celebration, before he eased her down to her feet.

The messenger held up his hands to get their attention again. "We're all ordered to return to our housing. We'll be forming up outside NORAD to take custody of the prisoners when they open the gates to surrender."

Nico wanted nothing more than to go find Zach and celebrate. There was no way the Jugs were going to relent on the siege unless the military government handed over McClosky and any other high-ranking personnel involved in the implementation of Project Juggernaut. They would finally see justice for what had been done to them and for all the deaths that had followed.

The walk back to their apartment complex was a long one, though Nico took it at a jog. He would need to shower anyway while they waited for the order to join Foxtrot outside the mountain. Nico took his time bathing, stroking his dick leisurely as he imagined what he'd do when Zach got home from working at the clinic.

This was it. It was almost over. The waiting would be done, and after over a year of being in limbo, they could settle into whatever would pass for "normal" lives in the postpandemic world.

In his mind, he was spread out on the bed, in the process of being screwed into the mattress by Zach, when the building caved in on him.

29

DIASPORA

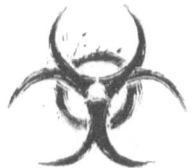

The first explosion shocked Zach out of his moping as he pedaled along the perimeter security causeway, past the quarantine zone, to the neighborhood the Jugs had claimed. He'd been staring at the road, watching it blur beneath his wheels, and he hadn't even noticed anything amiss until the explosion, which was answered by the sound of assault rifle fire, then followed by another boom.

Nico!

He pedaled faster, rushing toward home, rushing toward his husband. He stopped, though, when he heard the rumbling engine of a tank, when he saw its turret turn and take aim at the apartment building that housed Echo Company. Sierra Company's housing was farther up the road; he couldn't see it from where he'd stopped. All he could see were Jugs pouring out of the other intact buildings to confront suited soldiers who followed the tank, taking shelter behind anything they could as they tried to stop the Jugs' advance before they reached contamination range.

The need to get to the Sierra building and find Nico warred against the voice that cautioned him from stupidly running into a combat zone with bullets and mortars still flying, not to mention potentially wounded Jugs on the ground. He took shelter in an empty storefront, watching through the dusty windows as half the

Jugs charged the tank and the other half went after the soldiers on foot.

It wasn't a contest. Zach wasn't sure why the soldiers even tried. No doubt they were obeying some command from on high, ordering them to commit suicide as long as they took some of the Jugs with them.

This time, Zach noted, the Jugs didn't go after the masks of the attacking soldiers right away. Even now, under fire, they didn't want to infect anyone if they could avoid it, and there were Jugs bleeding everywhere. They disarmed the soldiers instead and used them as shields, threatening to tear their masks off if their comrades didn't lay down their arms. Another apartment building—Charlie Company's—was reduced to rubble before a squadron of Jugs got the hatch on the tank open and started dismantling the turret.

The firefight stopped, leaving behind a heavy haze of dust and smoke and gunpowder fumes that clouded the streets. Zach couldn't see very far, but he heard the shouts of the Jugs demanding the soldiers' surrender, and finally left his hiding place with his hands up in case anyone noticed him and questioned his presence. Even now, after months of living alongside them, he only knew the Jugs from Sierra Company and Nico's friend Kaleo from Delta Company.

He located his abandoned bike and rode back the way he'd come, circumventing the combat area to take the long way around to the opposite side of the apartment complex where Sierra Company was housed. When he got there, his heart stopped beating.

Another tank had been stopped and torn apart by Jugs, but Sierra Company's building was a pile of rubble, and some of it had fallen on the house next door that Zach and Nico shared. Jugs were digging through the debris, and all thought of his own survival fled as he dropped his bike and sprinted toward them.

"Nico!"

"*No*! Zach! Oh God! Keep him *away*!" The shriek was pained, like the cry of a panicked, wounded animal. Zach spotted a cluster of Jugs working on a thrashing man on the outskirts of the ruined building, trying to hold him down. Some of them had blood on their clothing.

A huge Jug grabbed Zach, preventing him from going any closer. He was too far away to see Nico's face, but he could hear those frantic screams, sobbing cries to get Zach out of there.

"You can't go near him," yelled a familiar voice, and Zach realized the Jug had to yell because Zach himself was shouting, arguing, trying to tell Nico it was all right.

Zach fell silent and turned to see Kaleo holding him back. He was covered in dust but not blood, his brown skin gray with streaks of grit and sweat. The sight of him was reassuring enough that Zach calmed.

"Do you know how badly he's hurt?"

"Compound fracture in his left leg," Kaleo said. His cheerful smile was long, long gone, his mouth pulled into a grim line. "The medics are trying to check him over for internal injuries, but if he's got any, he's going to hurt himself worse freaking out about you. Get the fuck out of here. Get to the Clean Zone where it's safe."

"I can't." Zach shook his head, swaying with relief and glad that Kaleo was still holding him upright. "I think I managed to avoid going near anyone who was bleeding, but I should probably go to quarantine. Just in case."

"Fine. We'll deal with that later. We're taking the wounded to Tango's quarters. Bravo should be safe. Get over there, tell them I sent you, and stay there, out of the way where no one is bleeding, until I come for you."

Zach nodded, taking a moment to pull himself together before he shrugged off Kaleo's hold. "Before I go, can you tell me what happened?"

"Ambush." Kaleo's mouth twisted. "Assholes inside the mountain were supposed to come out to accept the civilian government's terms and agree to a timetable to turn themselves over into custody. Instead, they launched a full-scale attack. Fuckers bowled right over Foxtrot. If it'd been twelve hours later, there would have been more of us there. Wiped 'em out and kept coming for the rest of us."

"Oh, dear Lord." Zach closed his eyes and thought a short, silent prayer for all the casualties. "How many have died?"

"We're still counting. But the first building they took out was housing Lieutenant Colonel Wallace and his staff. Pretty much anyone above the rank of company CO is dead." Kaleo shook his head. "They knew exactly what they were aiming for."

Zach swallowed hard and met Kaleo's gaze again. "You're sure Nico's all right?"

"I don't think he'd be making as much noise as he is if he weren't." Kaleo squeezed Zach's shoulder kindly. "Get somewhere safe. I'll come find you as soon as I can."

⋀ ⋀ ⋀

THROUGH THE CHATTER AROUND HIM, made fuzzy as it was by his pain, Nico learned of a second onslaught from inside the mountain. By then the Jugs had relocated, though; the buildings where they had made their homes for a year were empty. They launched a sneak attack of their own, rushing out of hiding to stop the tanks and foot soldiers with almost no casualties.

"Fuck this," he heard one of the medics say outside his room. From the sound of his voice, he thought it was Charlie Company's medic. "I say we head for the Clean Zone, hole up in there. Get ourselves some fucking human shields. Let's see them try to attack us, then."

"Have you lost your damn mind?" That strident voice he knew also. It was Xolani, Delta Company's medic. "Human shields?"

The argument moved down the hallway of the makeshift infirmary before Nico could hear any more. Eventually, he smoked another blunt—the Jugs had been supplementing their almost-depleted supply of analgesics with cannabis for months now—and drifted off with the pain in his leg a low, burning throb. He was glad Xolani had spoken up, because the thought of anyone using Zach as a human shield made him want to flop off his stretcher and rip Charlie Company's medic a new asshole.

If he had anything to do with it, Zach would never be in danger of exposure ever again.

His dreams since the attack, when he'd heard Zach's voice calling to him, coming closer while he was bleeding, were always the same. In the dream, Zach smiled at Nico as they whiled away a peaceful afternoon together, until a bullet tore through Nico out of nowhere and splattered Zach with his blood. Zach's beautiful face began rotting away, his eyes full of love and pain. Zach would lean in for a kiss and pull away with bruised-fruit patches spreading outward from where Nico's lips had brushed his.

He always woke up screaming.

The Jugs didn't end up hiding in the Clean Zone or using human shields, but they didn't give the military government a chance to attack a third time. Nico heard about the operation after it was over. The moment the gates opened two days later to let another tank pass through, a full thousand Jugs charged, gaining entrance to the underground facility before the gates shut again. By that point, the military government had expended most of their troops. Convincing them to surrender was, by all reports, easy.

And now, in a makeshift jail somewhere nearby, Logan McClosky awaited the decision as to whether or not he would be tried by the Jugs or by a Clean Zone civilian court. Nico couldn't decide how he felt about that.

A rap on his bedroom door caught his attention, drew him out of his morose musings.

"Nico?" It was Paula, Sierra Company's medic. She poked her head in with a small smile. "Zach is here to see you again. Want me to let him in this time?"

The pain in his chest put the ache in his leg to shame. "I thought he was going to quarantine."

She shrugged. "What's it matter if he passes quarantine here with us or in the pens? We're keeping him away from anyone who might be bleeding."

"Send him away. Tell him to get to the pens and stay there. I don't want him having anything to do with us again."

"I'm not going to do that." She gave him a censorious look. "If you want to send him packing, sooner or later you're going to have to face him yourself."

"Fine. But just . . . not now. Not yet. Tell him I'm still not safe to be around."

Paula frowned and did what she was told. Nico probably should have expected that her sympathies would be with Zach. Nico was breaking Zach's heart by refusing to see him. Hell, he was breaking his own heart. But he wasn't going to take any more chances with Zach's survival. When he closed his eyes, all he could think was what might have happened if Zach had gotten any closer to him that afternoon. What might *still* happen.

He should have never resumed his relationship with Zach. He'd been too lonely, too weak to remember the reasons he'd let them take him away from Zach to begin with.

No, that was a lie. He'd remembered the reasons; he'd simply downplayed them in his own mind. It was magical thinking, believing that if he just loved Zach enough, if he could just be careful enough, an accident wouldn't happen and he wouldn't end up killing the man he lived for.

Nico cried a lot during those weeks of recovery, until his leg was strong enough to stand on again. He hoped shedding those tears had been enough that he'd be dry-eyed and firm when he finally saw Zach again.

He was trying for the dozenth time to work himself up to going to see Zach when Kaleo stormed into his room one afternoon, letting him know something had shifted in the uncomfortable impasse between the Jugs and the civilians, following the surrender of the military government.

"They've done it. The fuckers have actually done it."

"Done what?" Nico blinked, trying to focus on the man-shaped mass of furious energy barging around his room.

"Ratified the constitution without us. As far as they're concerned, we're not Clean Zone citizens." He stopped his pacing and turned to Nico, confusion and pain lurking under the outrage in his soft eyes. "They've *exiled* us."

"*What?*"

Kaleo shoved a sheet of paper at Nico and flopped into a chair, shaking his head in disillusioned disgust.

Written on the page was an official act of the first, lawfully elected Clean Zone Congress. It declared that anyone infected with the Alpha strain of the Bane virus was forbidden entry into the Clean Zone and that they would neither be supported by Clean Zone resources nor protected by Clean Zone laws.

Nico let the paper fall from a numbed hand. "What are we going to do?"

"I dunno. COs are meeting now. Guess now that all the 1st Juggernaut upper brass are dead, they're trying to run things by committee. There's some talk about us forming our own settlement nearby, but . . ."

"But what?"

Kaleo sighed. "Schuyler says it might be interpreted as an antagonistic move. Like we're going to compete with them for resources. There we are, so much stronger than them and living so close. They'll always be looking our way, wondering what we're up to."

"She's probably right," Nico murmured. "They have to know we'll be pissed off by this. They're going to worry we'll take action. If we stay nearby, it'll seem menacing."

"That, and the fact that— I mean, what the fuck do we have to stick around *for*?" Kaleo ran a hand through his hair, making it stick up in spikes.

Zach.

Nico shut that voice in a steel box and shoved it to the very back of his mind. "Guess that's true too."

They fell into a morose silence, each brooding separately until Kaleo finally spoke again. "There's another option. Some of the Jugs have been talking about fanning the rev-hunting parties out farther, across the country. Hit all the population centers, especially in the south and on the West Coast, where the revs and the survivors are less likely to have frozen over the past couple winters." He snorted and shook his head. When he looked up, his face was blotchy and his eyes glistened. "We still feel like we need to *protect* them. How fucking sick is that?"

Nico sighed. "It's not. Someone has to get rid of the revs. As long as they're out there, there could be another outbreak. We're the logical choice, because we can't be infected. And as for the civilians?" He shrugged helplessly. "No matter how shitty they are to us, the fact is, if we don't look after them, humanity will die. They're our only hope for survival as a species. We *have* to make sure they make it, even if they reject us."

Kaleo sneered. "So we're basically infertile drones—stupid,

gullible worker bees protecting and supporting the members of the hive that can reproduce. Great."

Nico didn't know what to say to that.

△ △ △

WITH A GREAT DEAL OF RELUCTANCE, the Jugs agreed to turn General McClosky and the other high-ranking military officials over to the Clean Zone government for trial. Everywhere Zach went, he heard the arguments about it. Some Jugs recognized that it was too personal for them, that they wanted vengeance too badly to give McClosky and the others a fair trial. Others thought they were perfectly entitled to their vengeance and to hell with a fair trial.

Ultimately, the voices of reason won out. If the Jugs flouted the rule of law to satisfy a vendetta—however just that vendetta might be—everything they had fought for could crumble into chaos again.

And four weeks after that final surrender of the military government, Nico finally agreed to see Zach.

By then, Zach had gone into quarantine, and it was fairly certain he had escaped being infected. Gillett Morris had been promoted to chief of the new Department of Perimeter Security, and as such, oversaw the new quarantine operations. He quartered Zach in a unit apart from the others so that, if Nico requested to see Zach, he could be escorted in without going near any of the other detainees.

Zach spent a lot of his time in isolation praying, reconnecting with God. He thought he'd lost his faith somewhere along the way, but it brought him comfort now. Or maybe he just needed to not feel so alone. The people he'd thought were his friends had abandoned him in favor of fear and ignorance and bigotry. And Nico—

Nico would leave him. Zach didn't need to be told what would happen when they saw each other again. Nico would leave to keep him safe, and there would be nothing Zach could say to change his mind. He couldn't even offer to go away with Nico. And he would have done so in a heartbeat. Nico wouldn't hear of such a thing because it would still mean Zach was in danger of being exposed.

If only he hadn't destroyed the ampule of the Alpha virus. But it was gone, now. That wasn't an option anymore. He could ask Nico to *try* to infect him, but they didn't even know if it was possible, and he knew nothing short of an ironclad guarantee of safety for Zach would placate Nico's concerns now.

It was a hot, early summer day when he looked up from tending his little vegetable patch outside the house to see Gillett and Nico walking up the aisle between empty quarantine units toward him. Zach dropped his gardening gloves and closed his eyes, whispering a prayer.

Lord, help me get through this without falling apart.

Nico stopped on the other side of the fence, shaking his head when Gillett offered to unlock the gate and let him in. Gillett slipped away, and he and Zach stood there on opposite sides of the chain-link, staring at each other.

He looked wrecked, and not just because he was walking with a crutch. He'd lost weight, and his face was lined with grief and turmoil. All the emotions Zach had been praying for God to help him control were there in Nico's bloodshot eyes.

"I'm leaving with the Jugs," Nico said finally, and Zach nodded. "I know."

A tear escaped the corner of Nico's eye, but Zach's own burned dryly. "I don't want to. I want to stay more than I want to continue breathing. But it will *destroy* me if I end up being the cause of your death, when all it takes to keep you safe is—"

"Condemning us both to a life alone?" The anger in his own voice astonished him, and the words that poured out were bitter utterances he'd never even let himself think before. "A life without being touched? Without the tiny bit of happiness we've been allowed to have in this whole damned *nightmare*—" He broke off when his voice cracked, biting his tongue when he realized just how fragile his control was.

"You don't have to be alone, Zach."

"*Don't.*" He gave Nico a savage glare. "You can play the martyr and walk away but spare me the whole, noble 'find someone else' scene, all right?"

Nico looked like he wanted to argue for a moment, but he finally nodded. "Okay. Just don't refuse a chance to be happy, if you get one," he said, stuffing his hands in his pockets.

"No, you're doing that for both of us."

Nico swallowed. "It's okay if you hate me—"

"Fuck you!" Zach stopped himself from charging the fence when he realized he'd taken a step forward. "I don't hate you and you know it. I wish I could. I wouldn't feel like I was *dying* right now if I did."

Nico's breath was so ragged Zach thought he might dissolve into sobs right there. He shuddered and hunched his shoulders, like he was trying to gather all his parts close to keep them from flying apart. "This isn't what I came here to say."

"Then what?"

"I just got done watching the transfer of the prisoners we took from Cheyenne Mountain over to the Clean Zone authorities and I saw someone. Zach, *Secretary Littlewood* is here."

It took Zach a moment to place the name, and then the blood drained from his face. "You mean, the man you—"

"Your serial rapist. I'll bet anything it's him."

"Oh God." Zach let his head fall back, gulping in a deep breath. "How am I going to get anyone to listen to me about *that?* I've lost all my credibility with everyone I knew in the Clean Zone."

"You have to find a way. *He saw me*, Zach." Nico's eyes were huge with terror. "He looked right at me. If he finds out you're connected to me—"

Zach nodded, clenching his fists to keep from reaching out to Nico, trying to comfort and reassure him. "I'll be careful."

Nico fell silent again, still hunched in on himself, until he finally murmured, "I should go. We march first thing tomorrow. Sierra Company is going to be working its way east across the plains states toward Chicago. So that's where I'll be, if—"

"Take me with you." Zach had sworn to himself he wouldn't beg, that he'd let go, but the plea slipped from him before he could stop himself. "Nico, *please.*"

"I *can't.*" Nico's voice was raw, his face tormented. "God, Zach, I wish I could. No matter where we go, if you're with me, you're in danger. There's nothing we can do to change that."

"That's *my* risk, and it's worth it to me."

"I could never live with it. I'd be terrified all the time. Maybe if there were still a *sure* way to infect you with Alpha, but without the ampule . . . It's not about being together, Zach, don't you see? I helped kill *billions of people*. But I can save you. Just one life. *Your* life. I can make sure you're safe from what I've done." He shook his head again, dashing tears from his face. "I love you too much to risk it. I'm sorry. Good-bye."

He rushed away, wobbling on his crutch, before Zach could even respond.

"Good-bye, Nico," he whispered, finally letting himself reach out and brush the chain-link with his fingertips, just inches from where Nico had stood, and let the tears fall.

EPILOGUE

ALLIANCE

FOUR YEARS LATER

The sound of gunfire was muffled through the thick walls of the ritzy Gulf of Mexico resort where Charlie Company had set up their base of operations. The smoke, too, was dampened, now that Nico had closed the door.

The same couldn't be said for the scent of blood and the accompanying stench of death. Bladders and bowels had vacated after bullets penetrated skulls, and the odor accompanied that of vomit from the other slaves who had watched their fellow captives be executed before their very eyes. They had only hesitated a moment, though, before they rose up and stopped Charlie Company from eliminating the remaining witnesses to what they had done.

Then there was this poor bastard in front of Nico, glaring up while he tried to hold his intestines in with his hands. Four gore-covered slaves surrounded him, one armed with the knife that had unzipped the Jug's belly and killed his comrades. The slaves had broken off their attack when Nico requested it, but blood was in their eyes both literally and figuratively, and they quivered with the need to finish what they had started.

They were Jugs. Nico was still grappling with what he'd seen, the way the supposedly cowed "slaves" had risen up to attack their captors from the rear.

They were *Jugs*.

Outside the condo, Delta, Bravo, and Sierra Companies were mopping up the remnants of Charlie Company. It had been almost a year since a squad of Charlie Company soldiers escorting a group of survivors to the Clean Zone had attacked a squad of Sierra Company people they'd come across on a similar mission. Nico's friend Marc had been one of the two surviving members of Sierra Company to bring back the news. He had died of an infection from his wounds shortly after he'd reached Sierra Company's base.

What had happened to push Charlie Company to commit such an atrocity was a question for someone else to answer. Nico had more pressing concerns.

"You've got a choice," Nico said, nudging the gutted man on the floor with his foot. "Tell me what I want to know, and I'll put a bullet in your head. Or you can stay silent and I can let your slaves hang you from the chandelier by your entrails before you die."

The man licked his parched lips, sweat pouring down his temples. "What do you want to know?" he whispered.

"How did these people end up infected with Alpha?"

The dying man at his feet glared at him. "How the fuck should I know? We didn't know they were until they fucking attacked us." He coughed, blood splattering his lips. "Why do you care? After what they did to us, threw us out after we *helped* them—"

It took all Nico's restraint not to kick the motherfucker. "*These* people didn't do that. How long has this been going on?"

"Two years." Another defiant glower. "Why the fuck are we wasting our time chasing down revs and helping these people? Make 'em work for us for a change. Knock 'em up and make a few babies we can raise, since we can't have any of our own. Couldn't even do that, though. Babies kept getting infected and dying. We thought it was us causing it."

One of the slaves growled and dashed forward, her hands curled into claws, but her fellows stopped her, though their own fury leaked through.

"But it wasn't," Nico prompted. "You infected your slaves with Alpha."

The man on the floor smirked. "The ones we fucked, at least."

The temptation to lift his foot and just crush the man's skull to erase that gloating look was strong, but Nico had one more thing he needed to confirm.

"Who else knows Alpha is sexually transmitted?"

Those bloody teeth sneered. "We didn't even fucking know until a couple hours ago, asshole."

The back of the wounded man's head splattered against the floor beneath him almost before he finished speaking, and Nico raised his eyes from the barrel of the gun he'd used to finish the fucker off to look at the slaves still in the room. "You. What's your name?"

A boy who couldn't have been more than seventeen stepped forward. Pretty, haggard, half-starved, but with a sober, rational look in his eye that said he wasn't as far gone as the rest of his companions were. "Bailey." He nodded to a young woman next to him, who was holding the sobbing woman who would have finished tearing the man at Nico's feet limb from limb if they hadn't restrained her. "This is my twin sister, Brenda."

"Bailey, I need you to listen close. Other Jugs are going to be coming along soon, and they'll help all of you. We're not all like this guy was, okay?" Bailey nodded, a quick dip of his head, his face pale beneath the spatter of blood. "I need to go, all right?"

The boy nodded again, and so did his sister and the two other slaves, all listening intently.

"Good. As far as you're concerned, you never saw me. Please?"

He watched them process that. They had no reason to trust him, none of them. For all they knew, he could be just like the people in Charlie Company. But eventually they all nodded again.

"Good. Now here." He dropped his rucksack and pulled his spare set of fatigues out. "Put these on a corpse and throw it into one of the burning buildings. If anyone asks, you last saw a guy matching my description running in there, trying to rescue someone who was trapped."

Nico turned on his heel and walked away. Marc had been his only true confidante, after all this time, and Marc was gone now. He had friends in Sierra Company who would miss him, but he couldn't let them know where he was headed, or why.

Last year, it had been all the Jugs could talk about when the Clean Zone's newly formed Department of Pandemic Research and Prevention had had the gall to issue a request for the Jug medics to put together field reports of their observations on the transmissibility and spread of the Bane virus. Too many Jugs were still bitter about how the civilian population had treated them that they'd resented the fuck out of being asked to do a damn thing for the Clean Zone. The medics were hardly less bitter, but they had seen the benefit of contributing what limited knowledge they had in the interest of preventing another outbreak.

Two things had been nagging at Nico ever since, though.

The first was that the letters asking for field reports from the Jug medics had specified that the DPRP wanted to know about the transmissibility of the Alpha strain as well.

The second was that the request came directly from the head of the DPRP—Secretary Stephen Littlewood.

He'd spent months convincing himself that it was irrelevant. It didn't matter if Littlewood wanted to know about the transmissibility of the Alpha strain, because no one knew for sure if the Alpha strain even *was* transmissible.

But now they had confirmation. And God only knew what Littlewood wanted with that information.

He needed to know what Littlewood was after. And he knew exactly one person positioned to help him do it.

Shrugging his rucksack onto his back once more and shouldering his assault rifle, Nico put the Gulf of Mexico behind him and set off for Colorado Springs.

Zach and Nico's story isn't over!

Don't miss *Strain* and *Bane*, the continuing story of Zach, Nico, and the troops of Project Juggernaut!

STRAIN

In a world with little hope and no rules,
the only thing they have to lose
is themselves.

AMELIA C. GORMLEY

STRAIN

In a world with little hope and no rules, the only thing they have to lose is themselves.

Rhys Cooper is a dead man. He's spent years hiding from the virus that wiped out most of the human race, but an act of futile heroism has him counting down his remaining days. The timely arrival of superhuman soldiers offers some feeble hope—but only if Rhys can reconcile himself to doing what is necessary to take advantage of it.

Sergeant Darius Murrell has seen too much death and too little tenderness, seeking out survivors only to put the infected out of their misery, or send the uninfected to a safe haven he and his fellow Juggernaut troops can never enjoy. Rhys's situation is different, though. Not only is there an improbable chance that Darius won't have to put a bullet in Rhys's head, but he has somehow managed to get under Darius's skin.

The virus Rhys must infect himself with is sexually transmitted, and optimizing his chance of exposure requires him to submit as often as possible to Darius—and the other soldiers. Though the boundaries of morality have shifted in this harsh new world, what they must do has them asking if their humanity is too high a price to pay for Rhys's survival.

A STRAIN NOVEL

BANE

The weapon that nearly
destroyed humanity
may be their
only salvation.

AMELIA C. GORMLEY

BANE

A STRAIN NOVEL

The weapon that nearly destroyed humanity may be their only salvation.

RHYS COOPER once thought he was a dead man. Instead, he's proven immune to the virus that nearly wiped out humanity.

Now the Clean Zone's scientists want to know why. Summoned for testing, Rhys is about to learn first-hand why his Juggernaut partner, Sergeant Darius Murrell, and the rest of his superhuman comrades in Delta Company don't trust the uninfected survivors in the Clean Zone—or the remnants of the government that unleashed the epidemic in the first place.

For a decade, Zach Houtman has yearned for his lover, Nico Fernández, but fear of infection has kept them apart. Separately they keep tabs on the last vestiges of the corrupt government, particularly the head of the Clean Zone's virus research division. Secretary Littlewood seeks to unlock the secrets of the Bane virus. But Nico knows how dangerous Littlewood will be if that ever happens.

Now Zach and Nico have the perfect bait to draw Littlewood out: Rhys. But Delta Company isn't about to let Rhys walk into hell alone. They'll take Littlewood down together, or not at all. Even if they succeed, however, for Zach and Nico one question remains: can infected and uninfected people ever be together safely?

OTHER BOOKS BY AMELIA C. GORMLEY

THE IMPULSE TRILOGY

Inertia

Acceleration

Velocity

SEASONS IN SAUGATUCK

The Field of Someone Else's Dreams

Sea Change

Risk Aware

THE STRAIN TRILOGY

Juggernaut

Strain

Bane

Player vs. Player

(Coming Soon)

Amelia C. Gormley published her first short story in the school newspaper in the 4th grade, and since then has suffered the persistent delusion that enabling other people to hear the voices in her head might be a worthwhile endeavor. She's even convinced her hapless spouse that it could be a lucrative one as well, especially when coupled with her real-life interest in angst, kink, feminism, and pretty men.

When her husband and son aren't interacting with the back of her head as she stares at the computer, they rely on her to feed them, maintain their domicile, and keep some semblance of order in their lives (all very, very bad ideas—they really should know better by now.) She can also be found playing video games and ranting on Tumblr, seeing as how she's one of those horrid social justice warriors out to destroy free speech, gaming, geek culture, and everything else that's fun everywhere.

http://ameliacgormley.com
http://ameliacgormley.tumblr.com

facebook.com/ameliacgormley

twitter.com/ACGormley

goodreads.com/ameliacgormley